ADVANCE PRAISE FOR *POISON*

"Brimming with intrigue, action, and enough double-crosses to stump even the most venal of Renaissance popes . . . A fascinating page-turner as delicious and deadly as the poisons brewed up by its heroine."

—Lauren Willig, bestselling author of *The Secret History of the Pink Carnation*

"*Poison* presents the most unique heroine I have ever seen in a mystery series (a complex, angst-filled Renaissance Dexter). . . . The plot is as much a fast-paced thriller as a compelling mystery."

—Karen Harper, *New York Times* bestselling author of *The Last Boleyn*

"*Poison* delivers a fast-paced, gripping look at the wages of sin under the Borgias, as seen through the eyes of a troubled female poisoner. The seductive danger of Rome, lethal sanctity of the Vatican, and bitter taste for revenge all combine to produce an intoxicating brew that keeps us turning the pages, even as we glance fearfully at our fingertips for signs of residue."

—C. W. Gortner, author of *The Last Queen*

"An engrossing journey through the darker side of Renaissance Rome, *Poison* creates an elegant tapestry of mysteries and deceit and a resourceful, original heroine in Francesca Giordano."

—Susan Holloway Scott, author of *The French Mistress*

"*Poison* is an irresistible concoction of danger, mystery, and romance—a fast-paced thrill ride through the darkest intrigues of Renaissance Rome. I could not put this book down!"

—Jeanne Kalogridis, author of *The Borgia Bride*

"An impressive blend of story and history! . . . A complex and compelling heroine led me through the crooked streets of Rome—and of the human heart—into the bowels of a decaying St. Peter's Basilica to watch the struggle for ultimate power play out in an unforgettable climax."

—Brenda Rickman Vantrease, bestselling author of *The Illuminator*

POISON

POISON

A Novel of the Renaissance

SARA POOLE

ST. MARTIN'S GRIFFIN

NEW YORK

This is a work of fiction. All of the characters, organizations, and events portrayed in this novel are either products of the author's imagination or are used fictitiously.

 For information, address St. Martin's Press, 175 Fifth Avenue, New York, N.Y. 10010.

www.stmartins.com

Library of Congress Cataloging-in-Publication Data

Poole, Sara, 1951–
Poison : a novel of the Renaissance / Sara Poole.—1st ed.
p. cm.
ISBN 978-0-312-60983-2
1. Women poisoners—Fiction. 2. Revenge—Fiction. 3. Alexander VI, Pope, 1431–1503—Fiction. 4. Cardinals—Italy—Rome—Fiction. 5. Nobility—Italy—Rome—Fiction. 6. Borgia, Lucrezia, 1480–1519—Fiction. 7. Borgia, Cesare, 1476?–1507—Fiction. 8. Renaissance—Italy—Rome—Fiction. 9. Rome (Italy)—Fiction. I. Title.
PS3569.E43P65 2010
813'.54—dc22

2009047299

First Edition: August 2010

10 9 8 7 6 5 4 3 2 1

POISON

Prelude

ROME

SUMMER, 1483

The white bull charged down the chute into the piazza. Roaring, the crowd shook the tiers of wooden seats erected around the square. In their midst, the child clung to her father and felt the deep vibration within him as he shouted along with all the rest.

"Borgia! Borgia! Huzzah!"

Beneath a cloudless sky so bright as to be a pain behind the eyes, the red-robed prince of Holy Mother Church stood on a dais draped with the gold and mulberry silks of the House of Borgia. He spread his arms wide as though to embrace the crowd, the piazza, the travertine marble palazzo glowing golden in the sun, and beyond to the farthest reaches of the ancient city awakening to a new dream of glory.

"My brothers and sisters," Rodrigo Borgia proclaimed, his voice a thunderclap in the sudden stillness. "I thank you for coming here today. I thank you for your friendship and for your support. And I give to you—"

He paused and the girl felt the inhalation of the crowd, suspended upon the will of the man who, it was said, aspired to rule all of Christendom though he'd be better suited to reign in Hell.

"I give to you from the plains of my home, beautiful Valencia, the greatest of all bulls ever seen in our beloved Rome! I give you his strength, his courage, his glory! I give you his blood! Let it nourish our magnificent city! Roma Eterna!"

"Roma! Roma! Roma!"

The bull pawed the summer dust and tossed its great head, snorting as the black pools of its eyes caught the frenzied scene. A well of silence opened, so deep that the girl could hear the creak of harnesses on the horses closing in from all sides, thrust through their fear by the spurs of the men who led the companies of Il Cardinale's private army.

Trumpets sounded from high along the walls of the palazzo. A bevy of *campinos* in parti-colored costumes and garish red wigs ran into the piazza, waving at the bull with their fringed capes and capering as close to him as they dared.

"Andiamo, Toro! Andiamo!"

Driven before them, the bull turned toward the line of mounted men. One among them, gifted with the honor, rose high in his saddle and saluted Borgia. The killing tip of his *rejón* lance glinted in the sun as he surged forward.

The crowd screamed its delight. The bull, sensing danger, lowered its head and charged at horse and rider. At the last instant, the *rejonear* pulled hard on the reins, veered sideways, and, rising again in the stirrups, thrust downward.

The bull bellowed, blood spurting from between its heaving

shoulders, spilling over its white hide to splatter in the dust. It raced away, circling the piazza, looking—the girl thought—for a way out, but found instead the parti-colored men, who charged at it, arms waving akimbo.

"Andiamo, Toro! Andiamo!"

Again they drove the bull toward the *rejonear,* who, with measured thrust, drew more blood for the thirsting crowd. Again and again and again until the animal staggered and fell first on one knee, then another. At the last, its great hindquarters gave way and it collapsed in the dust churned to mud by the river of its life.

The girl stood frozen in the summer heat, unable to look away. She saw the white bull stained red, the red man on the dais roaring bull-like in his triumph, and all around her, spinning in the gaudy light, the contorted faces of the crowd, mouths agape with lust.

The *rejonear* lifted his lance to the sun before sending it downward in the final *colpo di morte.* A long spasm rippled through the animal. In its wake, the parti-colored men ran out, knives flashing.

The girl did not see them cut away at the carcass, taking ears, tail, testicles. She did not watch the dripping prizes held high to the cheers of the crowd. She saw only the river of blood, a crimson tide pulling her down, spinning round and round, heedless of the screams that drew the gaze of the red bull to her.

1

The Spaniard died in agony. That much was evident from the contortions of his once handsome face and limbs and the black foam caking his lips. A horrible death to be sure, one only possible from that most feared of weapons:

"Poison."

Having pronounced his verdict, Cardinal Rodrigo Borgia, prince of Holy Mother Church, looked up, his dark eyes heavy-lidded with suspicion, and surveyed the assembled members of his household.

"He was poisoned."

A tremor ran through guards, retainers, and servants all, as though a great wind blew across the gilded reception room shaded by the columned loggia beyond and cooled in this blazing Roman summer of Anno Domini 1492 by breezes from the gardens filled with the scents of exotic jasmine and tamarind.

Poison

"In my house, this man I called to serve me was poisoned in my house!"

Pigeons in the cotes beneath the palazzo eaves fluttered as the great booming voice washed over them. Roused to anger, Il Cardinale was a marvel to behold, a true force of nature.

"I will find who did this. Whoever dared will pay! Captain, you will—"

About to issue his orders to the commander of his condotierri, Borgia paused. I had stepped forward in that moment, squeezing between a house priest and a secretary, to put myself at the front of the crowd that watched him with terrified fascination. The movement distracted him. He stared at me, scowling.

I inclined my head slightly in the direction of the body.

"Out!"

They fled, all of them, from the old veterans to the youngest servant, tumbling over one another to be gone from his presence, away from his terrifying rage that turned the blood to ice, freed to whisper among themselves about what had happened, what it meant, and, above all, who had dared to do it.

Only I remained.

"Giordano's daughter?" Borgia stared at me across the width of the reception room. It was a vast space carpeted in the Moorish fashion as so few can afford to do, furnished with the rarest woods, the most precious fabrics, the grandest silver and gold plate, all to proclaim the power and glory of the man whose will I dared to challenge.

A drop of sweat ran down between my shoulder blades. I had worn my best day clothes for what I feared might be the final hour of my life. The underdress of dark brown velvet, pleated across the bodice and with a wide skirt that trailed slightly behind me, pressed down heavily on my shoulders. A pale yellow overdress was clinched loosely under my breasts, a reminder of the weight I had lost since my father's death.

By contrast, the Cardinal was the picture of comfort in a loose, billowing shirt and pantaloons of the sort he favored when he was at home and relaxing, as he had been when word was brought to him of the Spaniard's death.

I nodded. "I am, Eminence, Francesca Giordano, your servant."

The Cardinal paced in one direction, back again, a restless animal filled with power, ambition, appetites. He gazed at me and I knew what he must see: a slim woman of not yet twenty, unremarkable in looks except for overly large brown eyes, auburn hair, and, thanks to my fear, very pale skin.

He gestured at the Spaniard, who in the heat of the day had already begun to stink.

"What do you know of this?"

"I killed him."

Even to my own ears, my voice sounded harsh against the tapestry-covered walls. The Cardinal paced closer, his expression that of mingled shock and disbelief.

"*You* killed him?"

I had prepared a speech that I hoped would explain my actions while concealing my true intent. It came in such a rush I feared I might garble it.

"I am my father's daughter. I learned at his side, yet when he was killed, you did not consider for a moment that I should take his place. You would have for a son but not for me. Instead, you hired this . . . other—" I caught my breath and pointed at the dead man. "Hired him to protect you and your family. Yet he could not even protect himself, not from me."

I could have said more. That Borgia had done nothing to avenge my father's murder. That he had allowed him to be beaten in the street like a dog, left in the filth with his skull crushed, and not lifted a hand to seek vengeance. That such a lapse on his part was unparalleled . . . and unforgivable.

He had left it to me, the poisoner's daughter, to exact justice. But to do so, I needed power, paid for in the coin of one dead Spaniard.

The Cardinal's great brow wrinkled prodigiously, leaving his eyes mere slits. Yet he appeared calm enough, with no sign of the rage he had shown minutes before.

A flicker of hope stirred within me. Ten years living under his roof, watching him, hearing my father speak of him. Ten years convinced that he was a man of true intelligence, of reason and logic, a man who would never be ruled by his emotions. All down to this single moment.

"How did you do it?"

He was testing me; that was good. I took a breath and answered more calmly.

"I knew he would be hot and thirsty when he arrived, but that he would also be cautious of what he drank. The flagon I left for him contained only iced water, pure enough to pass any inspection. The poison was on the outside, coating the glass. He was sweating, which meant that the pores of his skin were wide open. From the moment he touched the flagon, it would have been over very quickly."

"Your father never mentioned such a poison to me, one that could be used in that way."

I saw no reason to tell Il Cardinale that I, not my father, had developed that particular poison. Likely, he would not have believed me anyway. Not then.

"No craftsman gives away all his secrets," I said.

He did not reply at once but came closer yet, so close that I could feel the heat pouring off him, see the great swathe of his bull-like shoulders blocking out the light. The glint of gold from the cross dangling against his barrel chest caught my gaze and I could not look away.

Cristo en extremis.

Save me.

"By God, girl," the Cardinal said, "you have surprised me."

A momentous admission from this man who, it was said, knew before any other which swallow would alight first on any tree in Rome and whether the branch could hold its weight.

I took a breath against the tightness of my chest, looked away from the cross, away from him, out through the open window toward the great river and the vast land beyond.

Breathe.

"I would serve you, signore." I turned my head, just enough to meet his gaze and hold it. "But first, you must let me live."

2

The servants came and went, removing all trace of the Spaniard. They carried in my chests, brought food and drink, and even turned down the covers of the bed framed in wooden posts of carved acanthus where once my father had slept and now I would.

Tasks completed, they filed out silently, all except the last of them, an old woman close enough to Heaven to have little to lose. Skittering away, she hissed:

Strega!

Witch.

A cold shiver ran through me, though I was careful to give no sign of it. Such a word would never have been applied to my father or to the Spaniard or to any man possessed of the fearsome but respected skills of a professional poisoner. But it would be applied to me now and forever, and I was helpless to prevent it.

They burn witches. The terrifying auto-de-fé is not limited to its point of origin in Spain. It has spread to the Lowlands, the Italian Peninsula, all of Europe. For the most part, the flames consume those accused of heresy, but how easy it is to indict a man or a woman—almost always a woman—or even a child accused of the even graver sin of trafficking with Satan. Anyone too conversant with ancient healing, too knowledgeable about plants, or simply too different from others may end as fuel for the fires that char human skin, sizzle human fat, crack human bones, and reduce to ashes all that is hope and dream.

I turned, intending to distract myself by unpacking the chests, then turned again suddenly, a hand clamped over my mouth. On my knees, I yanked the piss pot from beneath the bed and crouched over it as the contents of my stomach spewed out, a bitter stream that all but choked me.

Disgustoso!

Do not think I am prone to such infirmity, but the events of the day, the desperate gamble I had been forced to take, and the terror of mortal sin it brought overwhelmed me. I lay where I was, unmoving. Exhaustion bore me away as on a fast-running tide flowing swiftly beyond any sight of shore.

The nightmare came almost at once. The same dream that has tormented me all my life. I am in a very small space behind a wall. There is a tiny hole through which I can see into a room filled with shadows, some of them moving. The darkness is broken by a shard of light that flashes again and again. Blood pours from it, a giant wave of blood lapping against the walls of the room and threatening to drown me. I wake to my own screams, which I have learned from long practice to muffle in my pillows.

As quickly as I could, I clambered to my feet. My limbs shook and I could feel the hot wash of tears on my cheeks. Had anyone come in to see me in such a state? Was someone there now, waiting in the shadows? The Spaniard had died not far from where I stood. Did his spirit linger? Did my father's shade, unable to rest until I fulfilled my vow of vengeance?

Heart hammering, I lit the candle beside the bed but found no comfort in its meager circle of light. Beyond the tall windows, the moon rode high, casting a silver ribbon across the garden and far beyond. Rome slept, so much as it ever did. In the narrow alleys and lanes rats were at work, gnawing here, feasting there, noses twitching, claws grasping, all in the shadow of the Curia. I lifted my gaze, staring into the middle distance from which I fancied I could see, glowing in the silver light, vast, writhing tentacles stretching outward in all directions, grasping at power and glory through all of Christendom. The vision was no more than a figment of an overwrought mind, yet it was real all the same. As real as the whispers that the master of it all, the Vicar of Christ on Earth, Il Papa Innocent VIII was dying.

Of natural causes?

Do not tell me you are shocked. We live in the age of poison, of one kind or another. Every great house employs someone like myself for protection or, when necessary, to make an example of an enemy. It is the way of things. The Throne of Saint Peter is hardly immune, being no more than the ultimate prize the families fight over like yapping dogs maddened at the kill. No one perched on it should sleep too soundly. Or eat without having his food tasted first, but that is just my professional opinion.

Cui bono? If the Pope dies, who gains?

Still weary in body and mind, I pulled off my clothes and slipped at last into the bed. Hugging my knees, I felt the cool damask of the pillow beneath my cheek. Around me the palazzo slumbered and shortly so did I, safe within the stronghold of the man who had plotted for decades to make the papacy the ultimate jewel in his earthly crown.

In the morning, I retrieved the clothes I had abandoned on the floor, smoothed the wrinkles from them, and folded them carefully away in the wardrobe. Mindful of the dignity of my new estate but equally concerned with comfort on what promised to be a sultry day, I donned a simple white linen underdress and covered it with a blue overdress embroidered along the hem with a pastiche of flowers. The embroidery was my own poor effort, for I have never been skilled with a needle; the flowers were the deceptively benign blossoms found on various poisonous plants. So had I made more tolerable the tedium of stitchery, at which every decent woman is expected to excel regardless of her natural inclination.

Properly dressed and with my hair twined in a braid coiled around the crown of my head, I ignored the rumbling of my stomach and set about my newly acquired duties with what I hoped was a pardonable eagerness. First, I sought out the captain of the condotierri to review the security precautions my father had put in place. Every scrap of food, every drop of liquid, every object that conceivably could come into contact with Il Cardinale or any of his family had to be provenanced, vetted, and secured. That required the full cooperation of the captain of his guard.

Vittoro Romano was outside the armory in the wing of the palazzo that also housed the barracks. A dozen or so young guardsmen had dragged benches into the sun and were busy polishing their armor while keeping an eye on the servant girls who found reason to pass by, balancing baskets of laundry or kitchen supplies on their swaying hips. Several cats dozed nearby, raising their heads only to stare at the pigeons who stayed just out of reach. It had not rained in days. The sky held the lemony hue that comes to Rome in summer. The courtyard in front of the armory was dusty, despite being paved with cobblestones. I watched an eddy of dirt spring up in the wake of a passing breeze and dance across the space of several yards before collapsing almost at Vittoro's booted feet.

He did not appear to notice. In his fifties and of medium height with a saturnine temperament, the captain of the guard gave the impression of being neither very interested nor even particularly aware of whatever happened to be going on around him. Anyone foolish enough to be gulled by that deception could count himself fortunate if he lived long enough to regret it.

Vittoro was speaking with several of his lieutenants but sent them away when he saw me. I was apprehensive about approaching him, wondering how he would take to dealing with a young woman who had killed to attain a position of authority. To my relief, he greeted me with a cordial nod.

"*Buongiorno,* Donna Francesca. I am pleased to see that you are well."

By which I gleaned that the captain, at least, did not regret Il Cardinale's decision to let me live, as opposed to having my throat slit and my body tossed into the Tiber, or however he chose to dispose of those who displeased him. Even so, I was under no illusion that the rest of the household felt the same. The old woman who had branded me a witch was unlikely to be alone in her sentiment.

I stood before him gravely, mindful that others were watching. "Thank you, Capitano, and I you. If it is convenient, I would like to discuss our security procedures."

He sketched a small bow and straightened, smiling. "By all means. Do you wish to make any changes?"

"To the contrary, I want to make sure that no one mistakes the trust Il Cardinale has placed in me as a license for laxity. Were that to occur, I would have no choice but to take it amiss."

"How amiss?" Vittoro inquired. I did not mistake the twinkle in his eye. He had known me as long as I had lived under Borgia's roof and had seen me grow from a gawky child to a somewhat less gawky woman. He and his wife—a plumb, cheerful matron—had three daughters, all close to my own age. Being proper young women, each was married, but they all still lived in the neighborhood with their husbands and growing broods of children. They were a source of great contentment to their father. I had seen my own look at them wistfully on their frequent, clamorous visits to the palazzo.

"Very amiss," I replied.

Vittoro nodded. "I will put that about. Whatever anyone thinks of Il Cardinale's choice of you, no sensible person wants to be on the wrong side of a poisoner."

I allowed myself a small sigh of relief. His support was essential to my success and I was grateful for it. We went on to speak of the procedures that, thus far at least, had proven effective in safeguarding Borgia and his family.

Over the years, numerous attempts had been made to kill or at least incapacitate Il Cardinale, but all had failed thanks to my father's vigilance. One such effort had involved a round of cheese injected with a solution of arsenic. Another concerned a bolt of cloth tainted with tincture of thorn apple. There were others, but I see no reason to detail them.

Of a certainty, there would be more. It was only a question of time before an attempt was made to test the vigilance of Borgia's new poisoner. I knew that full well even as I lived in apprehension of it.

"D'Marco is looking for you," Vittoro warned when we were done.

I grimaced, to his amusement, and took my leave. My intent was to make my presence felt in what was, from my perspective, the most vital part of the household and of necessity the essential focus of my attentions, the kitchens. I got as far as the covered walkway leading to them when I was intercepted by a small, ferretlike fellow.

Renaldo d'Marco was Borgia's steward, roundly disliked for his tendency to peer into every nook and cranny in search of wrongdoing. A certain amount of skimming is a perquisite of employment in so august a household, but too much cannot be condoned lest it bankrupt the establishment and kill the golden goose. By at least pretending to insist that there should be none, the steward managed to keep what did occur within tolerable limits.

He darted at me from out of the shadows hanging beneath the walkway. Such was his regard for his dignity that he wore a crimson velvet robe and matching cap despite the heat. He clutched a portable writing desk to his meager chest, as though it would ward off whatever blows came his way.

Frowning, he said, "There you are, Donna Francesca. I have been looking all over for you. I must say I was surprised when I learned . . . but never mind, that is of no account now. You would have been well advised to seek me out directly this morning and in the future, I hope you will do so. His Eminence trusts me in all things, I know his will and can be of great assistance to you."

Having no wish for his enmity, I answered mildly. "I will keep that in mind, Master d'Marco. For now, what do you seek?"

Mollified, the steward drew himself up a little straighter and informed me, "His Eminence has instructed that you are to inspect arrangements in the household of Madonna Adriana de Mila without delay for such purpose as to confirm the safety and well-being of

Madonna Lucrezia and others domiciled there. Further, I am instructed to give you this."

With palpable reluctance, he handed over a small pouch, which, I quickly determined, contained gold florins. I had handled money before; when I visited the markets with my father, he often gave me coins and instructed me to pay. As I grew older, he taught me the fine art of haggling and trusted me to get the best prices. I mention this so that you will understand I was not surprised to be given money, only puzzled as to what I was to do with it.

"Your salary for this quarter of the year," Renaldo said. He turned the writing desk toward me. "Sign here."

I signed and was glad that my hand did not tremble. Of course, I had understood that I would be paid; I simply had not thought how much. My father had left a substantial amount of money on account in a bank in Rome. It had become mine upon his death. With that and with the addition of my new income, I was that rarity of my age, a woman of independent means.

That suited me very well, as I reflected when I had taken leave of Renaldo and, having returned to my quarters long enough to secure the greater portion of the florins in a chest, set off to do His Eminence's bidding.

By his own standards, Il Cardinale was a man of discretion. As an example, he did not quarter his current mistress or any of his various children by his past mistress in his official residence on the Corso. Instead, they were in the care of his cousin, conveniently a widow of the powerful Orsini clan who lived in suitably noble circumstances nearby.

Since my father's death, I had not ventured beyond the palazzo, which, with its vast main building and surrounding dependencies inhabited by hundreds of servants, retainers, courtiers, and clerks, could be thought of as a miniature city. Just outside it lay the gracious square that Borgia viewed as an extension of his own domain, using it for all manner of crowd-pleasing entertainments from bullfights to pantomimes and firework shows. He had even gone so far as to renovate the other homes facing the piazza in order to raise the overall appearance to his own exacting standards.

Like his own monument to himself, the buildings were newly faced in travertine marble, brought from the nearby precincts of Tivoli. You see it everywhere in the city now—on bridges, churches, palazzi, even the windowsills of humbler homes and the curbstones of the newly paved streets. Should you visit Rome or be fortunate enough to reside within it, I recommend that you find occasion to rise early and observe how each new day transforms the city from the monochrome of night to the blushing hues that the sun draws from this remarkable stone. Later, you will see the colors deepen almost to purple before finally yielding late in the day to muted gold. It is said that Rome possesses the fairest palette of any city and I know of no reason to disagree.

As always, leaving the confines of the square for the larger city involved a brief sense of dislocation. Rome was in its usual perpetual turmoil. Everywhere I looked there were throngs of people, some on foot or on horseback, others in litters or carts and wagons, creating a cacophony of sound and a sea of motion that can be dizzying. Priests, merchants, peasants, soldiers, and wide-eyed visitors alike jockeyed for space in the streets and lanes. It was said that every language on earth could be heard there and I believed it. The healing a few decades before of the Great Schism that had torn the Church apart has restored Rome as the center of the Christian world. What had been a scruffy medieval town of haunted ruins and greatly diminished population was being transformed seemingly overnight into the greatest city in all of Europe.

Nothing better exemplified Rome's rebirth than the grandiose palaces being built by the great families. While the towering palazzo of Il Cardinale, erected fittingly enough on the site of the old Roman mint, was the first among them, the vast and luxurious Palazzo Orsini bid fair to be its rival. Indeed, it should be called the *Palazzi* Orsini for it comprises several palaces built around a vast inner courtyard, with each belonging to a different—some would say rival—branch of the Orsini clan. My destination was the wing of the palace situated on a narrow street within sight of the Tiber.

Scarcely had I stepped into the blessedly cool marble entry hall and announced myself to the majordomo than I was assailed by a slender girl on the verge of womanhood whose heart-shaped face was framed by a riot of blond curls. This exquisite creature, smelling of violet with a hint of vanilla, threw herself at me and hugged me fiercely.

"I have been so worried about you! Why have you stayed away? I wept for you . . . for your beloved father . . . for you both! Why weren't you here?"

How to explain to the cherished only daughter of Il Cardinale why she had been so neglected? How to entreat her pardon?

"I am so sorry," I said, hugging the twelve-year-old. "I was not fit company, but I knew, truly I did, of your thoughts and prayers. From the bottom of my heart, I thank you."

So soothed, Lucrezia smiled, but her happiness faded as she beheld me. We had known each other virtually all of her young life. We shared the common bond of daughters loving and beloved of powerful, feared fathers. In the isolation that imposed, we had reached out to each other, finding a degree of sisterhood that comforted us both even as it could never erase the social gulf between us.

"You are too pale," Lucrezia declared. Though the younger by seven years, she did not hesitate to assert the authority bestowed by her superior position. "And you have lost weight, now you are too thin. And your hair, why must you always wear it in that braid? You have beautiful hair—such a lovely shade of auburn—you should let it down, the better to be admired."

I stepped back and smiled at her. "My hair is not beautiful and I am not seeking admirers, therefore I wear it up for practicality's sake."

Lucrezia's good humor fled, as did her brief interest in my own troubles. With a pretty pout, she sighed. "Perhaps I should envy you. Have you heard?"

"Heard what?" I replied, although I knew the answer already. Not even grief for my father had shielded me from the gossip of the household. We linked arms as we walked from the entry hall toward the family quarters.

"A second betrothal broken! Another husband gone! What is my father thinking? He has promised me to two men, both fine, upstanding lords, Spanish like ourselves, and then he changes his mind. I will die an old maid, I swear I will!"

"You will be gloriously wed and your husband will cherish you forever."

"Do you really think so?"

Did I? That Il Cardinale would arrange the most magnificent marriage possible for his only daughter could not be in doubt. Everything he did served but one purpose: the greater glory of La Famiglia. Perhaps he truly believed that through the advancement of the Borgias would come good for the Church and all of Christendom. Perhaps he did not care a whit. No matter, the benefit of La

Famiglia directed all his actions. As to whether that would result in any personal happiness for Lucrezia, who could know?

"It will be as God wills," I said. "Now I must speak with Madonna Adriana. Will you come with me?"

We chatted as we walked through the galleries filled with statues, some new, some recently reclaimed from the excavations going on throughout the city. Along the way, I tried to gauge if Lucrezia had any sense of the change the past day had wrought in my own circumstances. The younger girl made no mention of that as she prattled on cheerfully. Child though she still was in many ways, the Cardinal's daughter was skilled beyond her years in keeping her own counsel. It was impossible to be completely sure of what she knew or how she knew it.

At last we came to the wing of the palace occupied by Il Cardinale's household. The guard standing before the entrance bowed as we passed through the high, bronze gates. Beyond lay a world of splashing fountains, scented gardens, silk boudoirs, and gilded assembly rooms so utterly feminine that I thought of it as *il harem*. Where the Cardinal, prince of the Holy Roman Church, one of the most powerful men in all of Christendom, came to throw off the cares of his day and accept the comfort of his women.

And such women they were. Besides the sweet vivacity of his only daughter, he enjoyed the company of his cousin, Madonna Adriana de Mila, widow of the late Lord of Bassanello and a power to be reckoned with in her own right. Among her countless virtues practicality reigned supreme. So sensible was her nature that Madonna Adriana offered no objection when Il Cardinale took as his mistress the astounding Giulia Farnese, Giulia la Bella as she was called, said to be the loveliest woman in all of Italy, if not the world.

That she was also the wife of Adriana's stepson might have prompted some objection from the older woman. Instead, La Famiglia ruled, as always. Adriana agreed to the removal of her stepson to his country estate, leaving the sixty-one-year-old cardinal free to enjoy the charms of eighteen-year-old Giulia, who was herself happy enough to acquiesce.

Both women were enjoying the shade of the inner garden, seated beneath a plane tree, sipping chilled lemonade and watching the antics of a pair of fluffy Maltese pups at play in the grass before them. Blackamoors in pearl-trimmed turbans and silk pantaloons stood behind the ladies, fanning them with braces of pure white ostrich feathers.

Lucrezia darted forward, laughing as she fell in a heap on the bench beside Giulia and called for a cold drink. I hung back, waiting to be acknowledged. Madonna Adriana eyed me for a long moment before she raised a bejeweled hand and gestured to the stool at her feet.

"No need for such formality, *cara*. Sit, tell us your news."

I did as I was bid, smoothing my skirts as I murmured, *"Grazie, Madonna."*

"Such a warm day," Giulia said. She arched her slender neck and stretched languidly. "I can scarcely keep my eyes open." No surprise there, as rumor had it she was with child. The Cardinal was said to be pleased. He had I don't know how many children by various mistresses, but there was no doubt that he had his favorites. Likely La Bella's would be another of them.

I stared at Giulia in unwilling fascination. She truly was the most beautiful woman I had ever seen. Some combination of golden hair, dark eyes, perfectly harmonious features, and a manner at once warm yet aloof compounded to create within her an aura of sensual and spiritual perfection. The latter was entirely misplaced, but as for the former . . . perhaps only Il Cardinale could truly judge.

For all that, she was not without a brain.

"How clever of His Grace," Giulia said, looking at me. "How daring. I had no idea he believed women capable of such responsibility."

So they did know. Good, that made everything simpler.

"His Grace," I said, "is, as always, infinitely wise and just."

The two women murmured their agreement in the way of prayers reflexively intoned. Lucrezia merely watched, eyes darting from one to the other.

"But surely we have nothing to fear here," Adriana ventured with a glance around the garden nestled within sheltering walls.

"Of course not," I said quickly. "I only wish to make certain that everything is as it should be."

"For which we are truly grateful," Giulia said. "We live in such tumultuous times."

Adriana sighed in agreement. "Truly, who can say from day to day what new perils afflict us? But enough of gloom. Just this morning my servant brought word that the Holy Father is improved. His fever has broken and he is said to be in good spirits."

Giulia raised her glass to her lips. No doubt the hint of sourness in her reply was from the *limonata* and nothing else.

"Wonderful news."

"Who knows what causes such illnesses," I said carefully. "Perhaps the prayers of Christendom have improved His Holiness's condition."

"Do you really think so?" Lucrezia asked. She tossed a small red ball to one of the pups. It ran after it panting, its short legs laboring.

Did I? My faith at that time was still, in some ways, the faith of a child, yet already questions were stirring within me.

"We must hope for the Pope's recovery," I said noncommittally. "Now, if you would not mind, I would like to speak of more immediate matters. As you know, it has become my responsibility to help safeguard this household." Lest that sound pompous, I added quickly, "Not that there is any need for you to be concerned, of course. I only ask that if you hire a new servant, if you change your habits in any way, or if you just notice anything unusual, you tell me at once. Does that meet with your approval?"

Silence reigned in the scented garden for a moment . . . another . . . until Giulia's laughter, likened far too often to the pealing of silver bells, rang out.

"Dear Francesca, so serious! How glad I am not to have the duties of a man! But of course, fear not, we will tell you whatever we must."

"Oh, yes, of course we will," Adriana assured me. "But for now, let us put aside such dark thoughts." She raised her hand again, summoning one of the blackamoors. "Bring us some amusement . . . music, games, oh, I remember, there is a letter from Cesare. Fetch that."

I ducked my head, concentrating on the pattern of my skirt, the antics of the dog at my feet, the scent of lemons on the freshening air. Anything other than the unwelcome reminder of Cesare, the not-quite-seventeen-year-old son of Il Cardinale, handsome as a dark angel, dangerous as Satan. A memory I would be best advised to forget forever.

"Cesare," Lucrezia sighed. "How I miss him!"

Giulia laughed, as did Adriana. Only I remained silent, there in the walled garden of the Cardinal's harem. Beyond, ancient Roma seethed and roiled, baking in the summer heat, waiting eternally for whatever was to come.

3

A year before, when he was in Rome for a brief visit with his papa, Cesare kissed me. Such a foolish thing for me to remember! Foolish and dangerous. He would have done a good deal more—indeed, he had his tongue in my mouth and his hand under my skirt very close to where the memory of him makes me damp—when I remembered that I was not an idiot servant girl to be tumbled for a few minutes' rough pleasure.

Yet neither could I afford to anger him. I had known him most of my life as I had known his sister. Until three years before when he was sent off to school, we had seen each other almost daily. His frequent visits home confirmed that his nature had not changed with exposure to the wider world. He was mercurial, this son the Cardinal meant to make into a priest. He took offense easily.

Thank God I am no such slave to emotion, as women are so often said to be. Yet it is men, I have observed, who are more likely to think with their nether parts than with the brain the good Lord gave them. Certainly, Cesare was one such. I waited until he freed my mouth and had turned his attention to my breasts before I said, "Be careful you do not break the vial in my girdle. It contains a deadly poison."

He looked up, slack-faced in the grip of passion. Like his father, he had a highly carnal nature. At barely thirteen, he became an adept at the altar of Venus. From then, his conquests were legion. But for all that, he was not without some sense.

"Poison?" he repeated.

I smiled sweetly. "Did you not know? I assist my father now in making potions. He says I am quite skilled." In truth, I had long since ceased to be the assistant, having mastered all my father could teach me and far more. But, of course, I would not reveal that.

He dropped his hands and stepped back, staring at me. I held my smile and made no attempt to cover myself. Let him not think I was denying him lest vanity prick him to foolishness.

"Ay, Francesca!" he muttered at last and whirled away, his crimson cloak flowing out behind him as he strode down the corridor and disappeared.

Only to reappear from time to time in dreams I blush to recollect.

Thunderstorms rumbled to the west but no hint of rain fell to relieve the torpor of the day. Having finished my business at the Palazzo Orsini, I set off for the market. I kept my pace brisk and my gaze straight ahead, ignoring the sallies flung by the young men who favored parti-colored hose and exaggerated plumes in their hats, and who seemed to have nothing better to do than loiter in the streets insulting lone women and looking for fights. Because of them, there were times when I preferred to travel the city in boy's garb. I admit to this practice with some hesitation because, as we all know, the "crime" of dressing as a male was the principle charge upon which blessed Saint Joan was brought to trial only a few decades ago, found guilty of heresy and burned alive. That the Church has since reversed itself on her account is scant comfort to some of us.

Between the Basilica di San Rocco, the seat of the bishop of Rome—which is to say, the pope—and the Vatican lies the thriving Campo dei Fiori, the city's most important market and the place where it is said everyone in Rome eventually comes, if only to watch the frequent executions. Here the preference is not so much for travertine as for the good red brick made from Tiber mud, which, on a summer day, glows like blushing gold.

As always, the market teemed with sellers, buyers, gawkers, and the inevitable thieves who vied with the cudgel-waving patrols hired by the merchants to create at least the illusion of security. All this went on over and around piles of garbage, offal, and manure, adding their aromas to the hanging baskets and trailing trellises of flowers that filled even the most modest lane.

I passed by the streets of the crossbow-makers and coffer-makers, glanced briefly at the offerings of the cloth merchants and goldsmiths, and made my way finally to the Via dei Vertrarari, where the glassmakers clustered.

I had been there before, many times, but even so I hesitated before turning into the street. In a city that lives for gossip, news of my advancement in Borgia's household was bound to be in the air. Conscious of the glances following me, I walked quickly past a dozen shops, stopping finally in front of a modest, timbered building half-hidden between its neighbors on either side.

A young boy of almost six years with a mop of dark hair and the lingering softness of babyhood in his features sat cross-legged on the ground, playing at marbles as he guarded a small selection of glassware. He gaped at me for a moment before jumping up and running full tilt to fling his arms around my waist. I knelt to catch him and found myself smiling.

"Donna Francesca," he exclaimed and pulled away a little, the better to look at me. "Are you all right?" Patting my cheek with his grubby little hand, he added, "I am so sorry about your papa. You must be very sad."

My throat tightened and for a moment I could not trust myself to speak. I had watched Nando grow from a babe in swaddling clothes, laughing at his antics and cosseting his small hurts and disappointments. If there were ever moments when I yearned for a child of my own, they were in his company.

"I am sad," I said, because I would not insult him with dishonesty, "but I am also very glad to be here with you."

Satisfied, he let go of me and darted inside. I just had time to rise before a tall, powerfully built man in his late twenties, his bare chest covered by a leather apron, stepped from the shop.

"Francesca!"

I mustered a smile that I hoped concealed my unease. Rocco Moroni had appeared in Rome half a dozen years before, bringing with him a rare gift for glassmaking and his motherless son. My father was one of his first customers. I had stolen my share of glances at him during our frequent visits to his shop, for he was by any measure a handsome man. The previous winter, he had approached my father about the possibility of a marriage between us. I could only conclude that in the innocence of his own nature, he had not realized that my interest in my father's trade went far beyond that of a dutiful daughter, for what man would ever knowingly link himself to one skilled in such dark arts? Nor could he have sensed anything of the even greater darkness within me, that place where my nightmare lives.

For a fortnight after Rocco's proposal, I struggled to convince myself that I could be the woman he and Nando both deserved before conceding defeat with a mixture of relief and grief that haunted me still. Rocco seemed to accept my demurral with good grace, but he had become more watchful in my presence, as though realizing belatedly that I was more complex than he had thought me to be. Now, though, he seemed only kind and welcoming even as he cast a quick look up and down the street before stepping back toward the shelter of the shop.

"*Venite,* the air has ears. Come inside."

I followed him into the cool shadows of the single ground-floor room. He shut the door behind us and looked at me closely, his dark brown eyes alight with sympathy.

"I am so sorry about your father. We came to the palazzo—" he nodded at Nando, who stood nearby, looking from one to the other of us.

"We wanted to give you our condolences, but they would not admit us or even acknowledge what had happened."

"They buried him at night." I hadn't meant to speak of it, but in the presence of a man I knew to have been my father's friend and, I dared to hope, my own, the pain of my loss would not be denied. "In the graveyard at Santa Maria. All in a rush, as though they thought they could hide what had happened to him."

Rocco nodded. He reached out a hand as though to console me but let it fall in the air between us. Gently, he said, "Giovanni is with our Lord now. He has left the trials of this world for the eternal joy of paradise."

His certainty pricked me, who had none. I envied him at the same time that I resented his acceptance of what I could only question.

As though understanding the fear such doubts provoked in me, he added, "Your father was a good man at heart. Surely, the blessed Lord will receive him. Besides, he—"

"Did the bidding of Il Cardinale," I interjected, "prince of Holy Mother Church, who gave him absolution. So I tell myself. I can only hope that is enough."

As for myself, who had killed without the bidding of Il Cardinale, indeed in opposition to his wishes, I could only wonder what price I would pay in the world beyond.

The glassmaker's broad chest rose and fell in a deep sigh. "*Cara,* I believe in a loving God, a God who forgives—"

Mindful of the presence of his son, he stopped there, but I understood. Rocco, too, had his own need for forgiveness. While still a child, little older than his son, he had been pledged to the Dominican Order and had lived as a friar for several years. Only love for a young woman had driven him to leave the Order to marry her and then to care for his son, the child of that love left motherless at birth. For those loving acts, he still could be hunted down, scourged, and branded as a betrayer of his faith, all this by the same men who kept their priestly offices at the same time they kept their mistresses and plotted to advance the children they had by them.

So much for the state of Holy Mother Church. As to the state of any person's soul, who could say?

With a reassuring smile for the boy who could not take his eyes from us, I moved away, pretending interest in a glass vase set in a niche near the far wall. "But I forget myself. I came to discuss business."

Rocco glanced at his son and nodded. "Nando, go down to the bakery and get us a nice fresh loaf, all right? Tell Maria I want it warm from the oven, and while you're there, get yourself a biscotto. "

He drew a coin from his pocket and sent it sailing through the air, to be caught by the child who, grinning broadly, took off out of the shop and down the street.

When we were alone, Rocco opened a cabinet and took out a bottle of wine along with two goblets. Having filled both, he handed one to me.

"We have a few minutes before he gets back. Tell me, is it true what I hear? Did you—"

I had dreaded this moment, when I had to admit what I had done and face the possibility that Rocco would turn away from me in disgust. As I had when confronted by Borgia, I spoke in a rush.

"I did what I had to do. My father was murdered and no one has lifted a hand to bring his killers to justice. It is left for me to do so. But as a woman without power or influence, how could I? I had no choice. Besides," I added, emboldened as he continued to look at me with deep concern but no sign of abhorrence, "the Spaniard was no innocent. By all repute, he had killed many times."

Rocco studied me for a moment before he asked, "Is it justice you seek . . . or vengeance?"

I understood that the question was critical for him, speaking as it did to the condition of my soul. Yet I was reluctant to confront it.

"Is there a difference, at least where my father is concerned?"

Had Rocco remained a Dominican, I believe he would have shown a talent for theological debate. His propensity for it annoyed me at times yet I will not deny that when I was most troubled in my conscience, I sought him out. He was, and will always remain, the lodestone guiding me through dark waters.

"Of course there is a difference," he said. "Justice serves the good of all. Vengeance is purely personal, therefore selfish. It cannot find favor with God."

"Do not expect me to feel *impersonally* about my father's murderers. When they pay, and they will, the world will be the better for it."

Rocco did not dispute that, but he raised another concern. "All well and good, but what of Borgia? Now that you are in his service, won't he expect certain things of you?"

I took a sip of the cool, crisp wine in the hope that it would steady me and shrugged. "He can expect whatever he wishes, but contrary to rumor, he deployed my father very sparingly and only as a last resort. I see no reason for that to change."

To my great relief, Rocco appeared reassured by my responses, at least enough to move on. "What is known of your father's killers?" he asked.

"The Cardinal's steward informed me that they were thugs bent on nothing more than robbery. And why not? We all know that Rome is a dangerous place."

"Yes, of course, but still . . ." he looked at me carefully. "You don't believe that?"

I hesitated. I trusted the glassmaker but was unsure if I wanted to involve him in my troubles any more than I was already doing simply by being there.

"Something weighed on my father in the final days of his life," I said finally. "Whatever it was, it drove him to prayer at all hours, which was very unlike him. Several times, I found him on his knees, almost in tears. He would not tell me what tormented him, but he was making plans to send me to the country when he was killed."

"You think it had to do with Giovanni's work for Il Cardinale?"

"It is hard to think what else could have been involved. My father lived for his work and for me. There was nothing else in his life, at least not that I know of."

"But he served the Cardinal for many years. Why would he be so troubled now?"

"I don't know," I admitted. "Perhaps it became too much for him." Would it for me as well?

I set down the goblet and looked out into the backyard, where the furnace that Rocco used to turn ordinary sand into works of unsurpassed beauty burned night and day. Through its open vent, I could see flames flickering and could almost feel their purifying heat. Even so, the sight made me shiver as though I were in the grip of deep, uncontrollable cold.

"But I do know," I said, "that I will not rest until I find who killed him. Find them and make them pay. I cannot do less."

Nando returned moments later, lurching with a child's eagerness into the silence that followed my declaration. He stood, uncertain, until his father smiled. Taking the loaf of bread he had brought, Rocco made a show of smelling it appreciatively.

"Well done, *mi figlio*. Come, sit, let's eat."

Over bread, cheese, sausage, and more of the good wine Rocco poured, I relaxed a little. Certainly, I was in better humor by the time we finished and pushed the plates away.

"What is it you wish?" Rocco asked when we were done refreshing ourselves.

Wasting no more time, I said, "Tubing mainly, very thin, such as you made for my father last year. It is very good quality but inevitably it breaks after awhile. I need to replace it and I also need more of the pipettes you made, as well as beakers, bulbs for heating, and several lenses."

I drew a paper from my pocket and laid it on the table. "I have the list here. The Cardinal has been very generous, payment won't be a problem."

Rocco waved that aside as though it were of no matter, but I was proud all the same to be able to say it. Proud, too, when he looked over the list carefully, giving it his full attention.

"It all seems in order apart from the lenses. I may have to find someone who can make those for you."

I nodded. "So long as he is discreet."

"He wouldn't last long in our business if he wasn't."

Unspoken between us was the knowledge that equipment such as I sought and Rocco made was believed by many to be used by servants of the Devil. Who else would want to plumb the secrets of nature so thoroughly, transform matter in new and possibly dangerous ways, and even try to understand the very essence of Creation? Such was the province of God, not Man, as any right-thinking person should surely know.

Yet here in Rome and elsewhere in the Italian states, reaching up into La Francia and the Low Countries, even, it was said, as far away as L'Angleterre, there were daring men and women willing to give their lives for the conviction that faith is not a substitute for knowledge.

It was even whispered that some had dared to band together in mutual support, calling themselves that which they most longed to bring into the world: Lux—Light. If my suspicions were correct, my father had been one of them.

With my business concluded, I lingered, enjoying Rocco and

Nando's company. The love so evident between them reminded me of all I had lost, yet it was still a comfort to know that such love remained possible in a world that seemed to be spiraling into ever greater darkness and danger.

When I finally rose to leave, Rocco walked me to the door. Keeping his voice low so the boy could not hear, he touched my arm lightly and said, "Giovanni's murder shocked everyone, yet so far there has been very little talk. That won't last. If I hear anything, I will send word to you. In the meantime, guard yourself well, Francesca. Your father would want nothing less."

I nodded in gratitude. Rocco might seem a simple, even humble man, but the nature of his work meant that he had contacts in the universities, among the great families, and, it was even said, within the Curia itself. Inevitably that meant he was also privy to a great many secrets. It was possible that he knew those my father had been associated with, who might in turn have information regarding the circumstances of his death. It was even within the realm of possibility that Rocco himself was part of Lux, assuming that it truly existed. As not even my father had ever confided in me directly concerning it, I could hardly expect Rocco to admit any such involvement. But I could and did count on him to deal with me honestly.

I pressed his hand in thanks, bade a fond farewell to Nando over his father's shoulder, and set off for the Palazzo Borgia. It was in my mind that I needed to unpack the chest I had so hastily filled after learning of my father's death, all that I was able to secure before the Cardinal's guards sealed the apartment. They had searched the chest, but finding only my own clothing, had seen no reason not to let me take it. Had they known of the compartment hidden beneath the false bottom, they would have acted differently.

The thunderheads were passing off toward the west and a freshening breeze blew out of the north. The relative coolness lightened my step and may, along with my general preoccupation, have contributed to my failure to pay proper attention to my surroundings. Whatever the cause, I was taken by surprise when, almost within sight of the palazzo, a trio of men appeared suddenly from an alley.

Blocking the street in front of me, they looked me up and down and sneered.

"Puttana," the largest of them said. "What do you think you are doing, whore?"

"Get away from me," I snapped. At that moment, I was not yet afraid. They seemed just three more idiots bent on harassing women. My clothes marked me as not of the nobility but still far from poor, a woman who would have a degree of protection. They could be bold enough to verbally assault me but nothing more. Even so, I did not wait for their response but began to go around them.

Only to be stopped when the one nearest me grabbed my arm.

"Puttana," he repeated and threw me to the ground.

In that instant, everything changed for me. The illusion of safety built on my success challenging Il Cardinale shattered. I had taken a terrible risk, even killed a man, only to come to this? That seemed impossible and yet it was happening, right then and there. Even as my mind screamed that I had to regain my feet and flee, shock paralyzed me.

Before I could recover and act, one of the men kicked me in the stomach. Pain and disbelief made me cry out even as I instinctively curled into a tight ball, trying to protect myself.

"What are you doing? Stop!"

I was a servant of one of the most powerful men in all of Christendom, protected by his might and my own skill. They were insane to attack me. Yet my father had been similarly protected and he was dead, beaten to a pulp in a street very like the one where I lay, helpless to shield myself from the blows that fell like crimson rain.

"Stop!"

"Get yourself to a nunnery, *puttana,*" one of the men said. He leaned down and yanked on my skirt, pulling it up to expose my bare legs and beyond. The primal terror of rape filled me and I stopped thinking entirely, becoming only a desperate animal struggling to escape.

They laughed, the sound enveloping me. I looked up just then, saw the medal dangling from around the throat of one of them, and heard myself moan. It was a papal medal, identical to the one given to my father the previous year by the hand of Pope Innocent VIII himself, an honor the Cardinal had procured for his trusted servant. My father had worn the medal faithfully but it had not been found on his body. Its disappearance had been a mystery—until now.

"Don't cause any more trouble," a different voice said, and another blow landed, the metal-tipped boot driving hard into my ribs. "Or you'll end up the same way your father did."

I couldn't breathe, my heart hammered so frantically I thought it would burst. Pain filled me, vying with maddened fear. As though from a great distance, I heard:

"We're going easy on you. Learn from this and you might even live."

I cringed, hating them, hating myself, hating the horror of what had happened to my father, what he must have felt as he died.

And then it was over; the attackers were gone. There was only the damp cobblestones hard and sharp under me, the stink of the street, and the cool breeze on my bared skin.

That and the old woman looking at me from the terrace of an

apartment above a shop from which everyone else had fled at the first sign of trouble. Just an old woman with her knitting, her toothless mouth wide open as she grinned, vastly entertained by the doings in the filth below.

4

I slipped back into the palazzo through a little-used door. Clutching my bruised side, I made my way up a narrow flight of stairs hidden in the wall. Having regained my rooms without being seen, I slumped, shaking, on the bed. For a brief time I gave into the storm of emotion that threatened to consume me.

The men had lain in wait for me, either that or they had followed me without my being aware. In either case, I had been singled out deliberately for attack as it was now beyond doubt my father had been. But why? What had he been doing that had led to his murder? What did someone want to prevent me from doing?

Even as such questions tormented me, grief for my father more than equaled fear for myself. Before, I had merely imagined what had happened to him. Now I knew for certain what his final moments had been like. That knowledge fueled the hatred that grew within me, becoming stronger with each labored breath.

Hatred for the men who had made me cringe and sob. Hatred for my father's murderers, who, if they were not all the same men, were surely allied with them. And above all else, hatred for whoever had given the orders. That man in a quiet room somewhere with his clean hands, he would have to suffer more than any other. I would see to it.

At length, I sat up and wiped my eyes. Unwilling to call for help and set off a maelstrom of gossip and speculation, I resolved to see to my injuries myself. Removing my clothes, I winced and had to bite my lips to keep from crying out. My ribs and stomach had taken the worst of it, but bruises were forming on my arms, my legs, and when I looked over my shoulder into the mirror, I could see that my back was already a patchwork of darkening splotches the size and shape of boot tips.

With great difficulty I managed to apply salve to most of the worst areas and to get a bandage around my ribs, which I suspected were cracked. By the time I was done, and had dressed myself again in clean garments, my hands were shaking and I was so exhausted that I could do nothing but lie back on the bed, propped up by a bolster, and pray that sleep would take me.

It did, but only briefly. Too soon the acute discomfort over every inch of my body woke me. I considered taking an opiate but decided against it. With the easing of pain would come a loss of control that I could not afford. Instead, I forced myself off the bed and knelt beside a carved wooden chest. Opening the lid took almost all my strength; I had to pause and inhale slowly against the stabbing pain that came with every breath. Pacing myself, I removed each item of clothing until I reached what appeared to be the bottom of the chest.

Anyone suspecting that the bottom was false would look for a slit to pry up the wood and reveal a hidden compartment. But they would look in vain, for the chest itself was an ingenious mechanism designed to keep the false bottom in place. To free it, the right sequence of steps had to be carried out on the four outer sides of the chest itself, a procedure that involved sliding separate sections of wood in different directions until at last the hidden lock was released. Only then would the bottom tilt slightly, revealing itself. One misstep and the lock would reset.

My father had taught me the secret of the chest while I was still a child. He said it had been crafted by a sailor from the east whom he had befriended and who claimed that such chests were common in his homeland. Whatever its origins, it was more secure than any strongbox and had kept its secrets inviolate throughout the years.

When the bottom was freed, I lifted it out carefully and set it to one side. The compartment beneath was fitted to hold sealed vials and bottles, each labeled in my father's neat hand. As important, it also contained the records we had both kept of our experiments and discoveries.

The supplies and records were all I had been able to gather up and hide in the moments immediately after learning of my father's death and before the Cardinal's guards rushed to secure the apartment. In the small, tidy workroom hidden behind heavy curtains, the condotierri had found shelves of chemicals and several tables holding equipment—some of the sort Rocco made but also scales, mortars, grinding stones, and the like. To their untrained eyes, it would have appeared that nothing had been disturbed. Satisfied, they had backed away hastily, several going so far as to make the sign of the cross.

Given a few hours, the Spaniard would have realized that there were gaps among the supplies, certain compounds that should have been present but were not. Questions would have been raised. However, he had not lived long enough to make that discovery. It remained my secret.

Sitting on the floor, I read slowly and carefully through the last entries my father had made, dating back to several months before. So far as I could see, there was nothing unusual except for the lack of more recent entries. While maintaining a careful watch over the Cardinal's households, he had been free to pursue his search for the *alchaest,* the universal solvent in which all substances could be dissolved and which, he believed, could be used to produce medicines capable of curing every illness.

That a man who made his living as a poisoner sought to find the key to saving lives did not strike me as odd, knowing my father's complex nature as I did. However, I had been concerned that his investigations were leading him to question the very nature of illness itself, a highly dangerous undertaking in a world that decrees such suffering to be the will of God. But I found no indication of that in his notes. Indeed, I found precious little.

Frustrated, I put everything away again and closed the chest. Standing required all my will and strength. I was reconsidering the opiate when there was a knock at the door.

I opened it to find the captain of the condotierri. He inclined his head graciously even as his keen eyes missed nothing.

"*Buonasera,* Donna Francesca. His Eminence requires your presence."

And he had sent the captain of his guard to fetch me? Highly unlikely unless the Cardinal had reconsidered his act of clemency toward me, in which case Vittoro Romano would not have been smiling.

"How good of you to come yourself, Capitano Romano."

The officer made no effort to deny that his presence on so menial an errand was unusual. "There was a report of a disturbance nearby a few hours ago. I wondered if you knew anything about it."

As he spoke, his gaze focused on my face, which, being as stiff and sore as the rest of my body, I thought must also be bruised.

"A disturbance, really? Of what sort?"

"That's unclear, but a woman may have been accosted."

He waited, giving me every opportunity to tell him what he had undoubtedly already concluded for himself had happened. But I had made up my mind to say nothing. Beyond the humiliation, I did not want anyone, least of all the Cardinal, to know I was aware that my father had been targeted for murder. Unlikely though it was, there was a possibility that Borgia himself might have been involved. Certainly, he was most probably the source of whatever had so tormented my father in his final weeks of life.

"How terrible," I said. "If only there were more men such as yourself, Captain, Rome would be far safer."

Vittoro blinked in surprise at the compliment. He was far too astute a man not to know that I was deflecting him, but neither was there anything he could do about that. At least not at the moment.

"Let us not keep Il Cardinale waiting," I said, and stepped out of the apartment, shutting the door behind me.

The Cardinal's apartments were on the first upper story of the palazzo facing the river. No expense had been spared in their decoration and furnishings. Parquetry floors were covered with lush carpets in the Moorish fashion, the walls displayed magnificent tapestries devoted mainly to scenes from the hunt, velvet upholstered couches and gilded tables were scattered throughout. At every turn, the palazzo announced itself to be the residence of a lord at least as powerful as any secular prince.

Vittoro left me in the antechamber decorated with murals displaying the fall of man. Unwilling to sit—and betray my soreness when I had to stand again—I sought distraction studying the scenes that, though drawn from Scripture, were imbued with earthy sensuality.

Eve in all her naked glory seemed of far more interest to the artist than did the hapless Adam, who appeared only once, in the act of receiving the fateful apple. Until then, his feckless wife was shown disporting herself beneath a waterfall, on a bed of wildflowers, and anywhere else she could show off her lush figure. The serpent made a prominent appearance, mostly leering at her. I studied the snake carefully, trying to decide whether the rumors were true that it had been fashioned to resemble a certain rival cardinal.

I was still considering that when the concealed door to the inner sanctum opened and a secretary beckoned me into the Cardinal's presence. Borgia sat behind a desk of burled wood and inlaid marble. He looked younger than his years and appeared filled with vigor despite what had undoubtedly already been a busy day.

Watching me walk across the thick carpet toward him, Il Cardinale frowned. "What happened to you?"

"I had a fall," I replied. "It's nothing."

Borgia looked unconvinced, so much so that he waved me into a chair opposite his desk. Such an unusual favor could only have been prompted by a reluctance to see me collapse in a heap at his feet.

Perched on the edge of the chair, keeping my back ramrod straight, I asked, "How may I serve you, signore?"

"You may begin by telling me how you found things in my dear cousin's household."

This, at least, I had expected and was prepared to answer. "Madonna Adriana gave me the kindness of an audience. I asked to be informed of any changes, new servants and the like, and she agreed. I assured her that there was no particular cause for concern."

I broke off and looked at the Cardinal carefully. "I hope I was correct in that, signore?" A second audience in just two days was, of course, a great honor, but it also signaled that Borgia had matters on his mind that concerned his poisoner.

"I know of no particular threat," he said. "However—"

Ah, yes, here it came. The reason for my summons. In truth, the likely reason for my survival. The Cardinal had need of my skills.

"However," he continued, "we live in precarious times. The Holy Father's health is failing—"

"I heard just this morning that he is improved."

Borgia frowned, whether at my presumption in interrupting him or because of what I said, I could not tell. "Market gossip, nothing more. Giovanni is fifty-nine years old and his constitution has never been good."

I resisted the urge to note that the Cardinal himself was two years older than the allegedly dying Pope. Comparisons between the two men were irrelevant. Borgia was a bull of a man who seemed to thrive on excess whereas Giovanni Battista Cibo, as he had been called before mounting the Throne of Saint Peter, seemed worn down by his own indulgences. Father to at least a dozen children, would-be crusader to free the Holy Land at the same time he was in the pay of the sultan of Turkey, exploiter of the practice of simony, the selling of papal offices, in a bid to replenish his constantly emptying purse, the Pope was said to fear death and the reckoning to follow so greatly as to be willing to commit the most despicable acts in order to avoid it.

"In such times," the Cardinal continued, "heightened vigilance is merely prudent. May I trust you to see to that?"

Solemnly, I nodded. "Of course, signore. You may trust me in all things."

Borgia appeared less than convinced. However, for the moment he would at least pretend to believe me. "Good, then tell me what you know of the work your father was doing at the time of his death."

I had to answer carefully, of course. On the one hand, I could not afford to expose my ignorance. On the other, I could hardly claim to possess knowledge I did not have and hope to retain the Cardinal's trust in any measure.

"He was pursuing various alchemical interests," I said. "Perhaps you could tell me to which you refer?"

This ploy proved less than successful. The Cardinal sat back in his chair, eyed me directly, and said, "So he did not tell you. Yet the two of you worked closely together, did you not?"

"I . . . assisted my father, yes."

Borgia cast me a look that for a moment made me wonder if he knew more about me than he chose to reveal. For all that I had watched him in the ten years I had lived in his house, was it possible that he had also watched the poisoner's daughter, drawn so irresistibly to her father's trade by the darkness within her? I would have thought myself an unlikely subject for his interest but it was possible that I was wrong.

"Did he leave no records?" Borgia asked.

I swallowed against the dryness of my throat and met his gaze forthrightly. "There are records but they break off several months ago. He wrote nothing of what he was doing more recently."

"Do you find that odd?"

I answered honestly, for once. "Yes, I do. My father believed that study and experimentation are never enough by themselves. Only with good records can results be understood in the perspective of larger efforts."

"A sensible approach. It stands to reason then that he did leave records, just not with you."

I doubted that. The nature of my father's work—which had become mine—makes it very difficult to form friendships, much less have confidants. If he would not trust me with knowledge of what he was doing, it was unlikely that he would have trusted anyone else.

"It is important that those records be found," the Cardinal said. Again, his gaze locked on mine. "I expect you to secure them without delay."

"I will do my best, signore, of course. But until I know what inquiry occupied my father, I cannot say with assurance that I will be able to discover whether he kept records at all, much less what he did with them."

I hoped that the Cardinal would simply tell me what my father had been doing, assuming he himself knew. But instead he slid a folded piece of paper across his desk toward me. Opening it, I found a name—S. Montefiore—accompanied by an address in the Quarto Ebreo, the Jewish Quarter. Borgia's interest in that area surprised me. Like every other prince of Holy Mother Church, I assumed him to be no friend of the Jews.

"Go there," he instructed. "And when you do, remember that you go as my servant, not as your father's daughter. Is that clear?"

No, of course it wasn't, yet I assured him that it was entirely so.

I had risen and was being ushered out by a secretary when Borgia had a final instruction.

"Francesca," he said, startling me by the use of my given name.

I turned so quickly that every muscle in my bruised and battered back clenched in pain. Through gritted teeth, I replied, "Signore?"

"From now on, do not go out without an escort."

Who would watch my every move and report to the Cardinal where I went, who I met, what I did. Everything within me rebelled at the notion. Almost everything. With the memory of the attack I had suffered still uppermost in my mind, a small part of me accepted the relinquishing of my freedom. It was not, after all, as though I had a choice. Il Cardinale willed it.

"So be it, signore," I said, and took my leave.

The entrances to the Jewish Quarter being sealed between sunset and sunrise, I had to wait until the following morning before carrying out the Cardinal's instructions. Even then, I needed an hour's soak in a hot bath before I could move with anything resembling ease.

My ribs still hurt acutely, but the rest of me had settled down to a dull throb. The bruise on my forehead, thankfully the only one on my face, had darkened considerably but could be covered by a swathe of my hair. However, to achieve that I had to forgo my usual braid.

I was fiddling with my hair, trying to get used to it being down, as I left my rooms. In the corridor, I all but walked into Vittoro Romano.

"Captain, what a surprise." The more so because he was not wearing his usual uniform. Instead, the captain of the condotierri was dressed in a nondescript doublet and hose such as a modest merchant or tradesman might wear.

"*Buongiorno,* Donna Francesca," he said with a smile. "I trust you are feeling better this morning?"

"Yes, certainly. May I ask why you are here?"

"You have an errand to run outside the palazzo, is that not so?"

Of course it was, just as it was true that the captain knew of it and of Il Cardinale's order that I have an escort. However, I had not anticipated that he would provide that escort himself.

"I thought you would assign someone to accompany me," I said as we walked down the corridor toward the stairs. Indeed, I had hoped to steer him toward someone young and callow, likely to be uncertain how to deal with a woman of authority and therefore easy to manage.

Vittoro seemed to be following my train of thought for he smiled, a rare disturbance of the normally somber folds of his face. "I haven't been to the Jewish Quarter in quite awhile. I am curious to see what is happening there."

I understood what he was referring to. In the almost three months since their most Catholic Majesties, King Ferdinand and Queen Isabella of Spain, issued their edict expelling all Jews from their kingdom, tens of thousands of desperate refugees had streamed into other parts of Europe, including Rome. There, as in other cities, they had to cram into the already overcrowded ghettos where increasingly the Ebreos were forced to live. Conditions in the ghetto, situated on marshy tidal land beside the Tiber, had never been good, but it was said that now they were rapidly becoming deplorable.

"Do you know what we will find at the address the Cardinal gave me?" I asked as we stepped out onto the street. Rain showers during the night had washed away the dust and grime from the cobblestones and left the air cooler than in recent days. A light breeze carried the scent of the lemon and olive orchards just outside the city.

"I do not," Vittoro replied promptly enough that I believed him. "However, I am certain that whatever may be there, you will deal with it properly."

The frank expression of his confidence surprised me. I did not know the captain well, having only observed him during my years growing up in the palazzo. But I was aware that he had been friends with my father. The two men had played chess together regularly.

"Thank you," I said quietly. "I will do my best."

With Vittoro at my side, the walk down to the Sant'Angelo district where the ghetto was located was uneventful. Even so, I could not shake off my sense of apprehension. At the entrance to every shadowed alley and lane we passed, I relived the moment when my attackers sprang out at me. By the time we neared our destination, my palms were damp and I was breathing rapidly.

"Do you need to rest?" Vittoro asked. He took my arm lightly to steady me.

"No," I assured him. "I am fine." I looked ahead to the walls rising before us and the rooftops beyond. Despite the sunny day, a grim shadow of despair seemed to hang over the ghetto. I could not wait to be done there.

"I would just like to finish with this," I said.

"Of course," he said, nodding.

At this time, there was not yet a single wall around the ghetto, although many of the streets that would have led out of it were blocked by piles of stone and rubble. Since the announcement of the edict expelling the Jews from Spain, talk had increased of the need to build an actual wall, but thus far it was only talk.

Even so, it was no easy matter to come and go between the ghetto and the rest of Rome. Wagons were allowed through only one checkpoint, guarded by condotierri who decided who could pass according to what was pressed into their palms.

Those on foot passed a little more easily but not much. Only Vittoro's air of authority and the Borgia insignia he did not hesitate to display assured that we were admitted without harassment. That proved to be a mixed blessing. The moment I stepped inside the ghetto, I feared I would gag. The smell of so many people packed together in so small a space was overwhelming. Garbage and offal lay everywhere, the stinking piles covered with swarms of mosquitoes drawn from the river. With every high tide, filthy water washed into the lower floors of many of the ramshackle shops and tenements, leaving deposits of mud and waste. Hardly a breath of air stirred between buildings so closely packed together as to all but block out the sun.

But all that paled beside the mass of humanity that spilled from every doorway and packed the streets—spindly, dull-eyed children; men and women stooped and worn far beyond their years; and the very few elderly, huddled despite the heat, rocking back and forth as though trying to escape the unbearable grief that was their lives.

"My God," I whispered and gripped Vittoro's hand.

He nodded somberly. "The priests say the expulsion from Spain is only God's latest punishment of the Ebreos for killing Christ."

I had heard this but could not claim to understand it. The house priests who conducted Mass at the Cardinal's palazzo rarely mentioned such matters. They favored sermons exalting the wisdom of authority and the necessity of obedience to it. But occasionally they would mention, almost in passing, that the Jews were to blame for every ill in the world because they had killed the Redeemer of Mankind, Christ.

Once I had asked my father why the Jews had done that, but he had only smiled sadly and reminded me that it was Roman soldiers at the foot of the cross.

Was it then really Rome that was being punished? The Rome of Holy Mother Church with its plague of princes and palaces? With men like Rodrigo Borgia who aspired to be its ruler?

I shied away from such thoughts. They were matters best left unquestioned by anyone hoping to remain alive. But they were also distracting enough that I failed to feel the hand slipped lightly into the slit in my skirt and from there into the pouch I wore beneath where I carried coins, my keys, and a few other important items. If I hadn't stumbled on a jagged cobblestone at just that moment, the pickpocket relieving me of my purse might have gotten away unnoticed.

Instead, I felt the hand against my leg and instinctively cried out: "Thief!"

The culprit attempted to dart away into the crowd but Vittoro, despite his age, was faster. His hand lashed out, closing on the scruff of an unwashed neck.

"Not so fast!" The captain gave a hard shake to the thin, ragged creature dangling a foot or two off the ground. "What do you think you're doing?"

Incredibly, the boy—who looked no more than six or seven years of age but was probably several years older—made no effort to plead for mercy. Instead, he kicked fiercely, trying to land a blow anywhere he could and at the same time shrieked:

"*Bastardo!* Let go of me! Let go!"

Vittoro raised his free hand to strike the child but I grabbed hold of his arm. "Best not," I said softly and inclined my head toward the surrounding crowd.

The captain followed the direction of my gaze and saw what I had seen. No one among the Ebreos was making any sort of threatening gesture toward us, much less attempting to rescue the boy. But the great mass of them on all sides and their silent watchfulness raised the question of what exactly they would do if they thought the boy in danger of arrest or worse.

"This won't help us," I said, still keeping my voice very low.

Vittoro nodded. He set the boy on his feet but kept firm hold of his thin arm.

"What is your name?" he asked the young thief.

The answer was a great wad of phlegm, remarkable for so small a boy, that landed precisely an inch beyond the tip of Vittoro's boots.

The captain sighed and shook his head. "What way is that to act? I asked you a civil question." He looked down at the boy, who was beginning to frown through his defiance as the scene failed to play out according to his expectation. "But perhaps you don't know your name," Vittoro suggested. "Perhaps you don't know your father."

"I'm not the bastard," the boy shot back. "You are."

"In fact, I am not," Vittoro replied patiently. "My name is Vittoro Romano. This lady is Francesca Giordano. Who are you?"

Grudgingly, the boy replied, "Benjamin Albanesi."

"Good," Vittoro said. "Benjamin Albanesi, I am going to release you. When I do, you have two choices. You can run off and be done with this. Or you can stay, help us find the place we seek, and earn a silver penny for your trouble instead of trying to steal one."

Benjamin stared at him suspiciously. "Let me see the penny."

With a sigh for the demands of children, Vittoro did as he was bid. The pickpocket looked carefully at the coin, then held out his hand. When it was placed in his palm, he weighed it with equal caution before he finally nodded.

"*Bene.* I will help you."

The crowd, apparently satisfied, moved on. Vittoro released the boy who remained where he was, looking at us both.

"What is it you seek?" he asked.

I drew out the paper the Cardinal had given me and showed it to the boy, assuming that I would have to read it for him, but Benjamin surprised me. He took a quick look and nodded.

"I know the place. Come on."

We followed him down one crowded street, around a corner into a narrow lane, and out again onto another street. Deeper and deeper we went into the maze of the ghetto until I began to wonder if we were being taken in circles. Along the way, we saw streets of another sort, where the tidal overflow from the river did not impinge, nor did the teeming masses. Behind high, featureless walls constructed to give no hint of what they concealed, Jewish merchants who did business from L'Angleterre and the far-off lands of the Rus to the souks of Morocco and Istanbul lived in what was whispered to be unbridled luxury. Though they might have greater comforts than others of their tribe, they were no more free to live outside the ghetto than was any other unconverted Jew. The only route to such freedom lay in the denial of their faith. More than a few Jews had taken that path and become *conversi,* but not without great peril. They were the first to be proclaimed heretics and the first to burn.

At last, we came to a crooked lane all but hidden in shadow. A straggling line of people waited in front of what appeared to be an apothecary's shop. Several held sick children in their arms. Others supported friends or family members who were unable themselves to stand.

"Cover your face," Vittoro ordered as he quickly pulled up a length of his shirt and did the same.

I obeyed. My eyes darted back and forth, narrowing as I took in the misery on every side. In quick succession, I saw suppurating sores, unhealed wounds, breathing that racked skeletal bodies, and people so close to death as to be insensible. With difficulty, we reached the apothecary's door just as a middle-aged woman opened it.

"Binyamin," the woman exclaimed. "What are you doing here?"

The boy, who had not bothered to cover his face, eyed the woman confidently. "Benjamin, Signora Montefiore. *Per favore,* my name is Benjamin."

"Such foolishness. You have no business here. It is not safe."

"I do have business, signora. I have brought these two to meet you." He stepped aside and with a flourish, indicated the two of us.

Seeing us, the woman frowned. Her gaze settled on me as, without thinking, I lowered my shawl from in front of my face. After studying me for a moment, the woman asked softly, "What brings you here, lady?"

Remembering the name on the paper the Cardinal had given me, I replied, "I seek Signore Montefiore, your husband, perhaps?"

A faint smile touched the woman's exhausted face beneath the cloud of silver hair emerging from a roughly tied kerchief. "Then you seek in vain. My husband died ten years ago. I am Sofia Montefiore. I think it is I you want to see."

She stepped aside for us to enter.

Once in the apothecary shop, I looked around quickly. What I saw confirmed what I already suspected: The shop was functioning as a hospital for the very sick. Almost every inch of the floor was taken up with patients lying on litters or on the floor itself. Most were wrapped in threadbare blankets. Others, those in the throes of fever, had thrown off their blankets. A handful of men and women went among them, offering what comfort they could.

Vittoro tugged hard on my arm. "We must leave. *Now.*"

Tempted though I was to agree with him, I shook my head. "Not yet. I must find out why the Cardinal sent me here."

To Sofia Montefiore, I said, "My name is Francesca Giordano. I am—"

"I know who you are," the woman said. She wiped her red, worn hands on the apron covering her simple gown, both clean despite the chaos surrounding her, and gestured toward the rear of the shop. "We can talk in there."

With a quick glance at Vittoro, she added, "Unless you are afraid to linger."

The captain flushed but I did not hesitate. I followed the woman toward the back, mindful that Vittoro did the same. Briefly, I considered asking him to wait outside, but to do so would be to offend both his pride and his sense of duty. Together, we accompanied Sofia Montefiore into a small workroom.

When the door was closed behind us, shutting out the mass of suffering humanity in the front of the shop, I asked, "You recognized me. How?"

Sofia Montefiore leaned against a cluttered table. She appeared to be inexpressively weary yet her voice remained strong. "I knew your father. One day when you went with him to the Campo dei Fiori, he pointed you out to me while you were looking at spices. He was a good man. His death is a terrible tragedy."

"Thank you," I said, and immediately pressed on. "How were you acquainted with him?"

I truly could not imagine what would ever have brought Giovanni Giordano into contact with the Jewess, much less that they could have become friendly enough for him to point out his daughter to her. Not that my father had ever expressed any sentiment against the Jews. It was just that he scarcely mentioned them at all.

"My late husband was an apothecary," Sofia said. I had the impression that she was choosing her words with great care. "He and your father knew each other as young men. They resumed their acquaintance when Giovanni came to Rome to serve Cardinal Borgia."

"That must have been shortly before your husband died." My father had been ten years in the service of Il Cardinale, which meant that he and Sofia Montefiore's husband could not have had long to renew their acquaintance before the latter's death.

"That is true," Sofia said. "When my husband died, Giovanni came to offer his condolences. As I took over Aaron's work, we remained in touch."

"You became an apothecary?" I asked, unable to hide my surprise. I had heard of women in some of the guilds—dyers, brewers, and the like—who succeeded to their husbands' positions upon becoming widows. But they did so only with great difficulty and then only until any sons they had became old enough to take their places. The Jews, of course, were not allowed in the guilds. Presumably, they had their own rules.

"I did," Sofia said with a faint smile. "Surely, you do not disapprove of a woman in a man's profession?"

The way she said it made me suspect that Sofia Montefiore knew of my own recent ascension to the ranks of women doing men's work. Given that rumor is the chief product of Rome eclipsing all else, that was not surprising.

"Of course not. What you do is your own affair. But I do want to know what contact you had with my father in recent months as well as anything that he may have told you or left here with you."

A look of bewilderment came over the older woman. She shook her head slowly. "I have no idea what you mean. It was winter when I saw your father last."

I stiffened. Sofia Montefiore was telling me that Borgia had sent me on *una ricerca vana,* a wild-goose chase. Given that Il Cardinale had the most extensive and highly skilled network of spies in Rome, the Papal States, and beyond, it was highly unlikely that he would do any such thing.

"It would be a mistake," I said carefully, "to underestimate the Cardinal's interest in this matter."

Calmly, Sofia said, "I assure you I would never do that. Now, if you will excuse me, I must return to my patients."

With no better choice, Vittoro and I left through the back door of the shop. It gave onto a dank and narrow alley, which took us finally to one of the larger streets and from there to the gate leading out into the city. Once we were free of the ghetto's stifling confines, I all but sagged with relief. Nothing had prepared me for the suffering of Rome's Jews. Even as I walked away quickly, I knew I would be haunted by what I had seen.

Under the circumstances, and given that I had nothing of any substance to report to Il Cardinale, I persuaded Vittoro to escort me only so far as Rocco's shop in the Campo. There the captain left me with my promise that I would not return to the palazzo without the guard he would send to fetch me.

You may wonder why I went there. To put it plainly, I was overwhelmed and had no idea where else to turn. To all intents and purposes, I had failed in my first mission for Borgia, having discovered nothing to indicate what my father had been doing, much less records of his work. Sofia Montefiore claimed complete ignorance of his activities. The only other person I could think of who might know was Rocco.

He was occupied at the furnace in the back and did not see me at first, giving me the opportunity to study him as he worked the massive blowpipe he held as easily as though it were a feather. The sculpted muscles of his bare back flexed as he filled a molten lump of sand with breath, transforming it into a shimmering glass bubble streaked with crimson and azure.

According to Pliny the Elder, the Phoenicians discovered the art of making glass, although some say it was known even earlier. The Moors in Andalusia refined the technique, producing works of astounding purity. But it fell to the Venetians to create glass of such breathtaking beauty as to be likened to the exhalations of angels. Rocco was a true master of the art and it was for that reason, and surely for no other, that I found him so fascinating to watch.

I held back, not wanting to startle him, until he clipped off the finished goblet and set it on a nearby rack to cool. Only then did I muster a smile and step forward.

For just a moment, as he caught sight of me, his expression was unguarded. I saw there—what exactly? Surprise, of course, for he could not have expected to see me again so soon, but something more. A flash of wary pleasure, perhaps, or was that merely a trick of the speckled sunlight filtering through the plane trees shading the yard? Surely there was nothing to merit the sudden flush of warmth that stained my cheeks and made me look away.

"I need your advice," I said simply and was relieved when he put down his tools and nodded.

We sat again at the table near the back door, well away from the busy street. Nando was out playing with friends. For the moment, we were alone. Briefly, I described what had happened in the past day. I said nothing of the attack on me but saw him frowning at the bruise on my forehead, revealed when I absently brushed my hair aside.

"Are you all right?" he asked.

"Yes, of course. I am fine." Uneasy beneath his penetrating gaze, I moved quickly to the reason for my visit.

"Do you know what my father was working on at the time of his death?"

"I do not," Rocco said. "Why do you ask?"

"Questions have come up," I said carefully. "I am endeavoring to find answers."

"For Borgia? Is he the one asking questions?"

"Well, he would be, wouldn't he? It's not as though I would run about asking at anyone else's behest."

That was tarter than I had intended, but Rocco did not seem to mind. He leaned back, studying me, and said, "I made equipment for your father a few months ago, but it was of the same sort you just ordered and could be used for any number of purposes."

"He said nothing to you of why he wanted it?"

The glassmaker hesitated a moment before replying, "Giovanni was always very discreet. He rarely spoke of his work in any but the most general terms."

"Were there never circumstances when he felt able to speak in greater detail? Perhaps in a gathering of like-minded friends?"

If I hoped that Rocco would respond to my clumsy attempt to bring up Lux, I was disappointed. He merely shrugged and said, "I would help you if I could, Francesca, but I truly do not know what your father was doing. If Borgia also does not, perhaps Giovanni had reason to keep it to himself."

"I am not so certain that His Eminence doesn't know," I confessed for, having failed yet again, I had little left to lose. "He may or may not. I think his interest runs more to whether my father left records of his work."

Briefly, I told him of the mission I had been sent on. When I was done, I asked, "Have you ever been in the ghetto?"

"Occasionally. I have customers there, or at least I did before all the trouble started."

"You mean the refugees?"

Rocco nodded. "I hear it's a real mess there now."

"And likely to get worse. In little more than a month, any Jew left in Spain will be subject to immediate execution."

"They're mad, those Spaniards."

"Maybe so, but it's not as though the Jews are welcome here. Conditions in the ghetto are terrible."

Something in my voice must have revealed my distress at what I had seen, for Rocco got up, went to the cabinet, and poured wine for us both. Returning to the table, he set a goblet in front of me. "Drink that before you say anything more."

Grateful, I did as he said. The wine hit my empty stomach hard, but it also gave me a small sense of distance from the reality I had witnessed.

"Did you know that my father went there?"

"To the ghetto?"

"He knew a woman there, an apothecary."

"How do you know this?"

I told him about Sofia Montefiore. When I was done, Rocco shook his head slowly. "She says it was winter when she last saw your father, but the Cardinal believes he was there much more recently?"

I nodded. "I have to assume that is the case since Borgia sent me to see her at the same time he said he wanted any records of recent work that my father might have left."

"Do you think she is telling the truth?"

That was the crux of it. Sofia Montefiore had showed no surprise at my sudden appearance. It was almost as though she had been expecting me.

Slowly, I said, "No, I don't."

Rocco sighed and sat back in his chair. He twirled the stem of his goblet between his large fingers scarred by so many years of work with fire and glass. His eyes met mine.

"The Jews have a rough time of it. She won't tell you anything unless you can convince her to trust you."

I finished the last of my wine and pushed my glass toward him. As he refilled it, I said, "And to do that—" The images of what I had seen flowed through my mind—the suffering, the horror, the grinding hopelessness of the ghetto from which there seemed to be no escape except death itself.

"To do that," I said, "I have to go back."

6

Steeled in my resolve to discover whatever Sofia Montefiore knew, I returned to the ghetto the next day. Vittoro came with me—for protection but also to carry the medicines I brought. I would like to tell you that I intended them as an act of charity in obedience to the injunction that we are to do unto others as we would have them do unto us, but the truth is I brought them in order to bribe the apothecary.

Perhaps bribe is too harsh a word. Call them an inducement to convince her to tell me what I needed to know, and in so doing spare us both a great deal of trouble. But before I could approach her, I had to run the gauntlet of suffering that was the ghetto and find again its Via di Miseria where her shop was located.

Although we looked around for Benjamin as soon as we passed through the gate, we saw no sign of him. I had a flicker of concern that he was picking pockets in the city beyond and risking dire punishment in the process, but before we had gotten very far, he popped out from behind a pile of garbage with a nonchalant grin on his face.

"Everyone's talking about you," he said.

Vittoro merely grunted but I have a tendency to chatter when I am anxious. "What are they saying?"

Benjamin took a deep breath, significantly expanding his scrawny chest, and launched into his recitation. "Some think you are a witch, signorina. Others say it is too soon to tell. Some say you are a spy for the Cardinal, and no one really disagrees with that, but there is argument over why so illustrious a personage would feel the need to spy on us. As for you, signore—" He indicated Vittoro. "Some say you are a military man, others believe you are the signorina's familiar."

That got the captain's attention, but he merely grunted again and kept going. We came at last to the apothecary shop. If anything, the line in front was longer than it had been the previous day. There were also several shrouded bodies lying near the street, waiting for whoever disposed of corpses in the ghetto. In the city beyond, the dead are buried in the churchyards. Except in times of plague, even paupers go to a decent grave. But dead Jews . . . I had no idea what happened to them.

"We should not tarry," Vittoro said as Benjamin opened the door and we stepped inside.

This time, I did not bother to cover my face. While many believe that disease is caused by bad air, I am not convinced, although I gladly would have protected myself from the stench had not hiding behind a scented pomander seemed a poor approach to winning Sofia Montefiore's trust.

As it was, she was in no position to give me her attention. A young woman in the throes of childbirth lay in a corner of the room crowded with the sick and dying. She was on her back on a thin pallet, her face the pasty gray of approaching death, seemingly slumped in insensibility. Sofia Montefiore knelt between her spread legs. The young man at her side, clutching her hand, was weeping.

"Push," Sofia urged. "For love of your child, you must push!"

I heard her but I could not tell if the young woman did. The pool of blood seeping out from beneath her suggested she was already beyond such cares.

I stumbled back toward the door and bumped instead into Vittoro. He set down the medicine chest quickly and grabbed hold of me.

"Donna, are you all right?"

For pity's sake, I was the poisoner of no less than Cardinal Rodrigo Borgia, one of the most feared men in all of Christendom. I had, only three days before, killed a man to attain that position. I had survived a beating and sworn to avenge my father. I was not and never had been weak.

But I was terrified. Having lived only with my father—without mother, aunts, sisters, cousins—I was not inured to the reality of childbirth as every young woman is expected to be. On the contrary, I saw the suffering that had killed my own mother as bizarre and hideous.

I did not answer Vittoro but did manage to recover myself enough to stand on my own. The young man was bent over sobbing. Sofia said something more that I did not hear; it may have been a curse. When he did not respond, she reached around behind her, took hold of a knife she must have hidden there and—

The young woman screamed. The sound went on and on, seeming to echo off the walls pressing in so close around and set the very air to vibrating. A scream of such anguish that devils in the pits of

Hell must have heard it. It took her life's breath and left her slumped, eyes wide and unseeing, in the young man's arms.

Another cry was heard, far more feeble, the whimper of a new life born out of death. I saw the baby stained with his mother's blood, saw the bloodstained knife Sofia dropped, saw her face, and then I saw nothing but the floor.

Such humiliation! For a long time afterward, I insisted to myself that I had not fainted at the mere sight of blood. I had merely sat down abruptly, forgetting there was no chair. Vittoro, bless him, never spoke of it. I had the comfort of my lies even as I knew the truth.

By the time I regained myself, the young woman's eyes had been closed and her body decently covered, her distraught husband was being led away; the exhausted Sofia had handed the baby, wrapped in a length of grimy blanket, to a pale young woman who wearily offered him her shriveled breast.

Do not ask if the child lived; I have no idea. But in keeping with my new policy of honesty, let us admit that his chances were slim.

Half an hour later, I sat at the table in the back room across from Sofia Montefiore and told her that she could take the help I offered or she could face the wrath of the Cardinal, the choice was hers. I was not certain at first that she understood me, so withdrawn was she from the world into the place we go when life becomes too much. It was a place I knew well, having inhabited it myself after my father's death and been tempted back toward it after I was beaten. In kindness, I might have let her stay there a little while, but kindness was not in me then.

"You must decide," I insisted. "I can help you with medicines and with food, but in return, you must tell me everything my father said and give me anything he left with you."

Sofia looked up, her eyes sunken and her lips ashen. So softly that I had to bend closer to hear her, she said, "I told you, he left nothing."

That much, at least, I knew might be true. My father had ever been a careful man, and besides, such was my vanity that I did not want to believe he could have trusted anyone more than me.

However, I was also certain she was not telling me everything.

"This," I said, indicating the medicine chest, "is only a small sample of what you can have. I will bring you—"

"I will tell you what you will bring," Sofia said. Her voice remained very low yet her strength was unmistakable. "Most of what is called medicine is useless. I will give you a list of what I require."

When I nodded, she said, "Once you have what you want, why should I believe that you will keep your part of the bargain?"

"I will give you my word—"

Her laugh was hoarse and strained, as though it did not get much use. "Your word? The only Christian I ever knew who cared about keeping his word to a Jew was your father, and I do not see him here."

That stung. While it is true that I do not resemble my father—he was darker than I am and of stouter build—I like to think that I have his nature. That stands to reason as he raised me.

"He may not be here," I said coldly, "but I would never betray his memory."

Sofia thought about that for several moments, long enough for me to begin to believe that she would reject my assurances. Finally she nodded.

"We must speak alone," she said, and looked at Vittoro. "Entirely alone."

"I will be right outside," he told me. With a warning glare at her, he left, taking Benjamin with him.

Silence hovered in the small room where the scent of herbs hanging from the rafters fought a futile battle against the stench of sickness and death. I heard the creaking of a cart in the lane beyond and a muted shout from far away.

Finally, Sofia said, "I last saw your father in March, right before the festival of Purim. Do you know what that is?"

I shook my head. Apart from the charge that they had killed Christ, I knew nothing of the Jews.

"It is when we celebrate our salvation from the one called Haman, who served the mighty emperor of Persia and who sought the annihilation of the Jewish people."

Despite myself, I was curious. That, too, is a part of my father in me. "Why did he do that?"

Sofia pretended to look surprised. "Isn't it enough that we are Jews? Does anyone need another reason to kill us?"

When I merely stared at her, not knowing how to respond, she took pity on me. "As it happens," she said, "we were saved by a woman. Her name was Esther and her story is told in your Bible, but I take it you are not familiar with it?"

I shook my head, resenting the need to respond to so foolish a question. It is well known that only priests know the Bible, and they share only those parts of it they think beneficial for the souls of their flock.

"Never mind then," Sofia said. "Let us speak of more recent matters. As I said, I saw your father in March. Giovanni came to say good-bye."

"Why would he do that? He had no plans to leave Rome." At least, not as far as I knew, but already I was beginning to sense that there was much my father had not told me.

"He did not say that he was leaving," Sofia told me. "But he was concerned that matters were developing in such a way that anyone known to be connected to him could be in danger. Because of that, he told me that he would not be coming to see me again."

"What matters?" I asked even as I thought that was about the same time my father had begun to talk of sending me to stay at the Cardinal's residence in the country. I had protested so vigorously, having no wish to be separated from him, that he had agreed to postpone a decision. But I had feared that he really had made up his mind and would only tell me at the last moment in order to avoid argument. That I argued with him at all shames me still.

Sofia did not answer at once. She sat back in her chair and stared at the wall over my shoulder as though seeing something far removed from our surroundings. Slowly, she said, "You know that your father was very interested in the cause of disease?"

"He spoke to you of this?" On reflection, I should not have been surprised. My father must have realized that one of the very few people he could talk to safely about such matters would be a Jew or, failing that, a Muslim. Certainly, both peoples are known for producing physicians of great skill, perhaps because they are willing to entertain thoughts forbidden to Christians.

"He knew that I shared his interest," Sofia said. "You must understand, Giovanni truly did want to find how to cure illness. But more recently he was seeking a way to bring about a death that would seem entirely natural."

I had difficulty comprehending this, and the reason for my confusion is simple enough: When a decision is made to kill—whether by poison or any other method—it is not enough to remove the victim from this world. Usually, it is also desirable that everyone knows or at least fears that the person was done away with deliberately. Only in that manner can the proper level of respect be assured.

Seeing my bewilderment, Sofia put out a hand and covered mine. "I am sorry, but there is more."

And it would not be good. She would not have breached the distance between us to offer me the simple comfort of her touch if she had anything to say that was less than terrible. I knew that, but even so, I had not begun to grasp the enormity of what Sofia Montefiore was about to tell me.

I was silent on the walk back to the palazzo. Vittoro respected my mood and kept his thoughts to himself. We parted in the courtyard. I went not to my rooms but to the small chapel where I was accustomed to hearing Mass on Sundays. At that hour, it was empty. The scent of incense lingered on the air. I knelt before the marble and gold altar, raised my eyes to the jeweled crucifix, and I prayed.

I am not a pious woman. The gift of deep, abiding faith eludes me. Perhaps my mind is too restless, too inclined to question. Or perhaps I simply haven't tried hard enough. Whatever the case, prayer does not come easily to me.

But that day, I prayed, clumsily to be sure, but with utmost sincerity. I prayed that the Redeemer of the World would save me from the knowledge I had so thoughtlessly acquired. Or, failing that, would show me what to do with it.

No sign came, of course. I am always envious of those who claim that their prayers are answered, often with great flourishes of scent, sound, and sight. Saint Catherine of Sienna, for example, she who helped to heal the Great Schism and bring the papacy back to Rome, spoke of experiencing a mystical marriage with Christ and receiving visions of Heaven, Hell, and Purgatory. The great Saint Thomas Aquinas, master philosopher and theologian—said to have died from poison, by the way—credited all he knew to the power of revelation. And there have been others, the long line of saints the Church holds up as models for us all.

Obviously, I am no saint, but I did, that day, pray for a glimmer of divine insight. At length, becoming aware that I was both exhausted and bereft, I rose. Only then did I realize that I must have been kneeling a very long time in the chapel. My knees throbbed as though hot coals had been burned into them and day had turned to evening. As I slipped out, the monks were filing in for vespers.

I did go to my rooms then. I ate supper alone. I bathed and eventually I slept. The nightmare came again, even more vividly than usual. I woke from it shaking and rubbed the tears from my face.

Any further thought of sleep being impossible, I sat at the small table by the window and read through the night, seeking in my father's journals some insight into the great and terrible thing that had come upon me.

But you want to know what that was. What Sofia Montefiore told me there in the ghetto's charnel house.

Very well, but you have been warned. Knowledge such as this is a curse, ripping us from the paradise of ignorance we so blithely occupy, never suspecting that with one misstep our lives can be torn apart utterly.

7

The last time I saw your father," Sofia had said, "he was weighted down with worry and more distraught than I had ever known him to be. He spoke with the greatest difficulty, understandably enough, for when we speak of evil, we give it life."

She passed a hand over her face wearily and adjusted her posture in the chair before continuing. "You will ask me how he knew what he did so I will tell you now that he did not say and I did not ask. It was enough that he had discovered what he had."

"And that was?" I was growing impatient with what seemed to be her coyness. God forgive me, I still did not understand.

Her eyes were dark-ringed and bloodshot, but what I remember most was the deep, impenetrable sadness within them.

"It seems," she said, "that it is not enough that all the Jews be expelled from Spain, with all the suffering that has unleashed on us.

His Holiness the Pope is not content with that. For the sake of his soul, he is preparing an edict to expel us from all of Christendom upon pain of death for any who would remain."

Her voice grew a little stronger as outrage filled her. "Innocent will use his authority to expel all Jews from the Papal States. But he won't stop there. He will also call on every king, prince, and the like to follow suit and cleanse all of Christendom of the 'pollution' we represent. He is prepared to demand this in the strongest terms, even threatening excommunication for any leader who disobeys. And as though all that were not enough, he will unleash the faithful, encouraging them to wipe the Jews from the face of the earth."

She put her worn hands, still stained with the dead mother's blood, flat on the table and looked at me. "If this edict is issued, the Jewish people will face extermination."

I heard her, of course I did; I even understood more or less. Jews . . . trouble . . . extermination . . . Yes, yes, it was all very clear. God forgive me, all that really mattered to me at that moment was what any of that had to do with my father.

Sofia Montefiore claimed he had been distraught over the fate of the Jews. I supposed that was possible. He had a tender heart sometimes at odds with his profession. I can remember him nursing a bird with a broken wing back to health before releasing it at the same time we tried to give a quick death to the dogs and other animals we used for testing new poisons.

Suppose my father had discovered that such an edict was being prepared, what would he have done? Warned the Jews? That much I could believe now that I had discovered that he counted one of them as a friend. But if Sofia Montefiore was telling the truth—a question as yet unresolved in my mind—he had gone a great deal further. Far enough to worry that anyone associated with him would soon be in grave danger.

He had, according to her, been seeking a way to kill that would appear to be completely natural.

I wrapped the shawl more tightly around myself in a vain effort to contain the fear bursting within me. Beyond the window, rising as a dark shadow, I saw the towers of the Vatican, the citadel of Christendom where I fancied His Holiness the Pope slept well, his health much improved since my father's sudden death.

In the morning, I slipped out of the palazzo early as the street cleaners who found ready employment in the wealthier neighborhoods were spraying water over the cobblestones and preparing to scrub them with their thick bristle brooms. Mindful of the Cardinal's injunction, I dragooned a young guardsman into escorting me, refusing his tentative request to inform his captain before we departed.

"I have no time for that," I informed him loftily. "Perhaps you would like to explain to Captain Romano why I had to leave without you?"

"No, no, Donna," he said, and trotted after me as I strode past the watch gates and out onto the street.

I kept up a brisk pace all the way to the Palazzo Orsini, but the effort to outrun my thoughts failed. With every step, I struggled to convince myself that my suspicions were misplaced and my fears exaggerated. It did not help that my ribs still throbbed and that each breath I drew was a painful reminder of the beating I had received—and the warning that came with it.

My visit, as with everything I did, was certain to be reported to Il Cardinale. That being the case, I went at once to the storerooms, where I busied myself inspecting supplies that had arrived for the household in the past few days. Fresh food was less a concern for me since that is extremely difficult to poison without leaving telltale traces in smell and taste, and even in color. However, it is possible to hide small quantities of poison in the folds of meat, for example, so every carcass has to be checked carefully. Similarly, it is difficult to taint wine, although not impossible. Here clarity as well as bouquet are the best indicators of safety. Poisons added to wine will dissolve but only partially; they tend to leave a certain murkiness immediately evident to the experienced eye.

It is helpful to my purposes that any merchant supplying goods to noble households understands full well the terrible retribution that will fall on him and his family if he is even suspected of conspiring to do harm. Even so, no conscientious poisoner allows the purchase of very much in the way of prepared foods for a household he—or she—is guarding. Sausages, smoked meats, dried fish, and the like must all be prepared under my direction. This is simply good sense. So are the precautions taken with fabric. Poisons that can penetrate the skin, rather than needing to be ingested, are rare, but they can be very potent. I used one such to kill the Spaniard, but about that I will say nothing more.

I will say that the simplest way to deliver a poison is to conceal it within a spicy dish—a stew, for instance, or anything else expected to have a rich and complex flavor. As such dishes are a favorite of those who can afford them, they must be prepared with the greatest care.

As a matter of routine, all food and drink must be offered first to animals kept for that purpose. It was the part of my job I disliked the most and I was glad when it was completed without incident.

Once determined to be safe, the provisions were sealed until they were about to be used. I saw to the sealing myself using the small bars of wax and the insignia my father had kept for that purpose. After being unsealed, all household provisions became the responsibility of the master cook or, beyond the kitchens, the majordomo. Woe betide either if any harm came to a member of La Famiglia.

Having performed my duty, I tarried until the hour was respectable enough that I might ask to pay my respects to Madonna Adriana and the other inhabitants of *il harem*. But her ladyship, it seemed, was away visiting a friend in the country and Giulia la Bella, ever the late riser, remained abed. Only Lucrezia was in the garden, having breakfast.

She waved me over to join her. "Francesca, come and sit. I am so glad to see you. Are you hungry? The strawberries are delicious."

We sat in the shade of the loggia within sight of the fountain. Already, the day was warm. Lucrezia wore a light chemise of finely spun linen. The Maltese pups lay at her feet, their tongues lolling.

"What happened to your face?" she asked when I had taken my seat. She offered the bowl of strawberries, perhaps to sweeten the question.

I selected one and took a bite before responding. The bruise on my forehead no longer hurt unless I touched it, but it had darkened enough that my hair could not conceal it entirely.

With a smile, I told the same lie I had told her father. "I took a fall." As is the way with lies, I found myself elaborating. "I tripped really, nothing more. It was a little embarrassing." With the last, I hoped to deflect further inquiry.

Lucrezia's perfectly arched brows drew together. People raved about Giulia's beauty, understandably enough, but Lucrezia herself was also lovely. She had been a skinny child but, having become a woman in recent months, was beginning to sprout curves. Her features were delicate and very feminine but her hair was her crowning glory. Pale blond and coaxed into ringlets, it made her look like an angel surrounded by a halo of light. Later, when she was accused of such terrible crimes, people would remark on that.

"Does it hurt?" she asked, demonstrating the persistence that ultimately made possible her survival in the face of calamity that would have destroyed most anyone else.

"Not at all," I assured her.

"Good." She smiled mischievously. "I have a secret you will want to hear."

I suspected that Borgia's daughter was privy to far more secrets than the usual young woman her age, in fact, I was counting on it. But I was still surprised that she would offer one like a marzipan confection for my enjoyment.

"Tell me," I said.

"Cesare wants to come to Rome even though Father told him to stay in Pisa. He is so bored at university and afraid of missing something here that he says he may just come anyway."

Had she been speaking of anyone other than her eldest brother, I would have discounted that as mere bravado. But Cesare had the combination of impulsiveness and ruthlessness that could lead him to challenge the Cardinal and escape unscathed. Certainly, Borgia was known for indulging the son he expected to follow him into Holy Mother Church.

As always, the thought of Cesare as a priest made me smile. Lucrezia leaped on that at once. "My brother amuses you?" she asked.

Cesare did a great many things to me and in time I suppose I will speak of most of them. But yes, under certain circumstances, he could amuse me.

"Forgive me, Madonna," I said, very properly. "I was thinking of something else entirely."

"Oh, you were not," Lucrezia said, quite rightly. "Don't even try to pretend. You are as fascinated by Cesare as everyone else."

Fascinated? Yes, I suppose that was true, but I was also wary.

"I told him about your father," Lucrezia said. "He writes that he is most sorry but he is certain that you will fulfill your new responsibilities admirably."

God forgive me, I blushed. Seeing that, Lucrezia chortled. But a moment later, her mood grew serious.

"He is not really so terrible, is he, Francesca? When all is said and done, Cesare has a good heart."

If she meant a heart that beat strongly and gave its possessor no trouble, she was certainly correct. Apart from that—

"I am sure that he is the best of brothers."

"He is, but I have also heard that he is a very good lover. Isn't that also true?"

Are you shocked? Are you perhaps leaping ahead to think of the vile rumors that surrounded Lucrezia and Cesare in later years? Rumors that, allow me to assure you now, were entirely false.

"I wouldn't know—" Even to my own ears, my protestations sounded weak, inevitably so for they were not true. Let us suppose that following my first encounter with Cesare, when he backed away before the reminder that I was the poisoner's daughter, he found me worthy of pursuit. This speaks to his love of a challenge far more than to my own desirability, I am sure.

Let us further suppose that one night not long after I refused Rocco's offer of marriage, while yet my spirit was severely bruised, Cesare happened on me in the library. I was reading Dante again, ever my bane. You may assume, if you like, that I was seeking relief from my turbulent emotions in familiar intellectual pursuits. My father was above in our apartment. The Cardinal was away, visiting La Bella. It was very quiet.

Cesare was supposed to be in Pisa, where he was supposed to be taking the measure of his fellow student, the Medici heir, at the same time he was distinguishing himself as a scholar. By all reports, he accomplished both, having a versatile mind and a talented tongue. Very talented.

He had slipped away to Rome for a few days to try to persuade his father to change his plans for him. Don't laugh, or if you must, not loudly, but Borgia really did intend his eldest son for the Church. When Cesare was not yet seven, his father arranged for him to be made protonotary apostolic to the pope. I have no idea what tasks are performed by that august office and neither did Cesare, I am sure. Swiftly thereafter, he acquired rights in the bishopric of Valencia at the same time he became a rector and an archdeacon. In the following years, he acquired the bishopric of Pamplona with all the rich revenues of same. That he had not yet taken holy orders was a mere detail easily overlooked.

But his father intended for him to take such orders, to become in due time a prince of the Church, and eventually to follow Rodrigo himself as pope. That Cesare foresaw an entirely different future for himself made no difference to Il Cardinale.

Cesare had come to make the case for the military career he wanted but, per the talk in the kitchen, father and son had fought. He stomped off to who knows where, returned less than sober, and somehow found his way to the library.

Where I was. Imagine me as I was then, *virgo intacto,* whole and complete within my alabaster world where I was resolved, however regretfully, to remain. And imagine him, wild and dark, smelling of wine and leather, bringing the wind of the wider world into my maiden's sanctuary.

What shall I tell you? All of it? How he approached me with a smile in his wild eyes? How I thought to flee but somehow could not even manage to rise from my chair? How he knelt before me, his hands warm and strong as he lifted my skirts, stroked my skin, found the heat of me—

How I died there, in his arms.

How he smiled and told me I was beautiful, his precious girl, lauding my attractions even as he slipped into me? Yes, slipped, for all the talk of pain and rending I had heard whispered by eye-rolling serving maids.

How afterward, as he stroked my hair and crooned to me, the world seemed reborn in the light of the astounding discovery I had just made. I was not, contrary to what I had feared, barred from all intimacy by the darkness within. I had only to confine my experience of it to one such as Cesare, a being of purest physicality with no more interest in what lay in my heart than I had in his. Despise me if you will for lacking the tenderer feelings of a woman, but knowing myself as I did, I simply could not see how I could afford them.

"Please," I said to Lucrezia. "Let us speak of more important things."

That caught her attention, as I knew it would. She waved away the hovering servant. "Can we really? No one ever wants to talk with me about anything important. I am, after all, only a girl, therefore presumed to be ignorant."

"We both know you are far from that." I was not merely flattering her. Lucrezia had at least as good a mind as any man of her family. "Besides, you will be married soon and a married woman must concern herself with important matters whether men wish to acknowledge that or not."

The mention of marriage usually cheered her but this time she only sighed. "If my father does not become pope, I fear that he will never find a husband he thinks good enough for me. But, of course, if he does become pope, the same may be true."

The frankness with which his only daughter spoke of Borgia's ambitions took me aback. But it fitted well with where I hoped to guide our conversation.

"Truly, if it pleases God to call Il Cardinale to the Throne of Saint Peter, we will be blessed." Having expressed the correct sentiment, I plunged on. "But it must be daunting to contemplate the burden of responsibility that falls on the Holy Father."

Lucrezia selected another strawberry, took a bite, and swallowed it before she replied. "I suppose. Perhaps that is why my dear *papà* seems so distracted these days."

"Does he?" I asked with what I hoped was the right measure of polite interest and nothing more.

She nodded. "Giulia says he sleeps badly when he sleeps at all. He never used to be like that. Nothing ever seemed to disturb him."

"I am sorry to hear this. Do you have any idea what is troubling him?"

For a moment, I feared I had been too obvious, but then Lucrezia sighed and sat back in her chair, looking thoughtful. "I know that your father's death upset him greatly. He was here when the news came and I feared . . . let us just say that I have rarely seen him so angry."

Indeed? This from the man who had not raised a hand to find my father's killers, much less punish them.

Carefully, I said, "The death of any servant would be cause for distress, no?"

"Your father was far from just any servant," Lucrezia admonished. "*Papà* trusted him with our lives, to be sure, but also with . . . secrets, I think, that perhaps did not die with him?"

She looked directly at me, her eyes golden in the sunlit garden. It was then that I realized that Lucrezia was as intent on gleaning information from me as I was from her. Moreover, this daughter of Il Cardinale was more adept at the art of intrigue than I could ever hope to be.

In a bid for time to gather my thoughts, I asked, "What makes you say that?"

"No special reason," she assured me. "It is just that *Papà* was so upset when it happened and he has not been himself since."

"But he said nothing in particular about my father's death?"

Lucrezia hesitated. A servant stood nearby to attend to her needs. She waved him away.

"He said '*Alea iacta est.*'"

The die is cast. The words Julius Caesar supposedly spoke as he stood on the bank of the Rubicon, about to invade Rome and make himself its master.

Lucrezia, who was being educated to be a great lady, already spoke several languages, including Latin. She would have understood her father but it was not likely that anyone else in *il harem* could have done so. Even in his agitation, the Cardinal had sought instinctively to conceal his thoughts.

I, too, had been educated and I, too, understood, all too well. Even so, I asked, "What die? What did he mean?"

She tossed a sweet roll to the Maltese pups and shrugged. "Perhaps you can tell me."

Inexperienced as I was at the game of intrigue, I knew that I had to offer information in turn, otherwise I could not hope for her to be forthcoming in the future.

Slowly, I said, "I think it means that my father was doing something on behalf of Il Cardinale from which there is no going back."

"But what is that 'something'?" Lucrezia asked. This girl who, so far as I could tell, truly did love her papa, furrowed her brow in concern. "That is the question, isn't it?"

How I wish that it had been, but any doubts I might have had about the enormity of what my father had been doing were gone. He had served a man who would never be content until Peter's Throne was his own. But more than that, he had cared deeply about a people whose only hope of survival rested on removing the present occupant of that throne through the only means possible—death.

My father was gone, but all the rest remained: Borgia and his overweening ambition; the Jews and the knife-edge of extinction upon which they teetered; and my poor self, who had set out to avenge a murder only to discover that I was being maneuvered into committing another that would reverberate through all of Christendom and damn my soul for eternity.

8

I returned from the Palazzo Orsini to discover that I had won a brief reprieve. The Cardinal had departed for his offices at the Curia, but not before expressing his displeasure that I was not to be found when he summoned me. He would return in the afternoon; I was expected to be on hand. So Vittoro informed me at the same time he shook his head in admonishment.

"You took advantage of Jofre," he said, referring to the young guardsman I had bullied into accompanying me. "Now I have to put him on latrine duty for a week."

"I am sorry," I replied, with no hint of contrition. "But I did take an escort and surely that is what matters?"

The captain of the guard expelled a mournful sigh. "Francesca, you know perfectly well that what matters is what the Cardinal says matters and nothing else. I suggest you do not disappoint him again."

Advice I would do well to remember, but such was my agitation that I had difficulty doing so. In that state, which it must be said comes upon me only very rarely, I find it useful to keep busy.

Accordingly, I plunged into the day's work, inspecting provisions, checking seals, observing the servants as they went about their tasks. Did any seem particularly nervous or self-conscious? Was there any change in routine? Was there any sign, however slight, that an attempt was in the works against the Cardinal?

All the while I was doing this, guards patrolled outside the palazzo and within, keeping constant watch. Beyond in the city, spies were at work in the markets, brothels, trading houses, the Vatican itself, ferreting out whatever morsels might be useful to Borgia. All this in service to the one great goal: the preservation and advancement of La Famiglia.

But let us not forget that there were other families, the great and the would-be great, and that they were not at rest. Alliances formed and dissolved like the mists that rise above the Tiber at night only to vanish in the morning sun. Today's friend could as easily be tomorrow's enemy. Rome, like much of Christendom, was in foment, torn between two great forces. On one side was the ancient injunction to bow before God and tradition as defined by our betters. On the other, the new, still only half-formed impulse to lift our faces to the light of change, what some were calling a rebirth of the world and others deemed paganism. Any such challenge to their authority being terrifying to our earthly rulers, they responded by trying to smother it in its cradle. So far, at least, they had not succeeded; the struggle continued.

I had my own role to play in it. While the priests were chanting their offices at sext, I withdrew to my rooms to confront the terrifying question I knew could no longer be avoided: If my father had been trying to kill Pope Innocent VIII, as I now believed, how had he intended to do it? Sofia said he had been looking for a means of killing that would appear to be an entirely natural death. I knew of no way to accomplish that.

Not that some poisons aren't subtler than others. Arsenic is an old favorite, of course, and its symptoms can be confused with those of malaria, but such is the nature of our times that anyone of consequence so stricken would suspect poison immediately. Wolfsbane yields a useful substance that in the proper dose stops the heart; so does foxglove, such a pretty flower, but again not without arousing immediate suspicion. Hemlock, Socrates' slayer, is highly effective but not in the least discreet, causing paralysis and agonizing pain before bringing on death. Belladonna, which some foolish women use to brighten their eyes, can cause a rapid heartbeat, disorientation, and the like before it slays.

You see the problem? If the goal is simply to kill, there are no end of ways to do it. But to kill without raising suspicion, that is another matter entirely. I could say more, but I fear I am telling you too much. God forbid I give you occasion for sin.

My point is that if there was any thought that the Pope's death was unnatural, Borgia's reputation was such that he would come under immediate suspicion. He was of an age when this was his last chance for the papacy, and there were others, as strong as he, who would contend for it. No matter what incentives he might offer for their support, there was a line beyond which they would not go. Killing the Pope was on the furthest, darkest side of it.

My imagination would not venture there. Try though I did, I could not begin to fathom what my father had done, assuming he was actually responsible for Innocent's recent illness. I could not discount entirely the possibility that it had been a coincidence.

Which would not spare me the Cardinal's demands. They came shortly after nones—the priests again, did they do nothing but chant? Although he had been gone only a few hours, His Eminence was not a man to arrive or depart anywhere without due notice. The household turned out at the first shouts of the escort announcing his approach.

I went along to get a sense of his mood. It was not good. Amid the sharp ring of hooves on cobblestones, the jangle of harnesses, the clash of shields as the guardsmen sprang to attention, and the babble of voices from servants, retainers, and hangers-on, Il Cardinale was a dark and glowering presence. He threw his reins to the cowering stable boy and stomped off toward his apartments without a word to anyone.

Moments later, I was summoned. The Cardinal was still being divested of his heavy garments when I arrived. I hung back, gazing into the middle distance, until he was decently attired. He waved off his valet, accepted a cold, wet cloth to put at the back of his neck, and grunted in my direction.

"You saw the Jewess."

It was not a question and I did not take it as such. Nodding, I said, "As you instructed, Eminence."

Borgia took a long swallow from a goblet of chilled wine and nodded. "What did she tell you?"

We were not alone. One of his secretaries was present, the valet was still in the room, the anxious steward, Renaldo, was hovering nearby, and likely there were others just out of sight. Men such as Borgia tend to take the services they receive so much for granted as to be oblivious to the people who provide them. My silence was a pointed reminder that they had ears.

The Cardinal waved a hand and, like a magus, made them all

vanish. They might as well have evaporated as rain does on hot stone, so quickly were they gone.

"Well, then?" he asked.

"There are no records. I am certain my father stopped committing anything to paper months ago."

Borgia gave a quick, sharp nod. "What else did she tell you?"

I had thought long and hard about what I would say to him. Do not ask me why I had decided to protect Sofia Montefiore; I could not tell you. Perhaps it was simply because she had been my father's friend.

"She told me that His Holiness intends to issue an edict calling for the expulsion of all Jews from Christendom, or, failing that, their deaths."

I had not expected him to be surprised and I was not disappointed. Borgia merely nodded and went on. "Anything more?"

"That was all." I had to account somehow for the time I had spent alone with Sofia, so I added, "As you may imagine, she went on and on about it."

"And said nothing about what your father was doing? About his work?"

"I am sorry, Eminence, but she knows nothing about my father's activities. That was very clear." It was a lie, of course. Sofia knew what my father was seeking. She was an intelligent woman. It would not have been difficult for her to reach the same conclusion that I had. But if I told the Cardinal as much, he would see her for the danger she was, a means of implicating him in the planned murder of a pope. Sofia could be made to disappear with the greatest ease.

Borgia looked . . . how? Frustrated to be sure, but also in some measure relieved, believing his secrets were still safe.

Before he could resume, I jumped in. "Eminence, I am puzzled as to how my father learned of the edict." For certain, no one in the Pope's confidence would have discussed such a matter with the poisoner serving the great rival for Innocent's crown.

I give the Cardinal credit, he did not hesitate. "I told him."

"May I ask why?"

Borgia reclined in a large armchair, stretched out his legs, and regarded me almost benignly. I say almost because nothing involving the Cardinal was ever truly benign.

"Why do you think I did?" he asked.

He was playing me, of course, but there was more to it than that. Despite having lived in his household for ten years, I was still something of a stranger to him, at least in my newest incarnation as his poisoner. He would want to test my mettle.

Slowly, I said, "I think you knew of my father's friendship with Sofia Montefiore." Which was certainly more than I had done. "You judged that he would care about the fate of the Jews and would warn them about the edict."

"Why would I want them to be warned?"

Why indeed? Borgia had no love for the Jews. Why would he care if they lived or died?

The answer came to me in an instant, and when it did, I wondered that I had not seen it sooner, it was that obvious. To survive, much less prosper in the world we know, power is essential. Hadn't I gone to the greatest lengths to secure what I could of it in order to avenge my father? How much further would one such as Rodrigo Borgia go?

"The Jews are not without wealth," I said. The conditions in the ghetto were not the inevitable result of poverty. They came rather from the strict limits placed on where and how the Jews could live and work. Left to their own devices, they were more than able to earn their way.

Ultimate power, of the kind Borgia sought, required money. A great deal of money.

"You offered them your protection." I could not begin to imagine what amount of wealth would have to change hands for the Cardinal to extend his benevolence over so despised a people, but I was certain it would have to be immense.

"*If* I am pope," he said. "If I am not, there is nothing I can do for them. With the proper financing, I can buy the papacy."

"Once the Pope is dead." I felt that I had to remind him of this small condition that must be met first.

Il Cardinale smiled, as though at a student he had feared might be slow but who instead was proving to be apt. "Yes, Francesca, once Innocent is dead."

My palms were damp and I was certain that my voice would betray my state. I took a breath, willing myself to steadiness. "It would have been one thing for my father to warn the Jews about the edict. But the death of a pope—"

Borgia took a sip of his wine and smiled. Without any change in his expression, nothing to warn me, he said, "Your father was *converso*. Did you not know that?"

I stared at him dumbfounded, unsure at first that I had heard him correctly. I *knew* my father. I had been raised by him, a motherless only child. He had shaped my knowledge of the world, given me what wisdom I possessed, and always treated me with what I was certain was impeccable honesty.

Except that he had never mentioned his friendship with a Jewess or her dead husband, or his desire to protect the despised tribe of Israel.

Even so, it could not possibly be true that my father was one of *them*. A Jew who had converted to Christianity. A suspect turncoat imagined to be slinking about unholy rituals while pretending to be one of us. A candidate for the flames that devour heretics.

"I don't believe you." My voice was shrill and taut but I could not help that. I had been dealt a blow I could scarcely fathom.

Borgia didn't bother to take offense. He merely shrugged. "For all I know, his conversion may have been real. Stranger things have happened. He was born a Jew in Milan. He fell in love with a Christian girl, your mother, and converted for her sake. But he remained a believer after her death and he raised you in the true faith." His gaze narrowed. "Or so he assured me."

Swiftly, I said, "I am a Christian." Not pious, not exemplary, but not one of *them,* either. Not one of the Others, scapegoats for all our failings and our ills.

My profession of faith did not seem to matter one way or another to this prince of Holy Mother Church. "If you say so," Borgia told me dismissively. "Whatever else you are, you are your father's daughter."

And he expected me to take up my father's task. But if Borgia was to be believed—and I did not for a moment actually believe him, not then—my father had a motivation I lacked. As a Jew, former or otherwise, he would have had a natural inclination to prevent the extermination of his people. Of course, I didn't relish the thought of their suffering and death. But neither was I prepared to imperil my immortal soul on their behalf.

"I know what you want," I said, thinking it was far more likely that Il Cardinale was simply lying about my father to secure my cooperation. "I understand completely, but so must you understand: To kill a pope and survive, there would have to be no suspicion that the death was unnatural. I have no idea how to accomplish that. Even if I did, I would be courting eternal damnation."

"For killing Innocent?" Borgia looked amused. "For cleansing the earth of that depraved fool? Oh, yes, the angels will weep at his passing."

He rose and walked over to the high windows looking out toward the river. Transparent curtains billowed in the strengthening breeze. Another storm was brewing, perhaps greater than all the others that had swept Rome in this season of upheaval and disorder.

When he turned back to me, he looked not angry as I had feared but merely calm, as though he had come to a decision within himself. Almost gently, he said, "In memory of your father's faithful service, I will give you time to consider your decision. Do so carefully, Francesca."

I was foolish enough to believe him and, being a fool, departed with grateful speed to hide myself in my rooms and contemplate the enormity of what he asked.

9

The summons came a few hours later. A harsh knock on my door, the hard smack of it being thrust open, and then a light above me as I woke, befuddled, not understanding what was happening.

"You must come now, signorina," a familiar voice said.

"Vittoro—?"

"Put this on." He held out my robe for me.

"Why?" I asked, my thinking slowed by surprise and dread. I had denied the Cardinal. What punishment did he intend?

Vittoro did not reply. He merely thrust the robe toward me and said again, "Now."

I went; really, what choice did I have? Hustled through the dark hallway, down a flight of steps, down another, Vittoro's hand firm on the small of my back, I struggled against the terror threatening to engulf me. Dimly, I was aware of other guards, a small contingent accompanying us. Did they think I would attempt to flee? At the thought of that, a panic-stricken laugh began to bubble up in my throat. I clamped a hand over my mouth and kept going—down and down and down.

I had been in the cellars of the palazzo where the storerooms were located many times. But I knew, in the way we know things we do not wish to acknowledge, that there were other levels lower still. Levels where it was said traces of our ancient Roman ancestors had been found and where enemies of the Cardinal were sent to contemplate their sins.

With the realization of where we were going, I did try to turn around, but Vittoro was having none of that.

"I am sorry, Francesca," he said, very low so that only I could hear him. "But the Cardinal would not be dissuaded."

I was going to die, quickly if I was lucky, otherwise alone and starving in the dark. I was a fool to have crossed swords with Borgia—a poor benighted fool soon to be praying for death.

The stone staircase ended in a low corridor that ran off into darkness. One of the guards went ahead, carrying a torch. We followed. At the end of the narrow passageway, a cavernous room suddenly appeared, its arched ceiling looming far above. Water dripped from the stones, reminding me that we were near the river. Rats scurried in the shadows but I scarcely noticed them. The torches set in iron brackets along the walls illuminated a nightmarish scene that drove all else from my fear-haunted brain.

Why had I ever read Dante? Why wasn't romantic Boccaccio or lyric Petrarch enough for me? Why was I not content with the masterful poems of Lorenzo de' Medici, prince and visionary, dead these two months—of poison, it was said. Why did I have to put into my mind the writhing, tortured sufferings of the damned so vividly evoked by the author of *La Divina Commedia*?

The torments of Purgatory and Hell combined seemed to spring to life before me there in the torture chamber of Rodrigo Borgia. Red-hot coals glowed in braziers set on high tripods beside an array of instruments designed to wrest the greatest possible pain and suffering from a frail human vessel. I saw in quick succession racks, hooks, chains, and spike-filled metal coffins, but they passed in a blur for what I saw most, what I could not rip my eyes from, was the naked man stretched out on a rack, screaming hoarsely.

"Mother of God, save me! Jesus, save me! Mother of God, save me! Jesus—"

He broke off, choking on his own blood. His face was a swollen mass of bruises, his upper body and limbs webbed by cuts deep enough to show bone; his legs, arms, and shoulders were grotesquely arranged, having been pulled apart and dislocated. He had been racked, beaten, burned, and castrated, the last wound crudely cauterized so that he could not bleed to death. Maddened by pain and fear, he thrashed helplessly, his chest rising and falling in rapid spasms.

One of the inquisitors bent down, cupped the back of the man's head in his hands and lifted him enough so that he could see me.

"Tell the lady," the torturer demanded. "Tell her what you told us."

Vittoro pushed me forward. I stumbled, but he gripped my arm and did not let me fall.

"Tell her," the torturer said again and twisted the man's neck so that he howled.

"Innocent! He did it! He ordered your father's death!"

Drawn by forces I could not resist, I moved closer yet. The stench of sweat and blood and waste almost overcame me. I stared down into the face contorted in agony and felt . . . nothing? No, that would not be true. Certainly, I felt something, but it was far from the horror and pity that had filled me moments before. Those simple human feelings, the natural response to what I was witnessing, retreated behind the wall that was always there for me. In their place came a dark and howling emptiness that would have terrified me had I still possessed the capacity to feel anything at all.

A glint of gold off to the side drew my eye. Vittoro held a chain up for me to see. A medallion that I knew well dangled from it.

"They took this off him," Vittoro said, and pressed the medallion into my palm.

I closed my fingers around it and stared down at what had been a man. As though from a great distance, I heard myself speak. "The Pope ordered my father's death? Is that what you are saying?"

"Yes, yes!" he sobbed. "For pity's sake, help me!"

I scarcely heard him, for just then a figure emerged from the shadows. Garbed in scarlet and gold, his great shoulders blocking out the light behind him so that all was cast into darkness, His Eminence, Cardinal Rodrigo Borgia, prince of Holy Mother Church, smiled.

"Help him," he said, and having drawn a knife from beneath his robes, he handed it to me.

I do not remember going back upstairs. When next I recalled anything, I was sitting in Il Cardinale's office, in the same chair I had occupied scant hours before. The medallion was still in my hand, squeezed so hard that it had left its imprint on my flesh.

My other hand was stained with blood.

There was no sign of the knife; it was gone.

Vittoro handed me a glass of brandy. "Drink," he said, and I obeyed, swallowing it all in a single, long draught.

I felt very cold, which was ridiculous because the night was warm. It must have rained because the terrace beyond the high windows glinted wetly in the moonlight. A part of me marveled that the world had gone on so mundanely while all within me was shaken to the core.

Borgia sat behind his desk. Candles threw his weighty features into high relief. He toyed with a small blade, the kind used for opening the seals on letters. "You did better than I thought you would," he said.

When I say that I do not remember returning to the world above, that is the truth. However, I have a clear memory of what happened in those final moments in the bowels of the palazzo. I, who hated and feared blood above all else, slit the throat of my father's killer—only one of them, to be sure, and among the least.

Far greater prey awaited me.

The river of his life had poured out over the rack, onto the stone floor, almost touching my feet, reminding me of the images I had seen of ancient sacrifice. I had only moments to contemplate the stunning sense of satisfaction and relief that exploded within me before Vittoro yanked me back, snatched the knife from my hand, and threw it to the ground. Without waiting for the Cardinal's permission, he hurried me away.

Now he handed me another glass of brandy, which I took but did not drink. All my attention was on Borgia. If he had underestimated me, I had done the same with him. Never had I imagined how far he would go to secure my cooperation.

"I still prefer poison," I said with care to conceal the dark emotions roiling within me. Borgia saw too much as it was. I would not willingly give him more.

"Vengeance is vengeance," he said, "in whatever form it comes." The greyhound at his feet raised its head and looked at him before lying back down. It was one of his favorite hunting dogs, the pack kept at his country residence except for a favored few who were always with him. He was a great lover of animals, Borgia was, except for those he liked to see torn apart.

"Vengeance is mine, sayeth the Lord," I replied, and thought, for a fleeting moment, that Rocco would be pleased. Yet I could not ascribe to that belief, not while the man who had ordered my father's death still breathed on this earth.

The Cardinal raised a brow. "A few minutes ago you did not hesitate to take matters into your own hands."

"God's justice is for the world beyond. Here we have only what we make for ourselves."

I looked to Vittoro, who was watching me with concern. "Should we not speak in private, Eminence?" I asked.

I was thinking of myself, of course. The fewer people who knew what I was about to agree to, the better. But I also thought of Vittoro. I could not imagine that he would want any part of what the Cardinal and I intended to do.

Once again, Borgia surprised me. "The captain has my confidence," he said, and waved Vittoro into the chair beside me. It was a masterful gesture, putting us all on an equal level, as it were. Yet not equal at all, for behind the vast expanse of his marble and gilt desk, in the palatial surroundings he so effortlessly dominated, there could be no doubt that the Cardinal ruled all.

And so we talked late into that dark night. Borgia stressed what I already knew, that Innocent's death had to appear entirely natural.

I said again that I knew nothing of how my father might have contemplated bringing that about, but promised to do my utmost to determine how it could be accomplished.

"Don't take too long about it," the Cardinal said. "I can raise enough questions within the Curia to delay the edict for some little time, but not for very long."

"Do you have any idea how much time we have?" Vittoro asked. He had been silent until then.

"Innocent's recent illness has created a sense of urgency," Borgia replied. "We have a few days at most."

A few days in which to find a way to induce death that would raise no questions in the minds of the most suspicious and watchful people in all of Christendom, those most likely to see conspiracy in the most ordinary events, among which the death of a pope certainly cannot be ranked.

"That illness," I asked, "do you know if my father actually caused it?"

Borgia shook his head. "I have no idea, but Innocent must have suspected as much or he would not have ordered Giovanni's death."

If he had ordered it. Do not think me a fool. I understood full well that men under torture will say anything demanded of them. That is why, in my opinion, torture is senseless. I am clearly in the minority in believing this, as it remains so much in fashion.

Why ever the man said what he did, I knew that he had participated in killing my father and in the attack on me. He linked both to the Pope, which might or might not be true but which, along with what I had learned about the edict, certainly pointed in the direction of the Vatican. If I were to reach so high in pursuit of my father's murderers, I would need Borgia's help.

"Whether he already had the means to sicken the Pope or not," I went on, "my father must have had some plan for getting close to Innocent. But surely he knew that no one would allow him anywhere near the Pope."

"I have thought as much," the Cardinal said. "It is possible that your father knew someone in a position to help him—another *converso,* perhaps."

I let the reference to my father's supposed status go by without comment and concentrated on the possible usefulness of what Borgia had said. I could not pretend to be surprised. It was well known—or at least rumored—that those most determined to pass as Christians were inclined to take holy orders. Any priest who could not prove his lineage going back generations might be a secret Jew.

"Do you know this for a fact?" I asked.

Borgia shook his head. "I do not. As I am sure you understand, any such person would keep himself extremely well hidden."

Undoubtedly so, but I had to find him and without delay, at the same time I had to find what my father had sought. And I had to accomplish both before time ran out—for the Jews and for me.

I was suddenly very tired. "It will be light soon. I must consider how best to proceed."

With the Cardinal's permission, I withdrew. Before the door closed behind me, I saw him pick up a document and begin to read. It was said that Borgia was tireless in the pursuit of his ambitions, and I believed it.

Vittoro accompanied me to my apartment. On the way, I gathered my courage to ask him what I had to know. "Are you certain you want to be part of this?"

"I am a faithful servant of His Eminence."

"That's all very well and good, but what about your soul?"

He stopped abruptly. The young guard carrying a torch to light our way almost walked into his back. Vittoro took my elbow. Together, we walked a little ahead, enough for privacy's sake.

"My soul?" he sounded amused. "Do you have any idea how many men I have killed, Donna?"

When I admitted that I did not, he said, "Neither do I. As a young man, I fought in the papal war against Florence and against the Duke of Ferrera when he, too, offended the pope. Later, I fought against the Kingdom of Naples for the same reason. I would have fought against the Turks but they bought Innocent and own him still. I have watched him sell forgiveness for every manner of sin, including the greatest depravity. But then he himself is an expert on such matters. He has whored, stolen, lied, and blasphemed his whole life. The sooner he faces divine judgment, the better."

I glanced over my shoulder. The young guard hovered far enough away that we would not be heard.

"And you believe Borgia is different?" I asked.

Vittoro answered thoughtfully. "He is . . . practical. That's the word for him. Certainly, he likes his pleasures, what man doesn't? But you saw him just now when we were leaving, he was going to work. That's what he's like. Go full out and get the job done, that's his attitude. And that's what we need. Rome, Christendom, all of us. He'll see us right."

"He tried for the papacy before and lost," I reminded him.

Vittoro nodded. "And he'll lose again if he has to wait much longer. Once that edict is out, it will be too late. He needs the Jews' money."

And he needed Innocent dead.

Innocent who, it was very clear, Borgia was determined to set me on as the hound to the hare.

Vittoro left me at my door. In my rooms, I stood for a few

moments, looking at the bed with its covers tossed back in haste. I had left it one person and returned as another. It was not only the act of ending a life without the distance poison afforded, it was also what I had discovered about myself.

While my father lived, I was a loving daughter, sharing his interests, learning from him, ultimately far surpassing his abilities but always protecting him from loneliness even as he protected me from the harshness of the world. Since his death, I had lived to avenge his murder, as surely it was my duty to do. But something else was stirring in me now, watered by the blood I had shed that night.

I had killed the Spaniard out of need, to attain the position that had to be mine.

I had enjoyed killing the man on the rack. Were it possible, I would have killed him again and again. There was something in the stroke of the knife I wielded and the spurt of blood that followed it . . . something that made me feel a sense of power and, strangely, peace that I had never experienced before. Were I to sleep just then, I understood in a flash of insight that the nightmare would not come.

The thought drove me to the basin set on the table beside the bed. The water had cooled long ago, but I scarcely noticed as I scrubbed the blood from my hand and kept on scrubbing until my skin was raw and red. It did not matter. The fingers that had curled so eagerly around the knife would never truly be clean again. No amount of prayer or absolution could wipe out the sin of what I freely and knowingly intended to do.

"The die is cast," the Cardinal had said. So, too, I feared, was my soul into the pit of damnation.

It is a curious thing to think oneself damned. Fear fades away, doubt dissolves. There is a strange, exhilarating sense of liberation. On the cusp of it, I went out into the bloodred dawn rising over Rome.

10

Sofia was bandaging a festering wound on the leg of an old man when I arrived at the apothecary shop. Nothing seemed to have changed since the previous day—as many sick and dying people as before were lined up waiting for help while the pile of bodies out in front was as high as ever.

She looked up, saw me, and gestured toward the workroom at the rear.

"Wait for me in front, if you will," I told Vittoro, aware as I was that Sofia would not speak in his presence. He nodded, shot me a quick look that I interpreted to be a reminder of the need for caution, and went to take up his post.

Before he did, he placed the supplies we had brought in my arms. I walked to the back, behind the wall that separated the workroom from the rest of the shop. The battered table was cluttered but there was just enough space to set down my burdens. When I had done so,

I took a moment to look around more carefully than I had been able to do on my two previous visits.

Despite her desperate circumstances, I saw that Sofia maintained a sense of order and cleanliness. Everything was neatly labeled—salves, ointments, and balms on one shelf, pills and suppositories on another, and raw ingredients on several more. She had basic surgical instruments—scalpels, pincers, cauterizers, and the like—and a better than decent pair of scales. Overall, I was surprised that a simple apothecary would be so well equipped.

I was still thinking about that when the back door opened and Benjamin peered in.

"Signorina," he said, beckoning to me with a smile. *"Viene prego."*

"What is it, Benjamin?" I asked. But he was already backing out of the shop, still gesturing to me to follow. I went with some exasperation, uncertain what he wanted or why he would imagine that I could go with him just then. Surely he understood that I was far too busy for childish games?

Apparently, he did understand that very well, for scarcely had I set foot in the alley behind the apothecary shop than I was grabbed from behind. A hood was dragged down over my head, plunging me into darkness. With the memory of the beating I had suffered sharp in my mind, I fought frantically and tried to cry out, to no avail. Before I could draw breath, I was thrown into a rough conveyance, a heavy wood hatch banged down above me, and I could feel myself being rolled away.

For several minutes, I could do nothing except try to steady myself against the sides of what I rapidly determined was a large pickle barrel. Although it had been emptied out prior to my arrival, the wood was saturated with the smell of brine. I could barely breathe even through my mouth and had to use all my strength to keep from being slammed back and forth against the sides. Even so, I did try to drag the hood off only to discover that it had been drawn tight around my neck and knotted.

In that manner, I traveled a distance that, though short, seemed to take forever. Several more bruises were added to my collection as I was trundled down a flight of steps, coming to rest at last in what I guessed must be a cellar.

Wondering if perhaps it was God's mercy that I should die before I sinned unforgivably, I tried to steel myself for whatever was to come next. The lid of the barrel was wrenched open and I was hauled out as unceremoniously as I had been dumped in. Hard hands shoved me down onto a stool. For a moment, nothing happened, then I heard a man's voice.

"What is it you want?" he asked.

What *I* wanted? Hadn't I been brought there against my will? Why would he assume that I wanted anything?

And yet, there was something I wanted enough to accept that its price was eternal damnation. As I have said, that was oddly liberating.

"I want to avenge my father." My voice sounded muffled to my own ears, but the words were clear enough. I wondered what the man would make of them.

A moment passed. The hood was untied and yanked off over my head. I blinked in the dim light filtering through slits cut at street level near the ceiling.

"At least she's honest," another man said.

I realized then that there were several of them, all mere shadows in the dimness beyond the light. I could not make out any of their faces.

"Or she doesn't think enough of us to lie," the first man suggested.

He laughed without humor. "Is that it, poisoner? Are we so lowly in your eyes as to not be worth the effort of deception?"

"I don't know whether you are or not," I said. "I don't know *who* you are."

"We are Jews," the second man said. "Isn't that all you have to know to judge us?"

He had a point. All my life, I had heard, "The Jews this . . . the Jews that . . ." They were spoken of as a single entity, all carrying the same taint, enmeshed in the same plots, deserving of the same fate. Was it the knowledge that my father might have been one of them that made me begin to see them differently?

"What do *you* want?" I asked, hoping to conceal my confusion.

"The same as you," the first man said, and stepped out into the light.

He was young, only a few years older than I, tall and broad-shouldered. With his dark, curling hair, strong features, and sharp, black eyes, he looked like a Spaniard. But he was a Jew, a handsome Jew, a notion so novel that I could not help stare at him.

"Who are you?" I asked.

He sat on a stool facing me. Close-up, he looked even more like a creation of the painter Botticelli, all liquid eyes and fierce grace. Botticelli shares my fascination with Dante to the extent that he scandalized his peers by illustrating the first printed edition of *La Divina Commedia* a few years ago. No one seriously imagines that mechanical printing can ever replace the handwritten art of creating manuscripts, though it makes for interesting novelties. But I digress. I do that when I am unnerved, and the handsome Jew put me in that state.

"My name is David ben Eliezer," he said. "I apologize for the way you were brought here, Signorina Giordano, but we have to be careful."

"Yet you sent a child to lure me. Where is your care for him?"

With fear fading fast, I took refuge in the tart temper to which I am, admittedly, prone.

Ben Eliezer looked taken aback for a moment, but, give him credit, he recovered quickly. "Such tender concern for the well-being of a Jewish child? You astonish me, signorina."

Only a few days had passed since I had done the same to Borgia, or so the Cardinal had said just before deciding to let me live. Perhaps I would be equally fortunate this time.

"That's all well and good," I said, "but you haven't told me what I am doing here."

Although by then I had a fair idea. Even if my father had been a Jew, which I still could scarcely credit, I did not believe they would share my desire to seek vengeance for him, not under such desperate circumstances and given stakes so high. That left only one other possibility. I waited, scarcely breathing, on the hope that fate had conspired for us to share a common goal.

Ben Eliezer hitched his stool a little closer and dropped his voice. "You know about the edict, about what Innocent intends to do. That cannot be allowed to happen." His face hardened. "Enough Jews have died, are dying, will die. While the rabbis and the merchants dither, that madman will kill us all."

I understood what Ben Eliezer was saying, that the leaders of the ghetto were not willing to move against Innocent directly. They would go so far as to strike a deal with Borgia but no further. And who could blame them, really? If they were even suspected of considering so heinous a crime as the murder of a pope, all the hounds of Hell would be unleashed against them. There would not be a Jewish man, woman, or child left alive in Rome. Nor would it end there. All of Christendom would rise up in a bloodletting to rival anything seen in the history of the world.

Yet the edict Innocent was preparing would have much the same result. Ben Eliezer and the others gathered in the shadows behind him recognized that.

"There is only one way to stop him," I said.

We looked at each other. I knew, and I assumed he did as well, the enormity of what we were contemplating, each for our own reasons. But if what I believed was true, we were not the first.

"Do you know what my father was doing?"

Ben Eliezer turned and gestured to someone behind him. Sofia stepped out of the shadows. I was only moderately surprised. Obviously, someone had brought me to the notice of Ben Eliezer and his associates.

"I hope you can forgive us," she said. "We had to have a better sense of your seriousness before we could risk approaching you."

She took a stool beside us so that we formed a small circle, sitting huddled together in a small ring of light isolated from the darkness. I tried to muster some annoyance at the lies she had told me but could not. Matters were moving too quickly to allow for pettiness.

"I told you that your father was seeking a way to bring about a seemingly natural death." When I nodded, she continued. "You will understand that we don't know what causes disease. When plague strikes, people who seal themselves up in their houses are as likely to sicken and die as is anyone else. Those who flee to the countryside may or may not escape. When fevers come in the summer, some are stricken, others not. The pox kills some, leaves others blind and horribly scarred, and doesn't touch others. There is no rhyme or reason to any of it."

"God's will—" I began, but Sofia shook her head.

"If we say it is God's will," she said, "what does that avail us? All inquiry becomes pointless. Your father believed—and so do I—that we can use the reason God gave us to discover how to help ourselves. *That* is God's will."

It was a startling thought. The great Saint Augustine taught that Man possessed free will as a gift from God. But he also taught that God knows our fates from the beginning. How can what is divinely known be subject to human choice? But if there is no choice, how can we fairly be held accountable for our sins?

You see the circles we Christians entangle ourselves in with our effort to know the unknowable?

Better to concentrate on matters closer to hand. "What did my father's reason lead him to?" I asked.

"He came to the conclusion that some people are more likely to get some illnesses when they are in close contact with people who already have them."

That much seemed obvious. Most physicians, priests, and the like will not go near anyone they suspect of contagion unless they are richly paid, and even then they are fainthearted in their duty. Sofia was very much the exception in that regard.

"No one suspected of being ill would be allowed near the Pope," she went on. "Therefore, your father had to find another means to bring the contagion to Innocent."

"And did he find it?"

She hesitated for so long that I began to wonder if she would answer, but finally she said, "He thought that it might be possible to use blood to transmit disease."

"Why blood?" I asked. "Aren't all four of the humors equally important?" Certainly, that was what I had been taught, the knowledge dating back to the Greek, Hippocrates, and being upheld by every physician since.

"So it is generally thought," Sofia agreed. "Blood, yellow bile, black bile, and phlegm all have their part to play in temperament and well-being. Too much yellow bile, for instance, disposes one to anger easily, whereas an excess of black bile causes sleeplessness and a tendency toward irritability. Each of the four has a different but equal effect on the body."

"Why then did my father only consider blood?"

"Because," Ben Eliezer said, "that was our best hope for reaching Innocent."

The look on his face—he was enjoying this—warned me I would not like what I was about to hear.

"For several years now," Ben Eliezer said, "your Pope has sought to maintain his health and stave off death by suckling at the breasts of nursing mothers."

I had heard this, of course. Who in Rome had not? The city wallows in rumor; it is our sport, our entertainment, our tool, and our weapon. At times it seems to be the very reason for our existence.

But Ben Eliezer had more. "Recently," he said, "Innocent has become convinced that milk is not enough. He needs blood, specifically the blood of young boys."

I would like to tell you that I was shocked, but that was not the case. People do all sorts of things in an attempt to cheat death. The more powerful they are, the more bizarre the efforts they resort to. I myself have known those who dined on the placentas of the newborn, ingested gold, and engaged in all manner of other activities, some of which I suspect actually hastened their demise.

"You are aware of the *cantoretti* school in the Vatican?" Sofia asked.

I had heard the rumors, the same as everyone else. It was said that the choral masters of the Vatican were adopting the Byzantine practice of castrating certain promising boys. So altered, the castratos' voices remained extraordinarily pure and flexible, producing, it was claimed, the music of the angels.

The practice was very controversial, being both foreign—the Muslims favor it—and a violation of God's will that we should be fruitful and multiply. It also strikes visceral horror into most males.

"What about it?" I asked, without revealing the extent of my knowledge.

"Some of the boys dedicated to the school have been directed to another purpose," Sofia said, "one Innocent has decreed is higher."

"Keeping him alive?" I guessed.

Ben Eliezer nodded. "They are allowed to remain intact, apparently because the Pope fears his own virility, such as is left of it, will lessen if he receives the blood of castrati. However, few of them survive the procedure by which he is . . . supplied."

"Why is that?"

"Perhaps they are bled too often," Sofia said. "At any rate, your father had the thought that it might be possible to replace blood taken from the boys with the blood of someone who was dying of disease. The hope was that the Pope, too, would sicken and die."

"Was such an attempt actually made?" I asked her.

"We don't know. Giovanni broke off all contact with us for our own protection, as I have told you. But there is always sickness in Rome. It is possible that he acquired tainted blood elsewhere. Perhaps he even found a way to get it to Innocent."

"The Pope's condition did worsen at about that time," Ben Eliezer reminded me. "Unfortunately, we don't know for certain if that happened because of your father's efforts. At any rate, Innocent did not die."

No, he did not. He was still very much alive and, if the word on the streets of Rome was to be believed, currently enjoying improved health.

"How does he receive the blood?" Already, my mind was working to address the problem. How had it been done? How might it be done more successfully?

"He drinks it," Ben Eliezer said. "Perhaps he believes that God transmutes it into wine for him."

He did laugh then and several others still in the shadows did the same. The notion of the Holy Father, the leader of all of Christendom, engaged in such a travesty of the sacred Mass might have amused me, too, if I hadn't been thinking about the boys.

"Who prepares it for him?"

"His physicians, we assume," Sofia said. "And no, before you ask, none of them is a Jew. Innocent won't let any Jews near him, or Muslims, either."

"What about *conversi*?" I asked, remembering what Borgia had told me.

"That's a different matter," Ben Eliezer acknowledged. "There are rumors, to be sure, but we don't know for certain that there are any such in the Vatican."

"You would be the last to know." Any *converso,* being naturally fearful of discovery, would avoid any connection to the Jews. If my father had been one, and I still did not accept that he was, he would have been the exception. Much as I did not want to think it, that might help to explain what had happened to him.

We were all silent for a moment. I was thinking about what I had learned and how I might turn it to my own ends when Sofia said softly, "Will you help us?"

I did not hesitate. My reply was clear and unequivocal.

"No, absolutely not."

11

Those were either the most daring or the most foolish words I had ever spoken, perhaps both. Not even when I challenged Borgia to make me his poisoner had I gone so far.

Ben Eliezer, Sofia, and the others were desperate, poised as they were on the keen edge of catastrophe. With the knowledge I now possessed, they had every right to see me as an intolerable danger. If it had not occurred to them that I should not leave the cellar alive, it would soon.

Yet I felt I had no choice. "I will not help you," I said. "This matter is far too delicate to be in your hands." Before they could protest, I added, "However, I will allow you to help me."

Under other circumstances, the look on Ben Eliezer's handsome face would have been comical. It was clear in that instant that he had a trait in common with Cesare: namely he was not accustomed to hearing "no" from a woman.

Sofia, on the other hand, looked amused. "You think you should be in charge?" she asked.

"I think I have to be," I told her truthfully. "You have no contact inside the Vatican nor any prospect of acquiring one. That is key to our success. Moreover, you don't even have the support of your own people." I gestured at our surroundings. "If you did, we wouldn't be meeting in such a place."

"The rabbis think they can pray our way out of this and the merchants think they can buy our way out," Ben Eliezer began, but Sofia hushed him.

"She is just saying what is true, David. Be thankful. That will save us a great deal of time." Turning to me, she said, "Are you prepared to make an attempt?"

"No," I replied, "not yet. I don't know if my father even had a contact inside the Vatican. I will have to discover if there is such a person and, if there is, convince him to cooperate again." I did not add that at the moment I had only the faintest idea of how to accomplish that.

"We have very little time," Ben Eliezer warned. "The edict could be issued at any moment."

"We have no more than a few days," I told him. "Borgia made that clear."

A look passed between Sofia and Ben Eliezer. I saw how dismayed they were.

"The Cardinal is said to know everything," Ben Eliezer said. "Surely, he can discover who your father was working with?"

"Borgia is going as far as he can by employing me in this affair," I replied. Everything I knew about Il Cardinale told me this. He possessed ruthlessness and prudence in equal measure. Only with both had he risen so high, within reach of the very pinnacle of power in all of Christendom.

"He will have nothing more to do with the matter," I went on. "If we are caught, he will throw us to the wolves. Be sure you understand that."

"I would expect nothing less from a prince of Holy Mother Church," Ben Eliezer said drily.

That was as well, for once embarked on so deadly a mission, we could count only on ourselves to see us through. As it was, we would be very lucky if any of us survived.

I was about to say as much when I stopped myself. Though Sofia, Ben Eliezer, and the rest showed great courage, they might as well have been in a waking nightmare. Death and despair were all around them, with the prospect of even worse to come. I did not have to remind them of how bad things were.

"Sofia," I said, "in whatever time we have, can you try to determine how to improve our chances for success? Some way of discovering what blood might work best?"

"I can try, but in all honesty, I have no real idea how to go about that."

"Just do your best and I will do mine." If anyone had told me that I would make such a pledge to a Jew, I would have thought him mad, but there it was.

"You should get back," Ben Eliezer said. He rose and went to open the door leading up to the street. I stood and followed him.

Vittoro was waiting in the front of the apothecary shop when I arrived. Of Benjamin, there was no sign.

"I was worried," the captain said. "You've been talking all this time?" His nose wrinkled slightly, calling my attention to the odor of brine that clung to me.

"We had much to discuss," I told him but offered nothing more. To Sofia, I said, "I will return when I have news."

She nodded and reached out, taking my hand. Softly, she said, "Go with God, Francesca. He has made you a Righteous Gentile and as such you are blessed."

I had no idea what she meant, but her words reminded me again of Saint Augustine, who wrote that the Jews were a people specially chosen by God whose continued existence reminds us of the truth of biblical prophecy. Since they serve God's purpose, it would seem ill-advised to torment them, but then I am no theologian.

I arrived back at the palazzo exhausted and filthy. After a bath and a light meal, I was still desperately in need of rest. My ribs throbbed and numerous other bruises made every movement painful. Even so, the thought of sleep terrified me. To sleep is to invite dreams, or, in my case, nightmares.

Instinct drove me out into the sun and from there into the city itself. Vittoro sent along a young guardsman—not the hapless Jofre, who was still cleaning latrines, but another he assigned to me after I assured him I only wanted to walk a bit to clear my thoughts.

"Better you rest instead," he said, but he did not try to insist.

I went out into the day, the guard trailing behind me. The afternoon being very fair, the streets were even more crowded than usual. Wagons jostled for space on the Pons Aelius that spans the river just below Castel Sant'Angelo. Much as I tried to avoid looking in the direction of the vast fortress with its curved stone walls that has loomed over Rome since the days of the Emperor Hadrian, I could not. The news in the street was that Innocent was living there now, having left his pretty little palazzetto near Saint Peter's for the far more secure *castel*. No doubt his quarters had a more pleasant view than onto the inner courtyard where prisoners were brought to be executed. It was said that more and more such executions were taking place each day, and I knew of no reason to doubt it.

Halfway across the bridge, I stopped and glanced back over my shoulder. I had the sense that I was being watched. Seeing what I did, the young guardsman stopped, too, and looked around. He saw nothing to concern him in the throng of passersby and neither did I. Convinced that my anxiety was due to weariness, I went on.

Crossing the river, I came within sight of the once magnificent Basilica of Saint Peter. Nowadays, it is in such disrepair that visitors can be forgiven for looking up anxiously at its gabled roof as they scurry from one point to another in fear of falling masonry. Despite this, my father and I had been regular visitors. We shared a fascination with antiquity, which the thousand-year-old basilica offers in abundance.

As always, the courtyard in front of Saint Peter's teemed with priests, trades people, lawyers, and visitors of every degree. Many lingered in the atrium, admiring the magnificent Navicella mosaic depicting Saint Peter walking on the waters. I slipped past and gained the interior, pausing for a moment to gaze down the length of the central nave to the main altar. I have said that I am not a pious woman, but even I could not help be moved by the magnificent marble and gold table set to receive the sacrifice of the Lamb. It stood surrounded by columns said to have been taken from the temple of Solomon by the great Constantine himself.

But such glories were not for me. I moved off across the side aisles to one of the numerous small altars lining both sides of the nave. This one was sanctified to Saint Catherine of Siena, she who was said to have experienced a mystical marriage with Christ and who devoted her life to caring for the poor and sick. My father gave me her medal, cast at her canonization a little more than twenty years before. He said it had belonged to my mother. I have it still.

There in the relative quiet of the side aisles separate from the main part of the basilica, I tried to pray. The young guard moved some distance away to give me privacy. As always, praying did not come easily to me. The more I tried to concentrate on the holy image of the saint and the flickering prayer candles lit before her, the more my attention wandered. I thought of the Spaniard and the medallion man, of Borgia and Innocent, of the Jews in general and Sofia and David in particular, and hardly lastly, of Cesare who gave way in turn to thoughts of Rocco. Really, I have a most wayward mind. I was endeavoring yet again to direct it in more appropriate paths when the sensation of being watched returned.

For a moment, I remained with my hands clasped and my eyes raised to the saint, but all my attention was elsewhere. I was aware of the rustle of cloth to my left and behind me. A hint of camphor and citrus hung in the air. When I focused very hard, I could hear someone breathing.

I stood and turned all at once. The sudden movement almost wrung a gasp of pain from me as my bruised ribs protested, but I bit it back and stared into the face of an angel.

I do not exaggerate. His features were the classical expression of masculine beauty—straight nose, square chin, high brow, and chiseled cheekbones. His eyes were large and of the purest blue. His hair was a nimbus of golden curls clinging to his perfectly shaped head. He was, in short, an enticement to the purest virgin.

Fortunately, I was neither pure nor a virgin. Which is not to say that I was not tempted.

The golden angel looked to all sides before he bent closer to whisper, "Signorina Giordano?"

When I nodded, still not quite trusting myself to speak, he smiled. I missed the next few words he spoke and recollected myself only when he said, ". . . must talk but not here, it is not safe."

"Then where, Father . . ." Did I fail to mention that he was a priest? Only they wear the black cassock, although few look as virile in it as he did. Fewer still seem to remember the vows they put on along with their priestly garb.

"Morozzi, Bernando Morozzi. I was a friend of your father's. His death . . . what can I say?" His eyes glistened with tears. "I pray for him daily."

My throat tightened. Such were my worries for my father's soul that I felt profound gratitude. "Thank you, Father. That is very good of you."

I would gladly have stood there talking with him for any length of time, but his evident anxiousness—he continued glancing around—reminded me of the precariousness of our position.

"We have a mutual friend," Father Morozzi said. He looked at me expectantly. "The glassmaker, you know him?"

"Of course—" A spurt of excitement shot through me. If the priest considered Rocco to be a friend, was it possible that he was one of those seekers of knowledge rumored to risk the condemnation of Holy Mother Church from inside its greatest fortress? And if he had also considered my father a friend, was it too great a leap of faith to hope that he might be the one I sought?

"Meet me at his shop tomorrow in the hour after terce," Morozzi urged. He gestured toward the nave, where my escort waited, oblivious to what was happening mere yards away. "Cardinal Borgia must not know that we have spoken. Do I have your word on that?"

Thinking his caution both prudent and necessary, I nodded.

"Of course." A sound behind me caused me to glance away. When I looked back a moment later, the priest had vanished.

I remained kneeling before Saint Catherine a little while longer, struggling to calm myself. Morozzi had sought me out—I was certain now that he must have followed me from the palazzo. Surely, he would not have done so without good purpose. If he was my father's contact inside the Vatican, perhaps convincing him to go forward would not be so very difficult after all.

That could mean that very soon I would reach a point from which there would be no turning back. It was what I wanted, of course; what I had been working toward, and yet it terrified me. The plain truth is that at the same time I could not imagine living without avenging my father, neither did I want to die.

Most particularly, I did not want the kind of death to be found within Castel Sant'Angelo, whose grim walls had absorbed so many raw and hopeless screams.

With that in mind, I returned to the palazzo and finally did what I knew could not be put off any longer. In the quiet of the workroom I had shared with my father, using compounds taken from his chest, I ground dried monkshood, paternoster pea, and star of Bethlehem with a mortar and pestle. Any of the three alone is deadly; together they kill with lethal speed. When the mixture was ready, I added a small quantity of the sediment that is found at the bottom of wine vats. This substance has a binding effect on most anything it comes into contact with.

The final result was a small brown lozenge that fit neatly into the gold locket, a gift from my father, that I secured around my neck. He had meant it for a far happier purpose, but I was glad that it fit my need. Placed in my mouth or dissolved in anything I ingested, the lozenge would kill me within minutes. It would be an unpleasant death, to be sure, but at least it would be swift.

With that accomplished, I laid down. The nightmare came almost at once and was as bad as always. I awoke to my own cries. Instinctively, I reached for the smooth gold talisman lying between my breasts. Holding on to it, I fell at last into restful sleep.

12

I was awake before daybreak and ready to leave for Rocco's long before the appointed hour, but first I had to deal with Vittoro. Morozzi had made it clear that he did not want Il Cardinale to know his identity, a prudent measure under the circumstances. While Vittoro had no qualms about ushering Innocent out of this world, I doubted very much if he would agree to keep anything from Borgia. That being the case, I needed a means of escaping the captain's scrutiny.

I considered seeking him out but decided against it, fearing to arouse suspicion. Instead, I waited patiently until he came to ask my plans for the day.

"I have much to do here." I tipped my head in the direction of my workroom. "But if I decide to go out, I will send word to you."

If Vittoro wondered what could keep a poisoner busy all day, he was too sensible to ask. Indeed, after a glance at the table on which I had set a variety of bottles, boxes, and casks, he withdrew quickly.

Left to myself, I wasted no time. From the bottom of my chest, I drew the boy's clothing that I had worn on more than one occasion, though not so often as to be comfortable in it. The short tunic, shirt, and hose left me feeling exposed and self-conscious at the same time they transformed my identity, free to go where I must without fear of harassment or censure.

As I final step, I tucked my hair up under a broad-brimmed felt hat, a struggle I accomplished with the help of a handful of pins. A glance in the mirror reassured me that no one other than the closest observer would take me for anything other than a slender lad, an apprentice or a servant perhaps, hurrying about his master's business.

As soon as the corridor outside my rooms was clear, I slipped out and down the stairs set inside one of the exterior walls. From there it was only minutes before I reached the same door through which I had returned to the palazzo after being beaten. As before, I was not seen.

Mindful of my disguise, I was careful to move with the combination of brisk self-importance and slightly endearing clumsiness that seems to characterize the passage of young males through the world. Fortunately, this did not require a great effort on my part. My father had made only the most passing effort to instill in me the graces of a lady, and for that I am deeply grateful. Several times, I glanced over my shoulder, but I never had any sense that I was being followed. By the time I reached the Campo dei Fiori, my ribs throbbed and I was glad to slow down.

I was also desperately hungry. Unwilling to arrive at Rocco's in such a state, I stopped to buy fresh bread and grapes before going on, and was gratified when the women selling both scarcely glanced at me before taking my money and handing over their wares as brusquely as they would have with any boy. I finished a hunk of the bread and brushed the crumbs from my tunic before I turned into the street of the glassmakers.

It was still early enough that the shops were just opening. Rocco was propping up the awning that shaded the tables where he displayed a small selection of his most everyday work. Nando was helping him. I riffled the child's hair as they both greeted me.

"Are you a boy now, Donna Francesca?" Nando asked with a giggle.

I bent down, the better to address him, and smiled. "I am in disguise. Isn't that exciting?"

He frowned uncertainly. "Like at a masque?"

"In a way. What do you think, do I look like a boy?"

Nando hesitated. In my experience, children are vastly more honest than the most forthright adult. Too often they are condemned for it, so they learn to lie.

"You look like . . . Donna Francesca," he said at length.

I offered an exaggerated sigh and rose. Beside me, Rocco showed no surprise at my boy's garb, which he had seen before. He accepted the bread and grapes with a smile for the vanished heel and ushered me inside.

"Will you take cider?" he asked.

It being a little too early for wine, I accepted. Soon we were seated at the table looking out onto the inner courtyard where the furnace glowed. Rocco had just begun to build up the fire for the day's work. His dark hair was swept back and secured with a band around his forehead. As he moved about the ordinary tasks of pouring drink and setting out the bread and grapes, the muscles of his upper arms, left bare by his leather tunic, rippled lightly.

He turned, saw me watching him, and flushed.

When Nando had finished his drink, his father sent him out to play with a handful of grapes and an admonition not to go far. Rocco waited until the door closed behind him before he asked, "Have you been back to the ghetto?"

I nodded. "I believe I have discovered what my father was doing and why. There is a plan in the works to issue a papal edict expelling all the Jews from Christendom. Innocent hasn't signed it yet but he is about to."

Rocco's eyes darkened. He stared at me for a long moment as he absorbed the impact of what I had revealed. The expulsion from Spain had been terrible enough, creating tens of thousands of refugees, many of who were dying from starvation and disease. How many times greater would the horror be if the same fate befell all the Jews of Europe?

"Where would they go?" he asked.

I shrugged. "The Turks have allowed some to come from Spain, but I have no idea how many more they would accept. It probably wouldn't matter. The Jews I spoke with believe that the real intent is to destroy them completely as a people."

"And Giovanni knew of this?"

"He did." Hesitantly, I asked, "Did you ever hear that he might be a *converso*?"

In a gesture that took me by surprise, Rocco reached across the table and covered my hand with his. His touch was warm and strong. To pull away from him would have been churlish. Besides, the truth is I had no wish to do so.

"Your father loved you dearly and only ever wanted to protect you. If he didn't tell you everything about himself, that was why."

Mother Mary and all the Saints, had everyone known about my

father save me? Since Borgia had first made the claim, the possibility that it was true had been growing in my mind. Even so, I still had difficulty accepting it.

"He didn't tell me . . . but he told you?"

Rocco withdrew his hand and leaned back. Carefully, he said, "When I first met your father I was suffering a crisis in my own faith. He sensed that and he helped me. In the process, we got to know each other well."

"Then he truly was a Christian—?" How desperately I wanted to believe that. Everything I had ever been taught told me that if my father was not of the One True Faith, his soul was lost forever. Yet when I actually thought about it, I had trouble understanding why God would arrange for that to be so.

We are not supposed to wonder about such things. Yet I suspect that more than a few of us do, especially when we yearn for a God who loves all His children without condition or reserve.

Quietly, Rocco said, "Your father saw in the teachings of our Lord evidence that the Messiah truly had come. Yet he still honored the beliefs of his people and he wanted to help them."

And for that, I was now certain, he had died.

Later I would think about all this but just then there was nothing for me to do but push on.

"I think my father was seeking a way to stop the edict from happening."

"If Innocent is about to sign it—"

I waited, knowing that he would put the rest together but uncertain how he would react. We were, after all, speaking of the pope, God's own anointed, set by His divine hand to rule over us. What my father had contemplated was not merely assassination, it could also be taken as sacrilege of the worst sort. I would not have been surprised if Rocco had expressed shock and outrage, perhaps even ordered me from his home. But I should have had more faith in him. He paled, to be sure, but he did not falter.

"When Giovanni counseled me on matters of faith, he drew on the teachings of Saint Augustine, whose writings impressed him greatly. He agreed with Augustine's conclusion that evil has no independent existence. It is simply the absence of good. It comes into being only when good is rejected."

I had scant interest in theology, but even I understood that the undeniable existence of evil in our world would make belief in an infinitely good God impossible had not Augustine shown so brilliantly that it is not God who creates evil but Man himself through his rejection of God's goodness.

"How can Innocent embrace evil and still serve God?" I asked carefully.

Without hesitation, Rocco replied, "He cannot. No man can, not king nor prince . . . nor pope."

Greatly relieved that we were in such accord but still presuming nothing, I changed tack and said, "I met a priest named Bernando Morozzi. He says that he knew my father and knows you. He also has knowledge of what my father was doing and claims to have been willing to help him."

"I know Morozzi," Rocco said. "I've made apparatus for him."

"He is an alchemist?" I really wanted to ask if Morozzi was a member of Lux, the secret society of alchemists that I wanted to believe existed, and to which I hoped my father had belonged. But I could not bring myself to go that far.

"He may aspire to be one. I met him for the first time last autumn when he came here. He was very friendly, asked a lot of questions, even befriended Nando. At first, I couldn't make out what he wanted, but eventually he admitted to what he sought."

"He was being careful."

"I suppose," Rocco said. "At any rate, he's bought a few items and he seems sincere enough. He asked me if I could introduce him to others with similar interests."

"Did you?"

He thought for a moment. "Your father came by one day when he was here. I introduced them and they got to talking. He met one or two others the same way but that was the extent of it."

I nodded, understanding what Rocco was saying. One of the great hindrances to the advancement of knowledge is the need for secrecy. Scholars are either afraid to share their knowledge for fear of condemnation or unwilling to share it out of professional rivalry. Both make progress very difficult. If Lux truly did exist, it would be largely for the purpose of overcoming that.

"Father Morozzi suggested that we meet here," I said. "But I will leave now if you prefer."

Lest you think too badly of me, know that even then a part of me regretted the need to involve Rocco in any way. I knew full well that in doing so, I was taking advantage of his fundamental goodness. But the greater part, that which drove me, saw no alternative. Such was my nature. I have improved in years since but not so much as I could wish.

He hesitated as I contemplated the calculation I was forcing him to make: On the one side, the life he had managed to build for himself and his son that would be put at terrible risk if he helped me; on the other, the lives of uncounted thousands that were hanging in the balance and beyond even that, the possibility that so great an evil would overwhelm Holy Mother Church herself and cast us all from God's light forever.

"Stay," Rocco said. Meeting my eyes, he added, "Do what you must."

We finished the food and I helped him clear up. A few minutes later, the door to the shop opened and the priest entered. He was not wearing his cassock, being dressed instead in the modest tunic of a tradesman. I thought this a sensible precaution. While I couldn't be certain how much Rocco's fellow glassmakers knew about his activities, the appearance of a priest at his premises might have raised eyebrows. Even so, simply by virtue of his looks Morozzi was bound to be noticed.

"Father," Rocco said courteously. "It is good to see you again."

"And you, my son," Morozzi replied. His smile appeared warm and genuine but it gave way to a frown as he looked at me. "You are—?"

"It's me, Father, Francesca Giordano. I came without escort, as you asked, and took the precaution of concealing my identity."

Whatever good reason I thought I had for dressing as a male, it was clear that the priest did not approve. He stared at me in shock before quickly averting his gaze.

"It is not seemly," he protested.

Rocco raised an eyebrow but wisely allowed me to calm Morozzi as best I could.

"These are difficult times, Father. Surely we all understand the need for caution?"

When this failed to elicit more than another condemning glance from him, my patience faded. With some asperity, I said, "Please correct me if I am wrong, Father, but is it not the position of Holy Mother Church that a woman may wear man's garb without sin if she does so to preserve herself from the threat of molestation?"

I knew perfectly well that it was, the Church having been forced to declare that in order to nullify Joan of Arc's conviction for heresy and set her on the path to sainthood.

Rocco made a sound that might have been a chuckle. "I must see to the furnace," he said. With what I took to be a pointed glance at me, he added, "The fire waits for no one."

He was gone out into the courtyard while I was still wondering if he intended a hidden warning in his words. Morozzi appeared ill at ease but disinclined to argue doctrine with me. Or perhaps he was merely at haste to conclude our business and be gone.

He took a breath and finally seemed to relax somewhat. At least, my appearance no longer made him flinch.

Softly, Morozzi asked, "How much do you know of your father's activities, signorina?"

As I was wondering the same about him, I answered carefully. "Enough. Why did you want to see me?"

"His death was a great loss."

"So you have said." However anxious Morozzi might be, I was not prepared to indulge him very much longer. "Tell me what you know of my father's murder."

The demand—it could not be mistaken for anything else—surprised him. Clearly, he had presumed he would control our conversation. Instinct, honed in my years beneath Il Cardinale's roof, drove me to prevent that.

He fumbled for an answer. "It was very tragic . . ."

"I know all that. Tell me who ordered it."

The priest looked taken aback. His appearance and his holy office both assured that he would receive the utmost reverence from almost any woman he encountered. Clearly, I was outside his experience, but to give him credit, he rallied quickly.

"You don't know?" he asked.

"Perhaps I do, perhaps I do not. What do you know?"

As I have said, a man subjected to torture will say anything to stop the pain. That does not mean that what he says is necessarily false. Even so, a sensible person seeks collaboration.

"The Pope feared that in his eagerness to gain the papacy, Borgia intended to deploy his poisoner," Morozzi said. "By killing your father, he sent a message to the Cardinal that he would not succeed."

It was as I suspected, but even so, hearing it was very hard. I had to force myself to speak. "Why hasn't Innocent ordered my death since I assumed my father's office?"

"He does not fear you," the priest said. "Not as he did your father. You are only a woman."

God help me, I smiled. Innocent would have all of eternity to contemplate his error.

"When I realized that your father and I might have a common aim," Morozzi said, "I offered him my help. He accepted it. Unfortunately, he was not able to succeed in his endeavor. The . . . problem remains."

"Then an attempt was made?" I waited, scarcely breathing, to learn if my father truly had tried to kill the Pope.

Morozzi shook his head. "I know only that he was prepared to act. Tragically, he was killed before he could do so."

Oddly, I felt relieved. My father's soul was free of that sin, at least. But at the same time, I was now even less certain that the method Sofia believed he had intended to use could actually work.

"What do you mean that you shared a common aim?" I asked the priest.

Morozzi looked surprised. "Surely you know?"

"Perhaps I do, but I would still like you to answer."

Realizing that I continued to test him, he flushed. I could sense his patience wearing thin. "The edict . . . you know of it?"

I nodded. "Why would you care about the Jews?" I suspected that I already knew but I wanted to hear him say it.

He did so but not easily. For a moment, I thought the words would choke him.

"I am *converso*." Quickly, as though to cleanse the tongue that had uttered those words, he added, "I believe with all my heart and soul in one God, the Father Almighty, in Jesus Christ, his only begotten son, and in the Holy Ghost. I act only to prevent a great evil."

A part of me remembered the need for caution and yet I could not help be moved by what he said. Truly, I hoped that he spoke for my father as well.

"I understand," I told him. "Innocent is an old, sick man. In the natural course of events, he will not live much longer. Yet he may still have time to do much harm."

"Your father was determined to prevent that."

"He failed."

Morozzi nodded. He looked deeply unhappy yet still hopeful. "An attempt might still succeed . . . if you are willing?"

There it was, the offer I had sought. The path to vengeance for my father and achievement of the goal for which he had died, the survival of the Jews. If I was very lucky, I might even live long enough to have a chance to redeem my soul, but I wasn't counting on that.

"You can get me close to Innocent?" I asked.

Morozzi was very pale but he nodded without hesitation. "As close as is needed."

"How is that possible?" There were hundreds of priests within the Vatican. Very few of them had direct access to the Pope and even fewer would be allowed near him now that he had taken up residence in the *castel.*

"Since coming to Rome," Morozzi said, "I have been fortunate enough to draw the Holy Father's notice."

That did not surprise me. So far as I knew, Innocent was not a sodomist, but he had the same love of physical beauty that is shared by so many Romans. Morozzi looked like an angel. He would be noticed anywhere he went.

"The Pope is an old man terrified of death," the priest continued. "He is surrounded by people who are anxious for him to get on with it so they can secure their own positions in a new papacy. I encourage him to believe that he will be redeemed in the eyes of an all-forgiving God."

"Do you actually believe that?"

"As a Christian," Morozzi said, "I must believe that forgiveness is available to all. At any rate, the papal guards are accustomed to my presence in His Holiness's apartments. We will not be stopped."

I took a breath and let it out slowly. From this point, there was no turning back. Truly, the die would be cast. But then my decision had been made some time ago—when I knelt over the bloodied, battered corpse of my father and swore vengeance for his death. Every step I had taken since had been toward that.

"I will send word to you through Rocco when I am ready," I said. Much as I regretted using the glassmaker to such a purpose, I had no alternative.

The priest nodded. I could see that he was sweating but I sensed no weakness in him. "How will you do it?" he asked.

The question surprised me. I had assumed that he knew what my father had intended. "The same as before," I said carefully.

He nodded. "Poison then. Something quick and certain?"

My father could not possibly have intended to use poison against Innocent, not if his death was to appear natural. But apparently Morozzi did not know that. I had to wonder why even as I resolved to keep my own counsel in the matter.

"Yes," I said, "of course."

"Good, then I will wait for word from you."

"It shouldn't be long."

"I hope not. There is very little time."

I assured him that I understood the urgency and saw him to the door. Before he opened it, I asked as though in passing, "Tell me, is it true what I hear, that the Pope is drinking blood now?"

I thought he might deny the rumor, but instead he looked exasperated. "Innocent is convinced that it will keep him alive, but he grows weaker by the day."

"Perhaps Almighty God will be merciful and take him before he can sin further."

Morozzi shot me a sharp look. "Do not count on that. As I said, we must act quickly."

When he had gone and the door was closed behind him, I leaned back against it and took several deep breaths. My legs felt weak and I needed several moments to steady myself. By any measure, the meeting had been a success. I now had a means of reaching the Pope. But I also had more questions than before.

Why had my father not told Morozzi how he intended to kill Innocent?

Had he had some reason not to trust the priest?

Rocco returned just then from tending the fire. I was unprepared for the sudden urge I felt to seek the comfort of his arms. Instead, I wrapped my own around me in a vain effort to steady myself.

He did not hesitate but closed the distance between us quickly and stood before me, so near that I could see the steady rise and fall of his broad chest. Even at such dire times, there was a quiet strength about him, a steadiness that I could only envy.

"What did Morozzi say?" he asked.

I warred with my conscience. The easier path was to tell Rocco as little as possible. So do we descend to damnation by pleasant steps. I owed him more.

"That he will help me."

He paled and for a moment I thought he would cry out in protest. He was right, of course. What I contemplated was outrageous. Yes, popes throughout the ages had died in all sorts of unsavory ways, probably more of them even than we have guessed. But that was history, this was now.

This was me, Francesca Giordano, the poisoner's daughter. One lone woman seeking to upturn all of Christendom.

"Only say the word," I told Rocco, "and I will not come here again."

For a moment, I feared he would do just that. Certainly, he had no reason to further help the woman who had rejected him. But I had underestimated the courage of a good man who still believed in the power of the Church to save us all, if only it could be saved first.

His large hands, so powerful yet capable of the most delicate touch, closed on my shoulders. With utmost seriousness, he said, "Never speak of such a thing. I was your father's friend and I am yours. What Innocent intends is evil. Have faith, Francesca, that God has chosen you to stop him."

I was certain that had he even suspected my true nature—the darkness within me that howled for blood and death—Rocco would have never said what he did. But weak thing that I was, I could only be grateful for the false light in which he saw me.

He let me go then with murmured farewells on my part and a reminder from him that his door was always open.

Relieved by what my visit had accomplished, yet sensibly afraid of the course upon which I was now irrevocably embarked, I stole back to the palazzo. Scarcely had I regained my room than Vittoro appeared to tell me that Madonna Lucrezia had sent a message requesting my presence.

13

Is there a Roman alive who does not love *la campagna*? Proud city dwellers all, we nonetheless will seize any excuse to take a jaunt into the countryside to gape at the stolid tillers of the earth, chase after irate livestock, and generally make fools of ourselves. And what better time to do it than summer when the city swelters and, let us be honest, stinks.

Giulia la Bella had conceived such an excursion to bolster the spirits of her harried lover, and Lucrezia had invited me along. I was reluctant, feeling bound by duty to remain where I was, but my refusal would have raised suspicion. Besides, Il Cardinale was heading the party and where he went, so should I.

We traveled in several barges up the Tiber with what seemed like the whole of two households—guards, retainers, servants, musicians, chefs, and priests, not to mention dogs, several horses, La Bella's parrot who squawked the whole way, and a pig. I have no idea what the last was doing there, but as it was also on the return trip, I have to assume it was someone's pet.

A few miles north of the city, we put in at the pretty little villa La Bella had from her absent Orsini husband. It was far enough beyond the limits of Rome to be surrounded by lush forests and pleasant streams but convenient for a day's excursion. The servants were lined up along the bankside to welcome us and to help with the multitude of crates, baskets, and bundles required for even a day's visit to the country.

La Bella herself was assisted from the barge by no less than Il Cardinale, who hovered over her with tender regard. She had just begun to show but exaggerated the effect by thrusting her belly forward while she smiled at him. Borgia was far from a doting old fool, but he knew how to play one when the occasion called for it.

Lucrezia ran ahead, calling to me to follow her. I did so but not before I had a quick word with the villa's steward who broke off his harried supervision of the unloading to attend me. He knew who I was, word having spread through the usual channels. I perceived that I made him nervous but that is to be expected in my profession. Frankly, it is often an advantage. He accepted my instructions without objection—no food, drink, dishes, utensils, or linens except what we had brought with us unless inspected by me first—and confirmed that there was no new staff within the villa. Vittoro had sent along a lieutenant who I knew would inspect the Cardinal's quarters before Borgia entered them, looking for any concealed traps or weapons.

Having done all I could, I followed Lucrezia and found her in the small courtyard at the center of the villa. She was turning round and round in a circle, her arms flung out and her head tilted to the sky. Doves rose from their cotes, fluttering in the branches of the trees. It was a pretty sight.

"Isn't it wonderful here, Francesca?" she exclaimed. "Wouldn't it be lovely to live in the country all the time?"

"Don't you think you would become bored?" I asked, smiling at her.

She stopped turning and at the same time, turned serious. "Of course I wouldn't. After all, I would have a husband and children to tend to."

If you find it ironic that the woman who wanted only to be a devoted wife and mother is condemned by the world for licentiousness and worse, be assured that I do, too.

Her mood lightened at once. She gave me a teasing look, which I knew from experience meant that she had a secret that she was bursting to share.

"La Bella has a surprise for *Papà,*" she said.

I would have thought that informing her sixty-one-year-old lover that he was going to become a father yet again had been surprise enough for Borgia, but apparently Giulia had more in store for him.

"A masque," Lucrezia announced and clapped her hands. "We brought costumes and we've been rehearsing scenes from the *romanzos.* The musicians have composed a special piece and there is even scenery. It will all be quite wonderful."

"I'm sure it will be," I said, though privately I dreaded such things. My aversion was inherited from my father, who disapproved of such events on the grounds that once people are in costumes and masks, you cannot be sure who they are or what threat they may present. Also, the inside of a mask is a particularly good place to put poison, which will enter quickly through the membranes of the eyes, nose, or mouth and—

My apologies. It is not my purpose to provide you with such instruction. Heaven forbid. Let us just say that my dour thoughts could not survive Lucrezia's enthusiasm. She seized my hand and drew me off to help with this and that, needing me to hear her lines, review her dance steps, and generally make myself useful, not in the least by inspecting everything they intended to use. It was only after several hours that I realized she was diverting me deliberately.

"You have been so sad," she said when I challenged her. "I only wish to raise your spirits."

"That is very kind of you," I replied even though I did not believe her entirely. Not that Lucrezia was given to lying; she was far more honest than most people I have known. But like all of us, she could have more than one reason for her actions.

At the moment, she seemed interested only in getting me into the costume that she had brought along for me.

"You must," she insisted when I protested. "Everyone will be someone else tonight. *Papà* is Jupiter, Giulia is Venus, of course, and I am to be Diana. I have the most clever silver bow. You are Minerva. I even have an owl for you, but don't worry, it is in a cage."

Being chosen to portray the goddess of wisdom was sufficiently flattering to still my objections. Even so, I was not entirely comfortable in the thin linen chiton fastened at the sleeves with small gold clasps and belted at my waist that she had brought for me. It was undeniably far more comfortable in such warm weather than my usual clothing, but it left me feeling as though I wore almost nothing.

I saw no sign that anyone else was self-conscious in such garb as we all gathered for supper and the entertainment. On the contrary, Borgia looked entirely at ease in his purple-trimmed toga, which seemed to suit him much better than any ecclesiastical robe ever would. He was laughing with La Bella who, I must say, made an exquisite Venus. Her chiton was considerably thinner than mine, so much so as to reveal the dark aureoles of her nipples. She wore it with aplomb.

The masque itself went off splendidly, everyone applauding with much appreciation for the effort. Even the servants, garbed as they were in costume, seemed to be having a good time. I confess to being a little concerned that the party would be as ribald as some the Cardinal was said to enjoy. But perhaps because of the presence of his as yet virgin daughter, there were no naked dancing girls or other entertainment of that sort.

I was actually beginning to relax and enjoy myself when, from the corner of my eye, I noticed a man I had not seen before. His features were entirely hidden by a mask of hammered silver but I could see that he was tall, black-haired, and very well built, as was evident in the short toga he wore. He had a sword at his side and a shield strapped to his back, by which I guessed that he was meant to depict Mars, god of war.

We were dining in the courtyard, reclining in the old Roman style on couches. The man had emerged from the shadows cast by the torches set at intervals around us. At the same time that I saw him, the Cardinal rose, said a word to Giulia, and went into the villa. "Mars" must have done the same for when I looked, he was no longer in sight.

Some instinct brought me to my feet. I told myself that I was being foolish, the villa was under guard, no one could have entered it unseen. There was no danger. Yet I kept going, hoping to spot Vittoro's lieutenant, who would know better than I what to do.

Unfortunately, he was nowhere in sight. Ahead of me, down the length of a paneled corridor, I saw a door close. I crept nearer, scarcely breathing, and pressed my ear to the carved wood.

Was I eavesdropping? Yes, of course, but not out of puerile

curiosity, or at least not entirely. While I did not expect Borgia to confide in me everything he did and everyone he saw, I could not hope to protect him properly if strangers could come and go in his vicinity without restriction. At the palazzo, there was an entire regiment of guards under the very able Vittoro to prevent any such thing. But here in the villa was another matter entirely.

All I needed was some indication that Borgia knew the man and that his presence was benign. Then I could take myself off with a clear conscience, leaving them to talk—more likely conspire—to their hearts' content.

The door being very thick, the voices coming from the other side reached me only faintly. And yet I was certain at once that I was hearing an argument. Two voices, both male, both raised, both angry.

And then a crash.

I thrust the door open and stepped into the room without a second thought. Do not ask me what I intended to do, I could not tell you. I had no weapon, and even if I had, what use would it have been against the god of war? But I had taken on the task of protecting Borgia and I would not let him be harmed without making at least an effort to prevent it.

"Signore—" I began only to stop abruptly at the scene before me. The Cardinal was there in his guise as Jupiter and he was not alone. Mars was with him, or should I say Cesare?

Father and son turned from the broken vase one of them must have just knocked over to stare at me. Borgia spoke first. "What the Devil—?"

Cesare, quicker on the uptake, raked his dark eyes over me and smiled. "Signorina, how charming. By all means, come in."

Only then did I realize that unlike the two men, I still wore my mask.

Quickly, I tried to back away. *"Scusa,"* I said, and even managed a giggle. "I am in the wrong place. *Scusa.*"

It might have worked. Borgia was distracted, surprised by the presence of his son, who was supposed to be in Pisa seeing to family interests, and Cesare was . . . Cesare. I had no reason to think he would recognize me, mask or not. Surely our encounter in the library had not made such an impression that I would linger in his thoughts all these months later?

"Francesca?"

Ay, il mio dio! I turned cold, then hot, and felt my cheeks flame even as I fumbled for the door.

The deflowerer of my virginity was having none of it. Laughing, he came to me, took both my hands in one of his and with the other, snatched off my mask.

"Francesca!" he said triumphantly. "I knew it was you."

"I made a mistake," I said quickly. "I thought . . ."

"That my father was in danger," Cesare said. "Isn't that so?"

I only just managed to nod but it was enough for him. Still holding on to me, he turned to the Cardinal. "And to think, I had doubts about trusting her with your safety. I should have known better."

Borgia grunted. He looked neither pleased to see me nor particularly displeased. His attention was on his son.

"You have no business being here, Cesare," he said. "I made it very clear that we must be discreet, at least for the moment."

"I know, *Papà,* I know," he said without a hint of remorse. "But there are things that cannot be trusted to letters, as you well know."

"Your complaints can wait for another time," the Cardinal said.

He waved a hand wearily. "I cannot believe Giulia arranged this behind my back—"

"She didn't," Cesare said. "Lucrezia suggested it. She is a good sister."

"She is too indulgent of you," Borgia snapped. "As I have been. Go, Cesare, and do not let me see you again until I have sent for you. *Capisca?*"

Cesare's fingers tightened around my wrists so painfully that I almost cried out. Heedless of what he was doing, he said, "I understand, Father. But you must understand. I will not—"

"Go!" Il Cardinale roared.

We went, me wincing and trying to pull away, Cesare dark-faced and too preoccupied to notice that I was still his captive. Until, that is, we were in the passage, the door to Borgia's quarters closed behind us. Then he paused, looked down at his hand holding mine, and pushed me up against the wall.

"He will not listen to me! Why won't he? I am his son! I have a right—"

He was hard against me, this boy for whom pride, ambition, jealousy, and lust were all part of the same fury that drove him, not just then but all his life. As a man, he had somewhat better control of himself but not much and not yet.

That being the case, I saw only one way the encounter would end and it was not to my liking. I, too, had pride.

I leaned forward, put my lips close to his ear, and hissed, "Let go of me." At the same time, I brought my knee up to rest against his privates.

To this day, I cannot recall the look on his face without laughing, although at the time I felt very far from humor. He stared at me dumbfounded. I pressed harder.

"Remember who I am," I said.

Bravo, Francesca! Bravo to the young and vulnerable me! And to think that I was only just learning my way both as a woman and professionally. Bravo!

Cesare dropped my hands. He took a quick step back and stared at me as though I was some species of being he had never seen before.

"I wasn't going to—" he began.

I dismissed that with a flick of my hand. Having gained my ends, I had to move quickly to restore his pride.

"For heaven's sake, Cesare, what were you thinking? Isn't it enough that you come here without your father's permission? You want to get caught in flagrante with his poisoner? They'll have to declare a holiday in Rome, what with everyone too busy gossiping to work."

He stared at me a moment longer before throwing back his handsome head and laughing. I was convinced the Cardinal would hear and tried to hush him, but he grabbed my hand again, gently this time, and together we sped down the passage. Cesare's unbridled energy, his enthusiasm for life, and his disregard for the strictures that limit ordinary mortals never failed to bedazzle me. He swept into—and out of—my life like a great wind blowing through a house, banishing the cobwebs and rearranging the furnishings at will. Afterward, there is always much straightening to be done, but the moment itself is glorious.

I was out of breath and laughing myself by the time we stopped in a corner of the garden within sight of the party but hidden from it in shadow. A servant passing by was startled when Cesare reached out and grabbed a flagon of wine. Two goblets and a tray of meats followed.

"I'm starving," Cesare said as he flopped down on the grass. "I've ridden all day, worn this getup"—he plucked at his toga—"and for what? I tell you, my patience is wearing thin." Yet his mood, always mercurial, seemed to be improving. He patted the ground beside him.

"You don't have to run off right away, do you? Keep me company."

As I have said, the notion of damnation is oddly liberating. That and the fact that I am sufficiently Roman to believe it is best to take life's pleasures when and where one can. I sat and accepted the goblet he offered, watching him over the rim as he devoured the meats. He truly was a beautiful man.

In between bites, he said, "I really am sorry about your father. It was a shock when Lucrezia wrote to tell me. Without her, I don't think I'd know half of what is going on."

As ever with the Borgias, sympathy for anyone else was subsumed in their own needs. But I understood that just as I thought I understood Cesare.

"Your father only wants to protect you," I said. "These are difficult times."

"When have times not been difficult?" he asked, scoffing. "But this is *our* time, the time of the Borgias. My father must gain the papacy now or his chance for it will be gone."

"Innocent—" I began but Cesare was having none of that.

"That rotting eunuch." His lip curled with disgust. "Why can't he have the decency to die?"

"People say he is afraid to face divine judgment."

"As well he should be! The things he's done . . ." He refilled both our glasses and looked at me earnestly. "He can't really last much longer, can he?"

I hesitated, unsure how much Cesare knew or at least suspected. Preferring to err on the side of caution, I said, "It is in God's hands."

Cesare frowned. He leaned close enough that I could feel his breath along the curve of my cheek. "What kind of poisoner are you?" he whispered.

I pulled away a little, only to encounter his hand warm against the small of my back. I had no memory of him placing it there yet neither did I try to dissuade him. For just an instant, I saw in my mind not Cesare but Rocco, he who spun fire into crystalline light. A path flowed out before me, tempting in its sweetness yet one I felt unworthy to walk. I was who I was, what Cesare had named me: poisoner. Nor did my sins stop there. My hands had literally been drenched in blood. I woke regularly screaming from the nightmare I could neither control nor understand. I was, however much I might wish otherwise, a creature of the dark.

As was Cesare.

He embraced his nature. I could not quite manage the same for myself, but neither could I deny the only comfort I could find.

Our lips were almost touching when I said, "The most dangerous kind . . . daring, unpredictable . . ." I reached down, cupping him under the short tunic. "Imaginative . . ."

He was laughing when he laid me down on the fragrant grass. Across the garden, musicians were playing. Fireflies swirled above my head. I watched them for a little while and then I watched nothing at all.

14

We returned to the city the following day, all of us that is except Cesare, who was gone when I awoke in the morning. Back to Pisa, I hoped, with enough sense to stay there until his father said otherwise.

The company was more subdued than we had been the day before, but that is ever the way with a journey. Anticipation is always a headier pleasure than actual experience.

Well, perhaps not always. Sometimes experience lives up to the highest expectations.

When I came to breakfast in the courtyard, Lucrezia took one glance at me and giggled. I attempted what I hoped was a quelling look but doubt that I succeeded. At least she was kind enough to say nothing. If anyone else had noticed Cesare's presence or with whom he spent the night, they were too preoccupied with their own intrigues to comment.

The only exception was the Cardinal himself. As we were boarding the barge to return to Rome, he turned to me and said, "See if you can't reason with him, will you?"

I was not surprised that Borgia knew of my relationship with Cesare, much as I would have liked for it to remain private. He had eyes everywhere. But neither was I willing to take any responsibility for the wayward eldest son chomping at the bit for the power he was certain was his birthright. To get between Cesare and his father in any sense would be lunacy.

"I doubt very much that I will hear from him, signore," I replied, quite properly I thought.

Borgia frowned but said nothing more. Shortly, I saw him sitting with La Bella under an awning near the prow. She was feeding him berries and he appeared to be in better humor.

The same could not be said for myself. I had succumbed foolishly, albeit most pleasurably. But now I had vivid memories of the unpleasant week I had endured after my earlier encounter with Cesare in the library and before discovering to my great relief that there would not be consequences from it. This time I could not decide if I should worry or not. If I succeeded in what I intended to do, there was every chance that I would not survive, thereby rendering all other concerns moot.

Nonetheless, I had taken the first possible opportunity afterward to douche with vinegar and anisette, a combination some thought effective but about which I had doubts. Certainly, there were more drastic measures available to me, but as a poisoner I knew how difficult it was to use any of them effectively without risking permanent damage to my health. I resolved that for the future, should it turn out that I had one, I would make a pessary of beeswax, the favorite resort of sensible women, and keep it close to hand.

You may conclude from all this that I arrived back in Rome torn between determination to continue on my chosen course and a natural desire to remain in this life. You would be right but know, too, that I was unshakable in my resolve not to waiver.

With Vittoro as escort, I returned to the ghetto and made my way quickly to Sofia's shop. Although scarcely two days had passed since my last visit, it was clear that conditions had worsened even further. Not that all the refugees streaming out of Spain were coming to us. A few other cities were willing to receive them—Amsterdam, most notably—while the fortunate few made sail for Turkey and the protection of Sultan Bayezid II. However, enough were coming to make it clear that if something did not change soon, there would be a very real risk of plague, which always seems to erupt wherever the poor and desperate are packed together, although no one knows why.

If plague did appear, I shuddered to think what would happen. The Jews would be blamed, of course, and the outcry against them would be horrific. It was not inconceivable that the entire ghetto would become their funeral pyre unless there was a pope willing to protect them.

Such thoughts were in my mind as I passed the line of people waiting in front of the apothecary shop. Sofia was inside, tending to a sick child. She joined me in the back room as soon as she could. I had brought the promised supplies and more. She acknowledged them but got straight to the point.

"We have bloody flux, dropsy, the ague, and I fear at least one case of influenza."

That last brought me up short. The disease that causes chills, high fever, and fluid in the lungs had appeared in Florence a few years ago but had not remained there, making its way to Milan and

Rome. It tends to spread rapidly but also to die away quickly. Many stricken by it perish but most survive. Physicians attribute the disease to malignant astrological influences, hence its name. To me, that means they have no more idea of what causes it than they do any other disease.

"Dropsy takes too long to kill," I said. The congestive edema of the tissues, particularly around the heart, does tend to be fatal but can take years to do its work, or so I understand from the very few authorized dissections that have taken place in the universities of Bologna, Padua, and Salerno. There have been others, too, unauthorized, but I will not speak of those.

"The ague and the bloody flux both have symptoms too similar to poisoning," I went on. "If Innocent dies of either, Borgia's involvement will be suspected immediately. As for the influenza . . ."

It did not mimic poison at all but unfortunately it seemed a disease of the phlegm rather than of the blood.

"I don't think it will work," I said, and told her why.

Sofia agreed. She drew me a little way off, far enough to be sure that Vittoro could not hear us. "Are you certain that you want to go through with this?" she asked.

I nodded quickly. "Time is running out, we must act now. I believe I have found a way to reach Innocent, but there is no point unless I have the means we seek."

She hesitated a moment longer before nodding abruptly. Taking me by the arm, she led me over to a pallet set in a corner away from the other patients and surrounded by a curtain.

"See there," she said.

I saw a man who may have been in his mid-twenties. It was difficult to be sure because he was so ill, but at any rate, he was young. His dark hair was matted to his head, his skin was flushed, and he gave off a rank, sweetish odor. I knelt beside him and touched my hand to his forehead, pulling it back quickly when I felt his burning skin.

"What is wrong with him?" I asked.

"I don't know," Sofia replied. Among the many aspects of her character that I was to come to value, her willingness to admit ignorance stands out as among the rarest.

She, too, bent down beside him and very gently moved away the blanket covering the man, enough to expose his arm. What I saw made me grimace.

His upper arm still showed that it had been heavily muscled, but much of the flesh was being eaten away by a black rot that appeared to be spreading, sending red streaks down the entire limb.

"What happened to him?" I asked.

"His name is Joseph. Yesterday, he came here at his wife's insistence. He had a cut to his arm, a week old or so. You can't even see it now but it was there, clear enough. The skin all around was hard and hot to the touch. He had a fever and appeared disoriented. I convinced him to lie down and he has not risen since. His wife has gone home to tend their young children, but I have sent word for her to return soon, at least if she wishes to see him again while yet he lives."

"Do you have any idea what is killing him?"

"I do not," Sofia said. "His pulse became very rapid but has now weakened. The swelling itself spreads with the red lines that trace the path of blood in the limb. I have listened to his heart and it is weakening, too. His lungs are congested and he can no longer pass urine. He will be dead within a few hours."

She sighed and sat back on her knees, looking at what had been a young and vigorous husband and father. "There is nothing I can do for him."

"You think whatever is killing him has poisoned his blood?"

"I don't know where else it could be." She looked at me. "It is very fast, whatever is doing this, and it does not look anything like poison as we know it, does it?"

No, it did not. No poison that I knew of caused such symptoms. Moreover, I believed she was right that the disease was in his blood.

But I could not be sure.

And that brought me to what I had not wanted to think about but that, in the way of such things, had become uppermost in my mind.

"We are likely to have only one chance," I said.

Sofia pressed her lips together tightly. In that simple gesture I knew she had been thinking along the same path.

"It will be difficult enough to get close to Innocent even once," I said, for I was trying to convince myself as much as her. Looking again at the suffering young man, I said softly, "We must be sure."

There was only one way we possibly could be.

"You want to do what?" David ben Eliezer said a short time later after Sofia had sent for him. Understandably enough, she did not think the decision could be entirely hers. We were meeting in the back room, keeping our voices very low to avoid any chance of being overheard.

"We have to test it," I said. The very idea sickened me but I saw no alternative. "We have to be sure that this man's blood really carries a disease powerful enough to kill. If it does not, there is no point for us to go forward, not with the risk so high."

"Test it on an animal? That's what you mean?"

I shook my head. "We know that there are diseases that affect humans without touching animals, and the reverse is also true. It has to be tested on a person."

"Are you volunteering?" he asked.

I understood that I was hearing his justifiable horror at what I proposed, but I could not indulge it.

"I will take it into Castel Sant'Angelo. I will find a way to substitute it for the blood the Pope drinks. I cannot do that if I am already dead."

Sofia laid a hand on his arm. Quietly, she said, "It is not easy for any of us to speak of this. I can hardly bear to think of it. But we have known all along that there would be a high price for what we must do."

"Not this," David said. "We never thought of anything like this."

He was right, of course. However much I feared for my own soul, the Jews were only trying to save their lives. Surely God would understand that and forgive them.

But now I was asking them to kill someone who had done no harm, a true innocent.

"I will test it," David said. His eyes were dark pools, so pale had he gone. "This was all my idea to begin with. I can't ask anyone else to take such a risk."

"And we cannot afford to lose you," Sofia said. She looked at him as kindly as a mother would. "Who else will be our lion, David. Who else will protect us?"

His eyes glistened, as I was surprised to realize did my own. Before he could argue further, I said, "There is no point testing it on someone who is young and healthy since the Pope is neither. He is old and frail. It should be tried on someone in the same condition."

"That doesn't make it right," David said. "The old must be protected, too."

A dark weight bore down on me. I understood how he felt, indeed I approved wholeheartedly of his sentiment. But I also knew that in the world as it truly is, rather than as we wish it to be, it can be necessary to do terrible things. Sometimes there is no good choice. We can only do what is least bad.

Even so, I had to wonder what sort of person I was whose kinder impulses could be sealed off behind such cold practicality.

"We cannot ask anyone to do this," Sofia said, "without explaining it fully."

There was risk in that, of course. Even the suggestion of such a thing could spark an outcry. If the rabbis and merchants found out what we were doing, they would certainly move to stop us.

"Do you . . . have someone in mind?" I asked tentatively.

David flinched and looked away but Sofia met my gaze. Slowly, she nodded.

15

The old woman lay on a pallet in the back room, where she had been moved from the front of the shop. Despite the warmth of the day, she was covered with a blanket that, beneath a layer of grime, looked spun from the finest lamb's wool. Her gray hair was spread out beneath her. Although her cheeks and eyes were sunken, and her skin crisscrossed by a web of fine lines, I could see that she had once been beautiful.

"Rebecca," Sofia said softly, kneeling beside the woman and holding her hand.

The eyelids fluttered and slowly opened.

"Do you remember what we were talking about?" Sofia asked. She spoke in Catalan, a language I understood because it was the private family language of the Borgia, who had been Los Boryas in Spain. The Romans had never let them forget their Spanish origins, and so they clung to them out of defiant pride.

When the old woman nodded, Sofia said, "This is Francesca. She will help us."

"I didn't dream it?" Rebecca asked. Her voice was so faint and weak that I had to bend closer to hear her, but as she spoke, she seemed to gain strength. "What you told me . . . it is real?"

Sofia had talked with her for a time in private. I do not know what was said between them but I was glad that the task of explaining what was needed had not been mine.

"The threat to us is all too real," she said. "I wish it were otherwise but it is not. I know that what we are asking of you is terrible—"

Rebecca lifted a blue-veined hand weakly. "All my family . . . my husband, my children, my beautiful little grandchildren . . . all gone—" Tears slipped down her worn cheeks.

"She came to us a week ago, brought in by people who found her in the street," Sofia said to me. "She is from Lisbon. Her family was stopped as they were leaving the city. They were accused of trying to take money with them. I don't know the details of what followed, but witnesses said that she was the only survivor."

I was not surprised. Granted, their Most Catholic Majesties Ferdinand and Isabella had decreed that the Jews could leave their realm alive, if they did so before the deadline that was now only a few weeks off. But they could not take anything of any real value with them—no coins, no gems, nothing that might help them continue their lives elsewhere. They were to leave as paupers with little more than the clothes on their backs.

Of course, many were managing to smuggle out wealth, but those unlucky enough to be caught by the rapacious *mercenarios* hired to patrol the ports and border towns rarely survived the encounter.

Deliberately, I turned my thoughts from what the elderly woman had suffered and concentrated on what had to be done.

"What is her condition?" I asked Sofia.

"She is malnourished and her heart is weak."

I had expected her to say more and could not conceal my surprise. "But with proper care, she could live?"

"No," Rebecca said suddenly. "No, please God, no! I cannot . . . I will not . . ." In her agitation she gripped my arm. "The God of Abraham and Isaac is a just God. He knows my suffering. He will not begrudge my release."

"She has refused to eat or drink," Sofia said quietly. "I have seen this before. Many of the old do it. There is no way to stop them."

"Even so—" Face-to-face with the reality of what I insisted had to be done, I was overcome with doubts. The Spaniard, the medallion man, even Innocent were all a different matter. But there was a far cry between talking of testing a method of killing on an anonymous person and actually doing it to this frail old woman who already had suffered so much.

Rebecca's hand tightened on my arm. Very clearly, so that I could not mistake her, she said, "Do not deny me the chance to keep others from the fate that has overtaken those I love."

I had to get up and walk away then, out into the alley where I remained for several minutes until I had control of myself. When I came back in, I went to Vittoro.

"Go back to the palazzo," I said. "If the Cardinal asks where I am, tell him I am pursuing his interests. He will not want to know anything more."

Far from looking offended by my presuming to give him orders, Vittoro merely shrugged. "The Cardinal likes to know everything."

"Not about this. If he is ever questioned, he will want to be able to say that he knew nothing."

I had concluded that in deciding to set me against Innocent, Borgia acted with consummate cleverness. If the attempt on the Pope's life went wrong and we were caught, the Cardinal could always say that I was deranged over the death of my father and had acted entirely at my own initiative. He might even claim that I was a secret Jew, out to destroy him as well as Innocent. That wouldn't be enough to keep him in line for the papacy, but it would create sufficient doubt to save his power and prestige, not to mention his life. Mine, on the other hand, was entirely disposable.

"Is there anything else I should tell the Cardinal?" Vittoro asked.

I started to say no, thought better of it, and said, "Tell him *Alea iacta est.*"

Vittoro had not had the benefit of a classical education. He repeated the words three times to be sure he had them exactly. Then he was gone, leaving me in the charnel house of my memories.

I have always had an aversion to blood, don't ask me why. Bleeding is supposed to be a remedy for all manner of illness, yet I have avoided it at all costs. Nor does my abhorrence stop there. The Mass has always been difficult for me. I can tolerate the bread that becomes flesh well enough but wine into blood . . . I cannot drink it, can hardly bear to let it touch my lips.

When I knelt beside my father's corpse and bathed my hands in his blood, something in me changed irrevocably. Or perhaps I should say that something awoke. I had to kill twice, the Spaniard and, more important, the man whose throat I had slit, before I acknowledged what was happening to me. However, that made it no easier for me to watch as Sofia bled the dying Joseph.

David carried him into the back room and laid him on a pallet near Rebecca. Mercifully, he was unconscious and did not react at all when Sofia slit his uninjured arm, making a deep, wide cut so that his blood flowed swiftly out into the bowl she had placed on the floor directly beneath. The smell of copper made me gag.

"How much do you think?" she asked as she worked.

I had my face averted and a hand over my mouth. Through my fingers, I said, "I doubt that Innocent can be drinking very much at any one time."

Seeing me, David asked, "Are you all right?"

I nodded mutely and concentrated on breathing. If I thought about doing that and nothing else, perhaps I would not disgrace myself.

It was done at last, the bowl filled and covered with a clean cloth. Sofia bandaged Joseph's arm, though it continued to bleed through the linen. She took the bowl over to Rebecca and knelt down beside her.

We had discussed what to do next. David had suggested mixing the blood with wine to make it more palatable and that seemed a reasonable course to me. Even so, I swear I could still smell the copper as the strong red wine was prepared.

Sofia lifted Rebecca's head so she could drink. She gagged at first—apparently the taste was not completely concealed—but soon enough the wine took effect and she finished all of it.

We waited. The day wore on. Sofia went to tend those in the outer room, but David stayed with me. Joseph's wife came at midday and spent an hour or so with him. She left in tears, comforted by her sister, who had accompanied her. I was not present when she said her farewells; we gave them that much privacy. So far as I could tell, Joseph was not there, either, being too gone with fever.

Benjamin brought food and drink, and urged both on me. I sipped a little wine and ate a crumb or two of bread. My stomach rebelled at anything more. Toward midafternoon I was holding Joseph's hand. David was praying in a language I could not understand. I prayed after my own fashion, to the Madonna, reminding her that Joseph had a mother, probably already dead, and that he had been a babe like her own. I asked her to watch over him.

He died a short time later. I suppose his death was peaceful as such things go, but that was scant comfort. By the time we covered his face, Rebecca was unconscious. She had deteriorated very quickly after receiving the blood. Within an hour, she no longer knew us and within two she was burning with fever. When Joseph was gone, I moved over to her, bathing her face and limbs in cool water.

"She is past feeling that," David said. He was very pale, as I suppose I was, too. His hands shook as he held the basin for me.

"You don't know," I countered. "Neither of us has been close enough to death to know what it is like."

"How do you know?" he asked. "Perhaps I have been close."

I looked at Rebecca and shook my head. "She is very far from here, too far to ever return."

Sofia came then and sat with us for the remaining time that Rebecca lived. Right at the end, the old woman's eyes opened, giving us all a start. But whatever she saw, it was not us or any world in which we dwelled. I can only tell you that she died quietly, without a struggle. Kneeling beside her, I said a prayer that she would find those she had loved and lost.

Barely was her face covered with the worn blanket than I called Benjamin to my side. I gave him the note I had written on paper Sofia provided and instructed him carefully.

"Go to the Via dei Vertrarari. Find the glassmaker named Rocco and give him this. He will know what to do."

When Benjamin was gone, I waited as Sofia drew Rebecca's blood. We had decided to use hers because we thought the blood should be as fresh as possible when I reached the Castel Sant'Angelo.

By that time, a blessed numbness was settling over me. "I must be gone from here before the checkpoint is closed for the night," I said as Sofia poured the blood carefully into a large vial and sealed it.

All through that long and painful day, I had been conscious of the sun slanting westward. Wait too long and I, too, would be sealed in. The blood would begin to spoil. My chances of substituting it, hardly great to begin with, would grow slimmer with each falling grain of sand.

"I'm going with you," David said.

I made a halfhearted effort to argue, which he rightly ignored. We got out through the gate minutes before it was closed, trapping the Jews in the ghetto until the sun rose on a new day. If we failed and were exposed, what would that sunrise bring for them? The rage of a rampaging mob? Fire and death? All that and more were far too possible.

I glanced back once over my shoulder, thinking of Sofia and Benjamin, of the sick and dying in the apothecary shop, of all the suffering people I had seen in my visits.

Truly, the ways of the Lord are mysterious.

David took my hand. Together, we walked into the night descending over Rome.

16

We were halfway to Rocco's shop before we saw the first foot patrol. Until then, we had passed only the usual revelers, prostitutes, and rats that make Rome's nighttime streets their own. The humans cluster around the taverns and brothels while the rats spill from their hiding places in the ancient sewers and catacombs. No matter how many steaming heaps of their carcasses the rat catchers pile in the public squares, there are always far more live ones just out of sight, waiting to rise with the night.

I abhor rats, which surprises me a little because in general I like animals. Not snakes, but even they are better than rats. And both are better than the foot patrols paid by wealthy residents and merchants to strut about with swords and cudgels, extorting money or worse from any lesser mortal they come upon.

David and I pressed into the shadows near a tavern on the edge of the Campo dei Fiori as one such patrol passed. When they were gone, we waited several minutes before stepping back out onto the street. The moon was in darkness, not a sliver of light showing. But a stiff wind from the west had cleared away much of the cloud of smoke and haze that hangs over the city on still days. By starlight and memory, we were able to find our way to the street of the glass-makers.

Rocco had left a lamp burning at the front of the shop, hopefully too small to attract the notice of his neighbors, who would be busy in any case having supper and preparing for bed. When we knocked, he opened the door and waved us in quickly before shutting it again behind us.

At first, he appeared to see only me and the warmth of his gaze brought an answering warmth to my cheeks. But quickly enough he widened his attention.

"Who is this?" he asked, looking at David.

"A friend," I said. "You got my note?"

Rocco nodded. "I have sent word to Father Morozzi. He should be here soon."

"Nando . . . ?" The thought of the danger I was bringing into Rocco's house clawed at me even as I saw no alternative.

"I have sent him to the countryside to stay with his grandmother."

I nodded in relief. We waited, seated at the table, largely in silence the brief time until the priest came. He slipped in nervously and frowned when he saw David.

"What is this?" A small thing and petty of me to mention it, yet it lodged in my mind. Rocco, asking the same question, had said "Who?"

I credited it to the priest's fear, which under the circumstances was not unreasonable. He looked startled enough to flee and I could not blame him. I thought that as a *converso,* he must live every day on the edge of discovery and disaster.

"A friend," I said quickly. "He can be trusted."

"You should not have—" Morozzi began but he got no further before David stepped forward.

"I am no danger to you, Priest. I have to hope you are none to me."

Silence hung between them before Rocco decided the matter. "Let's get on with this."

"Very well," Morozzi said, though his reluctance was evident. He turned to me. "Are you ready? Do you have what is needed?"

I assured him that I did and was about to ask him how he intended to get us into the *castel* when Morozzi interrupted.

"Let me see it."

"See what?" Taken aback, I did what I always do in such circumstances and stalled for time to get my thoughts in order.

"What you intend to use. I want to see it." When I continued to stare at him, he said impatiently, "You can't expect me to risk everything to get you close to the Pope without being sure that you can actually do it."

"It isn't enough for you that she says she can?" David demanded, frowning.

Rocco, too, appeared uneasy. "Francesca wouldn't be here if she was not prepared."

I put a hand on David's arm in silent caution, smiled reassuringly at Rocco, and reached under my gown. Slowly, I drew the golden locket from between my breasts.

The priest's gaze focused on it intently.

"You want to see it?" I asked. "Very well." I snapped open the locket, exposing the lozenge I had made for myself. "Don't get too close. This is the most deadly poison I know of, capable of killing in minutes. It will not fail."

Morozzi stared at it for a long moment, his avid regard making me uneasy. It seemed out of keeping with our serious and desperate business. Finally, he said, "Good, then we can go."

As I closed the locket and slid it back under my clothes, David looked at me curiously. Had we been alone, I would have told him that I thought it best for the priest to know no more than he had to. As it was, I spread my hands just a little, so that only he could see, hoping that he would understand why I had done as I had. I was trusting Morozzi with our lives and yet I was not trusting him to know the means of Innocent's death. Whether David understood or not, he seemed to accept my decision, for after a moment, he nodded silently.

Meanwhile, Morozzi had produced a brown robe and held it out to me. "I had no idea that there would be two of you," he said. "I only brought one of these."

He handed me a monk's robe, the all-encompassing brown wool more than sufficient to hide my womanly shape. As I shook it out and prepared to don it, I asked, "What about David? We must find a way to disguise him."

A priest and a monk entering the *castel* together might draw attention but would not be challenged. A man in ordinary clothing, without the livery or insignia of a great house, would be treated very differently.

"Wait," Rocco said, and went to the back of the shop where a small ladder led up to the storage loft. He returned in a few moments carrying a white robe and a black cloak. Handing both to David, he said, "I think these will fit you."

"This is the habit of a Dominican friar," Morozzi said. "How did you come by it?" Clearly, he did not know Rocco's history.

"It was left here," Rocco replied shortly.

David hesitated before donning the garments. I understood his reluctance to put on anything associated with the Dominicans, who claimed among their own the loathsome Tomás de Torquemada, inquisitor general of Spain and one of the chief authors of the edict expelling the Jews from that land. But there really wasn't any alternative and David knew that.

The garments covered him from head to toe. When he had them on and had pulled up the cowl, he became just one more of the anonymous mass of clergy who came and went between the *castel* and the Vatican without notice or question.

"Thank you," I said, and squeezed Rocco's hand. Despite the warmth of the night, his skin felt cold. With a glance at the other two, he drew me aside so that we could speak privately.

"Whatever God intends, you have done enough, Francesca. Let me go in your place. You can explain to me what to do and I will do it."

Before I could reply, he went on, "Morozzi won't object; he's not comfortable with you being a woman anyway. And surely if you tell ben Eliezer to trust me, he will have no choice but to do so."

The magnitude of what he was offering almost undid me. To not only take my place in such dangerous circumstances but to also take on his own soul the act I intended to commit, the murder of a pope, was more than I could contemplate. As much as Rocco, I wanted to believe that it was God's will that Innocent die before he could commit an act that would bring about hundreds of thousands of deaths. But what if we were wrong? I was willing to risk my own immortal soul, but I would not risk Rocco's.

Besides, there were other considerations.

I smiled faintly and raised a hand to touch his cheek, roughened by the day's growth of beard. "From the bottom of my heart, I thank you. Truly, you are a valiant friend. But you are also a father, and I could never agree to anything that could leave Nando an orphan."

I let my hand drop and stepped back. "This is my struggle and I must wage it." Without giving him a chance to reply, I turned away.

We went—Morozzi, David, and I—out into the darkness. Rocco stood at the door and watched us go. For a moment, as I passed him, I saw his hand rise and thought he would try to stop me. But he let it fall, the sorrow in his gaze telling me that he accepted what could not be changed.

Morozzi moved with speed and confidence through the streets. He showed no concern about the foot patrols, and indeed, when we encountered one, they gave way quickly before him. His manner—he possessed the natural arrogance of those who have received a superfluity of nature's gifts—as much as his clerical garb warned off any who might have challenged us.

We crossed the Pons Aelius, to use its old Roman name, and moved directly toward the main gate of the *castel*. The dark mass of stone rising above the city was illuminated by a hundred torches, their reflected light creating pools of rippling silver in the slow-moving river. I had thought Morozzi might know of some secret entrance, such as must surely exist in a structure more than a thousand years old. But if he did, he did not care to use it. Instead, he walked us right past the guards who, as I had hoped, made no effort to impede our entry.

The massive structure looming above us could not have been better designed to strike fear into all who approached it even for the most innocent of reasons. Intended as the mausoleum for the Emperor Hadrian and his family, it still had traces of classical elegance, but most of that had vanished centuries ago when it was transformed into a fortress and prison. The moment we passed into the small courtyard just beyond the entrance—the Courtyard of the Savior as it was called, ironically for those who never left the *castel* alive—I felt a sense of the walls pressing in on us, cutting off all hope. From there, the ground descended slightly into the entrance vestibule. The temperature dropped and I shivered, although not entirely with cold. Here, too, guards were stationed and here, too, they let us pass.

"You are well known," I said to Morozzi, keeping my voice very low.

He nodded. "I have taken pains to be. What is familiar and customary raises no suspicion."

We continued on, past the immense statue of Hadrian, little more than a crumbling shadow of its former self after being badly damaged when the Visigoth Alaric sacked Rome. The emperor appeared to glare down at us, the descendants of those who had failed to safeguard his legacy. Ahead lay the vast spiral ramp built by the ancients to coil around the entire cylindrical fortress and give access to the upper levels. Torches in wall brackets lit our way as we began to ascend over the broken black-and-white-tiled floor, past crumbling marble columns that whispered of another, greater era.

I knew, as did everyone in Rome, that the first floor of the fortress contained prison cells. I saw no entrances to them, adding weight to the claim that prisoners were lowered by rope into these living tombs. The thought would have filled me with horror had not the events of the day left me almost numb. As it was, I was very glad of David's quiet presence beside me.

The next level housed the military quarters and armories. Here at last there was open air in the form of large courtyards, but before we could reach them, we had to pass through the windowless crypt where the imperial remains had been interred. There was nothing left of them, of course, again the result of long-ago looting, but the oppressive sense of death still lingered.

I breathed a little more easily when we stepped out into the Courtyard of Honor. The *castel* being a military fortification as well as a prison, the courtyard housed several impressive cannon that could, if need arose, be pointed out over the city to repel attackers. The quarters of the officers and troops faced inward onto the courtyard. I had to hope that no one, happening to glance out a window, would question our swift passage.

Just before we left the courtyard, I glanced up at the statue rising above the *castel*. The Archangel Michael in all his glory, sheathing his sword to proclaim the end of the plague that had devastated Rome almost a thousand years before. With its passing, the castle had been renamed to his glory and ever since his image, or various incarnations of it, had ruled over the Roman sky. I saw him now in silhouette against starlight, and I said a silent prayer that his might and fury would protect us.

Beyond the courtyard, we entered the officers' hall, furnished with large tables and benches, the walls painted with appropriately martial scenes and hung with banners. Several captains and lieutenants were there, drinking at their leisure. They looked at us as we passed but again, no one challenged us.

I had time to think that the *castel* was well designed to force invaders who managed to breach its walls into the very heart of its military strength, where they could be picked off one by one. The Courtyard of Honor itself would provide a convenient killing zone in which to trap any enemy luckless enough to enter it.

Morozzi increased his pace once we were through the officers' hall. I assumed he was as anxious to reach our destination as I was, and followed swiftly after him, as did David. Catching up to him, I asked, "Is it much farther?"

His face looked flushed and his eyes were hard as he shook his head. "We are almost there."

I nodded, trying to gather myself for what was about to come. Very soon, I would have to tell Morozzi what I truly sought. I had to find the boys being bled, more particularly I had to locate the blood so that I could substitute what I had brought. If a physician or anyone else was present, that person would have to be dealt with. I did not relish the thought but I understood the necessity for such action. Any cry of alarm, any signal that something was amiss and the entire garrison would descend upon us.

We went through one room, then another. Before the third, Morozzi stopped and raised a hand. Carefully, he stepped forward alone and peered into the chamber. What he saw must have satisfied him, for he gestured for us to go ahead.

David went first, I followed. Just as I passed Morozzi, he reached out and yanked the locket from around my neck. In the same moment, he pushed me into the chamber.

"What are you doing—?" I gasped but in some way I already knew. Our passage had been too easy, our path too smoothed. What I had wanted to believe was the favor of God for our enterprise or merely good luck was in fact betrayal.

Morozzi grasped a lever in the wall to the side of the entrance and yanked it down. At once, an iron portcullis descended, trapping us within.

"Deus vult!" the priest cried, his face transformed with religious fervor. God wills it! The cry of every crusader and inquisitor. The excuse for every atrocity done in the Redeemer's name.

Sara Poole

David made a dive across the room, trying to get under the portcullis before it completed its descent. He almost made it and for just an instant, Morozzi looked terrified that he would. But the heavy metal lattice thudded into place before David could squeeze under, leaving him sprawled on the floor at the priest's feet.

Morozzi threw back his head in exaltation. "First Giordano and now his witch of a daughter and a Jew to boot! I will bring your master down, destroy him utterly, and at the same time raise the fury of all Christendom against the betrayers of our Lord. You—"

My hands clamped on the bars of the portcullis, I confronted the mad priest without regard for anything other than the sickening suspicion roaring through my mind. From the moment I stood before the medallion man and heard the confession tortured from him, I had entertained doubts. But never had I imagined the truth.

"What do you mean, first Giordano? Did Innocent order my father's death . . . or did you?"

"Innocent?" Morozzi all but spit the name. "That disgusting old man can do nothing but weep over his sins and beg me to tell him how he may yet escape the damnation he so richly deserves."

A chill enveloped me. Even twisted by hatred, the priest still had the face of an angel, but one who, now I saw, wielded a terrible sword.

"What did you tell him?" I demanded. "That he could be saved by condemning all the Jews to death?"

"God's will is made manifest in me!" Morozzi proclaimed. "I am His messenger. All the slayers of Christ must die for what they did to our Lord!"

David had heard enough. He hurled himself at the priest, who jumped back from the portcullis just in time to avoid being seized through it.

"God protects me!" Morozzi shouted. "I do His holy work!"

Have you noticed that those who murder in the thousands invariably claim divine favor, while those who kill on a far more modest scale, myself included, know in our hearts that God weeps for our sins?

Morozzi carried no such burden. Having trapped us, he darted away—I presumed to summon the guards—leaving us to face the torments shortly to come.

17

The stark horror of what awaited us when Morozzi returned stripped the protective cloak of numbness from me and spurred me to action.

"Quickly," I said, my voice echoing faintly off the stone walls. "We have to find a way out of here."

Remarkably, David already had a plan. "Go left," he said. "I'll go right."

I spared a moment to be grateful that if I had to be trapped in such a place, it was with a man who could keep his head. We spread out in opposite directions, feeling along the walls of the dark, windowless room. My hands were cold and slick. Morozzi would be back within minutes and he would bring help. He would have witnesses to our being in the *castel* in disguise, and he had my locket with the poisonous lozenge. Nothing we, or Borgia, said would explain any of that away.

I was hoping to find a door, a passage, anything that might help us, but I reached a corner of the room and continued on without finding anything but stone wall.

"I think I know where we are," David said in the darkness. To my great relief, he sounded entirely calm.

"Where?" My own voice shook slightly.

"This is the room where prisoners are lowered into the cells. I just stumbled over one of the trapdoors set in the floor."

So there was a way out, but it would leave us entombed, exactly as Morozzi intended.

"There has to be another door," I insisted. "A way to reach the chambers beyond this one."

"There could be other passages leading to them," David said. "This place is a warren. It's been built and rebuilt for centuries. Rooms have been sealed up, walls shifted, whole floors dropped or raised. I doubt anyone knows the whole of it."

I feared he was right. A person would have to live in the *castel* for years, free to explore it at will, in order to have any real grasp of everything it contained.

At that point, the dark thought descended on me that we would not get out. I tried to push it away but it clung remorselessly, forcing me to confront what could not be denied. While I did not question David's courage and I thought I possessed a fair measure of the same, I feared that either of us could be made to talk under torture. Certainly, I could not withstand such torment as I had seen in the torture chamber beneath the palazzo.

When I talked—not if but when—the Jews of Rome would be doomed. Sofia, Benjamin, all the rest would die. The horrible truth was that Morozzi was right. Once he could present evidence of the plot to kill Innocent, the mob itself would rise up against the ghetto and destroy everyone in it. But it would not stop there. With the edict or without, Jews would face attack across Christendom.

Do not mistake me, I value my own life as much as the next person. In my anguish over my father's murder, I was willing to risk everything to avenge him, but that, in its own way, was a selfish act driven by my own need. This was different. If the Jews died, what was it to me? They were, for the most part, faceless, anonymous people to whom I felt no connection. Or did I?

I stopped moving along the wall and let my hands fall to my sides. Carefully, as befitted a situation in which my soul hung in the balance, I considered my course. Suicide is a mortal sin, so Mother Church tells us. Because all that comes to us in life is by God's will, the act of suicide places the human above the divine. This violation of nature makes it the ultimate offense against God.

Too vividly, I remembered Boccaccio's writhing visions of Dante's Seventh Circle, where suicides are transformed into thorn bushes and trees. For all eternity, they are torn at by the Harpies, the winged death spirits. So unforgivable is their sin that alone among all the dead, only they will not be resurrected at the Final Judgment.

And yet . . . what if the decision to end one's life was not a purely selfish one? What if by that act, thousands and more might be saved? Surely God would count the weight of one life as a feather against the lives of so many?

Within the great well of my sorrow, a light glimmered. Quietly, I asked, "Do you have a knife?"

In the darkness, I could barely make out David's shape nearby, but I heard him clearly. "Have you found something?"

"No." Only that, nothing more. He was an intelligent man; he knew the situation as well as I did. I trusted him to understand me.

Silence followed before I heard his reply. "I have a knife."

My chest was tightly constricted. I wrapped my arms around myself to try to stop the shaking that seized me. The poison in the lozenge wasn't pleasant but at least it wouldn't have involved blood.

"We have very little time," I said.

Silence again before David asked, "Have you ever heard of Masada?"

I thought he was trying to distract me and was grateful for it. "Is that in Lombardy?"

He laughed, he actually did, before enlightening me. "It was a fortress on the top of a hill in the Holy Land. A group of Jewish rebels held out there for years. Right as the Roman general sent to crush them was about to overrun the stronghold, they committed suicide."

"What, all of them?" Was not suicide also a mortal sin for the Jews? There was so much about them I did not know.

"All of them," David said. "They drew lots among the men. Those chosen killed all the others, including the women and children, and then killed each other. The last man left took his own life."

My heart hammered painfully against my sore ribs. I could not imagine what it must have been like to go among those you loved, killing them one by one. Did the children cry out in fear? Or did their mothers lull them into the final sleep first before baring their own throats to the knife? And what of that last man? How long had he stood on the silent hilltop among the dead before ending the nightmare that life had become?

God grant him forgiveness and good rest in the light of the Lord.

"Do you want to draw lots?" I asked with, I admit it, great trepidation as to how I would manage if he agreed and it fell to me to do.

Without hesitation, David put his arms around me. With equal certainty, I hugged him back. We were two human beings in the darkness, on the verge of the abyss, giving each other what support we could.

"No, Francesca," he said softly. "It will be all right."

Perhaps I am a coward after all, for relief flooded through me. Relief and gratitude for the burden this good man was willing to take on himself.

Even so, I said, "I need a moment."

To pray? To try to bargain with God or to rail against him? I'm not sure, but I think I tried to do all three at the same time.

And was still trying when a voice from above said, "Finally! I've been looking all over for you."

You may mock my foolishness but for just an instant, there in the darkness on the brink of death, I was overwrought enough to think that I heard the Almighty and that He was not remotely what I had been taught. Far from the omniscient majesty before whom we must tremble in blind adoration, He sounded a caring, if somewhat exasperated shepherd who went in search of us, His straying flock.

Of course, I know I was wrong. And yet I know no such thing. The thought lingers: Surely the God who created Heaven and Earth can speak through the mouth of a man? Indeed, how else would he speak to men? Or, for that matter, to one particular woman?

I looked up in astonishment. A square of light pierced the darkness, revealing an opening almost twenty feet up the wall, very near the ceiling. Within that light, peering down at us, I saw a familiar face.

"Vittoro," I exclaimed. "How . . . ?"

A rope dropped directly in front of us. "Later, Donna. Right now, we have to go."

David grabbed me around the waist and boosted me up. I seized the rope and, hanging on for dear life, climbed. My heart hammered painfully and my arms burned from my exertions but finally, after what seemed an interminable time but likely was no more than moments, my nose cleared the opening to the passage. Vittoro grabbed hold of me and pulled me into a stone-lined passage too low for us to do anything other than crouch.

A heartbeat later, David followed. We squeezed together near the narrow opening. Vittoro seized the lamp he had brought and gestured behind us into the darkness.

"This way leads to the outer wall. You'll be out of here in no time."

Below I could hear the portcullis rising. Morozzi had returned with guards. "Bring more torches," the priest shouted, and then, "Where are they? *Where are they!*"

We fled as quickly and as silently as possible, bent over almost double as we skittered after Vittoro, who moved with astonishing speed for one his age. My knees and elbows banged repeatedly against the stone and soon throbbed. I could only imagine how much more difficult it was for David, who was taller than either Vittoro or I, but the steady cadence of his breath close behind me reassured me that he was managing and at the same time urged me on. The passage sloped upward, making the going even more difficult. My monk's robe kept tangling around my legs, making the ascent even more arduous and exhausting.

When we were far enough away from the prison chamber to speak safely, I caught my breath and asked, "Where are we?"

Over his shoulder, Vittoro replied. "Inside one of the air shafts that run all through the walls of the *castel*. The old Romans who built this place weren't fools. House of the dead though it was intended to be, people came here to honor the old emperor. Without air, they wouldn't be able to burn torches, much less breathe. These shafts were the solution."

I thought of the windowless chambers we had come through and nodded.

"How did you find us?" David asked from behind me.

In the flickering lamplight, I saw Vittoro's smile. "I had a fair idea what you intended and I thought I'd keep an eye out in case your 'friend' back there turned out to be a problem."

Thank God he had, but even so, I was bewildered. "I don't understand. How did you even know where to look?"

"I served with the garrison here for ten years, most of it deadly dull duty. To keep from going mad, I amused myself by climbing all over this place, discovering everything I could about it. There are only a handful of places where Morozzi could take you unaware and trap you, if that was what he intended. I just kept looking until I found you."

So easily did he dismiss the accomplishment that had saved our lives and a great deal more besides. I was about to say so when we came alongside a cutout in the exterior wall and I found myself staring out over the city in the direction of Saint Peter's. I could see the crumbling basilica clearly. To my left, the river curved away into darkness.

"Does anyone else know about this?" David asked. I understood what he was thinking. Morozzi had sounded the alarm. If guards entered the air shaft, we could be trapped again.

"Damn few," Vittoro said. "Most of the lads were never as curious as me. But no one who does know will say anything to that crazed priest."

David looked unconvinced. "Why not?"

The captain grinned. "Because they want Borgia to be the next pope, that's why. They know he'll take better care of them than any of the other cardinals would."

"Borgia can't be pope," I said. "Not now. Morozzi will accuse him of sending us to kill Innocent. No matter how much gold he has, it won't be enough to make people forget that."

"Morozzi won't say a word," Vittoro said. "Oh, he'll want to, but he'll understand that with you gone, he has no proof."

I was mulling that over, realizing that it just might be true, when David said, "That still won't help my people, not if Innocent lives long enough to issue the edict."

He looked at me as he spoke. Knowing as I did now that it was Morozzi, not Innocent, who had ordered my father's murder, David could be forgiven for doubting that I would be willing to proceed. But in that he was mistaken. Somewhere in the days between when I had first entered the ghetto and when I left it carrying Rebecca's blood, the Jews had become human to me. My new sense of them did not lessen my thirst for vengeance, but it did create a fierce need to complete the task for which my father had given his life and in so doing deny Morozzi his victory.

Grasping Vittoro's arm, I said, "We can't leave, not yet. We have to finish what we came here to do."

Vittoro looked at me like I was a mad woman. "I can't get you to Innocent, especially not now. Morozzi won't make any accusations, but he will make sure that the Pope is secure."

"That may be, but he thinks he has the means by which I intended to kill Innocent." Briefly, I told Vittoro about the locket. "He'll believe that we've been disarmed, but he's wrong."

"How so?" Vittoro demanded.

From a padded pouch hidden beneath my gown, I drew the vial Sofia had filled. Vittoro stared at it as I said, "Because I still have the means and I don't have to get to Innocent. I just have to get to wherever the boys being bled for him are kept."

The captain took a deep breath and let it out slowly. I saw the uncertainty play across his face. He knew that the safest course was to get us out of the *castel* as quickly as possible. Innocent would die under any circumstances, probably sooner rather than later, and Borgia would have his chance to become pope.

But none of that would happen quickly enough to stop the destruction of the Jews. Now more than ever, the mad Morozzi would be determined to see to it that the edict dooming them was issued without further delay.

"The Cardinal—" Vittoro began.

"Did he send you here?" I interrupted, anxious to stop him from saying what I feared he would. He was Borgia's man, that much he had made clear to me. But did that mean that he would put Il Cardinale's interests above all others?

"No," Vittoro said. "He doesn't know anything about this." With a shrug, he added, "I thought about what you said, that he wouldn't want to know. I decided you were right."

Praise God. Perhaps there was a chance after all.

"I can do this, Vittoro, I truly can. The method is not foolproof but it has a good chance of succeeding. I don't even need much time." That last part was not necessarily true. If I found what I needed right away, well and good, otherwise . . .

"Get Francesca out," David said. "Just give me an idea of how to find the Pope's apartments and I'll do the rest."

Before I could protest, Vittoro was shaking his head. "You'd never find your way. The rats get lost in this place." With a heavy sigh, he said, "If Morozzi gets what he wants, he won't stop at the Jews. His kind never does. He won't be satisfied until we're all under the boot."

"It's too bad most people don't realize that," David said drily.

"Most people don't know their ass from their elbow," Vittoro replied. At once, he added, "Sorry, Donna, I'm an old soldier and plainspoken."

I squeezed his hand, aware that my eyes were damp. "Don't apologize, Vittoro, and for heaven's sake, stop calling me Donna. I'm as much a lady as you are."

Both men laughed, more with relief, I think, than at my poor wit. That readily the matter was settled.

We climbed—Vittoro, David, and I—as the air shaft continued steeply upward and around the curve of the *castel*. Twice more we passed cutouts in the walls and I glimpsed the city slumbering below. Finally, the shaft ended in a large square opening through which I could see only the night sky.

"Where are we?" I asked as Vittoro began to pull himself out. David followed and hoisted me up onto what I discovered with one startled glance was the roof of the *castel*. We stood at the feet of the Commander of God's Army, patron saint of warriors, he who I have since learned the Prophet Daniel calls the great prince who will stand for the Jews at the time of tribulation to come. Above us, the Archangel Michael rose in majesty, a stern and determined gaze on his handsome face. And below—

Fortunately, I have a good head for heights but it was tested that night. Even David looked less than at ease as we scrambled across the roof and down into another shaft that brought us out on the fourth and uppermost level of the fortress. We descended into a small passageway lined with flaking frescoes of sunlit villas where men and women with dark, liquid eyes gazed at us mutely from across time. Finally, we came to a small paneled door.

Vittoro pressed his ear to it, listening intently. After a moment, he straightened and nodded to us. "On the other side is a corridor that leads to the papal apartments. If Morozzi isn't there already, he will be soon, but first he'll have sent for the edict."

"What do you mean, sent for?" I asked.

"It isn't here," Vittoro explained. "It's at the Vatican. Borgia's managed to keep it tied up in the Curia, but Morozzi won't wait any longer, not with a threat to the Pope. He'll insist that Innocent himself has called for it and he'll try to get it signed without further delay."

"But first he has to get it here," David said, grasping the situation even as I did.

"So we have a little time but not much," I concluded.

Vittoro nodded. "Borgia has left instructions that the edict isn't to go anywhere without his permission, but by morning—"

He left the rest unsaid yet I was hopeful all the same. The Vatican was a bureaucracy to rival any in the world. Morozzi could utter all the demands he liked in the name of the Pope, but proper form had to be followed. Some official would have to be awakened and the situation explained to him. That person in turn would have to send word to Borgia, who would have to be found. My guess was that he would be spending the night in fair Giulia's bed rather than his own. Once he was located, he would have to array himself properly—Il Cardinale never went anywhere without due regard for his dignity. By then, he would know that I was missing along with Vittoro. He would conclude that something was in the works and he would move cautiously, which invariably meant slowly.

Which did not mean that we could do the same. "Do you know where the boys are?" I asked.

"At the opposite end of the corridor from the Pope's apartments. Innocent is squeamish, he doesn't like them too close to him, but he wants them kept nearby all the same."

"Is there likely to be a physician with them?" David asked.

Vittoro nodded. "From what the lads told me, this is the hour when they are bled."

"Why so late?" I asked.

"Innocent fears the night," Vittoro said with a shrug. "He has turned it into day."

We crept out of the narrow passage and down the corridor. David went first with me following. Vittoro stayed behind to play his part in the plan we had quickly worked out. It was not much of a plan, but given what we knew, it was the best we could hope for.

We had gone only a little way along the corridor before I stopped and grabbed David's cloak. "Do you hear that?" I whispered.

He started to shake his head but listened instead and, after a moment, nodded grimly. "We're close."

We had heard the whimper of a child, a small and plaintive sound that tore at my heart. Try though I did to steel myself, I could not manage it. For reasons I did not begin to understand, I had a sudden sense of being immured behind the wall of my nightmare, peering out through a tiny hole that revealed horror.

The whimpering grew stronger. My breath was labored but I pressed on, following David. At the end of the corridor, we stopped before a closed door. The sound came from the other side. I took a breath. David did the same and eased open the door.

Beyond lay a small, windowless chamber lit by lamps set in niches in the walls and simply furnished with four narrow beds, a table, and several stools. The beds were all occupied by young boys, about eight or nine years old. Three of them were huddled under the covers but the stiffness of their bodies indicated they were not asleep. The fourth was awake. He was a thin, pale boy of about the same age as the others, with a mass of dark curls and eyes filled with terror. He lay on his back, his left arm stretched out over a bowl into which his blood dripped from a deep cut. Other unhealed cuts were visible all along his arm.

A physician in a crimson velvet gown and embroidered cap was attending to him. He ignored the boy's weak cries as he squeezed his thin arm to make the blood run more thickly. I turned away, feeling sick. With my back pressed against the wall, I closed my eyes and struggled for calm. There was nothing we could do to help the boy, absolutely nothing. He and the others like him could be saved only by Innocent's death.

When I looked again, the physician had finished the bleeding and was transferring the blood from the bowl into a jar on the table beside the bed. Unattended, the boy continued to bleed. He whimpered once more and I had to put my knuckles in my mouth to keep from shouting.

David pressed my shoulder, tilted his head in silent warning to stay back, and stepped into the room. The friar's robe and hood covered him entirely. His arms were folded and concealed in the sleeves of the robe. He kept his head bent and his voice soft.

"Signore dottore," he said to the physician, "Father Morozzi wishes to have a word with you."

The doctor looked up, stared at David for a moment, then frowned. "He knows I am busy."

"Of course, signore, but he says this is urgent. If you would come with me, I am certain it will only take a few minutes."

The physician appeared to waiver. The thought of refusing Morozzi seemed to trouble him, but so did the need to complete his task. "The Holy Father's treatment is not yet ready. I cannot simply leave—"

"My brother in Christ will watch over it for you," David said, and moved aside so I could enter the room.

I, too, kept my head down and my hands concealed, knowing full well that the sight of them would betray me as a female.

For a moment, I thought the physician would refuse, but he only shook his head in exasperation and stepped away from the bed. "Touch nothing," he said to me in passing. Leaving the room, David gave me a quick glance, all the reminder I needed that I would have very little time.

As soon as the physician was gone, I sprang across the room. The boy who had just been bled stared at me. I put a finger to my lips, praying he would stay silent, and quickly drew the vial of blood from underneath my gown. The other boys did not move at all; I suspect they were too terrified or weakened by what had been done to them to take any notice of what was happening.

That left the problem of what to do with the blood already in the jar. The smell of copper rising from it made me gag. I held my breath, took hold of the jar, and looked around frantically. Out of the corner of my eye, I saw the boy move. He lifted his other arm, also showing signs of many cuts, and pointed under his bed.

I dove down, careful of the vial, and found the piss pot. With a sigh of relief, I poured the blood into it and shoved the pot back under the bed. With that done, I shook the vial several times as Sofia had instructed me so that the blood, which had begun to separate into a thin, yellowish serum floating on the top and a thicker, almost solid red base, would be mixed together again. As soon as I saw that it was, I poured it into the jar and set that back on the table exactly where it had been.

Through all this, the boy continued to watch me silently. By the time I finished, I could hear Vittoro's voice out in the corridor where he had waited to intercept David and the physician.

"A thousand apologies, *dottore,*" Vittoro was saying. "Father Morozzi had to leave unexpectedly but I am sure he will want to speak with you later."

"Damn nuisance being called away like that," the physician complained. "The Holy Father is waiting. I really can't be expected to be everywhere at once."

He stepped back into the room to find me pressing a bandage to the boy's arm. Of course, I should not have done it. No, I do not have any explanation for why I did. Except that he was a child, terrified and in pain. You would have done the same, surely?

"What are you doing?" the doctor demanded. "I told you not to touch anything."

David stepped forward quickly. "Brother . . . Francis means well, *dottore.* He used to care for . . . horses. I'm sure he didn't mean any harm, did you, Brother?"

Mutely, I shook my head all the while wishing the *dottore* and his kind to the seventh circle of Hell. Indeed, it pleased me to imagine him immersed there in the Phlegethon, the river of boiling blood, where I heartily hoped he would spend eternity.

"We'll be off then," Vittoro said. "Again, apologies *dottore.*"

The physician was still grumbling as we sped down the corridor.

"Were you successful?" David asked as we went.

I assured him that we had been and we slipped back into the

passage, following it to the roof, which we crossed again, coming down into another passage from which we emerged into a second courtyard on the military level. By this time I fully appreciated what Vittoro had said about even the rats getting lost in the *castel*. I was completely disoriented and would have had no idea where to go had not the captain been there to guide us.

We had just reached the courtyard when we came across the patrol—a dozen guards in breastplates and plumed helmets, armed with pikes and scabbards. They were moving at a trot across the open space. Elsewhere, we could hear the sound of pounding feet.

Pressed back into the shadows along the wall, we waited until the patrol had passed. My heart pounded against my protesting ribs. If we were caught now, Morozzi would have everything he needed to accuse us and more. Someone would realize that we had been near the blood meant for the Pope. The boys would be questioned—

Bile rose in my throat. I prayed as I have never prayed in my life, but my prayers were not very good all the same. They consisted mainly of warning God that if He allowed any such thing to happen, I would know that he was a fake and a fraud, a trickster god undeserving of our adoration. That is probably not the best way to win the favor of the Almighty.

"They'll be sealing off the exits," Vittoro said when the patrol had moved on. "Morozzi's one chance now is to stop you from getting out of here."

"But you already thought of that," David said. "Right?"

The captain shrugged. "To tell the truth, I was more interested in finding you. I figured I'd work out the rest afterward."

"Perhaps there is somewhere we can hide," I suggested quickly. "Until the furor dies down. Then we could just slip out."

Vittoro shook his head. "There are a hundred places, maybe

more, but you risk being discovered in any of them. It would be smarter to get you out now. I'll stay behind and sow as much confusion as I can. The lads won't mind. As I said, they're on Borgia's side."

"The captain is right," David said. "Besides, if we succeed and Innocent dies, the *castel* will be locked down until the fight for the spoils is decided."

I had to agree with that. Too well, I remembered what had happened eight years before, when Pope Sixtus IV died. Along with my father and most of Borgia's household, I had evacuated to the countryside while the Cardinal fought his great—and losing—battle to take the papacy. Gangs had rioted in the streets, fires burned throughout Rome, and chaos reigned until the conclave of cardinals finally chose a compromise candidate. It could be much the same again.

"You have to go," Vittoro said. He looked around quickly and came to a decision. "This way."

We went on, down a few steps, a few more before we had to stop to let another patrol go by. Pressed against the wall, I held my breath as a young guardsman glanced back over his shoulder and frowned, as though he had seen or heard something. He went on after a moment and I breathed again, but it was clear to me that we could not remain in the *castel* much longer and still hope to go undetected.

We came at last into a vast room filled with clay pots that came as high as my waist and were set in wooden frames that held them upright. This was the *castel*'s oil storage area, at the far end of which Vittoro stopped.

Off in the distance we could hear the tread of patrols on the move, interspersed with shouted orders.

"This is where it gets a bit tricky," Vittoro said.

Those were not the words I wanted to hear just then, but I kept that thought to myself as he continued.

"There is a shaft. It cuts straight down through the walls and comes out above the moat." He looked at both of us. "Can you swim?"

I nodded, as did David. Neither one of us showed much enthusiasm at the prospect of diving into the moat, which was bound to be as filthy as such places always are.

"Won't we be seen?" David asked.

Vittoro shook his head. "The shaft comes out on a side of the *castel* where there are no gates, no passages, nothing but what looks to be solid wall. Standard procedure is to mass guards at the main gate and deploy smaller forces to the two other sides, where there are hidden entrances. That's where they'll be watching."

As he spoke, Vittoro uncoiled the rope he had used to hoist us out of the prison room. "Another reason they don't bother guarding this side is that the shaft is almost vertical. Anyone falling from this height would be killed."

"So we can't just slide down it?" David asked.

"Not unless you're eager to meet your Maker." Hefting the rope, Vittoro grinned. "Who wants to go first?"

19

David unfastened the black cloak and pulled the white robe off over his head. He dropped both onto the floor of the storage room. "They will weigh me down in the water," he said, misinterpreting my look of surprise. I understood perfectly well why he was taking off the garments. However, if he assumed he would be going first, he was wrong.

"We don't know how wide the shaft is, do we?" I pointed out. "I stand a better chance of being able to get through and at the same time discover if you can make it. Otherwise, you could become stuck, trapped in there with no way out."

"She has a point," Vittoro said reluctantly. "I've dropped a rope down the shaft but I've never been down it myself. I can only guess at its width."

"It's too dangerous," David insisted. "She'd be in the water alone."

"I'll be fine," I said. Without waiting for them to agree, I stripped off my own robe and for good measure also removed my overdress. Vittoro had fixed a loop in one end of the rope. I took it and dropped it over my head, pulling it snug under my arms.

With a glance into the dark shaft, I took a breath. "I'm ready."

Of course, I was not, but there is no way to prepare for such a task. Far better to simply get it over with. Following Vittoro's instructions, I sat down on the edge of the opening.

"Lower yourself slowly," he directed. "I'll let the rope out little by little. If it's too tight around you, you can take some of your weight off by pressing your legs and arms against the sides of the shaft. If there's a problem, tug on the rope and I'll bring you back up."

I nodded as though I understood, when in fact all I knew was that I was going into a dark, dank hole that, if I survived the descent, would dump me out into a filthy moat. At the last moment, just before I grabbed hold of the rope, I looked up at David.

"When you reach the water, whatever you do make sure not to swallow any of it. If you go under, don't inhale. Any surface water brings the flux, but what is in that moat will kill us for certain."

"Too bad we couldn't give it to Innocent," he said with a strained smile.

Vittoro stood ready. I could see the worry in his eyes and mustered a smile. "Don't worry, I'll be fine. You didn't save us from Morozzi just for me to drown in a few feet of fetid water."

His voice gruff, he said, "I pray that is so."

I reached over and squeezed his hand. "My father considered you a friend. Now I understand why."

"Giovanni would be proud of you," Vittoro said. "Any father would be."

My chest tightened. I nodded once, then took as deep a breath as I could manage. Putting my trust in God, Saint Michael, and above all, in the stalwart soldier who had gone into the lion's den to save a sinner, I lowered myself into the shaft. Instantly, the air turned clammy. From far below, I could smell the stench of human waste, offal, slime, dead carcasses, and heaven only knew what else that was tossed or fell into the moat. I swallowed hard and tried not to think about the absence of anything solid beneath my dangling feet or the protests of my abused ribs.

Too soon, the light of the chamber above narrowed to a small square and I was in darkness. Vittoro let the rope out very slowly. Afraid that he would be left with little strength to lower David, I stretched out my limbs to the sides of the shaft and began to inch downward. The process was both painstaking and painful. The sharp stones scraped my skin as darkness closed in from all sides. I would not say that I have difficulty being in small spaces, not in the way I have heard some people describe, but such surroundings tend to provoke thoughts of my nightmare, which I would gladly have dispensed with just then.

In an effort to collect myself, I closed my eyes. Behind my shuttered lids I saw the falling flash of steel and for just an instant, I thought I smelled blood. Quickly, I opened my eyes again and discovered that they had adjusted to the darkness enough for me to make out the rough stones lining the shaft. By watching carefully, I was better able to place my hands, knees, and feet to lessen further injury.

As I continued to descend, I was heartened that the shaft was wide enough for David, but I still feared that I would encounter some obstruction before I reached the bottom. When I was able to proceed without incident, it seemed that my prayers were being answered. Excitement filled me as I realized that I could see a patch of dim light below where the shaft ended. I was preparing myself as best I could for the moment when I would be lowered into the filthy water when suddenly the rope pulled tight, halting my descent. From high above, I heard Vittoro curse.

A moment later, the problem became evident. The rope was too short. I could go no further. If Vittoro had to haul me back up, everything would be for naught and we would still be trapped.

Twisting around, I managed to wedge myself against one side of the shaft as best I could with enough of my weight on my feet and knees to give a little slack on the rope. With difficulty, I pulled it off over my head. For a moment, I held on to the rope with both hands. I had no idea how far the distance was to the moat or whether the water would be deep enough to cushion my fall. Neither did I have any choice.

I took the deepest breath I could manage, clinched my eyes and mouth tight shut, and let go.

I fell a heart-stopping distance that was probably not more than ten feet. Landing in the moat, I sank quickly. My feet touched a disgustingly soft bottom that seemed to tug at me. With all my strength, I swam for the surface, breaking through a thick layer of slime.

Once my head was clear of the water, I shook off as much as I could before opening my eyes and drawing breath. The stench was overpowering. I struck out for the opposite side of the moat only to discover that the level of the water was several feet lower than the adjacent ground. For a horrible moment, I thought I might be trapped. When I saw the glint of iron rungs driven into the stone, I almost cried out in relief.

By the time I had scrambled up them and collapsed flat on the grassy verge opposite the *castel,* David had dropped into the moat. I watched, hardly breathing, until he surfaced, then pointed him to the rungs. He joined me, both of us dripping with malodorous ooze, and together we ran for the riverbank.

"The bridge is guarded," David said as we went. "We can't cross there."

He was right, of course. We had to find another way, but where? Looking around frantically, I pointed. "The Ponte Sisto, half a mile upriver, if we can reach it."

And if we didn't find it, too, occupied by condotierri.

We went as carefully as we could, dodging in and out of the bank-side shadows. The tide was low, adding to the stench, but, God's mercy, I was quickly becoming insensible to all smells. With every step, we sank in mud that slowed us. Twice I stumbled and would have fallen if not for David's strong arm. Where one of the ancient sewers ran into the river, we disturbed a colony of rats who poured out all around us, their high-pitched squeaks filling the darkness. Under other circumstances, I would have frozen in terror. But after all the events of the night and the desperate danger still hanging over us, David and I both ran right through and over the rats, startling them so that they fled before us like the parting of a great, gray tide.

"We have to warn Rocco," I said as we ran. And please God, let it be in time.

Within sight of the bridge, David pulled me down beside him. Carefully, we searched for any sign that the span was guarded. The commander of the *castel* could have sent men to secure it and might well have done so if Vittoro was wrong. But if he was right, if there was sympathy for Borgia within the garrison . . .

"It's empty," David said. Nothing stirred across the Ponte Sisto and no one stood guard at either end.

Together we ran across the bridge. Beyond lay the ancient walls of Rome. Built to protect the city from the barbarian hordes, they had failed so miserably that they have not been considered worth rebuilding. We slipped through what would once have been a gate and sped on.

A little farther on we entered the Campo dei Fiori. Several taverns and brothels around the market were still doing business but otherwise the area was quiet. We gained the street of the glassmakers but stopped again to make sure that no guards were about.

All seeming quiet, we went on, turning down an alley that took us around the back of Rocco's shop past the furnace. I knocked softly on the door and called his name, "Rocco . . . it's us."

Instantly, the door was thrown open. The glassmaker looked disheveled and weary but infinitely relieved to see us. "Francesca!" he exclaimed and seemed about to throw his arms around me when he took a quick step back, driven no doubt by the sudden realization that I stank.

"Where have you . . . what is . . . ?" At a loss for words, he simply stepped aside so we could enter.

When the door was closed safely behind us, Rocco lit a lamp and took a long look at the pair of us. I cannot imagine the sight we made but I recall too well the smell.

"We were in the *castel* moat," I said. "But that's not important. It was a trap. Morozzi isn't one of us. He's a madman who wants to bring down Borgia and kill all the Jews. We have to get out of here, all of us."

I give Rocco credit, confronted by such a claim he did not hesitate. Blowing out the lamp, he grabbed his cloak off a peg and said, "Let's go."

"Do you have any particular place in mind?" David asked as we hurried from the shop and headed back out into the night.

"Only one I can think of," Rocco replied, and without saying anything more, set off at a trot. David and I followed, the pace leaving us without breath for questions. Beyond the Campo dei Fiori, we passed within the shadow of the domed Pantheon, the only ancient building in Rome that has been spared so much of the depredations of time and a reminder of what greatness actually looks like. A few streets on we entered the Piazza Minerva, sacred to the ancient goddess of wisdom.

All the while we stayed close to the stone and timber buildings, listening for any hint of an approaching patrol. It was now past the hour when the hired thugs, tired of strutting about showing off their authority, like to retire to the all-night taverns. Those who didn't drink themselves into a stupor would be out again later, fueled on raw red Umbrian wine and more dangerous than ever.

Before then, we had to find sanctuary. A moment later, I realized where Rocco was taking us.

"Are you sure?" I asked, keeping my voice low in the hope that David would not hear my doubts. Of all the places to hide, him in particular.

Santa Maria Sopra Minerva, the church built by the Dominicans that also serves as their chapter house in Rome, stands on top of a temple to the goddess of wisdom. The body of Saint Catherine, of whom I have spoken, is buried there but not her head, which is in Siena. I find that troubling but the arrangement seems to satisfy her adherents in both places.

"I have a friend here," Rocco said. I had to hope that he was right.

It is a sad fact that many churches in Rome, as elsewhere, are locked at night to prevent their despoliation. Anyone in need of spiritual sustenance is expected to wait until morning. But such is the authority of the Dominicans, and the fear they inspire, that the house shared by the Mother of our Lord and the Goddess of Wisdom is an exception.

We stood at a small side door surmounted by a stone lintel carved with the images of hounds at the chase, a play on *Domini canes,* which styles the Order as the hounds of the lord. For a moment I feared that David would refuse to enter. His extreme distaste and suspicion were writ clear on his face.

I seized his hand and said urgently, "Rocco is a good man. There is nothing I would not trust him with, and he endangers himself by coming here."

David looked far from convinced but he did consent to enter. We found ourselves in an aisle off a side nave near the altar to the Mother of our Lord. Candles burned in front of the statue of the Virgin, illuminating the interior. I had been in the church before but had forgotten its full glory, a stark contrast to the simple façade without. The arched vaulting vivid with red ribbing framed a blue, starry sky. Polished marble columns to either side of the main nave reflected the light of the sanctuary lamp, the reminder of Christ's eternal presence. I tried to calculate how long we had been in the *castel* and in flight from it. By my reckoning, we were sometime in the hour between compline, that so gently welcomes night, and matins. Before the friars arrived for the service that heralds the coming day, we had to hide.

"This way," Rocco said, and gestured toward stone steps leading from the altar down into the crypt. I went reluctantly, having had my fill of dark, narrow spaces. Fortunately, perpetual lamps burned before a dozen tombs, including that of Saint Catherine herself. Her effigy showed her in serene repose but I thought of the headless body within and shivered.

Catherine was not alone in her apparent tranquillity. Toward the back of the crypt, where David and I finally collapsed, the carved face of a woman emerged from the wall. Her features were noble, her hair coiled in braids around her head. She had a no-nonsense look about her.

"Minerva?" I asked Rocco.

He nodded. "Probably. When this was her shrine, there was a well here. The friars have kept it in repair." He disappeared into the gloom for a few minutes and returned with a bucket of water.

David and I fell on it. We drank, and when our thirst was slaked we washed as best we could given the requirements of modesty and the lack of clean clothes. Exhausted, we slumped back against the wall. My eyes were closing when I heard David ask, "How likely is it that someone will come down here?"

"Someone will," Rocco replied. "I'm counting on it."

Beside me, David stiffened. I could not really blame him, given that we had been caught in one trap already that night.

"Your friend?" I asked.

Rocco nodded. "A few years ago, after Guillaume was transferred to the chapter house here, we happened to pass each other on the street. He recognized me, as I did him, and I wondered if he would expose me. But he has kept my secret."

"What secret?" David asked, clearly still doubtful.

I left it to Rocco to answer, which he did with simple dignity. "I used to be a Dominican."

David made a sound somewhere between incredulity and disgust. It was not difficult to understand his reaction. From his point of view, he might as well have entrusted his life to the Serpent himself.

"I didn't know it was possible to leave the Order," he said finally.

"It isn't," Rocco replied. "I ran away. Recognizing me, Guillaume could have caused much trouble, but he did not. He has kept his silence."

"Why?" I asked.

"He has his reasons," Rocco replied, and leaning back against the wall, closed his eyes, effectively ending the conversation.

We remained in silence for some time. I drifted in and out of sleep. When I was awake, I thought of Nando, sent to the countryside for safety, and of the possibility that his father would become a hunted man because of me. How carelessly I had involved him in my troubles, convincing myself that I had no alternative when the truth is that we always have choices. If harm came to Rocco, I would bear full responsibility for it.

I was dwelling on that unpleasant possibility when I heard footfalls on the stone steps leading to the crypt. Rocco heard the same and stood up immediately. I nudged David, who had been dozing. We crouched down behind a sarcophagus as Rocco moved to intercept whoever was coming.

A moment later, I heard the low murmur of voices. I could not make out the words but there was no sound of argument. Shortly, Rocco returned bringing with him a man in the white habit and black cloak of the Order. He was of an age with Rocco but a few inches shorter and slighter in build with a dark, neatly trimmed beard and mustache. His expression was open and frankly curious. He did not appear alarmed to see us.

"This is Friar Guillaume," Rocco said. "He will help us."

"Rocco says you escaped from the *castel,*" the friar said, looking from one to the other of us. So intent was he that he did not so much as wrinkle his nose at our stench. "However did you manage that?"

David stood up. He flexed his shoulders, curled his hands into fists, and looked at Guillaume quellingly. "Why do you want to know?"

Guillaume flushed slightly before the none-too-delicate threat but did not back down. "I'm curious. The *castel* is a kind of puzzle. To unlock it, you need wisdom, insight, and perhaps a little luck."

"Guillaume likes puzzles," Rocco said with a smile. With a glance at me, he said, "Most particularly, he likes the puzzles to be found in nature. Ask him about bees."

"Bees?" I repeated, at a loss.

The friar looked a little abashed but such was his enthusiasm that he could not restrain himself. "Bees are the most amazing of God's creatures, far more than Man himself. They toil diligently and selflessly toward their appointed purpose. In the course of which, they engage in several fascinating forms of behavior. For instance, a bee, upon returning to the hive, may alight outside and perform what appears to be an intricate dance, the exact steps of which may vary in ways I suspect are to different purposes. Other bees, watching this dance, will then depart, often in the same direction from which the first bee came."

"Fascinating," David said. He had unclenched his fists and was looking at the friar with something close to amusement.

"But that isn't all," Guillaume went on. "I am almost certain that there is a pattern to the breeding of bees, by which I mean to their number. The count in any hive advances according to the sequence of numbers discovered by the great mathematician Leonardo Fibonacci. That same sequence appears in myriad other natural settings . . . the petals on a sunflower, for example, the spirals formed by the scales of a pinecone, the—"

"Amazing," I said, and truly I did find it so. But time was passing too quickly and a plan for our escape had yet to be devised.

"Forgive me," Guillaume said, looking not at all abashed. "I do tend to go on and on. Perhaps that is why the master of our Order allows me the freedom to pursue my studies in private—to the greater glory of God, of course."

Only then did I recall that the same Dominican Order that had spawned Torquemada had, in its better days, nurtured the likes of Saint Albertus Magnus, who argued that science and faith could exist side by side in accord, and, supreme above all, the great Saint Thomas Aquinas, upon whose shoulders the Church can fairly be said to stand. How far the Order had fallen from such heights of brilliance into the fevered passions of the Grand Inquisitor

"You have found a strange place to do your work, Friar," David said.

Guillaume spread his hands in simple acceptance. "I am where God has set me. Now, as to the present circumstance, you are safe to remain here for the time being. I tend the crypt lamps, checking them before we pray each of the offices. It is now almost matins. My brothers will be in the church above but none will venture down here. Come daylight, we will see how matters stand and, if need be, we will make other arrangements. Is that agreeable to you?"

When we had assured him that it was and more, he added, "Before prime, I should be able to return with food and, if at all possible, news. Until then remain here and try to rest."

Rocco walked back with him toward the steps as David and I sat down again. Just before I fell into exhausted sleep, it occurred to me that I had finally met the man I had hoped Morozzi to be, a seeker of truth hidden within Holy Mother Church itself. If there were others like him, and if they had Guillaume's courage, there might yet be hope that the Torquemadas of this world would be defeated.

On that thought, I slept, deeply and without dreams, rousing only a little when I heard, drifting down the steps from the altar, the friars chanting the holy office: *Rest in God alone, my soul. He is the source of my hope.*

20

"Francesca?" A deep voice, very low. A gentle touch on my arm. I opened my eyes. Rocco crouched beside me, his face creased with concern. Above, at the top of the steps leading to the altar, I saw faint daylight.

"What hour is it?" I asked as I struggled back to full consciousness. I had slept deeply but to little good. My mind remained fogged with exhaustion and I ached everywhere. Rocco extended a hand to help me rise. I took it, grateful for his strength and the steadiness of his presence.

"Almost prime," he said. "Guillaume brought food and, as promised, news."

"What news?" David demanded, waking at the same time. He rose to his feet just as though he had enjoyed a full night's rest in a sumptuous bed.

"The city is quiet," Rocco said. "There is no hue and cry about anyone escaping the *castel* last night, nor is there any sign of trouble near the ghetto or anywhere in the streets. All seems to be in order."

A blessing, to be sure, so far as it went. Vittoro had been right: Without hard evidence of a plot to kill the Pope, Morozzi could not say anything without baring his own throat to Borgia's revenge. However, that would not prevent him from getting the edict signed and the Jews doomed. Only Innocent's death would do that.

"No word about the Pope?" I asked.

Rocco shook his head. "Nothing new."

I could not believe that we had gone through so much only to fail, and yet I knew that there had never been any guarantee of success. Although I had managed to switch the blood, I could not be sure that Innocent had received it. Even if he had, it might not have affected him as it had Rebecca. On the other hand, he might yet die from his own dissipations, which were legion. Or God, in His infinite mercy, might decide to remove his servant by some other means before he could do yet more harm. With so many unknowns, there was only one course open to us.

"We have to find out what is happening at the *castel,*" I said, intent on setting off at once. My stomach had other ideas. Sensing food, it emitted a growl that would have done a hungry wolf proud. At the same moment, the bells rang for prime.

As we waited for the service to be over and the friars to leave the church, we devoured the bread and cheese Guillaume had brought. When the way was clear, we slipped up the steps from the crypt and out the same door through which we had entered. Emerging from the bowels of the earth, we stood blinking in a morning so bright it hurt the eyes. A fresh breeze carried the scents of the lavender fields south of the city, softening the edges of the stench that clung to us still.

Near the Pantheon, we parted. I feared for Rocco's safety and pleaded with him not to return to his shop, but he dismissed my concern out of hand.

"Let Morozzi come after me," he said. "It will keep him from you long enough for Borgia to bring him down."

I would have suspected another man of bravado but not Rocco, who was the very soul of strength and determination. Even so, I gripped his hand tightly.

"Please, be careful. I would never forgive myself if—"

"Send word," Rocco said as he squeezed my hand in turn, "if anything is amiss. But do not trouble yourself over me."

I meant to answer but unaccountably my throat was thick and my eyes stung. By the time I might have spoken, he was hurrying off. But he looked back once, catching me looking after him, and smiled. I did the same but I don't think he saw for he was already gone.

Filthy and bedraggled, David and I made our way through the crowd that, as always, thronged the streets. Our odor preceded us. More than a few passersby gave us startled looks and a wide berth.

By the time we reached the palazzo, I had worked out a plan of sorts.

"We must find out where Borgia is and what is happening with the edict. You can hide in my apartment while I—"

David took my arm gently, stopping me. "I will not hide anywhere, Francesca. Once you are safely within the palazzo, I am going back to the Quarter."

I started to protest but he would not hear me. "If the edict has been signed," he said, "it will be proclaimed very soon. Once that happens, we will be attacked as the Jews of Spain were as soon as the order for their expulsion was given. They were not prepared to defend themselves but we are." His face set grimly. "The time for killing Jews without cost is over."

Dread filled me. Humans being children of the Fall, there will always be some eager to take out their own fears on those they see as too weak to retaliate. But if what David was promising came to pass, the consequences would be horrible in the extreme. However many Gentiles died attacking the warren of streets and lanes that was the ghetto, Christendom as a whole would not rest until every Jew in Rome was dead.

"You must know the cost of what you intend," I said.

"We will die. But if we don't fight, most of us will die anyway. The survivors will be like Rebecca, facing death alone in a world where we are denied any right to exist at all. If by our deaths we embolden Jews elsewhere to rise up or even cause those who would attack us to think twice, our deaths will not have been in vain."

My eyes burned. I scarcely trusted myself to speak. "The children . . . Benjamin . . . all the others?"

The sorrow in David's eyes was unbearable to see. For a moment, I thought his resolve might weaken, but I should have known better. What arrogance on my part not to understand that this was a battle he had fought within himself long ago. Fought and won, however terrible the burden that victory laid upon him.

"Forgive me," I said before he could answer. "I have no right to assume that I know better."

He smiled faintly and squeezed my hand. "You are a surprising woman, Francesca. A professional poisoner who values life far more than others, who would toss you into the pit of Hell without a second thought. But don't despair quite yet. While I have very little faith in God, I have more than a little in Rodrigo Borgia. His ambition may yet carry this day."

I could only pray that he was right, assuming I could pray at all.

We parted then, David disappearing quickly back into the streets. I made my way up the walled staircase and managed to reach my rooms unseen. With a groan of relief, I stripped off my clothes, stiff and stinking from the moat. Naked, I stood in front of the copper sink in a corner of the room, scrubbed myself from head to toe and washed my hair as well. Time was precious, to be sure, but I could not approach anyone in the household before I was clean without rousing intense suspicion as to where I had been. When I had dressed in fresh garments, I braided my wet hair and coiled it around my head. I was still sticking the pins in as I hurried from my rooms in search of answers.

My hope was to find Vittoro and discover what had happened in the *castel* after our escape, but there was no sign of him. Nor was the Cardinal at the palazzo; his office was empty and his secretaries were not in evidence. A shame, as one of them might have been able at least to tell me his whereabouts.

With no other choice, I made my way to the cramped room just off the main entry to the palazzo, situated to give its occupant a constant view of all comings and goings of importance. The steward Renaldo was there, hunched over his ledgers. He did not look up when I arrived, so engrossed was he in the columns of figures, but he stiffened at the sound of my voice.

"Your pardon, signore. Do you have a moment?"

I had resolved on courtesy but I had also brought patience, which was just as well in dealing with the small, anxious man who ever seemed on the verge of leaping out of his own skin. Strangers assumed that he feared the Cardinal, but the truth was at once broader and sadder. Renaldo was one of those poor souls who went through life in terror of ever making a mistake. The least thing—a misadded column, a misplaced digit, a lost receipt, an illegible bill, anything—might become an occasion for him to be questioned by someone in authority and that he could not bear. Accuracy was the protection he had chosen against the world, the shield behind which he crouched.

He turned and looked at me with suspicion. "What do you want?"

"Nothing very great," I assured him. As soothingly as I could, I said, "I merely thought you could tell me where I might find His Eminence."

Renaldo shrugged and returned his attention to his ledgers, giving me his back. "If he wanted to speak with you, you would know where he is."

His logic was irrefutable, as was the intense rush of annoyance it brought. Despite the few hours sleep I had enjoyed, if that is the word, in Minerva's crypt, I remained exhausted. The strain of the previous night had taken more of a toll than I cared to recognize, especially when added to all that had gone before.

Forcing myself to pleasantness, I said, "You are correct, of course, signore. But a matter has only now come up that requires the Cardinal's attention."

"Really? And what would that be?" His voice suggested that he found pleasure in frustrating me.

Desperation steeled my resolve. I bent down so close to him that he started, though whether only with fear or with some added emotion I could not have said.

Softly, as though to an intimate, I whispered, "I have completed the new poison sooner than I had hoped. It is astoundingly effective. His Eminence left instructions to be informed the moment it was ready so that he could tell me who to use it on."

God forgive me, the poor man blushed beet red, then swiftly

paled. He dropped the ledger, knocked his quill onto the floor, bent over to retrieve it, and banged his head on the bottom of the desk. The jolt jarred his ink pot, which skittered toward the edge and would have fallen had I not caught it in the palm of my hand and gently set it back in place.

By now, I had Renaldo's full attention. He stared at me wide-eyed.

"You won't tell anyone, will you?" I asked. "People get so flustered at talk of poison."

"No! That is, no, of course I won't . . . tell anyone, that is. What do you want me to do?"

"Just tell me where the Cardinal has gone." Before he could demure, I added, "I know that you know, Renaldo. I see how you watch everything. Nothing escapes you."

Sometimes I embarrass myself, but there are moments when shame must be thrown to the winds.

His color brightened, he took a deep breath and straightened such shoulders as he had. "Yes, well, I suppose I do keep a good lookout, but it's necessary to do that in a household of this sort. After all, His Eminence counts on me."

"He does, Renaldo, he surely does. As do we all. I am counting on you right now."

His Adam's apple bobbed in agitation. "I don't actually know anything officially about where His Eminence went, but—"

"But . . . ?"

He dropped his voice to an urgent whisper. "Messengers came to find him in the middle of the night. No one knew what to tell them. We all knew where he was, of course, he was with La Bella. But no one was about to say that."

"Of course not," I agreed. "We all know His Eminence values discretion above all else."

"Exactly! I hope he knows that not a one of us spoke." Voice dropping, Renaldo continued. "He finally came back here at dawn. The messengers must have found him. He was in a terrible mood, let me tell you, roaring like a bull. He was shouting for you and for the captain. When he learned that neither of you was here . . . it was as though Vesuvius was erupting! Finally, he was dressed and out he went . . . to the Curia, I believe, although I could not swear to it."

"How long ago did he leave?" I asked, struggling to conceal my excitement.

Renaldo thought for what seemed a very long moment. Finally, he said, "Not an hour ago. Does it matter?"

It might . . . or it might not. Borgia would delay as long as possible but ultimate authority still rested with Innocent. If he was determined to sign the edict, he would do so . . . assuming he had breath left in his body.

Despite the gathering warmth of the day, a chill swept over me. Standing in Renaldo's cluttered burrow—surrounded by stacks of ledgers, contracts, scrolls, and the like, all the effluvia of everyday existence—I had the sense of standing on the edge of an abyss. Almost, I could hear the ground falling out beneath my feet.

So many people, so much pain, and all of it hanging on what might happen in an instant, the space of one heartbeat to the next.

Please, God . . .

"Are you all right?" From a great distance, I heard the steward. He had risen without my noticing and was staring at me with concern.

Please . . . for David, Sofia, Benjamin, and all the rest . . .

"Signorina . . . ?" Vaguely, I heard his alarm and wondered what could be causing it.

Suddenly, I knew. Behind him I saw in my mind a vast and terrible landscape blighted and seared in which nothing lived that could be recognized as human. A world in which smoke belched from the earth to blacken the sky. Where wolves howled in grief.

In horror, I recoiled and cried out. Only then did I see the slender ray of light that offered me escape. Saw and seized.

Lord, I beseech you, if my soul is the price, I give it gladly . . .

"Signorina!"

A great sound tolled in my head. A vast, cavernous peal blocking out all thought, all fear, filling every breath, expanding to encompass everything that had ever been or ever would be. A sound unlike any I have ever heard before or since.

On and on and on . . . the bells of each of the hundreds of churches in Rome joining in with another and another until the very air shook with their power. Closer, feet came running, enough to make the earth tremble, and then voices from within the palazzo, from outside in the streets, from every quarter of Rome and ultimately the great world beyond.

So many voices crying out as one: *Il papa è morto! Il papa è morto!*

The Pope is dead.

The answer to my prayers? Perhaps, but certainly the question I have lived with ever since in the dark quiet of my soul: By whose hand?

21

Borgia did not return to the palazzo for three days after Innocent's death. The Cardinal remained within the Vatican, overseeing preparations for the papal funeral in his capacity as vice chancellor of the Curia.

Meanwhile, Rome ran wild with rumor. The Pope had been murdered. No, he had died from his own dissipations. Or by the curse of a gypsy whore. Or because of an ancient prediction found within the tomb of one of the Caesars. Or . . .

Uncertain of my own guilt, I was unsure how to feel other than relieved. Innocent was dead, by my hand or nature's, it did not matter except to me. The edict had not been signed, that much I was able to glean from the hastily scrawled message David sent from the Quarter. The vast wealth the Jews had assembled from throughout Europe was flowing into Borgia's accounts in the Spannocchi banks in Siena, where Cesare had gone. Ostensibly, he was preparing his horses to run in the Palio races held each summer in that city. In fact, he was watching the money.

Well and good, or it would have been if not for the shadow hanging over all. The man I now knew to be the true architect of my father's murder remained at large, in all likelihood still somewhere within the precincts of the Vatican. I could not begin to imagine how enraged Morozzi must be that his plan had been thwarted by Innocent's death. If he even suspected that the death had not been natural, his fury would be all the worse. There was no telling what he might do next, *and* he was in possession of the lozenge. That, above all, I could not forget. Whether he had access to other poisons or not, he had the most deadly form that I myself had created to end my own life if need be.

Now it might well end Borgia's—and in such a manner as to implicate me in his death. I had a professional responsibility to protect Il Cardinale, and make no mistake, I took it seriously. Equally, at the very least, I was interested in protecting myself. But paramount above all, I was determined to fulfill my vow to avenge my father and deny Morozzi his victory before I killed him. How exactly I might accomplish that eluded me, at least for the moment.

With such dark thoughts nipping at my heels, I sought out Vittoro. He was busy giving orders to his lieutenants regarding the defense of the palazzo, but broke off when he saw me.

"Francesca," he said with a smile, "you are well?"

"Tolerably so, and you?"

"Never better. No ill effects, I trust?"

Having assured him that my plunge into the *castel* moat had done me no apparent harm, I glanced around at the preparations that were under way. Guards were in evidence everywhere, from the entrance hall to the watch towers. Many I recognized but others I did not, indicating that Vittoro was bringing in more men from the Cardinal's outlying estates. That surprised me.

"We are not leaving?" I asked. During the last papal conclave, following the death of Sixtus IV, Borgia had sent his household to the country and, not coincidentally, sent all his most precious household goods along with us—every tapestry, painting, piece of furniture, chest of treasure, every plate and goblet that could be was packed up and transported outside of Rome. It had been a sensible precaution for a man considered by one and all to be *papabile,* a candidate for the papacy. One of the stranger customs among the Romans is to fall upon and loot the residence of a new pope. This is not seen as a sign of disrespect or even necessarily illegal, being merely the reasoning of the populace that, once elevated to the Throne of Peter, a man has no further need of his private property.

This being the case, *papabili* are in the habit of emptying their residences before the start of any papal conclave. By watching the cartloads of belongings being trundled out of Rome, one can determine what each Cardinal thinks of his chances. Indeed, the emptying out of one's residence can be taken as a declaration that one is running for pope.

Therefore, what was I, or anyone, to make of Borgia's decision not to send his household goods to safety?

"He's lying low," Vittoro said. "Proclaiming that in his modesty and humility, he cannot consider himself a candidate for pope."

I all but choked. Borgia had been a cardinal for almost forty years, and for most of that time he had encouraged talk of himself as a future pope.

"That's nonsense."

Vittoro grinned. "Of course it is, but it's good nonsense. It sows confusion and in situations like this, that's always helpful."

"What is the situation?" I had a general idea but I wanted the particulars.

"As you would expect. There are two factions. Della Rovere leads the one and Sforza the other."

He named two of the most powerful cardinals in Christendom. Giuliano della Rovere was the nephew of Sixtus IV, the pope who preceded Innocent. He was a man of fierce temperament, even more so than Borgia himself, who had led troops into battle personally and delighted in crushing any who rose in rebellion against the Church. Endowed with vaunting ambition and endless confidence in his own abilities, he was said to believe that it was his destiny not only to be pope, but to lead the Church to greater glory than it had ever known.

Eight years before, he and Borgia had contested for the papacy following the death of Sixtus. When della Rovere realized he did not have the backing to make himself pope, he threw his support to the dissipated Cardinal Cibo, for no better reason than to deny Borgia the papal throne. It was an offense Borgia had neither forgiven nor forgotten in the years since. This time, della Rovere had secured the support of the French crown, the Venetians, and the powerful Colonna and Savelli families with ties to the Kingdom of Naples. Anyone could be pardoned for thinking he was unstoppable.

By contrast, Ascanio Sforza was the brother of Ludovico Sforza, the formidable Duke of Milan. His faction enjoyed the support of the Orsinis and Contis, as well as a host of cardinals opposed on principle to interference from either France or Naples.

At first glance, it was not an even struggle. Della Rovere had more allies, seemingly more money, and significantly more chance of success. Yet one dismissed the power of the Sforzas at one's own risk. And then there was Borgia . . . the bull . . . a man who had learned a hard lesson from defeat and vowed not to experience it again.

"The betting in the taverns is five to three for della Rovere over Sforza," Vittoro said. "A lot of the action is going to side bets that della Rovere will win even if he has to throw his support to another nonentity he can control like he did Innocent."

This was no small matter. If gossip is Rome's primary industry, gambling is its second. Vast amounts of money would change hands in the coming days as sums great and small were bet on who would become the next pope.

"What about Borgia?" I asked. "Where does he stand in the rankings?"

"Third, maybe fourth, but some of the smart money is starting to trend his way, the rumor being that he will spend to the heavens and beyond to win the papacy this time."

"Who's putting that rumor out, I wonder?"

Vittoro grinned. "Borgia himself, of course. He wants the cardinals to understand that he is open for business."

"Even as he proclaims himself too humble to stand as a candidate?" I asked.

Vittoro smiled. "Even so. The Cardinal said to bring you back with me. He wants to talk to you."

"You aren't staying here?"

"Not until His Eminence returns. I think it prudent to be where he is."

We looked at each other in silent agreement. With Morozzi at large and possibly soon to be allied with della Rovere, Il Cardinale could not be guarded too closely.

"How much does he know about what happened?" I asked as we left the palazzo. Vittoro was mounted on the gray he favored. I rode a mild chestnut mare, one of those kept on hand for riders like me who, let us say, lack a certain equestrian skill. I don't dislike riding;

I merely see no reason to do it very often. God gave us feet for a purpose.

The day was overcast and leaden, lacking a breeze to blow away the pall of smoke that hangs over the city even in summer from cookfires, furnaces, and the like. The streets were unusually quiet, in no small measure due to the squadrons of troops brought in to patrol the city. With the memory of what had happened at the last papal death still fresh in many minds, people were inclined to stay in their homes and shops, keeping to themselves as they waited to find out whether Rome would once again erupt into violence.

"I had a quick word with him," Vittoro said. "There wasn't time for anything more. He and della Rovere were both at the deathbed. They nearly got into a brawl even as the pope was taking his last breath."

That was a scene I could envision all too easily—the two cardinals, sworn enemies, each determined to wrest the ultimate power for himself. Absently, I wondered if either of them or anyone at all had thought to give Innocent the rite of extreme unction before his demise. Not that I believed anointing him with holy oil and saying a few prayers over him would spare the Pope when he was called to account for his earthly deeds.

However, I did have another interest. Hesitantly, I inquired, "Do you have any idea of his condition at the end?"

"You mean what killed him?"

Put that baldly, I had no choice but to nod. "I did wonder."

Vittoro shot me a look. "Don't dwell on it, Francesca. You did what had to be done."

"Then it was the blood?" I, too, would be called to account someday. I could justify killing a man poised on the edge of committing a great evil. But how did I account for killing the Vicar of Christ on earth? Where did the man cease and his holy office begin? I truly had no idea but I feared the answer all the same.

"Maybe it was, maybe it wasn't," Vittoro said in a tone that made it clear that he did not think it mattered. "What counts is that he's gone. Let's be glad for that and not worry about the rest."

We were approaching the Pons Aelius, the bridge we had crossed with Morozzi to enter the *castel*. I stared at the brooding walls of the fortress and marveled that David and I had managed to escape from within them. Lifting my gaze to the statue of Saint Michael, I gave silent thanks. At the moat, I did not so much as glance.

A little farther on, we entered the precincts of the Vatican itself. Unlike the rest of the city, the vast square in front of Saint Peter's bustled with activity. Clergy and laity from throughout Rome and the outlying districts had hurried there upon first word of the Pope's death to sniff out whatever advantage could be found, campaign for their favorite candidate, or simply enjoy the intrigue and excitement. Hard on their heels would come delegations from the Italian States and much of Europe. Every inn in Rome and many private homes shortly would be bursting at the rafters.

The race was on to reach the city before the conclave began, the cardinals were sealed away in the Sistine Chapel, and there was nothing left to do except await their decision.

Somewhere in the complex of buildings that make up the Vatican, Morozzi was laying his own plans. He surely knew that his only hope now of getting the edict signed lay in the election of a pope who hated the Jews as much as he did. There were any number of candidates who might fit that description, but chief among them was Giuliano della Rovere himself. Borgia's great rival had been the power behind Innocent's throne. As such, Morozzi must have secured his approval for the edict before proposing it to the Pope. It was reasonable to believe that he was now the mad priest's patron and, as such, was protecting him.

There was little doubt that della Rovere would go to any lengths necessary to continue his control of the papacy. If he could not get himself elected, he was still young enough that he could settle for a candidate of his choosing and wait to make his own bid another time. For Borgia, it was a different matter. At sixty-one, he could not afford to lose again and still have any real hope of ever becoming pope. He had wanted the papacy for too long and with too great a fervor to restrain himself now. Only della Rovere matched him in the unbridled intensity of his ambition.

"A clash of Titans," I murmured, looking toward the unadorned façade of the Sistine Chapel, where the struggle ultimately would be played out. No one other than the cardinals themselves and their attendants knew exactly what went on during a papal conclave, but the process by which God is said to make the choice of his Vicar on earth known seems to me to be little more than an invitation to human avarice and venality.

"What's that you said?" Vittoro asked.

I turned in the saddle and looked at him. "How far do you think della Rovere will go to win?"

"As far as he has to, as will Borgia," he replied as we dismounted. "There will be no backing down for either of them."

Our reins were taken by a squire wearing the mulberry red and gold Borgia livery. Looking up, I saw the vice chancellery banner flying over the Apostolic Palace. For the moment, Borgia was supreme head of the Church in Rome. But that could change all too quickly. Would change, if Morozzi had his way.

We went up a flight of steps, passed between a brace of armed guards, and continued down a corridor and into a warren of offices teeming with clerks who paid us no mind whatsoever as they rushed about the business set to them.

"Wait here," Vittoro said, and disappeared behind burnished oak doors studded with brass.

Left alone, I felt the stares of the dozens of petitioners lined up along one wall of the outer office, awaiting the chance to entreat Borgia for some favor or other, never mind that he had larger matters to concern him. Lawyers, clerks, factors, and what looked to be an artist or two, perhaps a musician here and there, all subjected me to intense scrutiny. I was the only woman and it was clear that my presence was an occasion for comment. A particularly plump toad of a man, probably a lawyer, leaned toward a similarly well-fed personage and whispered. Together, they looked at me and laughed.

I restrained the impulse to inform them that I was not, as I was sure they assumed, one of the Cardinal's women. That I was instead his poisoner. Their reaction would have been most satisfying but not at the cost of drawing attention to my presence. Instead, I stared off into the middle distance for the little time it took Vittoro to return.

The Cardinal's office overlooked the square in front of the basilica. Tall windows were open to admit what air there was. The corbeled ceiling high above was decorated with carvings of seraph and seraphim. Tapestries lined the walls. Long tables were piled with documents—scrolls, ledgers, and the like. I saw Borgia's secretaries, all three of them, hard at work, along with a host of priests and monks who bustled in and out, no doubt on weighty errands.

Borgia himself sat behind a vast expanse of polished chestnut and marble. He looked up as I entered and smiled.

And then he stood.

The Cardinal rose at my arrival, came out from behind his desk, and greeted me warmly. "Donna Francesca! How good to see you!"

All movement stopped. The secretaries, the clerks, everyone froze in place and stared at us. Or more correctly stared at me. Such signal courtesy, virtually unheard of in this place where women count for so little, was sure to set tongues wagging. Since Il Cardinale never did anything without thought and purpose, that was clearly what he intended.

How long would it be before it was known that Francesca Giordano, the poisoner's daughter rumored to have taken over that position, had visited the Cardinal in his offices at the Curia and had been received by him with great friendliness and respect?

That they had, as in fact we did, withdrawn a little way off to speak in private for some time, observed but not overheard?

That it appeared they had matters of great importance to discuss?

"What do you want?" I asked Borgia when we had removed to a corner of the office where we had a modicum of privacy. I meant what did he have in mind in making our conversation so public, but the Cardinal took my inquiry differently.

He assembled a look of surprise and said, "To be pope, of course. I thought you knew that."

Before my exasperation could get the better of me, I saw the gleam in his eyes. But I heard, too, his seriousness when he added, "But first, you must see to it that I live."

22

The Greek general Thucydides, in his *History of the Peloponnesian Wars,* tells us that we must always assume that our enemy is competent rather than rest our hope on the belief that he will blunder. I had not yet read Thucydides when I set all my skills to the task of keeping Borgia alive, but I possessed sufficient instinct to know that I must not, under any circumstances, underestimate my adversary.

Morozzi was a crazed fanatic, but he was also an intelligent dissembler who knew the workings of Holy Mother Church far better than I could ever hope to. In particular, he knew the Vatican, the ground upon which the great struggle between Borgia and della Rovere would be played out. I had very little time to familiarize myself with it as best I could.

Vittoro was my escort. With him at my side, I concentrated my attentions on the chapel where the papal conclave would take place.

Sara Poole

The Sistine Chapel, named in honor of Pope Sixtus IV who had ordered its construction, had been consecrated a scant nine years before. This would be the first time it was used for a papal conclave, but it appeared well suited for that purpose. Modeled on King Solomon's Temple in Jerusalem—shall we pause for a moment to appreciate the irony of such reverence for the work of Jews?—it conceals a wealth of extraordinary art behind an almost blank façade interrupted only by a row of tiny windows under the roof and a series of doors leading from the lower level to an enclosed courtyard. Lacking any means of entry from the outside, the Chapel can be reached only through the Apostolic Palace. This design offers significant advantages for security while also emphasizing its role as the pope's chapel, set apart from the much larger public basilica.

As many times as I have seen it, the Chapel never fails to steal my breath. Say what you will about Sixtus, he had a gift for drawing the best from the artists of our age and turning it to his own purpose. My beloved Botticelli, as well as Perugino and Ghirlandaio all contributed to the extraordinary series of frescoes that bring the walls to life. Beneath a vaulted ceiling of blue painted with gold stars, Moses, Aaron, Christ, Saint Peter, and a host of others proclaim the unbroken lineage of papal authority from God giving Moses the Ten Commandments to Christ giving Saint Peter the Keys to Heaven. Throughout all, the arch of Constantine reoccurs, reminding us that the pope possesses not only supreme spiritual power but temporal as well.

I paused before the section that always fascinated me most on visits to the Chapel with my father. His position in Borgia's household had afforded us certain privileges, among them the opportunity to enter locations closed to the general public. I thought of him as I stood before the section of the frescoes devoted to the punishment of

Korah, he who challenged the authority of Moses and Aaron, God's appointed leaders.

"Nasty business that," Vittoro observed, standing next to me. He cast a soldier's eye over the fresco in which, after attempting to stone Moses, and being repulsed by Aaron, Korah and his followers suffer divine wrath as they are swallowed alive by the earth. To be sure no one misses the message, Aaron wears the purple robes of a pope and an inscription warns against the dangers of any man taking that honor upon himself except he who is given it by God.

"It is," I agreed, "and it makes the point well enough. But how many of them do you think actually believe it?"

By them, I meant, of course, the cardinals who shortly would assemble in the Chapel to divine God's choice of his next Vicar on earth. There would be twenty-some of them, it not being known yet how many would reach Rome in time. Almost all were intensely worldly men like Borgia and della Rovere. Only a tiny handful were driven by spiritual considerations, and they were all elderly men unlikely to have any real role in the proceedings.

"How many believe any of it?" Vittoro countered. "At least until they're on their deathbeds, afraid of facing their Maker. Until then, they act like a pack of pagan hyenas squabbling over a carcass."

"And yet you support Borgia," I reminded him.

The captain shrugged. "Better the devil you know." He turned to face the opposite wall, where Botticelli had painted his magnificent rendering of the Temptation of Christ. I stared at it as well. In his final attempt to lure our Lord into betraying his sacred mission on Earth, Satan offers him all the riches of the world, only to have them rejected. Would that we could find a pope who would do the same, but until then, we must make do with what we have.

Reminding myself of my purpose in being there, I studied the chairs—they are really thrones—in which the cardinals would sit for their formal deliberations. Ranging to either side of the altar, each is covered by a red canopy. Upon election of a pope, all but the chosen would stand and personally lower his canopy to signify his acceptance of the outcome. As dean of the College of Cardinals, Borgia's seat was closest to the altar, a position I am sure he thought apt.

Borgia would be touching the arms of his chair, the canopy string, and undoubtedly a great deal more. I could not possibly be the only poisoner with a means of killing through skin contact, such as I had used on the Spaniard. Nor could I hope to limit where Borgia touched. But I could be certain that he wore gloves of my providing. Similarly, I could assure that he ate and drank nothing except what was brought to him under my seal.

Which did not mean that he couldn't be killed. Any man is vulnerable provided the would-be killer is willing to go to any lengths, including giving his own life to achieve his ends.

How far would Morozzi go?

How far would I?

"It doesn't seem quite fair," I said.

"How's that?" Vittoro asked.

"If any of Borgia's opponents dies suddenly, he will be suspected just as he would have been if Innocent's death was seen as unnatural. As no cardinal is likely to give supreme power to a man who is willing to kill a cardinal, that would assure that he would no longer be a candidate for pope. But if he died, how many of his fellow princes would care?"

"Damn few. It certainly wouldn't put a crimp in their own ambitions."

I might have spared a moment's sympathy for Il Cardinale had

I not been well aware that he cared for nothing but La Famiglia and would sacrifice anything—and anyone—for it. As it was, I stared at the bier set up in front of the altar to receive Innocent's body, even now being prepared for internment in multiple coffins, lead nestled within cedar within white oak. I could only hope they would be sufficient to contain the stink since the funeral itself would not take place for several days yet. If I failed in my task and Borgia died at Morozzi's hand, another funeral would have to be held hard on the first.

"Let us see the rest," I said, and followed Vittoro out of the Chapel to the adjacent hall where accommodations were being prepared. Each cardinal would have a private apartment in which to eat, rest, and deliberate. A few might even pray. The suites were hardly austere but neither did they begin to compare with the unbridled luxury to which the princes of Holy Mother Church were accustomed.

"Bit of a comedown for them, I'd say," Vittoro observed.

I agreed and remembered what my father had told me about why it had to be so. "In the thirteenth century, a conclave lasted two years and eight months. It might still be going on if the faithful hadn't finally taken matters into their hands and locked the cardinals in until they made a decision. Ever since, no one has wanted them to be too comfortable."

All the same, it did not look to me as though they would suffer. Amid the furnishings of each apartment, I glimpsed such niceties as chamber pots enclosed in wooden cabinets equipped with padded seats, enameled boxes of sweets, elaborate salt cellars, and the like.

Examining the quarters intended for Borgia, I waved a hand to encompass everything within it. "All this has to go, of course. We will bring in anything the Cardinal requires ourselves."

The cleric supervising the preparations overheard me and looked outraged, but a quelling glance from Vittoro kept him silent.

Sara Poole

Shortly, we returned to the Chapel for a final look. Later, we would discuss which attendants Borgia would take into the conclave with him—he would be permitted three—and how communication would be maintained with the outside, in violation of all the rules, of course. But for the moment, I wanted to be sure I had the lay of the land.

The sudden appearance of an honor guard at the entrance to the Chapel signaled that Innocent's body was about to be delivered to the bier in front of the altar. As I preferred not to be there when that happened, I had to complete my survey quickly. I was standing in the center of the Chapel, looking up at the ceiling, which has always struck me as rather plain compared to the rest, when a movement along the uppermost level of the building caught my eye. That story accommodates wardrooms for the guards, but it also has an open gangway that encircles the inner dome, providing an excellent view of everything going on below.

A man stood on the gangway, looking down at us. I recognized him all too readily. Remote in his black cassock, Morozzi was backlit by the light streaming through the small high windows behind him. He appeared surrounded by a nimbus of gold, as though enveloped in an ethereal cloud.

Then he moved and the impression dissolved. Without the light, he appeared as I knew him to be, an inordinately handsome man embarked on a vastly ugly evil. Our gazes met and in that moment, he smiled.

"Bastard," Vittoro muttered. Instinctively, his hand went to his sword.

I caught the motion from the corner of my eye and leaned over slightly, putting my hand on his. For the priest to appear so daringly before us confirmed my suspicion that he was, once again, well protected. That put him beyond my reach until such time as Il Cardinale no longer needed the support of his fellow cardinals in order to become pope. Then, and only then, would I be free to act.

"In due time," I said softly. "But not yet."

The priest saw my gesture to restrain Vittoro and his smile widened. He went so far as to raise his hand and give us a mocking wave before he disappeared into the upper reaches of the Chapel.

I was left below, beside Innocent's bier, wondering how much further I would have to imperil my soul in order to assure that God's choice fell upon Rodrigo Borgia.

23

A day passed during which I hastened between the two palazzi—Borgia and Orsini—doing my utmost to assure security for both of the Cardinal's households. Madonna Adriana was back from the country and received me with what passed for warmth from her. I sensed a new respect in her manner toward me, which I suspected had its origin in her private assessment of what had happened and my own role in it. Not that she made any reference to the Pope's death, she was far too adroit for that. But she did bid me sit on a chair rather than a stool in her presence, and she went so far as to compliment my gown, a nondescript gray serge I had thrown on for comfort's sake.

Lucrezia was more direct. She sought me out in the storerooms just as I finished going through the last of the bottles, baskets, bales, bundles, and casks recently arrived in the household, sealing each and every one against the threat of tampering.

"Is it true?" she demanded. "What they are saying?"

I looked up from my ledger—Renaldo had provided me with one to use and instructed me how to do so, for which I was genuinely grateful. Since the incident in his office—that was how I thought of it, as the incident, nothing more—he had extended himself to me most courteously. As I appreciate organization and accuracy, and Renaldo was a master of both, it was my hope that we would work together smoothly in the future.

Assuming I had one, of course.

"I don't know," I replied. "What are they saying?"

"That you are the greatest and most audacious poisoner who has ever lived. You dared to kill the Pope and made it look natural."

I gasped and dropped the ledger. It clattered to the stone floor at my feet, where it remained as I was far too dumbstruck to pick it up.

"People are actually saying that? It is in the streets?" Were that true, it would mean disaster. Borgia's entire hope of the papacy rested on his viability as *papabile*. Had I truly gone to such terrible lengths—Rebecca remained ever in my thoughts—for nothing?

"Well . . . no," Lucrezia admitted reluctantly. She gave me a charming smile as though to excuse herself. "But I did wonder. *Papà* was becoming so impatient and now at last he has a chance to attain his dearest desire."

I exhaled, bent over, and retrieved the ledger. Clutching it, I said, "Listen to me, Lucrezia. Never, ever say again what you just did. Whatever you think, whatever you imagine, you must know that your father must never be suspected of having had a hand in Innocent's death."

"Of course I know that," she said, looking offended at the notion that I could think her so ignorant. "But just between us . . ."

"There is no 'between us,' not on this matter." Seeing her pout, I softened just a little. "But only on this. We can talk about anything else."

"Good," she said. "Then you will tell me who the handsome fellow is who waits for you in the courtyard."

"I have no idea who you mean—" But I did or at least I hoped, so wayward was what passes for my heart.

I went on a wave of trepidation, then forced myself to slow, intent on looking the soul of calmness and self-possession. But when I saw the man I had rejected as a husband yet who had stood with me through trials from which almost anyone else would have fled, I hurried forward to greet him.

"Rocco! Are you all right? What brings you here? Nando—?"

"My son is still in the country," he said. Looking down at me, he smiled, which I observed transformed his features, making him appear at once younger and carefree.

"I came to make sure that you are all right," he said. "A man at the palazzo, I think he was the steward, said that you were here. I hope you don't mind—"

"For Heaven's sake, Rocco, how could I mind? But tell me that nothing is wrong." I did not think I could bear it if anything was. He had risked so much at my careless behest, if I had brought him harm, I would never forgive myself.

He laughed, a sound I had heard so rarely that I paused to relish it, and looked toward Lucrezia. She stood off to one side, eyebrows raised, smiling broadly.

"Who is this, Francesca? Have you forgotten your manners? You must introduce us."

I did and Rocco sketched a more than credible bow. I could see that Lucrezia approved of him and that made me blush, which was ridiculous because obviously he must have sought me out on important business. It was not as though we were lovers, after all, and given to foolish fancies of the heart. Nothing at all like that.

"A glassmaker," she exclaimed. "How fascinating. I have often wondered how such marvels as I have seen are created. Perhaps you could show me?"

That was Lucrezia, seductress and charmer, but through all of it of good and kind heart.

Rocco laughed, amused by her but glad, too, I think that I had such a friend. For a moment, there in the sun-drenched courtyard, it was just the three of us, young and at ease.

It could not last, of course. But it was sweet while it did.

His smile faded as he recalled himself. Quietly, he said to me, "We must talk."

I nodded and looked to Lucrezia, who nodded in turn and vanished back into the palazzo, but not without a glance over her shoulder and a smile.

Rocco and I walked a little distance away, toward the fountain. "Guillaume came to see me," he said. "He is very worried."

"Was our presence at Santa Maria Sopra Minerva discovered?" I hated to think what would befall the gentle friar if it became known that he had given us shelter.

Rocco shook his head. "No, not at all. It is what he is hearing." He glanced around to be sure there was no one to overhear us, then said, "Torquemada is on his way to Rome."

I inhaled sharply. Of all the news I could have received at that moment, this was the worst. As though matters were not in sufficient foment, we must now bear the presence of Spain's Grand Inquisitor? One of the primary authors and supporters of the edict expelling the Jews? An implacable fanatic who made Morozzi look almost mild-mannered?

"Why? What purpose would he have in coming here now?"

"Guillaume isn't certain, but from what is being said in the chapter house, it sounds as though he is coming to make sure that the next pope is one who will be willing to act against the Jews."

"Then he comes to defeat Borgia."

Rocco looked skeptical. "Perhaps, but rumor has it that Ferdinand of Spain was on the verge of canceling the edict expelling the Jews in return for an immense payment from them. If the story is to be believed, just as the king was about to act, Torquemada burst in upon him, hurled a crucifix at the floor, and demanded to know if Ferdinand wanted to make himself into the new Judas. That was enough to stay his hand and ensure that the edict was enacted."

"Borgia is no Ferdinand." If Torquemada thought he could dissuade the Cardinal from taking the Jews' money by threat of eternal damnation, the Grand Inquisitor was in for a rude awakening. For all that he was a prince of the Church, Borgia was unabashedly worldly and secular. Some would go further and say he showed pagan tendencies, and they might not be entirely wrong. This was, after all, the man who had looked entirely at ease garbed as Jupiter.

"The Cardinal has utter contempt for Torquemada and everything he represents," I assured Rocco. "I have heard him say as much myself." And on more than one occasion. Borgia could be the most discreet and adroit of politicians, but on certain subjects he did not hesitate to speak his mind.

"Then you are right," Rocco said, "and he comes to defeat Borgia. If he and Morozzi are not already in league, they will be soon."

"The Cardinal must be warned." But in truth, it was likely that he already knew. Borgia had the finest intelligence service of anyone in Christendom, better than any pope, fellow cardinal, king, or prince. He took great pride in it, for all that he complained constantly about the cost. There was every chance that he had heard rumblings of Torquemada's plans before the Grand Inquisitor himself knew them fully.

Rocco nodded but his brow was furrowed. "Promise me that you will be careful, Francesca. Torquemada makes a very dangerous enemy."

He did not have to convince me of that. Only the previous year, the Dominican had accused eight Jews and *conversi* of crucifying a Christian child. Despite the complete absence of a body or any evidence that a crime had even taken place, the accused were all burned at the stake. Torquemada had proclaimed their deaths to be a great victory for Christ who, in my estimation, was more likely to have wept over them.

Clearly, the Grand Inquisitor had a taste for the flames and the agony they inflicted.

"I will be careful," I promised. "But I cannot hide from this." We were standing very close together in the courtyard of the palazzo. Nearby, the fountain burbled as hummingbirds swooped down to drink. It was an idyllic setting, so harshly at odds with our troubled times.

"I would that you could," Rocco said, and drew me closer.

Hardly aware of what I did, I cupped his face in my hands. "None of us can hide from what is happening," I said. "We can only hope to turn events in the right direction."

"I have other hopes," he said, and kissed me.

24

As all Rome awaited Innocent's funeral and entombment in the crypt beneath the main altar of Saint Peter's, Il Cardinale announced his intention to host a dinner party. Let us not go so far as to call it a celebration. It was merely an opportunity to solicit votes under more gracious circumstances than would be available once the conclave began.

I was far too caught up in preparations for the event to think about what the kiss Rocco and I had shared meant, assuming that it meant anything at all, which I told myself, repeatedly, it did not. More than ever, I was convinced that he deserved far better than I could give him. Indeed, knowing me as he did, I marveled that he did not see that.

In the midst of assuring the safety of everything the Cardinal would take into the conclave with him, and securing both of his households, and worrying over what Morozzi intended, and anticipating the Grand Inquisitor's arrival in Rome, and thinking about Rocco, and wondering when Cesare would arrive, as he surely would—

In the midst of all that, I went to Renaldo for help.

"I cannot manage this dinner party by myself," I told him when I had tracked him down to his burrow, a place he seemed of late to be avoiding.

Renaldo turned bright red, ducked his head, and peered up at the ceiling, bypassing my poor self. "It has nothing to do with me."

"It has everything to do with you! You are steward here. Ultimately, everything that happens in this household is your affair."

"It is a political matter," he tried weakly. I perceived from his expression that he would be pleased to be involved. But worried, as Renaldo always was.

"Someone may try to kill Borgia," I said. "Can you imagine what the consequences of that would be?"

Personally, I could not, the implications being so vast. But apparently Renaldo's imagination exceeded mine. He blanched, then nodded hastily.

"I will do anything I can, of course."

I set him to oversee the food and wine being delivered in vast quantities. "I will inspect everything," I assured him. "But it is vital that nothing slip by without my knowing."

He assured me solemnly that nothing would and I hurried off to examine the setting for the event, the courtyard being rapidly transformed to resemble a room in a Moorish palace. Like so many Spaniards, Borgia had a great fondness for the styles brought to that land by its infidel conquerors, only lately expelled by the *reconquista* of their Most Catholic Majesties, Ferdinand and Isabella. Given his nature, he no doubt would have enjoyed having four wives, assuming he could still have had his choice of concubines. As it was, he had to satisfy himself with a night of Moorish luxury.

And what a night it was to be. There were no limitations on pleasing the Cardinal's guests, yet given the circumstances, a certain decorum had to be maintained. Therefore, the "dancers" who would perform at the party would restrict their other activities to discreetly arranged assignations. So, too, would the acrobats, jugglers, musicians, and the sword-eater hired specially for the occasion, but I didn't particularly want to think about that.

Even so, they all had to be vetted, which would have been an impossible task given the shortness of the time available had they not been provided by the same *maestro dei maestri,* the impresario beloved of the Roman elite, who had he not been forced a few years hence to flee the city after a scandal involving a beautiful boy, might still be staging the extravagant entertainments beloved by all.

I found Petrocchio, as he styled himself, in the courtyard, where he was supervising the installation of a billowing tent complete with luxurious carpets and intricately carved tables and settees, the latter to be covered with plump pillows for the comfort of eminent behinds. Servants waved incense burners to scent the air and chase away the bugs. Musicians were arriving and tuning up. Acrobats were turning practice flips on the nearby grass. The overall effect was at once alien, chaotic, and enticing.

Petrocchio was a tall, stocky man with the girth of a *goloso,* one who loves his food too well, and the vocabulary of a dockworker. He was shouting curses at the workers struggling to erect the tent. So vivid was his invective that I paused for a moment in admiration. When he reached the point of describing exactly how the workers' mothers had coupled with apes, I interrupted.

"It seems to be going well," I said.

"Well! They're all idiots! I can't get anyone to do the slightest thing without—" He broke off, only belatedly noticing who had spoken. "Oh, it's you, Donna Francesca, a thousand apologies. You caught me at a bad moment, but be assured, everything will be as it should be."

"I'm sure it will. I just wanted to speak with you about the entertainers."

The Maestro wiped his face with a kerchief and managed a tight smile. "Yes, of course. Every one of them is known to me, obviously. All professionals I've used countless times. Not a novice among them and no one who might be contemplating retirement and looking for a large purse to finance it, if you take my meaning."

I assured him that I did before asking, "And they all understand . . . should anything untoward occur . . ." I paused delicately, confident that I need not say more.

Petrocchio blanched. He waved a hand for an assistant who ran up and put a flagon of chilled wine into it. When the Maestro had refreshed himself, he said, "Absolutely they understand, Donna Francesca. They are all, as I said, professionals. You have nothing to worry about, nothing whatsoever. You have my word on it."

Given that he had been the most successful and sought after impresario in Rome for almost ten years without a single incident to besmirch his name, I was reassured that the entertainment, at least, would pose no risks.

That only left the food, wine, and the guests themselves. The first two kept me busy the remainder of the day and earned me more enmity from Il Cardinale's chefs than I will be able to erase in a lifetime. On a more positive note, I acquired an impressive vocabulary of obscenities, which I still find useful on occasion.

The matter of the guests was more intractable. Renaldo reported that Borgia was being coy about who was coming, saying only that "various and sundry princes of the church and other personages" would be in attendance. I took that to mean that he wasn't absolutely sure who would accept his invitation and didn't want to admit as much. All well and good, but at some point, he and I were going to have a serious discussion about the need to keep me properly informed.

As the hours wore on, I could not shake off a sense of nervousness but attributed it to the circumstances. The dinner was the first large event I had supervised since obtaining my position. Naturally, I was concerned that everything go well. Between one thing and another, I barely had time to bathe and dress before returning to the courtyard moments before Il Cardinale descended to greet his guests. He had made it clear that my presence was required. Almost at once I discovered why.

Lucrezia was with her father. Understand, at this time the Cardinal was considered the soul of discretion when it came to his children. Never had he flaunted them, as certain other princes of the church were known to do, the late Innocent among them. Lucrezia and her three brothers, Cesare being the eldest, lived apart from him in their own households. Although the sons received preferential treatment, titles, and benefices to which they would otherwise have had no claim, most Romans could only speculate about their true relationship to Borgia, who claimed straight-facedly to be their uncle. All this was taken as evidence of Il Cardinale's good sense and, remarkably, even as a sign of his self-restraint.

Yet here was Lucrezia, looking excited and lovely, at twelve a child woman trembling on the brink of whatever future her father decreed for her.

"Francesca!" she exclaimed and rushed to hug me. "How marvelous you look! Those colors are very good for you."

I was wearing a mauve gown and topaz over robe, the gifts of my father at Easter. The last gifts I had received from him. I had worn them for courage, and because I had nothing else grand enough for the occasion.

Francesca was in royal blue embroidered with silver in perfect counterfoil to the golden fall of her hair. Had she stood perfectly still, she would have looked like a statue carved of ivory, precious metal, and gems, except for the slight flush of her cheeks and the eager rise and fall of her breath.

Turning, she gazed at her father with such adoration that it tore at my heart. "It is so good of *Papà* to allow me to come tonight, don't you think? My first truly grand party. He says I will be meeting many important men."

Oh, yes, I was certain that she would. One look at Borgia watching his only daughter with benign indulgence and I knew her true purpose in being there that night.

Il Cardinale was about to play for the greatest prize of all and Lucrezia—sweet, lovely Lucrezia—was merely one more chip for him to lay on the table.

"Stay with her," he said as he passed me, speaking under his breath so that she did not hear. "She will be seated next to Sforza. Make sure nothing untoward occurs."

Only Borgia would see nothing amiss in appointing his poisoner as doyenne to his daughter. Not that Madonna Adriana was absent; she was very much there in crimson silk draped with ropes of lustrous pearls, her head topped with a crown of golden plumes. She had just taken the hand and kissed the ring of— Did my eyes betray me? Was that youngish man with the watchful gaze and taut smile really Cardinal . . . ?

Professional discretion requires that I draw a veil over certain of the events of that evening, particularly as they concern personages who, though present, played no direct role in what unfolded. Suffice to say that it was an odd company that gathered at Borgia's table, made up of the great and greater, scions all of noble houses frequently at war with one another yet capable of amiability when it suited them.

No wonder Petrocchio, whom I glimpsed hovering nearby, had been so nervous. He, far better than I, swam in the river of rumor that floods Rome in every season. He, far better than I, had anticipated who would be attending. The Maestro and I shared a glance, mine no doubt shocked, his worldly and resigned. He went so far as to spread his hands and shrug as though to say, "What did you expect?"

"Open for business" was how Vittoro had put it, and clearly he was right. But Borgia's audacity went beyond mere opportunism. By gathering together so many powerful men at odds with one another, he could be seen as proclaiming his intent to end old feuds and heal old wounds. That was an outcome devotedly to be wished for by all of Christendom. Certainly, it would make Borgia the favorite of the Roman populace itself, usually the first to suffer from the internecine struggles of Holy Mother Church's princes.

Of course, there were also notable absences—della Rovere, naturally, and half a dozen cardinals most closely linked to him. Other cardinals were still en route to Rome and therefore could not have attended even if they had wished to. The remainder of those in attendance were bishops in positions of authority within the Curia, which was to say mainly Borgia's men, and a handful of clerics, well-positioned men assumed to be on the way up. Madonna Adriana, Lucrezia, and I were the only female guests.

"Isn't this wonderful?" Lucrezia whispered as we took our seats within the silk tent scented with jasmine and patchouli. The tables gleamed with gold place settings and the finest porcelain. Turkish carpets covered the ground underfoot. Footmen waited behind each chair to attend to us, spreading squares of the finest white linen across our laps and hastening to offer wine in goblets studded with precious gems.

"Incredible," I replied, though, truth be told, I spoke more to the sight of so many vain and ambitious men than to the unbridled luxury on display that night. With so many rivals and enemies gathered around the same table, I could only pray that no one would take the opportunity to slip something into a cup, onto a plate, or anywhere else. Done with proper finesse, such poisonings are all but impossible to detect in time to prevent their deadly effects. Moreover, if the culprit possesses sufficient daring, he can deflect suspicion by assuring that several others, himself included, receive a small dose of the poison, enough to appear also to be intended victims. A good show of vomit makes for an excellent alibi. But you have no need of such instruction and I should know better than to provide it.

As we were being seated, I had a chance to study Sforza, who was busy for the moment chatting with the bishop to his right. Rumor had it that the banquet the Cardinal had given for the Neapolitan prince Ferdinand of Capua several months before at His Eminence's palace in Trastevere was of such unbridled opulence and magnificence as to defy all description. Surely, Borgia had heard the same. I wondered how Il Cardinale would strive to outdo him.

The brother of the Duke of Milan was in his late thirties but looked younger. Although fit enough, he had a smooth, round face with a soft double chin. He was said to aspire to win the papacy for himself, but not even his brother's power could obscure the fact that he was far too young for serious consideration.

The danger in electing too young a pope is obvious. Not that he will prove inept—ability is at best a secondary qualification for the papacy, far less important than animal cunning—but that he will live too long, thereby denying others their own chance at the trough. Older men, preferably dissipated in their habits and not likely to live many more years, tend to be the favorites.

At sixty-one, Borgia should have had the advantage, but he was known to be in robust health and more vigorous than many men half his age. That would count against him.

Sforza had turned his attention to Lucrezia, who blushed prettily. He was asking her if she enjoyed music, and she was assuring him that she did when I remembered that the Cardinal was cousin to the young, and at the moment unmarried, Giovanni Sforza, lord of Pesaro and Gradara. If my memory served, he was in his mid-twenties, which would make him twice Lucrezia's age. Even by the standards of our time, she was still too young to wed, but she could certainly be betrothed—yet again—if her father willed it.

But ties of marriage alone could not possibly be enough to assure Sforza's support, especially considering how he coveted the papacy for himself. I was wondering what else Borgia would promise him as the first course—larks' tongues in honey—was set before us.

Such occasions being an opportunity for *maestri della cucina* to show off their most exotic skills, it is prudent to eat well before sitting down to table. The arrival of the larks' tongues signaled that we were in for an evening heavy with the likes of swan, porpoise, and boar stuffed with venison stuffed with suckling pig, a popular dish that season, although do not ask me why. Give me a good chicken any day. But I digress.

I was sipping a pleasant claret, slightly chilled and not too robust for the warm evening, when I happened to glance toward the entrance of the tent. Much as I like to think it was a mark of my strong nature that the goblet did not fall from my hand, in fact it was a near thing. I barely managed to set it down safely as I stared at the man who had just entered.

A few paces from Borgia, within easy reach of him, having apparently gotten past every guard in the palazzo, Father Bernando Morozzi stood smiling.

25

At the sight of Morozzi, a gasp escaped me. At once, I began to rise from my chair but in the same instant, my gaze caught Borgia's.

Il Cardinale shook his head and made a small but unmistakable gesture with his hand, telling me to sit down. I obeyed with utmost reluctance.

Morozzi went at once to Borgia's side, made the merest inclination of his head, and said, "A thousand apologies for my late arrival, Eminence. I was unavoidably delayed."

At once, all ears were on him, though almost everyone pretended otherwise. A mere priest, albeit one very well connected, "unavoidably" delayed and therefore late for a party hosted by the vice chancellor of the Curia who was, at least possibly, the next pope?

The sheer effrontery was breathtaking. Even so worldly and blasé an audience was shocked into attentive silence. Along with all the rest, I waited for the scalding lesson in manners that I was certain Borgia was about to deliver.

Instead, Il Cardinale smiled and said, "Nonsense, my son, no apology is necessary. Sit, enjoy yourself."

For a moment, Morozzi looked taken aback. Clearly, he had been prepared for a confrontation with the Cardinal and appeared chagrined to be denied it. Under the circumstances, he had no choice but to take the seat he was shown to, which, surely not by happenstance, was directly across from me.

We stared at each other. If Morozzi felt any unease at being seated at his enemy's table, he did not show it. His golden hair framed his face in perfect, unruffled curls any woman would envy. His features were smooth and unlined, his smile seemingly both pleasant and unforced. He truly did look like an angel.

Studying the priest, I found myself wondering how old he was. It has been my observation that the truly deranged appear to age more slowly than the rest of us. Some would take that as proof of an unholy pact to preserve youth. I have come to believe it is more likely evidence that nothing they do truly affects them. They lack the essential sense of connection that animates our consciences and writes the story of our lives, for good or ill, on our countenances. That, more than anything else, is what makes them so dangerous.

And what makes it so essential that we never yield to them.

I turned and spied Petrocchio who, ever quick to sense trouble where there should be none, was studying Morozzi as intently as I was. The Maestro caught my look and hastened over. He bent close so that we could speak privately.

"Do you know who he is?" I asked, prepared to tell him if need be, but as I had expected, Petrocchio's knowledge surpassed my own.

"I have heard rumors. He was very close to Innocent, procured the boys to be bled for him, so they say. What is he doing here?"

"That is for Borgia to know." And for me to find out at the earliest opportunity, but first— "This priest needs to be taken down a peg or two, I think."

"More than that," wise Petrocchio said, "but it will do for a start."

He straightened, nodding solemnly as though I had been instructing him. Conversation around the table had resumed but the Maestro spoke loudly enough for all to hear.

"Yes, Donna Francesca, of course. Just as you say, at once, Donna Francesca."

He hurried off, making a show of snapping his fingers at several servers, who sprang to attention and followed him.

Moments later, a golden plate was set before Morozzi. On it was a sampling of each of the delicacies served so far that evening. Next to it was placed a jewel-studded goblet filled with the same claret that I was enjoying. Petrocchio hovered nearby, as though to assure that all was done precisely right.

Morozzi stiffened, looking from me to the delicacies and back again. An expression of wariness, even of fear, flitted across his handsome features. Surely I would not dare to attack him in so direct a manner, in front of so many prelates of the Church and in the presence of Borgia himself?

And yet, I was the woman who had gone into the *castel* to kill the Pope. And come back out again alive.

It was my turn to smile.

The entertainment began, the acrobats appearing first to appreciative applause. They were followed by jugglers, a fellow with a pair of trained monkeys, and the sword swallower. The monkeys in particular, fascinated me. Dressed in the exaggerated style favored by wealthy merchants who some say aspire to rule their betters, they hurried about, setting up a table for themselves, then sat down and dined with as much aplomb as many people I have seen.

Meanwhile, course followed upon course—*maccheroni* cooked in capon stock and flavored with saffron, eggs baked with spinach, grilled sardines wrapped in grape leaves, snails sautéed in wine, pickled eels, roasted heron, on and on and on, all accompanied by the superb wines of Tuscany and Liguria.

Through it all, Morozzi did not eat, nor did he drink. He did not so much as touch anything on the table before him. His hands remained out of sight, in his lap. Each course was brought to him, each taken away intact. So complete was his abstinence that Lucrezia broke off charming Sforza to voice her concern.

"Is the food not to your liking, Father?" she asked. I will swear with absolute certainty that she had no idea who he was. It was enough that he was a guest, therefore his comfort mattered to her. Anyone who has had the pleasure of supping at Lucrezia's table will tell you that she is always the most caring and attentive hostess.

Her innocent inquiry only heightened Morozzi's unease and drove him to answer rashly. His voice overly loud, he said, "I find it impossible to sup so grandly mere days after the death of our beloved Holy Father."

Had he emitted a loud and gaseous fart, he could not have more clearly pronounced himself a boor before such worldly company. A ripple of laughter went round the table, followed by the deliberate averting of eyes, as though from a display too embarrassing to be borne.

Realizing his mistake, Morozzi flushed. I did not help matters by making a show of tucking into my own food with rather more enthusiasm than I actually felt. Not that it wasn't delicious—some of it was—it was just that anyone foolish enough to indulge too heartily would regret it come morning. Either that or they would be following the old Roman custom and vomiting in the bushes.

"You must try this," I said to Lucrezia at one point and slid a slice a Bolognese tart onto her plate. She agreed that it was very good and encouraged me in turn to try the stuffed mushrooms, which I have to say were excellent.

The sword swallower withdrew to cheers and for a moment, silence fell. Into the sudden quiet came the soft, sinuous whisper of a flute, followed by the beat of a tabor. The music rose, grew more insistent, and suddenly the dancers were there, running lightly into the tent and taking up their positions where all could see them.

There were a dozen, mostly women but with three men, the latter with lithe, muscular bodies of breathtaking beauty. The women were wrapped in diaphanous fabrics that hid very little. The men were naked save for calfskin pouches holding their privates.

They danced . . . how shall I describe it? They evoked with the movement of their bodies the delight that comes to men and women alike with seduction's chase, the sweet moment of mutual surrender, and the triumphant joy that follows hard upon it. They moved with power that must, I suppose, be part of God's vision for us yet that seems to exist completely apart from the everyday world. They became, in the dance, more than merely human but something that soared above all mortal limits to become, dare I say it, one with creation itself.

They were very . . . exciting.

Mindful of my responsibilities, I tore my eyes away long enough to observe the guests. By then the wine had been flowing for several hours and all except Morozzi had partaken. If I was not alone in doing so sparingly, few had been equally cautious.

Sforza was leaning back in his chair, watching the performance intently. His breathing appeared somewhat ragged and I concluded that he would be visiting his mistress that night, whichever one he was currently keeping. Madonna Adriana was flushed, Lucrezia showed the expected unease of a virgin, and Borgia . . . Il Cardinale reclined in his chair, so heavy-lidded that he might have been thought to be all but asleep. It took me a moment to realize that his appearance notwithstanding, he was fully awake, but his attention was not on the dancers. It was on Morozzi.

The priest sat bolt upright in his chair. His face was red and he appeared . . . surely this could not be so? He appeared to be moving his hands urgently under the table.

I stared at him, first uncomprehending, then incredulous. His eyes, burning with the light of madness, met mine. In them, I saw a distillation of perverted passion and malignant pleasure such as I have never witnessed in another person in all the years since. For just an instant, pity rose up in me. It vanished in a wave of repugnance as the intimacy of his gaze filled me with a sense of violation.

I turned away, fighting nausea. My hand trembled as I reached for my goblet and took a little wine in hope of steadying myself. In desperate need of distraction, I looked again at the other guests. No one else appeared to have noticed him, so engrossed were they in the dancers. No one, that is, save Borgia, who continued to watch the priest from beneath half-shuttered eyes, only now with a faint smile.

The dance finished and so, apparently, did Morozzi, although I cannot say that he appeared to have found any relief. To applause, the dancers ran off to prepare for whatever assignations awaited them. I took several deep breaths. The priest had shaken me more than I would have thought possible. Having survived the confrontation in the *castel,* I had been buttressed by a sense of confidence that I now realized I could not afford. Morozzi's madness put him outside the bounds of normal human behavior and made him unpredictable. That, more than anything else, was his greatest strength and the most daunting obstacle I faced in overcoming him.

The music continued but more sedately. With the change of mood came the *dragée,* intended to close the meal and promote good digestion. Spicy hypocrase was poured and plates of sugared almonds offered around along with a selection of aged cheeses and fresh figs and oranges. There were marzipan cakes, sherbet flavored with rose petals, and my favorite, Turkish hats, the familiar name for fried tubes of pastry erupting with frothy cheese. Ordinarily, I enjoy a good Turkish hat, but that night they had lost their appeal.

The hour being very late, the air had cooled, reviving the guests somewhat. Tomorrow, they could return to being rivals, even enemies, but at the moment they laughed warmly when Borgia rose and made a little speech, something to the effect that friendship was one of God's greatest gifts and that we should all cultivate our friends as we cultivate our gardens. I only half-listened but I had the impression that it was well done.

As he spoke, servants appeared carrying gold—not gilded, they were made of solid gold lattice strips woven together as I discovered when I examined one—baskets filled with an assortment of thoughtful gifts for each guest. I glimpsed gem-studded penknives, crystal vials of rare oils, and most remarkable, miniature mechanical automata in the shape of birds that, when wound by the tiny key in their backs, flapped their wings and moved their heads. This last marvel provoked such delight that several prelates and princes were still playing with them as they took their leave, seen out by a beaming Borgia, who, having thrown off his heavy-lidded posture, appeared as fresh and energetic as though he had slept the night away.

Morozzi did not receive a basket, nor did he take his leave of Borgia, rather he endeavored to slip away into the darkness. I say endeavored because he was followed by Vittoro, who had appeared from the shadows just beyond the tent where I realized he must have been since Morozzi's arrival. I was comforted to know that he would assure the mad priest's departure from the palazzo.

Lucrezia was almost asleep on her feet as she embraced her father and thanked him warmly for allowing her to attend. Sforza stood just behind her. I saw the look that passed between the two men. Saw, too, that after she had left with Madonna Adriana, the cardinals walked a little distance away and had a few private words under the trees. Then Sforza, too, departed and Borgia went inside.

Petrocchio was slumped on a settee, a goblet in one hand and a leg of capon in the other, wearily overseeing the cleanup. I sat down beside him.

"It went very well," I said.

"It did, praise God. No thanks to that lunatic. Did you *see* what he did?"

I grimaced. "Unfortunately. What else do you know of him?"

The Maestro sighed, took a drink, and said, "He appeared two years ago, some say from Genoa, where he may have had family ties to Innocent, others say from Florence. He had a minor post in the papal household at first but he rose quickly in influence. It is said that he gained power over the Pope by promising him the secret to long life."

"And Innocent was fool enough to believe him?"

"More likely desperate enough. At any rate, with Innocent gone, he will be casting about for a new patron."

Petrocchio had said nothing of the edict or Morozzi's involvement with it. That confirmed my belief that it had been seen as so explosive even the rumor-ridden Curia had kept it secret. All the same, I probed a little further.

"Have you heard anything about Morozzi and the Jews?"

The Maestro shot me a look of surprise. "What do you mean? Are you saying—?"

"I am only wondering if he could be *converso*." Morozzi had, after all, claimed to be, but I had dismissed that as no more than a ploy on his part to win my trust.

Petrocchio's response confirmed that I had been right to do so. "Lord, that would be rich! But no, I've never heard it. There are always rumors of *conversi* within the Curia, of course, just as there are rumors of two-headed calves being born. I don't take one any more seriously than the other."

He tossed the stripped capon leg into the darkness and leaned toward me confidingly. "Speaking of *conversi,* have you heard the latest that della Rovere is putting about?"

When I shook my head, he grew serious. "He is saying that Borgia is *marano*."

A pig. A filthy swine. A secret Jew only pretending to be a Christian. To call a man or woman a *converso* was to cast doubt on the sincerity of their commitment to Christianity. But to label anyone *marano* was to throw that person into the doomed company of heretics and witches.

"Della Rovere is declaring war," I said. The conclusion was unmistakable.

Petrocchio sighed. "It will get worse before it gets better, mark my words. I'm thinking of going to the country for a while." He looked at me. "You would be wise to do the same."

I rose and gave him what smile I could muster. "Not while Borgia remains in Rome."

The Maestro gave me a sympathetic nod. He waved over an assistant, who helped him rise. "Seriously, Donna Francesca," he said as he prepared to leave. "Don't underestimate the forces arrayed against your master. More than a few of the cardinals are determined not to let a Spaniard take the papal throne. Even more fear Borgia himself. They suspect him of wanting to found a dynasty to surpass all the other families. There are even rumors that he dreams of uniting all of Italia under the rule of a line of Borgia popes."

I had not heard this but it did not surprise me. Ten years of living under Il Cardinale's roof had left me with no doubt that he was a man of boundless appetites and ambitions.

"Would unity be so bad?" I asked. It was a question I have pondered over the years. Divided as we are into city-states, minor kingdoms, duchies, and the like, we here in Italia are prey to the whims of our more powerful neighbors, France and Spain most particularly. Yet I remain of two minds as to what an end to our divisions would mean. In our distinctness lies the opportunity to find different paths, try different ways, and, just perhaps, throw off the oppression of fear and superstition. Unity under the wrong leader—and how often have we found the right one?—could destroy all that.

"Who knows?" Petrocchio said. He leaned on his young assistant, who bore his weight stoically. "Only don't count on anyone letting Borgia achieve it. Keep him alive, if you can. Help him become pope, if such is God's will. But never underestimate his enemies."

And so he went, the master entertainer who masked reality so brilliantly even as he saw it more clearly than most of us ever will.

I lingered a while longer in the courtyard, attempting to gather my thoughts. The first gray light of dawn crept up in the east but lamps still burned in the windows of Borgia's office. Il Cardinale found rest no more easily than I did.

Having delayed as long as I could, I went inside and shortly climbed the steps to seek him out.

26

A wiser woman would have gone to bed. Left the matter for another day. Thought twice and again before approaching Il Cardinale.

I was young and determined, and not entirely sober.

The double doors leading to Borgia's offices were unguarded and slightly ajar. I slipped between them and entered the clerks' chamber. Their high desks were covered with neatly stacked files and ledgers awaiting attention. Nearby, a counting table held a large abacus built into its surface, the fist-sized beads shiny with use. On the far side of the room, an inner door led to the reception area where I had waited on my first visit. Eve and the serpent still cavorted merrily. Beyond, the door to the inner sanctum stood open. On the far side of it, I saw the lamplight I had glimpsed from the courtyard.

Borgia was at his desk. He sat well back in his chair, his face in shadows. For a moment, I thought he was asleep. Were he, I would have left him undisturbed, one insomniac's consideration for another. But just as I thought of withdrawing, he stirred.

"There you are," he said, as though he was expecting me. Borgia being Borgia, that may well have been the case.

The Cardinal had cast off his robes and was in a loose shirt and trousers. When he straightened, I could see that the lines around his eyes and mouth appeared deeper than usual. For once, he looked his age, or close to it.

"Did Petrocchio get off all right?" You may think the question odd, but Borgia had a keen appreciation for the role appearance plays in winning and keeping power. He valued the Maestro highly.

"He did," I said. "He was relieved that all went well."

"I thought it did," Borgia agreed. "What is your opinion?"

I came a few steps closer. A flagon of wine and two goblets sat on the desk. One of the goblets was half empty. I had not known him to be a solitary drinker, but undoubtedly there were many aspects of his character to which I was not privy.

"You must know what I think," I said. "Why was Morozzi here?"

Borgia gave a dry laugh and leaned forward, resting his elbows on the desk. He stared off into the shadows, as though he could find the answer in them.

"I suppose I invited him. That must be it, don't you think?"

"Are you mad?"

Granted, it was not the most politic question. Not remotely so. But it was how I felt, exhausted as I was after all that had happened and all too aware that the greatest danger still lay ahead.

"Not so far as I know," Borgia replied with far greater mildness than I deserved. As though that was not magnanimity enough, he gestured to the chair in front of the desk. "Sit, Francesca."

Emboldened by his tolerance, and feeling an unexpected affection for him because of it, I did as I was bid. The litany of my complaints, simmering since the moment I looked across the tent and saw the mad priest standing so perilously close to the man I was supposed to protect, boiled out of me.

"I am your poisoner or I am not," I said with great earnestness. "You trust me to see to your security or you do not. To invite Morozzi here and not even to warn me that you were doing so . . ." I shook my head. "I cannot begin to understand why you would do such a thing."

Borgia waved a hand in the direction of the books that filled the floor-to-ceiling shelves along one wall of the office. Most were handwritten manuscripts, some centuries old. Others were products of the new printing presses that lately seemed to be appearing everywhere. He was a great lover of books, although he never had as much time to read as he would have liked.

"What is it Terence says? *Auribus tenere lupum.*"

I was not surprised that he found the words to describe his situation not in Holy Writ but in the works of a Roman slave manumitted in recognition of his genius as a playwright. Still, I was startled by his acknowledgment of the seriousness of the matter.

"Truly, you do hold a wolf by the ears," I said. "Let it go and it will devour you. But Morozzi—"

The Cardinal waved away my concern before I could fully voice it. "I have found," he said, "that the best way to know a man is to put him under pressure and see how he reacts, don't you agree?"

"I suppose, but—"

"Morozzi could have declined my invitation. What does it tell us that he did not, that in fact he came as he did, making a show of his insolence? Does it mean that he is vain and overly confident, the kind of man who, given the rope, will find a way to hang himself?"

"Perhaps but—"

"Or does it tell us that he believes he has reason for such confidence? That, in short, he has a plan he believes cannot fail?"

"A plan to kill you?" As the old Romans said, *in vino veritas*. My tongue seemed to have acquired a will of its own.

Before I could regret my frankness, Borgia poured wine into a second goblet and slid it across the desk to me.

"That would seem the logical conclusion," he said.

My concern for sobriety faded before the implacable truth of what we faced. I drank deeply before I spoke again.

"Morozzi is in possession of a deadly poison." I had delayed as long as I could in confessing this. To wait another moment would be a dereliction of my duty. Yet the admission cost my pride dearly.

The Cardinal raised a brow. "How do you know that?"

"Because I made it before I went into the *castel*. It was for my own use, if need be, carried in a locket that was a gift from my father."

"You were willing to kill yourself if you were captured?" He looked surprised, as though he had not considered that I would go so far.

"I reasoned that I would die under torture, but not before I was made to talk. Therefore, it was better to die first."

Unspoken between us was the specter of medallion man, who had perished in just the manner I had feared.

"A sensible conclusion . . ." Borgia said. "Yet one most people cannot face."

"Perhaps because they lack familiarity with the means of accomplishing death." And perhaps because they feared for their immortal souls thanks to the teachings of the Church he himself represented. The same Church so inclined these days to impose its will through torture and terror.

"At any rate, before we went, Morozzi insisted that I show him how I intended to kill the Pope. Rather than tell him the truth, I showed him what was in the locket. When he trapped us, he snatched it from me."

"When he trapped you and the Jew?"

"His name is David ben Eliezer." That he had a name, that he was a man, that he mattered, all had to be acknowledged by someone. The task seemed to fall to me.

Borgia shrugged. "I know what his name is and I know what he intends. An uprising in the Jewish Quarter is a lunatic plan."

That stung, all the more so because I could not deny it. I could only take refuge in the obvious. "Desperate people do desperate things."

"The Jews are right to be desperate. They stand on the knife's edge. If I do not become pope, it is likely they will face destruction here and throughout Christendom."

"Because Morozzi will convince whoever does become pope to sign the edict?"

Borgia refilled both our goblets and drank again before he answered. The wine seemed to make him loquacious.

"The edict against the Jews is only the most obvious sign of something much greater. The world that has existed for centuries, the only world we know, is on the brink of vast change."

His gaze fastened on me. "That is necessary and good, but there are many who want to keep the world as it is. They see change as a mortal threat and they are right to do so, for it will sweep them away."

To hear clearly what I had fumbled toward in my own inchoate reasoning was to see a candle lit in darkness.

"How far will they go to protect themselves?" I asked.

Borgia shrugged. "As far as they must. The Jews will be only the first to die. Their blood will cement the mortar that entombs us all."

Bile rose in the back of my throat. For a moment, I was enclosed in the wall, watching helplessly as the torrent of blood drowned my world.

"What can we do?"

Borgia emptied his goblet, set it down on the desk, and said, "We can make me pope, Francesca. Nothing else will serve."

"Della Rovere—"

"May have his turn, God help us, after I am dead and gone, but not until then. By heaven, not until then!"

He slammed his fist down on the desk so that the goblet and flagon both jumped from the force. As, for that matter, did I.

"Is Morozzi his creature?" I asked when I had caught my breath.

"So della Rovere believes, but he is wrong. Morozzi is the Devil's own and no one else's."

A breeze blew through the windows, setting the lamps to flickering. Light moved across his face, receded, and returned again.

"Another of his kind comes nigh," he said. "Are you aware of that?"

"Torquemada." The name scalded my tongue.

Borgia nodded. "I want you to go to the Jews and convince them not to do anything foolish. They must wait with patience and with faith. I will prevail, I swear it. But if they allow Torquemada to provoke them, they cannot look to me for help."

"I will try—"

"You must do better than that, and Francesca . . ."

I waited, bracing myself for whatever more was to come.

"Had you told me that Morozzi was your contact in the Pope's household, I could have warned you of him. You chose to keep that small bit of information to yourself and that almost led to disaster. You must never do anything of the sort again."

He was right, of course. I had no defense, although I did try to muster one.

"Without Morozzi, I would have had no way to reach Innocent. Surely, it was worth the risk?"

"Does that mean you killed him?"

Had I slain God's anointed Vicar on earth, the heir of Saint Peter and Moses, a small, despicable man set on perpetrating a great horror? Or had I not? Having acted to kill him, did it make any difference whether I had succeeded or failed? Was I damned either way?

"I don't know."

"And that matters to you?

The mockery I thought I heard pricked me. "Of course it matters! I believe I found a way to kill that would appear entirely natural. I tried to expose Innocent to it. Of all that, I am truly guilty. But whether I brought about his death or not, I just don't know. It is possible that he would have died when he did without my interference."

"It is also possible that you did God's work. Has that occurred to you?"

"No," I said honestly. "God has a thousand ways . . . a hundred thousand . . . to strike down a man without involving me."

"And you would prefer not to be involved?"

"Of course I would prefer it! Have you no care at all for my soul?"

Even then I knew the question was absurd. A few old men might cling to their mitres and mumble their prayers, but they were a dying breed. It was the new men like Borgia who were the Church now. They had transformed it into a mimers' play filled with posturing and pretense, a performance to distract the rabble while they went about their worldly business out of sight.

Where was the shepherd to stand against such wolves?

Borgia sighed deeply. "Do you want absolution? If that is it, you have only to say so."

"You cannot—"

"Of course I can. I am a prince of Holy Mother Church. I have the power to wash away sin. Or do you not believe that?"

If I did not, I was a heretic.

"Only say the words and you shall be forgiven." He looked at me closely, waiting.

"I cannot—"

"Why not, Francesca? Why can't you?"

Why could I not kneel before him, repent of my sins, and receive the blessing of God's forgiveness?

Ego te absolvo a peccatis tuis, in nomine Patris et Filii et Spiritus Sancti. Amen

"Because I am not sorry. Afraid, yes, for my soul's sake, but I cannot ask God to forgive me for what I truly do not regret."

He nodded, as though I had given him the answer he wanted. But he was not done yet. "Is there any other reason?"

Only one that I could think of and that was the darkest of all. My eyes burned. I blinked back tears. "Because I will kill again."

"Morozzi?"

I nodded. For my father, for David and Sofia and Benjamin, for the madness he wanted to unleash on all of us, I could not rest until the priest was dead.

"Morozzi for certain but others as well. God knows who they are. I do not, at least not yet."

"And this troubles you?" Just then, Borgia sounded almost like a priest. Certainly, he had drawn a confession from me that I had never intended to make.

"Yes, Eminence, it troubles me greatly."

He sighed again and leaned forward. "Kneel, Francesca."

Confused, I stared at him. He pointed to the floor in front of his chair. "Kneel and accept God's mercy. He loves us more than you know."

It was the wine. It was the hour. It was my heart, heavy as a stone dragging me down.

I knelt, my face wet, and lifted my head to see Borgia make the sign of the cross above me. As though from a great distance, I heard him.

"I absolve you from your sins in the name of the Father, and of the Son, and of the Holy Spirit. Amen."

I was and I remain a doubter; it is my curse. Yet in that predawn world, I discovered a truth I had not suspected. Whether by my own desperate need or just perhaps by divine intervention acting even through so deeply flawed a man, I found comfort and meaning in the act of forgiveness.

I rose Borgia's instrument and, I longed to believe, God's.

27

After my encounter with the Cardinal, there was no point in going to bed. Instead, I bathed and changed before leaving the palazzo. With Vittoro staying close to Borgia, I was accompanied once again by Jofre, the young guardsman who, having been duly chastised, was released from latrine duty to keep an eye on me. I felt a need to keep an eye on him as well, for, once inside the ghetto, the hand gripping his sword showed a tendency to twitch.

"There is nothing to be afraid of," I said. Of necessity, we went very slowly. With the edict expelling Spain's Jews about to go into final effect, the Jewish Quarter was even more crowded than before. The wealthier refugees, those who had managed to smuggle out gold or gems, found shelter behind the discreet walls of the merchants' houses, but for most the streets were their new home.

"We're perfectly safe here," I insisted, and truly I felt that way.

The ghetto was no longer an alien world to me, but beyond that, I knew that amid so many watchful eyes, my association with Sofia and David could not have gone unnoticed. I doubted that anyone would want to raise the ire of either of them by troubling us.

Jofre, of course, had no way of knowing that. He looked at me as though I were a madwoman. When we reached the apothecary shop and he saw the usual crowd gathered there, the color drained from his face. In the hope that the relatively fresher air would keep him on his feet, I set him to wait outside and went to find Sofia.

She was in the workroom preparing herbs. Seeing me, she pulled out a stool from under the table and gestured me onto it.

"You look terrible," she said.

I sat gratefully. Confession might be good for the soul but it seemed to wreak havoc on the body. Although, to be fair, perhaps a surfeit of rich food and far more drink than was good for me were the real culprits.

"I haven't been sleeping well." It was the simplest explanation and the only one I was prepared to give.

Sofia broke off what she had been doing to prepare a tea from fennel, dandelion, and mugwort. She ignored my protestations and set it before me to brew, then took a seat and eyed me narrowly.

"We have won a reprieve. I thought you would be glad."

Rather than tell her how far any semblance of happiness was from my troubled heart, I said only, "We must make sure that it is not just a temporary one. Do you know where David is?"

"I can make a few guesses. I'll send Benjamin to find him, if you like."

"Please. I need to talk with him."

She rose to see to it but not without a further admonition. "You also need to drink your tea. Don't let it get cold."

I drank and, after an initial impulse to retch, I did feel a little better. David arrived a short while later. He took one glance at me and shook his head.

"It was as bad as that?"

"What was bad?" Sofia asked. She busied herself crushing dried shepherd's purse with a mortar and pestle. I recognized the plant as one of those I had brought at her behest. Applied correctly, it restricts bleeding and can be very useful with wounds.

David sat and stretched out his long legs. He was unshaven and red-eyed, a good indication that he, too, had been up all night. Benjamin settled on his haunches near the door. I suspected he was making himself as unobtrusive as possible so that no one would notice him, but I lacked the will to send him away.

"The Cardinal's dinner party," David replied. "He's wasting no time spending our money." He looked to me. "Is it true the better part of the College of Cardinals was there?"

"Yes, and so was Morozzi."

David's gaze turned cold. "Why would Borgia allow him under his roof?"

"Something about taking his measure under pressure. I don't think it really matters. There are larger issues." I took a breath and said, "Torquemada is coming to Rome."

Sofia and David exchanged a glance. "Yes," he said, "we know."

I had expected as much. Borgia had his intelligence service, but the Jews had thousands of exiles streaming out of Spain. Certainly, word of the Grand Inquisitor's plans would travel with them.

"Borgia counsels patience." In point of fact, he had ordered it, but I saw no reason to stress that. "He cautions against any action on your part that could play into Torquemada's hands."

David was silent for several moments. Finally, he looked at me and said, "This is not La Guardia. The Cardinal must understand that. Under no circumstances will we allow Torquemada to do what he did there."

Despite the warmth of the day, a shiver ran through me. La Guardia was the Spanish town in which the Grand Inquisitor had claimed to uncover the crucifixion by Jews of a Christian child with the intent to use his heart in a ritual meant to poison the local water supply. Without evidence except what he could obtain under the most excruciating torture, he brought nine Jews and *conversi* to the flames. He had also used the alleged crime to convince Their Most Catholic Majesties, Ferdinand and Isabella, to issue their edict. In a real sense, all the Jews of Spain were the victims of La Guardia, and of Torquemada himself.

"You must have faith in Il Cardinale," I replied, the injunction more for myself as for them. "He understands the gravity of the situation full well and he will do everything necessary to ensure his victory." I saw no reason to mention that this included bartering his daughter in marriage and taking his sworn enemies to his bosom.

"Good," David said. "He has been paid to Heaven and beyond. Now let us see him earn it." He looked at me directly. "Tell him that, Francesca, and make sure he understands. He cannot ride to the papacy through our blood. If we fall, so does he."

Perhaps it was because Sofia's vile tea had not entirely banished my queasiness. Or perhaps sleeplessness was responsible for my ill temper. Whatever the cause, I answered him harshly.

"It is bad enough to be Borgia's messenger, I will not be yours as well. Tell him yourself."

"And where shall I do that?" David demanded. "Shall I stroll into his office at the Curia as you can do, or perhaps he'd like to invite me to dinner at his palazzo? Or better yet, I could invite him here. Sofia, you wouldn't mind, would you? You can rustle up something to please the Cardinal's palate, can't you?"

"David . . ." she began, but I interrupted. My patience, never in great supply, had evaporated.

"You have made your point," I said. "Now hear mine. Whatever you think of Borgia, he is right about this. Torquemada is coming to prevent the election of a pope who can be seen as favoring the Jews. Nothing less would get him out of Spain right now. The question is, with so little time left before the conclave, how can he possibly hope to assure that Borgia does not win?"

"You're going to say that he means to incite us—" David said.

But in fact I was not. Thoughts that had drifted in the back of my mind since I learned of the Grand Inquisitor's approach were coming to the fore now that I was finally able to give them the attention they deserved.

"Why would he think you can be incited at all?" I asked. Without realizing it, I had fallen into Borgia's habit of asking questions in order to work out puzzles. "Have Jews ever risen in rebellion, as you threaten to do here?"

Slowly, David shook his head. "There has been talk—"

"But no action. For centuries, Jews all over Europe have kept their heads down and suffered quietly no matter what is done to them. You want to change that, don't you? You want to show that killing Jews carries a price. Isn't that so?"

"You know it is but—"

"I think I understand what Francesca is saying," Sofia interjected. "Borgia knows what we intend, so do perhaps a handful of others. But Torquemada would never believe it. Given his experience with us, he'd be more likely to laugh at the notion that we would defend ourselves."

"Then why is he here?" I asked. "If he isn't planning to incite an uprising in the ghetto—"

"He is planning to incite the Christians," David said. "Just as he did in La Guardia. The result is the same. We will not allow that to happen here."

"But it won't," Sofia said slowly. "It can't. La Guardia took Torquemada almost two years. He had to work that long to convince the authorities to condemn those he claimed were guilty, and then he was only able to do it by subjecting the accused to extended torture. He doesn't have time for that now."

"Then what can he hope to achieve—?" David began.

"What did he not have in La Guardia?" I asked and answered in the same breath. "There was no body. For all the claim that a Christian child had been crucified, there was no proof. There wasn't even a rumor of a missing child."

My gaze drifted to Benjamin, who was watching us all attentively. Benjamin, a child who made his way in the streets like so many other abandoned or orphaned children, boys and girls alike, but ironically enough, one who would be protected in this incidence because he bore the mark of the covenant of Abraham on his body. Benjamin could never be mistaken for a Christian child and that was what Torquemada would need.

"My God . . ." Sofia murmured and pressed a hand to her lips.

Even David paled. That a priest would engineer the ritual murder of a child to achieve his perverted ends appeared too much for him.

But not for me for whom the idea had a clarity that made it indisputable.

"Not even Torquemada could arrive in Rome and within days perpetrate such a crime," I said, my mind racing ahead. "He has to have an ally, someone who is already here and prepared to act."

As one, David and Sofia said, "Morozzi."

I nodded. "It must be. With all he has to occupy him right now in Spain, how likely is it that the Grand Inquisitor would come all the way to Rome at his own initiative? Morozzi must be in contact with him."

"If the edict had been signed, Torquemada would be here to celebrate it," David said slowly. "Along with the edict in Spain, it would be a great triumph for those who seek our destruction. But with it as yet unsigned . . ."

"And awaiting the hand of a new pope," I finished his thought. "With all that, Morozzi has every reason to want the most famous Jew hater of our age nearby to lend his name and prestige to assuring Borgia's defeat."

I stood, clear now on what had to happen very quickly. "I must get word to Rocco. He can reach Friar Guillaume. Torquemada will be staying at the Dominican chapter house. Somehow we have to discover exactly what he and Morozzi intend, and how to stop them."

David was also on his feet. He appeared to have shaken off most, if not all, of his shock and was working out for himself what had to be done.

"We are not without our own resources," he said, and by that I suspected he meant *conversi* throughout Rome who, for the sake of maintaining their anonymity, could be pressured to cooperate with him. "I will find out everything I can."

Benjamin was at his side and looking at me solemnly. "So will I." He nodded in the direction of the gate leading from the ghetto. "Out there, no one knows I'm Jewish. Around the Campo, everywhere they think I'm just another street kid like them. If anyone's missing, I'll hear about it."

"Morozzi was recruiting boys to be bled for Innocent," I said. "If he could do that, he can—"

"Can Vittoro get someone inside the *cantoretti* school to keep a watch on the boys there?" David asked.

"If not he," I replied, "Borgia himself will have to do it."

Off in the distance, beyond the ghetto, I heard the bells tolling terce. The morning was aging and would soon be gone. In four days the cardinals were due to be sealed in conclave. Before then Morozzi had to convince the people of Rome to rise up against the Jews.

To do that, he had to kill a child.

"We have very little time," I said, and went out quickly, gathering the startled Jofre in my wake as I sped back to the palazzo.

By evening we had learned a great deal. But not enough.

Thanks to Friar Guillaume, we knew that Torquemada was in Rome. The Grand Inquisitor had arrived quietly that same day and was installed in the Dominican chapter house next to Santa Maria Sopra Minerva, ironically enough where David and I, with Rocco's help, had found sanctuary after our escape from the *castel*.

Rocco himself brought the news of Torquemada's whereabouts. He found me in the courtyard near the guards' quarters, where I had gone to speak with Vittoro. Amid the bustle of armed men and harried servants, we stole a small measure of privacy in the shadows of the loggia.

I had not seen Rocco since our last meeting at the palazzo. The memory of the kiss we had shared caused me to miss the first few words he spoke.

". . . slipped into Rome with only a dozen or so companions. They were disguised as friars arriving for the conclave. Since reaching the chapter house, Torquemada has not ventured outside but he has received visitors."

"Was Morozzi among them?" I asked, hastily recalling myself to the matter at hand.

"He was not, but Guillaume recognized two who came as members of della Rovere's household."

My stomach tightened. If Borgia's great rival was throwing in his lot with Torquemada, Il Cardinale stood in even greater danger than I had feared.

"I must tell His Eminence of this," I said. But before doing so, I lingered a moment longer, studying the man who put himself at such risk on behalf of people he had no particular reason to care about, including the woman who had rejected him.

"You have done enough and more," I said. "But now it might be wise for you to join Nando in the countryside." I thanked God that Rocco had had the foresight to send his son to safety.

He smiled and touched a hand gently to my cheek. It did not occur to me to move away, so preoccupied was I in looking at him. He was a handsome man, not in the way of mercurial Cesare or the false angel, Morozzi, but with a calm steadiness that sat well upon him and shown in everything he did. The creations he drew from fire and air were possessed of great delicacy, but I was coming to realize that the man himself was as an oak, unshakable in the greatest storm.

"My son is a child, Francesca. I am a man. I will be here to see this through."

Rather than risk speaking just then, and likely making a fool of myself, I squeezed his hand and nodded. A moment longer we lingered before the tug of the world, unrelenting in its demands, drew us apart. Even so, I watched Rocco go from the courtyard until he was lost from my sight. Only then did I seek out Borgia to tell him what I had learned.

"Damn Giuliano," the Cardinal said when I informed him of Torquemada's visitors. "Are there no depths to which he will not sink?" This from the man who had cheerfully solicited the death of a pope.

Of necessity, my suspicions regarding Torquemada and Morozzi's intentions had been revealed to Il Cardinale. He heard me out in silence, grunting once or twice, before pronouncing his verdict.

"Your father would be proud of you."

Startled, I said, "How so? He never wanted this life for me." To the contrary, he had wanted a husband I could accept and grandchildren he could spoil. That he got neither and died instead, cut down in a Roman street, was just one more of life's twists and turns.

"He saw things more clearly than most people," Borgia said. "Possibly because he had very few illusions."

Except the misbegotten belief that he could somehow keep his only child from following in his footsteps.

"What are we to do?" I asked, because he was there and not my father, whose advice I would have greatly preferred.

Borgia shrugged. "What can we do? I think you are right about what Morozzi and Torquemada are planning. Nothing else explains the Grand Inquisitor's presence here at this time. As to whether we can stop them, that remains to be seen."

"If we don't—"

"We will have a Holy Child of Rome," he replied, referring to the unknown child of La Guardia supposedly killed by the Jews. A shrine was being built to "him" that promised to draw the faithful in droves.

"Heaven forfend," I said, and truly meant it. If any such thing happened in Rome, Borgia's bid for the papacy was doomed and the Jews with it. Already, della Rovere was putting it about that he was *marano,* yet the public mood remained with Il Cardinale, thanks to his being seen as a practical man who would solve problems rather than cause them, as well as one open with his purse. Nothing less than a La Guardia–style event would turn the populace against him, and then it would do so not only in Rome but throughout Christendom.

"As far as we can tell," I said, "no street children are missing."

Benjamin had reported as much after his sortie beyond the ghetto. Passing as Christian, he had drifted from the Campo across the Tiber almost to the gates of the Vatican, all the while listening, watching, murmuring a question here and there in the right ears. Rome had its share and more of homeless children, but they were anonymous only to those who willed them to be so. To themselves, they formed a tribe of sorts, each being well known within it. Had any been missing, their absence would have been noted.

As for the *cantoretti* school, Vittoro had confirmed no boys were missing from there except those Morozzi had procured to be bled for Innocent. I had fears for the safety of those he had taken, but I was confident none of them would fall prey to Torquemada. Under other circumstances, the condition of their bodies, most particularly the obvious evidence that they had been bled over an extended period, would have encouraged the blackest accusations against the Jews. But this was Rome—rumor-swept, sophisticated Rome. Talk of the late Pope's desperate attempts to stave off death had swirled around the city for months. Let the body of a boy showing evidence of repeated bleedings suddenly appear, and it would be seen as a sign of the Church's depravity, not the Jews'. No, the child would have to come from somewhere else.

Wherever Morozzi was. Of him, there had been so sign.

"He hasn't been seen since leaving here after the party," I told Borgia when I met with him again in early evening. "He isn't at the *castel* or within the Vatican. No one seems to know where he is."

"That isn't good," the Cardinal observed. "He has to be found."

I could not have agreed more, but short of calling on the angels of Heaven to help us, I had no idea how to discover the whereabouts of the mad priest. He might be anywhere.

"We can put a watch on Torquemada," I suggested. "In case Morozzi goes to meet with him."

Borgia nodded. "Vittoro has seen to that, but why would they need to meet now? When the child is found, Torquemada will hear about it at once. He will appear, probably claiming that God brought him here miraculously, and arouse the populace to attack the Jews."

He sighed deeply and for just a moment, Il Cardinale looked old and tired, as though humanity's infinite capacity for sin, combined with his own, had worn him down.

"Short of putting a guard on every Christian child in Rome and the surrounding area," he said, "I'm not sure what we can do."

In the years since, I have accepted that it is the darkness in my mind that allows me to see so clearly under certain circumstances. But Borgia knew that already.

Certainly, he showed no surprise when I said, "The fact is, if worse comes to worse, we don't have to find the child. We just have to find the body before anyone else does."

The Cardinal eyed me closely. "But you would like to find the child, surely, to prevent his murder?"

"Of course I would. Morozzi is the monster, not I. But if we cannot—"

"If we cannot—" Borgia sat for a moment, lost in thought. "If you were Morozzi, where would you stage such an event?"

"What do you mean?" If I were Morozzi? Was he drawing a comparison between us? Seeing both of us as beings comfortable with killing?

"The whole point would be the discovery of the body," Borgia said. "It would need to be in such circumstances as to instantly point the finger of guilt at the Jews. Where would that be?"

I saw his point, however reluctantly. If we could deduce where the crime was likely to end, we might, with great luck, be able to stop it from taking place at all.

"I don't know," I said slowly. "Near the ghetto perhaps?"

Borgia shook his head. "Too obvious. Romans are vastly more sophisticated than the rabble in La Guardia. They would wonder why the Jews would be at such pains to implicate themselves. No, it has to be somewhere else."

"Where was the child supposedly killed in La Guardia?" I asked.

"On some mountainside. That doesn't help us here."

No, it did not, except . . . Rome was built on seven hills. There are more than a few steep inclines to be found in and around the city. Far too many to make any one the obvious setting for such an atrocity.

Despite my best efforts and the seriousness of the situation, I could not repress a yawn. Borgia looked at me chidingly.

"When did you sleep last?"

"Awhile ago, it doesn't matter—"

"It does. Go and lie down. If anything happens, I will send word to you."

I hesitated, reluctant to be banished to my room, where I was certain I would only toss and turn. But the Cardinal was not to be denied. He sent me on my way with a curt reminder that I would be of no use to him if I couldn't keep my eyes open.

By way of compromise, I took off my shoes but kept my clothes on and rested on top of the bed, not under the covers. For a while, I stared up at the ceiling, revisiting the events of the past few days. Doing so was hardly a recipe for sleep, and yet after awhile, I dozed, but so lightly that I was aware of being in a halfway state between consciousness and dreams.

True sleep eluded me. Morpheus is a capricious god; he comes easily to some and only with greatest difficulty to others. To lure him, it is best to pretend disinterest. Engage the mind in some pursuit unrelated to what is truly desired and allow no distraction from it. For me, nothing works so well as a walk through Rome.

My father was a great walker; he often took me with him on little trips of discovery around the city. I saw Rome through his eyes before I learned to see it through my own. It is not an idle boast to say that I can be set down in any quarter of the city and know where I am by sound and smell alone. On at least one occasion several years after the events related here, this ability saved my life. But I digress.

Courting sleep, I set off on an imaginary stroll, beginning at the palazzo and drifting eastward, past the ancient Servian Wall into the old city. In the distance, I saw the Quirinal, the hill from which the Sabine women were taken captive. My mother's marriage chest, preserved by my father and still in my possession, is decorated with scenes of their abduction. Do not think that a strange choice for a bride. No less an authority than Livy tells us that, in return for accepting Roman husbands, the Sabine women were guaranteed rights any woman of today would be glad to claim.

If I could, I would ask my mother what she hoped for in her marriage and whether she found the fulfillment of those hopes in the brief time she and my father were together. But she remains a faceless, voiceless shade who appears occasionally in my dreams only to vanish the moment I reach out to her.

My father is a different matter. In the dream where I shortly found myself, he walked beside me, a quiet presence at my elbow that I dared not turn to look at for fear that he, too, would disappear. Since his death, I had dreamed only of his murdered self, the battered and bloodied corpse I had wept over. It was sweet relief to feel what seemed to be his living presence. I would do nothing to disturb it.

We walked in silence past the Viminal, smallest of Rome's hills and its least interesting, as far as the Esquiline that rises steeply over the remains of the Colosseum. It is home to the Basilica di Santa Maria Maggiore, where my father and I often came to admire the interior and light a candle before the icon of the Virgin Mary, said to have been painted by Saint Luke himself. As I stared into it, the flickering candle flame swelled until it became the sun rising over the Capitoline.

"The highest of all Rome's hills, its glory," my father said. Palely as though light shone through it, his arm moved over all that lay before me. Beyond was the church of Santa Maria Aracoeli, atop the hill where it is said one of the ancient sibyls prophesized the coming of Christ.

I hung back, unwilling to mount the high wide steps leading up to the church. At their foot, condemned criminals are executed, it is said within sight of the Heaven they will not reach.

My father or perhaps his shade did not insist. We walked on, skirting the Caelian with its ancient ruins and moving south to the Palatine, where the infant twins Romulus and Remus were found, and where Rome had its beginnings. As in the way of dreams, we were suddenly elsewhere, atop the Aventine, where it is said Remus saw dire omens in the behavior of birds shortly before his brother killed him.

"Rome was founded in blood," I heard my father say. "It had its beginning here but its stain is eternal."

To the west, I saw the river, crimson beneath a drowning sun. I think I cried out although I cannot be sure. I was struggling to wake but some weight pulled me down, keeping me anchored in dreams.

"Do not be afraid, Francesca," my father said, and I turned suddenly, seeing him before me not as a ghost but as a man. He looked entirely real and solid, dressed in his usual hose and tunic, just as I had seen him the last morning of his life, as though he was not about to walk out the door and be gone forever.

"Forgive me," I said, but I doubt he heard me. The world in which he remained alive and well was dissolving. I was back in the world of my own making, following a path he had never wanted for me, one I believe he knew could lead only into darkness.

Sometime in the night, I must have awakened enough to cast off my clothes, but I have no memory of doing so. I slept fitfully, as if in a fever dream in which I saw the boys from the *cantoretti* hold out their scarred arms, as though to display stigmata, only for them to dissolve into the vision of Nando, holding a cross of glass that cracked as he offered it to me and drove bloody shards into his skin.

I woke shaking with cold although the day already promised to be hot. Woke to a banging at my door and Vittoro's urgent voice calling my name.

29

The room smelled of vomit and fear. Tall windows facing the river were unshuttered, admitting enough of a breeze to stir the white curtains but not sufficient to lift the oppressive stench. A pale young maid waving a censer filled with smoldering sandalwood had little more success.

Far too many people had crowded into the room, most of them doing nothing of any use. But that is always the way at such times.

Lucrezia bent over the bed, trying to push away the Maltese pups that were crouched, whimpering, amid the tangled covers. She lurched back suddenly as La Bella bolted up, retched again into the basin held by another hapless maid, then fell back moaning against the sweat-soaked pillows.

The midwives hovered, despite there being nothing more for them to do. The black-robed physicians, who as with all their brethren loathed being called in such cases, cast furtive glances toward the door and plotted their escape.

I stared at the evidence of my catastrophic failure and tried frantically to think of how I might salvage a life from it.

La Bella's face was pale, her eyes deeply sunken, her breathing shallow and her pulse weak. She was conscious but not fully aware of what was happening to her, which I supposed was a mercy. I might have ascribed all that to any of numerous possible causes had not her limbs and torso borne the telltale evidence of red lesions.

No natural agent had caused them. I suspected tartar emetic, otherwise known as antimony. Either that or arsenic, for they mimic each other in symptoms. But neither alone would account for the swiftness of the miscarriage that had taken her child. For that I thought of tansy, a powerful abortifacient when given in the right form and dosage.

I had administered juice of emetine shortly after arriving, having had the sense to grab a vial of it on my way out of my room after learning from Vittoro what had befallen Borgia's mistress. It may seem odd to use a potion designed to produce vomiting on one who is already doing so, but my instinct was to empty her stomach as quickly as possible. The results had been violent but, I hoped, sufficient.

The physicians clucked their tongues and shook their heads at my actions but said nothing. They were there because they dared not defy Madonna Adriana, who had summoned them and who stood off to one side, hands folded within the sleeves of her gown as though to avoid contamination. Attend they would—and present their bills for doing so—but none was about to say or do anything that might point the finger of responsibility in their direction when the death they all seemed to think was inevitable occurred.

Not so myself. In the face of such disaster, I had nothing left to lose.

"We must keep her propped up," I told Lucrezia, who, I sensed, was my only ally in the room and quite possibly La Bella's as well. "If she reclines too much, she will have even more trouble breathing,"

But that was the least of it. Had she vomited enough to expel as much of the poison as possible? Should I give more emetine or stop it and instead try to get liquids into her now before the lack of them became yet another threat to her survival? Had the midwives truly managed to staunch the bleeding or would she die from that before the poison could kill her?

The truth was that my knowledge of how to deal with the effects of poisoning was woefully inadequate. I knew how to prevent it from occurring, or so I had told myself in my vanity, and I knew how to inflict it. Apart from that, I was little better equipped than the physicians to save a victim of the poisoner's art.

La Bella's child—and the Cardinal's—had paid for my mistake with its life. Now it remained to be seen if the eighteen-year-old woman writhing in agony before me would survive.

The tansy had done its work. It would leave her body and, if she lived, she had at least a chance of healing from its effects. The tartar emetic—or arsenic, possibly both combined—was another matter entirely. Everything depended on how much she had ingested, but I had no time just then to try to determine that.

"She must drink," I said, making a decision to wait no longer. With luck, the liquid would flush her body and she would be able to expel the remainder of the poison before it harmed her further.

With Lucrezia's help, I held a goblet to La Bella's lips and trickled a little chamomile and peppermint tea into her mouth. Most of it dribbled out, but she managed to swallow just enough to let me hope that we had a chance. My heart all but stopped when she began to retch again, but despite several spasms, nothing more came up.

Throughout the remainder of that day, Lucrezia and I battled side by side. We alternately encouraged and forced La Bella to drink, cleaned up the inevitable results, kept her warm when violent chills struck her, and bathed her in cool water when she was fevered. No one else was willing to touch her, fearing to be stricken in turn. Maids brought a continual stream of fresh sheets, the physicians waited patiently for my efforts to fail, and Madonna Adriana remained where she was, ever watchful but silent.

Somewhere nearby, I was vaguely aware of prayers being offered and I knew that Vittoro was on watch but little else encroached on the all-encompassing struggle to save Giulia. She became that to me as the hours wore on—no longer the magnificent La Bella of song and story but only a young woman thrown into a treacherous situation not of her own making who had tried to manage as best she could. A woman who had depended on me to keep her safe.

By nightfall, I knew we had won, at least such victory as was possible under the circumstances. Giulia slept deeply, her breathing regular, her pulse improving, and her color returning. I thanked God for the youth and strength that I was sure had saved her as much as anything I had done. Lucrezia, by contrast, looked pale and drained. There were dark circles beneath her eyes and her lips were bloodied where she had bitten them in her anxiousness. I suspected that I looked worse. Certainly, I felt as though I had been beaten, every bone and muscle in my body being tense with pain.

But there was no time to think of that. I straightened from the bed, took one more look at Giulia to reassure myself that I was not wrong to believe that the worst was over, and turned my attention to Madonna Adriana.

She had remained throughout but was no longer standing. Instead, she was ensconced in a comfortable chair from which she could view the proceedings at a safe distance.

I wasted no time on niceties but went directly on the attack.

"What do you know of how this happened?"

Understand, I had no wish to try to evade my own responsibility. But young as I was, I already knew that the best answers come when the respondent can be taken by surprise and knocked off guard. Whatever she had expected from me—perhaps tearful contrition or a plea for her protection from the wrath of Il Cardinale—this was not it.

"What do you mean?" she demanded in turn, bristling.

"I have checked everything that has come into this house, every morsel of food, every scrap of cloth, every drop of drink. All has been under my seal as it was under my father's before me." I thought it did no harm to remind her of the long history of my family's service to Borgia.

"Something got past me," I continued, acknowledging the obvious before she could point it out. "I must determine what that was and how it happened. You are *Domina* here. I need you to help me." Deliberately, I used the title that acknowledged her as female head of the household, with both the rights and responsibilities of same.

A shadow passed behind her eyes, the merest hint of flinching. It startled me. I stared at her harder, trying to determine what had caused such a reaction. Swiftly, the conviction grew in me that Madonna Adrianna was not entirely innocent in this matter. Not that she had caused it in any way, I do not suggest that at all. Only that she knew or at least strongly suspected how it had come about.

"Tell me," I said.

She was worried, I could sense that, and perhaps more, but she was still Madonna Adriana and she was not about to be ordered about by the likes of me.

"How dare you—" she began, but I was having none of that. Precious hours had been lost—well spent in the struggle to save Giulia, to be sure, but lost all the same. Morozzi was out there somewhere, hunting his child victim or perhaps he had already taken him. I had to act quickly.

"I will dare whatever I must to find out how this happened," I told her. "I will look wherever I must and at whomever I must." Defiantly, I stared at her.

Her face reddened but, to give her credit, she kept a rein on her temper. I took that as a sign of the depth of her fear, that she had to control herself even with me.

Yet still she did not speak, though I could see her jaw working as though the words were struggling to get out.

It was left to Lucrezia, who remained by the bed keeping watch on La Bella but still attending to the scene being played out before her. Softly, she said, "The figs . . ."

I almost ignored her. It is true enough that fresh fruit can be deadly, causing as it will violent runs that rob the body of vital fluids. Washing or better yet peeling before eating seems an effective preventive. This notwithstanding, it is all but impossible to introduce poison into fresh fruit. Any attempt to do so mars its appearance and leaves a bitter taste sure to evoke instant suspicion. Besides, I had checked all the fruit in the house myself and put it under seal.

That close I came to thinking that she was only fumbling around in her young mind, trying to help. But the look on Madonna Adriana's face stopped me.

"What figs?" I asked.

Lucrezia looked to the other woman to answer. She did but not right away. Instead, she flicked a hand in the direction of the door.

"Out, all of you."

Servants, midwives, and physicians took to their heels. There was a crush right at the door as each tried to exit first, but finally the physicians—being male, of course—managed to push their way past all but the sturdiest midwives and the rest followed in a ragged stream until finally the last, littlest maid was gone.

"Shut the door," Madonna Adrianna ordered.

I did so, then turned back to look at her. She had risen from the chair and was pacing the floor near the windows. The air had cooled somewhat and the white curtains billowed around the bottom of her gown as though she walked through clouds.

She kicked them aside, stared at me, and said, "My stepson has done nothing wrong."

Giulia's husband, crowned with the cuckold's horns courtesy of the Cardinal's lust for his young wife. Orsino Orsini was scion of one of the most powerful families in all Italia, yet he was also singularly lacking in the qualities expected of a man of his position. Had such a nonentity finally dared to raise his hand in revenge for the insult done him?

"He has nothing to do with this," Adriana insisted. "Surely no one can blame him for caring about Giulia."

"Does he care for her still?" Already, I suspected the answer, but I needed to hear it from Adriana's own lips. "Are they in contact?"

"Letters," she said, biting out the word and only adding more with utmost reluctance. "He writes to her, sweet little letters asking after her health and telling her about his activities in the countryside."

"Does she reply?"

"Of course she does. She has no wish to hurt him any more than can be avoided. She sends a note back with the messenger. It is all very innocent."

"So Borgia knows of it?"

"No, he does not," Adriana said, not hiding her contempt for what she must have regarded as a truly stupid question. "Why ever would we trouble Il Cardinale with such an unimportant matter?"

The Cardinal's mistress and her husband had been exchanging secret letters under the nose of the cousin he had trusted to watch over both Giulia and his daughter. And truly, it had not occurred to either of them that he would want to know?

I shook my head at their idiocy but plunged on, anxious to get as much from her as I could. "What did he send besides letters?"

She pressed her lips together and refused to meet my eyes.

"By God," I said, "there is no time for this! Tell me or I swear I will go straight to the Cardinal and implicate you in everything that has happened."

"How dare you—" she began yet again, only this time with such fury that I thought she meant to strike me.

Before she could do so, Lucrezia leaped away from the bed and put herself between us.

"Stop!" she exclaimed. "A baby is dead, for pity's sake, and Giulia almost died as well. Francesca is only trying to help. We must tell her everything."

Adriana looked away, refusing to speak, but neither did she forbid Lucrezia to do so. With quiet earnestness, Borgia's daughter told me what I needed to know.

By the time she finished, I understood how poison had reached into *il harem* and done its terrible work. I also knew that I faced an enemy even more determined and resourceful than I had dared to believe.

30

Letters?" Borgia repeated slowly. "They were exchanging letters?"

He had returned to the palazzo from the Curia and had gone directly to his office. Not waiting to be summoned, I followed him there. Despite the late hour—it was after matins—his secretaries still trailed after him. They tried to stop me but he heard my voice in the antechamber and called out for them to let me enter.

Only a few lamps shone in the inner office. Shadows arched up the walls but left most else in darkness. Almost, I regretted forcing my way into Borgia's presence. Still dressed in his ecclesiastical robes, he looked like an old, stooped man weary in body and soul. But as soon as I began to speak, some of his usual energy returned. He gestured the secretaries out, threw off his heavy robes, and sat down behind his desk to hear what I had to say.

I had the sad duty to tell him that the child was lost but at least

I could reassure him that Giulia would recover. Having done so, I explained what had happened. I made no attempt to exonerate myself but I did hope to deflect the worst of his anger from the young woman who had suffered enough already for her ill-considered actions.

"I have the impression," I said carefully, "that they were merely friendly letters and that La Bella's responses were intended only as a courtesy."

In fact, I had seen Orsini's letters to Giulia and thought them embarrassing and sad. In them, he fretted over her well-being, confided his hopes that they would be together again soon, and went on and on about the hunting, which seemed to be his only activity in the country, and his loneliness. This from a man who had the means to do far more in his life than most of us could ever dream.

Her responses to him were not available since apparently she had not kept copies. But I did see the little gifts he sent her—a bolt of embroidered cloth as yet unused, a book of poems that looked as though no one had ever opened it, and most recently, a box of figs preserved in honey, a particular favorite of hers.

The poison was in the figs. Wearing gloves, I examined the fruit carefully once I got back to my rooms. At my worktable, under the brightest light I could manage with candles and oil lamps, and with the help of lenses my father had commissioned that had the effect of enlarging anything viewed through them, I carefully removed several figs and pried them open. Small flecks of white shone within the fruit, but so closely mixed with the seeds as to be invisible to all but the most discerning eye. Looking very carefully, I also found traces of a finely ground brown powder, which I suspected was the tansy.

In addition to the honey, the figs were flavored with saffron, cinnamon, and chopped almonds. It made for a delectable combination, which I had enjoyed myself on occasion. The combined flavors would have been sufficient to mask the taste of the poisons. Judging from the empty space in the box, Giulia had eaten three of the figs. Had she eaten more, I had no doubt that she would not have survived.

"And he sent gifts?" Borgia asked.

"Small things, no jewels or anything else extravagant." Don't ask me why I was trying to spare his feelings but it was not merely to avoid his anger. I truly felt sorry for him at that moment. His expression of deep melancholia and the way his hands trembled when he poured wine for us both suggested to me that he cared for Giulia in ways that went beyond the carnal pleasure of her body. To discover that he might have a rival for her gentler feelings, and that man her own husband, who had a moral and legal claim on her, must have disturbed him greatly.

"And yet," Borgia said, "you don't believe Orsini is responsible?"

This was the crux of it. The Cardinal was depending on support from the Orsinis to help him gain the papacy. If they were betraying him, he needed to know it quickly. By the same token, if one of them had gone rogue and struck out for his own reasons, Borgia needed to be aware of that as well.

But I was convinced that neither was the case.

"It is an attempt to drive a wedge between you and the Orsinis," I said with confidence. It was also an attempt to drive a wedge between Borgia and me, but I was not ready yet to mention that. Indeed, I hoped the Cardinal would reach that conclusion on his own.

"Orsini sent a letter to Giulia at least once a week," I said. "They were always delivered by a messenger wearing his livery. Anyone who had a watch kept on the palazzo would have known of this. The letter that came with the figs appears to be genuine but makes no mention of the gift. I believe the poisoned fruit was added by the same man who took the messenger's place."

"And that would be—" Borgia prompted.

"The maid who received the letter and the gift from the messenger is a very young girl, rightly terrified by the circumstances. It took some time to calm her down enough to tell us what she remembered."

In fact, it had taken the better part of an hour and the application of a stiff dose of brandy before she stopped weeping enough to answer my questions sensibly.

"She describes a tall, blond-haired man who she says was very handsome."

Borgia sat back abruptly in his chair. His eyes were hooded but I glimpsed the light in them. Despite the warmth of the evening, I shivered.

"Morozzi," he said, not a question but a statement of inescapable fact.

I nodded. "So it appears. I think that if we were to search between the Palazzo Orsini and their country estate, we would find the body of the real messenger."

I was not suggesting that we actually do so, the area being far too large to hope to accomplish anything useful. But Borgia took my point and nodded.

"For him to do this," the Cardinal said, "he must have planned well ahead."

"Indeed, but your relationship with La Bella is not precisely a secret, nor was her pregnancy. It would not have been difficult for Morozzi to discover where you were vulnerable."

Such vulnerability being the reason why he had sent me to the household in the first place. I waited for him to remark on that.

"You have no doubt that the figs are the source of the poison?"

I assured him that I did not, then added, "No one else ate from the box and no one else was stricken."

He stared off into space for several moments before he said, "Lucrezia likes figs."

I understood what he was thinking. In a single attack, Morozzi could have killed both Borgia's mistress and his only daughter. And he could have pointed the finger of guilt at a member of the same family whose support Borgia had to have in order to gain the papacy. Truly, the plot was brilliant.

"We have underestimated him," the Cardinal said quietly. He raised his eyes and looked at me. "How is it that you did not know of this?"

There it was, the question I had feared. Despite all my efforts to safeguard those precious to Borgia, how had I not learned that Giulia was receiving gifts from her husband? How had they gotten past me?

"From what I can gather," I said carefully, "La Bella did not want you to be disturbed by the knowledge that her husband was in communication with her."

"She wanted to keep it a secret?" Borgia was a man of secrets, keeping his own counsel to an extent I have rarely seen in another. But for everyone else the rules were different. He regarded the effort to keep anything from him as a betrayal and responded accordingly.

"So it seems," I said. "She knows the Orsini family is loyal to you and I'm certain that she never imagined there could be danger in the little gifts he sent."

"Then she is a fool."

Well, yes, she was, but to hear him state it so harshly was a shock.

Carefully, I said, "She has paid greatly for her foolishness."

Borgia sighed and drank some of his wine. He set the goblet down before he spoke again.

"The child . . . do you know . . . was it a boy?"

Men always want sons, so it is said, and value them more highly than daughters. But Borgia had two sons, possibly three if you believe what their mother claimed, and he had older boys by a mistress in his younger days. But he had only one daughter.

"It was a girl," I said gently.

He looked away but not before I saw the tears in his eyes.

I gave him what time I could before we had to return to the business at hand. "Morozzi must believe that you will blame her husband. He will be expecting you to strike him down and in the process, lose the Orsinis' support for your election."

Borgia's expression was inscrutable. "He will also be expecting me to strike at you."

A sudden image of the torture room under the palazzo sprang into my mind. I pushed it down as best I could.

"Yes, he will," I said with a calmness that surprised me. With all that had happened, I felt almost numb.

"In fact, he may be counting on it," I continued. "The conclave is due to start in two days—" A fact that caused me great concern as there had, as yet, been scant opportunity to plan how to keep Borgia safe within it.

"Four days," he corrected. "The Curia has received a message from the patriarch of Venice. He is en route to Rome and begs us to delay the convocation until he can arrive. Given his age and the great respect in which he is held, it was agreed."

I tried to remember what I knew of the patriarch, a man so elderly that mention of his name was usually accompanied by surprise that he was still alive. If memory served, he was in his eighties and had waited for his cardinal's red hat longer than any other prince of the Church, being named only in Innocent's final days. That Maffeo Gherardo was even attempting the journey to Rome at his age was a surprise. That he expected to arrive in good order, if somewhat tardy, astonished me. However, I was happy to take a delay any way it came, assuming that I would be alive to make use of it.

"If Morozzi can manage to remove me from your service"—how delicately I described my imprisonment and likely death—"he will be that much closer to success."

"Then you believe you can stop him?"

Did I? So far, the mad priest had been ahead of me with every step. I had escaped him at the *castel* only thanks to Vittoro and sheer luck. I believed that I had reasoned my way to his plan with Torquemada, but what if I was wrong? What if he had some other scheme in mind to prevent the Cardinal's election? It was impossible to really know what was in so twisted a mind. I could only keep my eyes focused on the ultimate goal, Borgia's elevation to the papacy. After that, God willing, there would be time to settle other scores with Morozzi, to which had to be added the death of Giulia's baby.

"I have to try," I said. "For all our sakes, you have to let me."

Telling Borgia what he had to do was probably not the wisest course at that moment, but greater delicacy was beyond my reach just then. I waited . . . for him to explode in rage, call the guards, do whatever he chose to do.

For several moments, he said nothing, only sat in his chair looking lost in thought. Truly, I had never seen him so weary or dispirited. I was beginning to wonder if he meant to answer me at all when, from the shadows near the door, a too-familiar voice spoke.

"She's right, you know," Cesare said as he stepped into the light.

31

Borgia's eldest son, the one he intended for the Church, was dressed for battle. He carried his helmet but still wore his breastplate of hammered steel. The sword belted at his waist lacked all adornment, being meant solely for killing. Beneath his armor, he wore austere, unrelieved black—shirt, doublet, hose, clothing chosen because it would not hinder him in combat. He could, when he chose, dress himself as extravagantly as any prince or prelate. But for the time I knew him, he always preferred to dress as what he was born to be—a warrior.

Borgia appeared to be expecting his son. He waved Cesare into the chair next to mine, filled another goblet, and slid it across to him.

Cesare drank, wiped his mouth, and said, "I got your message. Three hundred men-at-arms marched with me from Siena and I have two hundred more within easy reach. Fifty are here at the palazzo.

I've sent the rest into the city to search for that mad priest. Is there any word of him?"

These preparations for war did not surprise me; indeed, I was relieved by them. But I dreaded what was to come.

"Not yet," Borgia said. "But something else has happened."

Quietly, he related the events of the past few hours. I sat stiffly in my chair, waiting for the blame I was sure Cesare would rightly direct at me, but while he cast several glances in my direction, he did not speak until his father had finished.

"I am sorry about the child." The proper sentiment having been expressed between men, Cesare passed by my manifest failing and went on. "Morozzi will know we are hunting him. Where will he look for sanctuary?"

"With Torquemada," Borgia suggested so promptly as to leave no doubt that he hoped it was true. To take down two enemies in one fell stroke would be an auspicious beginning to the glorious papacy he anticipated.

I will pause here to say a word about the Grand Inquisitor. Undoubtedly, you have heard the rumors that Torquemada himself was descended from *conversi*. His followers—and make no mistake, he still has them—deny any such thing, but those in a position to know hold fast to the assertion that he had Jewish blood. They cite evidence that his grandmother was herself *converso,* having been born to a Jewish family in Castile.

We can speculate about the terrible pressures faced by *conversi,* especially after the uprising against them in Spain several decades past around the time of Torquemada's birth, but that is a distraction I do not seek. Suffice it to say that I remain convinced that the Grand Inquisitor was a deeply troubled man who strove to protect himself—in this life and the next—by basting his own guilt and fear onto those he consigned to the flames.

To return to the present circumstances, against the tightness in my chest born of mingled relief and regret, I said, "The Grand Inquisitor might give Morozzi shelter, but we have a friend among the Dominicans. If Morozzi goes to Torquemada, we will know of it."

Cesare nodded. "Good, but what about della Rovere? Might Morozzi not go to him instead?"

At mention of his great rival for Peter's Throne, Borgia looked thoughtful. "No doubt . . . but I suspect that as much as he may share Morozzi's objectives, Giuliano will be cautious about being tainted by him. He will try to keep his distance while maneuvering for whatever advantage he can grasp."

"He will be hard-pressed to find any," Cesare said. "The Jews have done as they promised. The amount you agreed to is in place. You will have no problems, at least not with money."

It was later said that the sum paid to Borgia by the Jews was no less than four hundred thousand silver ducats, an emperor's ransom to buy safety of a sort for a despised people. I cannot swear that number is correct, but it is telling that the amount was large enough for Borgia to send Cesare to keep a close watch over its receipt.

It was also said that Borgia kept the money in Siena in the care of the Spannocchi rather than bringing it directly to Rome because he did not trust the Medici, who had long dominated banking not only in their native Florence but in the Eternal City as well. I cannot vouch for that, either, but I will say that if it was true, it was a sensible precaution on his part, considering the trouble they were to give him in the future. Even at that time, with the great Lorenzo newly dead, they were the most formidable of the noble families arrayed against the upstart Borgias.

"We have Sforza," Borgia said. "He did not come cheap but we do have him."

Cesare raised his goblet to his father in salute. "At what cost?"

When Borgia told him, I really did stop breathing. Truly, the Milanese cardinal had not surrendered, or perhaps merely deferred, his own papal aspirations cheaply. In addition to fifty thousand silver ducats and a host of benefices and offices that would pay him easily ten times as much, including the vice chancellorship, Sforza would become the new owner of Borgia's pride and joy, his palazzo. There was no mention of a betrothal between Lucrezia and Sforza's cousin, Giovanni, lord of Pesaro and Gradara, but I did not take that to mean it was not agreed to. Borgia would be unlikely to mention it to his son, who, as he was to demonstrate so amply later, disapproved of anyone Lucrezia might marry.

Cesare whistled softly. "If this gets out, the vultures will be circling, demanding equal payments."

"They won't get it or at least most won't," Borgia said with confidence. "Once the vote is seen to run in my favor, the rest will scramble for whatever they can get."

If the vote ran in his favor, but I was not about to say that. Indeed, I did as Benjamin had done and strove to be as inconspicuous as possible. How often did anyone outside La Famiglia have the opportunity to hear the master plotter and his prize pupil at work? I could learn more about strategy and tactics in an hour with Borgia *padre e figlio* than I might from prolonged study anywhere else.

The discretion required of a professional prevents me from revealing the specifics of what I heard that night. Let it suffice to say that Il Cardinale understood better than any man the utter greed and venality that drove the princes of Holy Mother Church. He knew them all, each and every one, probably better than they knew themselves.

What did each most desire? What did he fear? What did he lust after in the most secret realm of his heart? Decades of diligent, devoted effort had prepared him perfectly for the moment when he, alone among all the rest, would make the Throne of Saint Peter his own.

If God loves ruthless ambition and cold brilliance, truly He must have loved Rodrigo Borgia.

After an hour and more, during which father and son exchanged information and plotted their strategy aided by several flagons of wine, Cesare said, "Francesca is almost asleep."

"I am not," I claimed, but my voice was slurred, and in truth, I had drifted off for a moment or two.

"Take her to bed," Borgia suggested, and Cesare appeared to consider it. He leaned over, took my hand, and raised it to his lips. His breath was warm, his gaze compelling. Time seemed to slow and for a moment, I was tempted. If a child's life and the entire future of Christendom had not hung in the balance—

I pulled my hand away, prompting a sigh from him that I heard as the surge of a wave reaching the shore. All my senses seemed strangely heightened.

The still air was weighted with the scent of candles and wine, yet for a fleeting moment I could have sworn I smelled copper and tasted on my tongue the tang of blood. The sensation roused me from my lethargy.

"Morozzi will not be resting." I heard myself as though from a distance. "We must find him before he acts."

"If the angels love us, he will be at the funeral," Borgia said.

I remembered then that the services for Innocent were scheduled for the coming morning. Those cardinals already present in Rome would be in attendance, along with a full complement of lesser prelates and nobles. Borgia himself would have a prominent role in his capacity as vice chancellor of the Curia. But I nurtured little hope that the man we had to stop would be so foolish as to expose himself at such a gathering.

Where then would he go? Not to the *castel* now that Innocent was gone, and with him his protection. To the chapter house then? Or to della Rovere, despite what Borgia believed. Where could Morozzi go that Il Cardinale's spies had not already found him?

Rome is a warren of streets old and new, a tumult of tearing down and building, perfect chaos on the best of days. It is also an ancient place, inhabited gloriously and ingloriously for thousands of years through the best of times and the worst. Beneath Borgia's own palazzo were the layers of the far earlier city. So, too, in the rest of Rome, stick a spade in the ground and you will unearth a hidden world we call the past.

More than anything else, it is a city of secrets made all the more necessary by the Roman love of gossip. Much of the city is hidden away behind walled gardens, down gated lanes, reached by passageways accessible only through innocuous buildings, the ideal hiding places for anyone who does not want to be found.

If I were Morozzi, where would I go?

As quickly as the thought surfaced in my mind, so did I reject it. I was not Morozzi, emphatically not. He was insane and I was . . .

The smell of blood grew stronger, so much so that I looked around half in expectation that someone somewhere nearby was bleeding. Looked but saw nothing save the landscape of my memories.

Giulia writhing on the bed . . . the boy holding out his mutilated arms to me . . . the man in the torture chamber spewing out his life's blood at the flick of my hand . . . the Spaniard with his black-foamed lips . . . my father lying lifeless in the street, his skull crushed . . .

"Francesca . . ."

I was back in the wall, watching the torrent of blood and feeling the world tilt, falling away into an abyss.

The scent of blood faded and I smelled candles—many, many candles, far more than lit the room where I still sat without being aware of it any longer. I saw instead a sea of flickering lights and far off I heard the chant of prayers.

I was on my knees, staring up at the statue of a woman who gazed down at me, a frown on her smooth face as though I had done something to perturb her.

"For pity's sake, Francesca!"

A hint of camphor and citrus hung in the air. I turned, looking over my shoulder, and saw Morozzi, the fallen angel, gazing at me.

"Signorina Giordano?"

"Yes?"

Cesare was kneeling beside me, his hands on my shoulders. He shook me urgently. "Francesca, are you all right?"

I blinked once, twice, and saw them both staring at me with grave concern. My throat was very dry. I could scarcely speak and when I did my voice sounded high and thin.

"I am fine." It was a lie. The nightmares were bad enough. These visions, I suppose they can be called, were an altogether different matter. Everyone has bad dreams from time to time, some more often than others. But to be taken out of this world so utterly, presented with sights, sounds, even smells and tastes from an entirely different reality . . .

Rocco claimed to believe that God had a purpose for me in eradicating the evil that was Innocent. I longed to believe him but my heart feared otherwise. Among all the souls in this world, why would the Almighty reach down to one so flawed as myself? You will say that His son reached out to the whore Mary Magdalene. But all she did, if the Church is to be believed, was lie with men, whereas I am driven to kill them. Surely, I am the far greater sinner?

"You are not," Borgia declared. "The strain has been too much. I should have known—"

"Do not!" I stood so quickly that Cesare had to do the same. The sudden motion made me dizzy but I ignored that and plunged on. "Do not say that I am not capable of doing what I must!"

Above all, I could not bear for him to say that there was something gravely wrong with me, some malady that explained the times when I seemed to step outside myself and become another, a creature of heightened senses and perceptions who far from abhorring blood was drawn to it.

Were he to speak so, he would give voice to my deepest and most secret fear that of late had grown stronger in me with each passing day. That I truly was damned not simply by my actions but by the dark nature of my soul, a stain not all the absolution of Holy Mother Church could ever wash away.

Before that fear could seize even greater hold, I took a breath and forced myself to speak calmly.

"There is nothing wrong with me. I am perfectly fine. What is wrong is sitting around like this, talking when Morozzi is out there somewhere preparing to act."

"We have hundreds of men searching the city," Cesare pointed out, not unreasonably. "In addition to my father's army of spies. What do you imagine we can do that they cannot?"

"I don't know," I admitted. "But two more sets of eyes and ears won't go amiss." On impulse and because I could think of nowhere else, I said, "We can start at the basilica."

"Why there?" Borgia asked.

Why indeed? I had wandered Rome in my imagination, trying to divine where Morozzi might strike only to find myself once again kneeling before the altar to Saint Catherine as I had the day the mad priest followed me into Saint Peter's. The holy woman had received visions of Heaven, Hell, and Purgatory in her communion with our Lord. My visions, if that was what they were, seemed of a far less blessed sort.

"Because Torquemada claimed that the Holy Child of La Guardia was killed on a mountainside," I reminded him. "If Morozzi seeks to re-create that crime, it is true that he has his choice of hills from the Capitoline to the Palatine and the Aventine, and more. All have great significance to ordinary Romans, but the Vatican itself was built on a hill, and besides, Morozzi is a priest. For him there can be no place of higher importance than Saint Peter's Rock."

Cesare looked skeptical. "I'd rather roust Torquemada from his bed and see what we can scare from him."

"A tempting thought—" Borgia said, but he did not give his approval. Instead, he looked to me.

"You understand there are hundreds of guards all through the Vatican, including in the basilica. How do you imagine Morozzi could get past them?"

"I don't know," I admitted. "But he all but vanished in front of my eyes near the altar to Saint Catherine of Siena. Perhaps that would be a good place to start."

"If he could disappear like that," Cesare said nervously, "he may be more demon than man." Instinctively, he made the sign of the cross to ward off evil.

"Take this," Borgia said and, having stripped off the gold crucifix he wore beneath his shirt, handed it to his son, whose nature he understood full well.

Cesare seized it and dropped it around his own neck. His faith, for all that it strayed wildly from Church dogma, was always far greater than mine, much good that it ever did him.

"Go with her," Borgia commanded. He stood, his energy renewed. "Do not let her out of your sight. Find Morozzi, take him alive if you can, kill him if you must. But do whatever is necessary to assure that I have no further trouble from him."

Cesare bent his head once in acknowledgment and in the same motion donned his helmet. With one hand on the crucifix and the other on the hilt of his sword, he went from the room.

I would have followed immediately had not Borgia stopped me. "What did you see, Francesca?" he asked, so softly that for a moment I was not sure he had spoken.

I turned and looked at him with studied innocence that belied the sudden rapid beating of my heart. "When, Eminence?"

"Just now when you were no longer with us. What vision was revealed to you?"

I took a breath and let it out slowly. He was watching me closely. I feared he saw far too much.

"With all respect," I said lest I appear to be instructing him in what he surely already knew. "Only those who find favor in the eyes of the Lord can hope to see beyond the veil of this world."

He sat back in his chair, a faint smile playing at the corners of his mouth. Not for a moment did I fool him.

"Is that what you believe?" he asked.

"It is what Holy Mother Church teaches, is it not?"

"And Holy Mother Church is never wrong, is she?"

A moth, drawn by the flickering candles, flitted into the room. It circled a flame, swooping so close I thought its fragile wings must surely be singed.

"You are far better able to answer that than am I, Eminence."

Softly, he said, "I should be able to, Francesca. I have known you since you were a child, watched you grow up in my household, taken note of your particular talents and, shall we say, your vulnerabilities. Yet in matters concerning you, I confess to a certain confusion."

"You should not," I said, startled by the notion that he had observed me so closely. "I am, above all, your faithful servant."

Before he could reply, I said, "Do something for me, if you will. Send men to the shop of the glassmaker Rocco Moroni in the Via dei Vertrarari. He has had dealings with Morozzi and may have some idea of where he would hide."

I hoped the predawn visit would not trouble Rocco overly much, but I was confident that he would understand the need for it. If I was wrong about Morozzi's likely whereabouts, I needed to know that as soon as possible.

"All right," Borgia said, and looked about to say more. Before he could do so I murmured my thanks and beat a speedy retreat from his office, down the broad steps into the night.

There Cesare waited, pacing impatiently, a splendid animal as eager as I to be loosed upon the hunt.

32

It is said that Rome was built on seven hills, yet these days only the Capitoline seems a true hill, the other six being much diminished by the draining and building up of the marshlands that once lay between them. But before Christ walked the earth, before there was a Holy Mother Church, there was an eighth hill that the old ones who were here even before the Romans called Vaticum. There, evil spirits dwelled close to the entrance to Hades, the mad Emperor Nero staged chariot races and executions, and the poor buried their dead. One such humble grave received the mortal remains of the martyred Peter the Apostle, companion and disciple of our Lord.

It is said, and I know no reason not to believe it, that as soon as Peter's body was laid to rest, his followers began to venerate his grave. They kept watch over it, buried their own dead nearby, and did their best to assure that the spot was not disturbed.

Of course, all of this happened centuries ago, and much is lost to us in the turmoil and darkness that followed. But the great Emperor Constantine left records of the church he built a thousand and more years ago to shelter Peter's grave, modeling it on the old Roman basilicas. It is whispered that to erect the monument to his own greatness as much as to the greatness of his faith, Constantine destroyed many other old Christian tombs, casting the bones of the faithful to the wolves. But it is best not to speak of that.

It is enough to say that from his vision so long ago sprang the great moldering pile of rock that these days threatens to crush us all.

Cesare and I entered through the atrium, past the Navicella mosaic, and continued on into the basilica proper. Despite the late hour, we were not alone in that vast and hallowed space. In addition to the several dozen men-at-arms who had come with us from the palazzo, Vatican guards were everywhere in evidence. Our arrival attracted some attention, but the sight of the Borgia livery discouraged anyone who might have challenged us.

The interior was lit by prayer candles and perpetual lamps burning in front of the altars lining both sides of the wide nave. Even so, it was very dark. Without the help of the torches carried by our guards, I would not have been able to see clearly more than a dozen or so feet in any direction.

"I was kneeling there," I said, indicating the side altar dedicated to Saint Catherine. "Morozzi appeared there." I pointed to the rear and left.

"Did you see where he came from?" Cesare asked.

I shook my head. "I believed he followed me from the palazzo, but I did not actually see him until he stood there."

"How long did you speak with him?"

"Not more than a few minutes. I looked away for a moment. When I looked back, he was gone."

"Anyone could vanish into these shadows." He spoke as though he wanted to believe that was what had happened, but his hand kept a firm hold on the cross around his neck.

"It was daylight when we met." I glanced up at the clerestory windows under the eaves of the gabled roof. At night, they did nothing to relieve the darkness, but during the day, they admitted enough light to make most of the interior visible.

Cesare glanced around uneasily. "Then where could he have gone to?"

"The foundations of the basilica are below us," I replied, remembering that my father, who had actually seen them, has described a vast maze of structures and debris roofed over when Constantine's construction began.

"Perhaps he went there," I added. Although how precisely he could have done so with such speed eluded me, at least for the moment.

"Or perhaps he vanished into the air," Cesare suggested. "If he truly does the Devil's bidding, he could possess such power."

Which would make him all but impossible for us to defeat. I could not accept that any more than I could allow Cesare to be overcome by such dark fears.

"If he is a demon," I asked reasonably, "how could he enter so holy a place as this? Surely, he would have been struck down the moment he crossed the threshold."

"Not if he did not touch the holy water," Cesare said with all seriousness. "As long as he avoided anointing himself, it is possible that he would be safe."

I had never heard anything of that sort, but then I am no expert on the power of demons. I do, however, possess a modicum of reason and attempted to use it then.

"He is a priest, Cesare. His holy office requires him to perform Mass daily. How could he transform wine and bread into the blood and body of our Lord if he is a demon?"

"No doubt he merely pretends. At any rate, you're the one who said he vanished almost in front of your eyes. If you have a better explanation, tell me what it is."

I had none, but spurred by him, I was determined to find an answer that placed Morozzi firmly in the mortal realm, which was to say within our reach. Otherwise, we were defeated before we began.

Gesturing to a guard to follow me, I moved slowly toward the altar to Saint Catherine and knelt before it. Having assumed the exact position I was in when I became aware of Morozzi, I looked over my shoulder in the direction where he had appeared. Without moving my eyes, I stood and walked a few feet forward as I had done before.

Cesare watched me closely. So, too, did the guards, who made no effort to conceal their unease. It is a curious fact that people are often uncomfortable in holy places, especially at night. Whatever they suspect lingers amid the altars, it is nothing they wish to encounter.

"We are wasting time," Cesare said nervously. "Torquemada—"

I ignored him and reached out my hands toward the air into which Morozzi had vanished. One step . . . another . . . I touched something solid.

"Bring the light," I said. Deep in the shadows, hidden between pillars, was a small door. It so closely resembled the paneled wall to either side of it as to be almost invisible. But when I put the palm of my hand against it and pushed lightly, it swung open without a sound. Apparently, the hinges had been kept well-oiled. Just within the door, I spied an iron bracket meant to hold a torch. A striking box sat on a small shelf next to it but the bracket itself was empty.

"So much for Morozzi's demonic powers," I said with a smile.

Cesare had the grace to look abashed. "It's a robing room," he suggested, speaking of the chambers in which priests don their vestments before conducting Mass.

But I had already glimpsed the steps leading downward and knew it was far more.

Cesare, all credit to him, let loose his grip on the cross and insisted on taking the lead. I followed, along with the guards who lifted their torches high to light the passageway to which we descended.

Cool, damp air struck my face. I took a breath and felt its thickness in my chest. Moisture trickled down the walls lined with ancient bricks. The floor was set with stones slick with lichen. I smelled the wet clay of the hill into which the basilica was built and spared a moment to pray that Constantine truly had emptied the ancient burial grounds.

We went on, the passage slanting downward at a gentle but steady angle until it widened suddenly. By the flickering torchlight I saw arched openings in the walls to either side with spaces beyond that were filled with tumbled debris. There was something familiar about it all that made me pause.

"Where are we?" Cesare asked in a whisper that seemed to suit the place.

"Still under the basilica, I think . . ." In the darkness lit only by darting flame, I had lost track of how far we had gone. Trying to orient myself, I narrowed my eyes and stared straight ahead as far as I could see down the passageway.

"It looks almost like a street," I said. "With shops to either side but all roofed over and buried underground. How could that be?"

Cesare was close enough for me to see that, despite the cool air, sweat was beading on his forehead. "Who knows? Who cares? Do you still think Morozzi is down here somewhere?"

"If he has taken a child, he has to hide him until he does whatever he intends. The funeral starts in a handful of hours. I don't think he will wait longer than then to act, but what better place to conceal himself in the meantime?"

He did not disagree but he did point out what I had just begun to realize for myself. "The basilica is vast. If this passage extends through much of it, there could be hundreds of places for him to hide, perhaps even more."

And if the passage extended farther, out beyond the limits of the church, we could search for days and find no trace of Morozzi.

Rather than let myself think that, I said, "We have to try. If he has been down here, surely we will find some sign of his presence."

"We could lose our way very easily," Cesare said.

The truth of that was undeniable. Even with the torches, after only a few twists and turns, we would have little idea of how to find the way back to our starting point. And if we should be trapped long enough for the torches to go out—

"You, there," Cesare said, pointing to one of the guardsmen. "Take your sword and carve the sign of the cross in the wall to your right every twenty feet. Make it large and deep enough that we can find it by touch if need be. On your life, do not fail to do so. Understand?"

The young man swallowed hard and jerked his head in acknowledgment. He drew his sword and quickly made the first cross.

Satisfied, Cesare faced down the passage, into the darkness.

Without hesitation, he said, "Let us go on and may the Good Lord protect us."

Unlike his father, who I am convinced truly was a pagan, Cesare was sincere in his faith. Yet he made no pretense of strict adherence to the teachings of Holy Mother Church, not even after he took the red hat and became a cardinal. As to what was in his heart when asked for the Lord's blessing, I will say only that there are hidden places in Rome and elsewhere, chambers well buried in the ground, where there are images of a young warrior god, whispered to have been a worker of miracles born to a virgin mother and to have ascended to Heaven in a golden chariot. I never heard Cesare speak his name but I do not doubt that he knew him in his heart.

We went on, moving within a small stream of light surrounded on all sides by impenetrable darkness. I was relieved that the torches continued to burn brightly. Although I cannot explain why, when a flame is placed in insufficient air, it will snuff out. Fortunately, as deep as we were underground, I could feel a slight current of movement past my face, suggesting that there were openings somewhere to the surface.

Glancing down at the floor, I saw that it was covered with swirls of dust that must have fallen from the ceiling above us. The dust was sufficiently disturbed to give me hope that others besides ourselves, most important Morozzi, had passed along the passage recently.

The passage widened suddenly and we found ourselves in a large space, the dimensions of which we could not make out, so far did it stretch beyond the reach of the torches. But I did take note that the walls we glimpsed to either side were curved and, unlike in the passage itself, the floor was dirt instead of stone. There appeared to be remnants of tiered seating along one of the walls, cut off where the space had been roofed.

A little farther on we reentered the passage and not long after that, it split in two directions, one leading straight ahead and the other going off to the right. Cesare stopped and frowned.

"Which way did he go?"

He did not seem to expect me to reply but I took it upon myself to find the answer. Staring down at the floor, I walked straight ahead and saw a coating of dust undisturbed except for tiny eddies such as would be made by the passage of the air over time. Having returned to my starting point, I walked to the right and saw immediately that someone had been along there recently.

"This way," I said, indicating the right.

"How do you know?"

When I pointed to the dust, Cesare flushed as though embarrassed that the explanation was so mundane yet had escaped his notice.

To soothe him, I said, "My father taught me to look at small details. I think it was the nature of his work that made him so attentive to them."

That was putting it mildly. It is the very nature of poison to be concealed in the simplest and most ordinary places where few ever think to look. It is the task of the poisoner to look into such places and understand what is to be found within them.

Mollified, Cesare nodded and we went on but not very far. Almost at once, the way ahead was blocked by what looked at first glance to be rubble. Cesare took one of the torches and walked forward. When he returned, he had an odd expression on his face.

"There is enough room for us to get through."

"That is good—" I began.

"But it won't be pleasant."

Without waiting for my reply, he turned to his men. "Remember who you are and what I will do to anyone who fails in his duty."

Before I could think of why he should find it necessary to give such a warning, he took my hand and with the torch held high, moved deeper into the passage.

33

I did not scream. To this day I take pride in that, although the plain truth is that my horror was so great that when I opened my mouth, only a tiny squeak emerged.

The pile of debris almost entirely blocking the passage was made of bones spilling from the rooms on either side where the walls seemed to have collapsed from the pressure of holding them. Leg bones, arm bones, pelvises, whole and partial rib cages some still attached to parts of spines, and above all, skulls. In all, there were thousands and thousands of bones of all sizes, some whole, some disintegrating, but all recognizable as human. Apparently, Constantine really had emptied the old Christian cemetery and he had dumped the pitiful remains like so much discarded trash.

So vast was this midden of the dead that it stretched above our heads several feet until it met the ceiling. The space in which we had to pass was little more than a foot wide, tight enough that we had no choice but to turn sideways in order to squeeze through. Bones crunched under our feet, poked into our sides, and caught in our clothing as we struggled to move forward.

The worst were the skulls with their leering smiles and sightless eyes. Some jutted out of the pile so close that my nose brushed where theirs once had been. God forgive me, I know they once were people like myself, but I shuddered in revulsion. Behind me, I heard at least one of the guards retching and really could not blame him. There was no stink of putrefaction, the bones all being far too old for that, but there was still a heavy smell of death coming from the crumbling, yellow remains, and along with it, the all too vivid reminder of our own mortality.

I have heard that there are people in far lands who burn their dead. It is forbidden by Church teachings, yet it seems a sensible practice, one that I would prefer for myself. Assuming, of course, that I am dead before the burning begins.

I clung to Cesare's hand as he moved forward, never faltering. Whatever his own fear, he understood full well the responsibility of a leader. Not for a moment would he show his men anything other than courage and determination. It is fair to say that he pulled us all through that horror, bringing us finally and safely to the other side.

Barely had the passage widened again than we all stopped and, responding to the must basic instinct, shook ourselves frantically. I held my breath lest I inhale even more of the dust of the dead.

Cesare gave us a few moments, then cut short our efforts.

"Let's go," he said, and continued on down the passage.

We followed and very soon found evidence that we were not the only people who had discovered the city of the dead beneath the basilica.

It is really not fair to say that Rome is a lawless place. There are times when the law is very much in evidence. Speak a word against Holy Mother Church, for instance, and prepare to face the fire. But as with so much else in life, it is all a matter of weighing risk and reward.

From time to time, an effort is made to tax various items Romans consider essential to our well-being. These are mainly in the category of luxury fabrics, fine wines, and the like. But even cheese has been taxed on occasion, and I can remember one misbegotten attempt to levy a tax on wheat.

As a result, every Roman aspires to know a good smuggler. I am no exception. However, I had never given any real thought to how exactly one goes about smuggling. Obviously, a place is needed in which to secure goods on their way to the customer. After running the gauntlet of the bones, we found ourselves amid a series of rooms that had been cleared of all debris and secured with iron gates in good repair. Behind the gates we caught glimpses of chests, boxes, and barrels hinting at all manner of luxuries.

"Something to remember," Cesare said with a wolfish smile.

"People have to earn a living," I reminded him. Should they gain power, I had to hope the Borgias would restrain themselves. We all need hope, however misguided it turns out to be.

By then, we had been below long enough for me to be concerned that we had found no trace of Morozzi. Time was fleeting. I had to wonder how much more effort we could expend without concluding that it was wasted.

I was about to say as much to Cesare when the passage curved again. Just beyond we found a room that, like the others, was used by smugglers, but in this particular case the chain holding the lock had been cut and the metal gates hung on their hinges partly ajar. This struck me as strange enough to be worth a closer look.

"Why would anyone do that?" I asked Cesare, gesturing to the severed chain.

He shrugged and followed me into the chamber. At the back of the room, several heavy iron rings were cemented into the wall. From one of the rings, a rope dangled. Not an old rope, frayed and worn, but a fresh rope, the end newly cut.

"Someone was tied here," Cesare said as he examined the end of the rope.

I nodded but did not let myself think too much of it. "A dispute between smugglers?" I suggested.

"Perhaps . . . but why a rope?"

"Does it matter?"

"It might . . . a chain requires a manacle."

One small enough to hold a prisoner securely. But a manacle made for an adult could slip right off the limb of a child.

"Oh, God—"

Cesare glanced at the rope again and barred his teeth in what an innocent might take as a smile. "Newly cut. With a little luck, he isn't too far ahead of us."

He plunged into the passage, his men racing after him. I followed hard on their heels, cursing the skirts that tangled around my legs. We ran . . . I don't know how far. Several times I thought I heard sounds ahead of us, but we were making enough noise ourselves that I could not be sure. The passage began to slope upward. I caught a faint whiff of incense on the air.

Cesare burst through a door, the rest of us tumbling after him. I heard a scream and the clatter of metal hitting stone. A wall of condotierri ahead of me blocked the way forward. Try though I did, I could not see past their broad backs and shoulders until finally a crack opened between them and I realized that we were in the sacristy filled with priests preparing for Innocent's funeral.

The sudden appearance of armed men with smoking torches and wild eyes emerging as though from the netherworld appeared to test the faith of more than a few of the holy men. There was an unseemly scramble to escape amid shouts, cries for help, and the like.

That all stopped abruptly when Cesare, sword drawn, shouted, "Halt!" At his order, his men fanned out to block the exit.

"We are in pursuit of a priest with a child," he announced. "Where did they go?"

Silence greeted this demand, followed swiftly by a babble of responses, some fearful, others outraged, none in the least helpful until one old priest, gathering up the shreds of his dignity, approached Cesare directly.

"Who are you, sir?" he asked. "By what right do you come here?"

For just a moment, Cesare looked uncertain. What right indeed? The right of the sword, of course, but did he really want to brandish that in such a place? Shouldn't there be at least the pretense of respecting the authority of Holy Mother Church, the ultimate arbiter before whom even mighty warriors must kneel?

"I am Cesare Borgia, son of Cardinal Rodrigo Borgia! You will do as I say or face my fury!"

So much for the renowned discretion of Il Cardinale, who by the standards of our time had gone out of his way to avoid flaunting his children.

The old priest paled but did not back down. While the others hissed and whispered among themselves, he drew himself up and confronted Cesare.

"This is a holy place! Sheathe your sword, son of Borgia, and do not draw it again beneath this roof!"

There are times when I dare to think there may be hope for Holy Mother Church.

Fearful of how Cesare would respond to so direct a challenge, I was about to say something about the priest meaning well, being an old man, not taking offense, and so on, but before I could utter a word, a cacophony of shouts and screams broke out that surpassed any that had gone before.

"A woman!"

"How dare she—!"

"Sacrilege!"

"Strega!"

Witch. For daring to set foot in God's holy sacristy. My presence alone was a source of pollution so vile as to make me deserving of death by fire.

To give the old priest credit, he ignored the others and said earnestly, "I would help you if I could, but truly no one appeared here until you and your companions. Now you must go."

Cesare's disgust was palpable. He looked around at the holy men, armored in their self-righteousness, and for a moment I truly did fear for what he might do. Squeezing his arm even harder, I tugged him toward the door.

"We're wasting time," I whispered. "Morozzi must have taken another way out."

Still, he hung back, staring at them all. None, not even the old priest, had asked about the child. None had expressed concern for anyone beyond themselves. Later, when Cesare was so criticized for his actions toward the Church, I remembered that moment and marveled that he did not act even more harshly.

We left the sacristy and found ourselves near the main altar. In the time that we had been below, the soft gray light of dawn had crept into the basilica. I could see that we were only a few dozen yards from where we had set out. As for Morozzi, he could be anywhere.

"How much time do we have left?" I asked.

Cesare sheathed his sword and looked around at the preparations going on around us. Already, servants were arranging benches in the vast nave to accommodate those of sufficient rank to merit seating. A bier on which Innocent's remains would rest was being set in place before the main altar. In the loft above, the choir was preparing to rehearse. Papal banners and the banners of the college of cardinals hung between the pillars separating both sides of the nave from the side transepts. Vast candles, some the size around of a fit man's waist, were being hoisted into place.

Amid all this, a few clerics already came and went, busy conferring with each other. Some of the lay guests had arrived early for the same purpose.

"A few hours," Cesare said.

Despite our failure to find Morozzi, I was more convinced than ever that he would not waste the opportunity presented by such an occasion. Prelates and lay alike, those attending the funeral were certain to be outraged by a supposed atrocity committed by the Jews within the very heart of Holy Mother Church. They were also best able to turn rage into bloody action in the blink of an eye. Yet how could he possibly hope to evade the notice of the hundreds of guards drawn up in and around the Vatican? However well he knew the netherworld under the basilica, he would have to emerge from it eventually.

Cesare must have been thinking along similar lines, for he said,

"I will set men to watch on the door by Saint Catherine's altar and outside the sacristy. If he comes from either direction, we will have him."

"But there must be other ways in and out," I said. Surely, the smugglers themselves could not be coming and going from within the basilica. Although given the ready complicity of so many priests, I could not rule that out entirely.

"We will do our best to find them," he said. With a true smile, he added, "Do not despair, Francesca. I count on you to keep my reason clear."

Which was as close as he would ever come to acknowledging the dark fears he had confronted before realizing that Morozzi was only a man.

My own spirits lifted with his words, but a few moments later, I had cause to feel less than cheered.

The men Borgia had sent at my request to inquire of Rocco if he knew of any place where the mad priest might be hiding had returned. They brought word that the glassmaker was not to be found. His neighbors on the Via dei Vertrarari reported that he had left suddenly the previous day and had not been heard from since.

34

I did not want to think about what could be behind Rocco's sudden disappearance, but the possibility that he might have come to harm because of his help when David and I escaped from the *castel* loomed large in my mind. I was questioning the guards, trying to discover exactly what the neighbors had said, when Cesare finished deploying his men and came over to join us.

"Why are you scowling?" he asked. He looked in ill humor himself, but that had less to do with the present circumstances than with the fact that the future cardinal was never at ease in any church.

"I fear something has happened to a friend," I replied. "He isn't at his shop and no one seems to know where he has gone."

The odds of Cesare having any interest, much less concern, for a shopkeeper were vanishingly small, such people barely existing within his notice. Yet he surprised me.

"Who is he?"

When I told him, he said, "You think Morozzi may have harmed him?"

I hesitated to say as much. Rocco was a strong and able man. Against a warrior such as Cesare, he might stand little chance, but against the priest—

"I don't know . . . it doesn't seem likely but—" But Rocco was not someone I would expect to go off without a word to anyone, especially not in such fraught circumstances.

Cesare looked at me closely. "You care for this man?"

The thought of him truly being in danger made it difficult for me to breathe. I could only nod and say, "He is a dear friend."

"And is his wife also a dear friend?"

"He is a widower with a young son—" Abruptly, I realized what was in his mind. So great was my surprise that I blurted out the first thought that occurred to me.

"For heaven's sake, Cesare, you can't possibly care that I—"

But apparently he did, at least enough to look like a sulky boy who thought that an amusement he assumed to be exclusively his own was, in fact, not.

"It doesn't matter to me one way or another," he claimed. "I just don't want you distracted right now."

"Then help me," I pleaded, in the hope that he could be mollified, his incandescent temper deflected in a more productive direction.

Something in my manner must have touched him, for he softened slightly and after a moment, nodded.

"Where could this Rocco Moroni have gone?"

Quickly, I tried to think where he might be. If he truly was in trouble, I hoped he would have come to me, assuming that he was able. But the palazzo and the Vatican both were surrounded by guards. He might well have been turned away. That left one other possibility.

"He has a trusted friend at the Dominican chapter house," I said. "Friar Guillaume. He might know Rocco's whereabouts."

"Is this the same friend you said would warn us if Morozzi tried to take shelter with Torquemada?"

When I nodded, Cesare turned to the guards who snapped to attention. Briefly, he told them about Rocco, then said, "Make inquiries at the chapter house but be discreet. Let no one other than the friar know why you have come."

They bowed and took their leave. I watched them go down the long nave of the basilica and out into the brightening day before I turned back to Cesare.

"Thank you for doing this."

He shrugged as though it was of no matter, but the look he gave me suggested that there would be a reckoning. Like his father, Cesare never did anything without a price.

"*If* you can concentrate now," he said, "my men have found half a dozen more concealed doors. The basilica seems riddled with them. But there is still no sign of Morozzi."

"Perhaps he is not here." My greatest fear was that I was wrong about the mad priest's intentions. He and Torquemada might have an entirely different plan that had eluded me.

My second greatest fear was that I was right.

If I were Morozzi . . .

Scarcely had the thought gone through my mind than I fought the impulse to dismiss it. The basilica was immense and the surrounding buildings even more so. If we were to have any hope of finding the mad priest before he struck, I had to steel myself to reason out his plan.

Assuming, of course, that reason can be applied to madness. That is a matter for the philosophers. For myself, I had more practical concerns.

"We must not make the mistake of underestimating him again," I said. "He is daring and clever, and he strikes where we do not expect."

"You are thinking of Giulia," Cesare said, looking grim.

I nodded. "All Morozzi cares about is the destruction of the Jews. He is at least as fanatical in that regard as is Torquemada himself. And he is unburdened by any sense of conscience or morality. We must assume that he is capable of doing absolutely anything in order to achieve his ends."

"He had an ally in Innocent. My father believes that had the Pope lived much longer, he would have signed the edict. Morozzi's failure to see that through must be as a fiery goad driving him onward."

"No doubt that is so," I said. "But when Innocent died with the edict still unsigned, Morozzi refused to take that as defeat. He came back immediately with a plan that, had it succeeded, would have assured that the one man he knows will not sign the edict could not become pope."

"By causing a rupture between my father and the Orsinis, whose support he must have if he is to have any chance of winning?"

"Exactly. If Morozzi had managed to turn them against each other, in all likelihood he would have assured della Rovere's election or, at the very least, that of someone else who would sign the edict."

"But the plan failed," Cesare pointed out.

"Yes, but it was that very failure that prevented me from realizing immediately that, in order to act as he did, Morozzi had to have knowledge that he could not possibly have acquired on the spur of the moment."

I was thinking out loud but at least I finally was thinking, seeing at last what shock and fatigue had prevented me from grasping earlier.

"He knew about the letters between Giulia and her husband," I said. "He even knew of her love for figs. I think he has been planning all along what he would do if Innocent died without signing the edict and it looked as though your father would become pope."

Cesare nodded slowly. It was clear that what I was fumbling my way toward made sense to him.

"Now he is regrouping again," he said. "This time with a scheme to rouse the mob against the Jews."

"And we can be sure that once again, he has worked out exactly how he will do that well in advance," I replied. "That is why Torquemada is here, to be present at the moment when the 'crime' is revealed so that he can announce to all that the Jews are to blame, thereby assuring that no cardinal seen as tolerant of them could possibly be elected."

Cesare's face had turned very dark. In sharp contrast, the knuckles of the hand gripping the pommel of his sword shone white.

"Della Rovere is putting it about already that my father is *marano*."

"Likely he knows what Morozzi and Torquemada are planning, though he will try to keep his distance from them both. At any rate, della Rovere doesn't matter; your father can deal with him. It is Morozzi we must stop at all costs."

"How?" Cesare demanded. "I can bring in more men and scour the basilica from top to bottom but we have very little time—"

"The mere fact of your doing that will raise alarm that should your father become pope, he—and his family—would abuse his power."

I did not say what I knew to be rumbling in the streets, that Borgia truly was the wolf come to devour the lamb. That no more rapacious or ambitious man had ever dared to seek the Throne of

Peter. Of course, all that was being put about on behalf of Borgia's rivals. So far, the Romans themselves, who by the mere threat that they could erupt into violence had influence in the election, were making mock of it. I had to hope that nothing would happen to make them change their minds—or their allegiance.

Never had I seen Cesare look so bleak or, for that matter, so close to despair. "Then we are finished," he said, "and Morozzi will have won."

"No! There is still time, granted not much, but we must make good use of every moment."

I looked around, driven by the sense that something eluded me, some fact I had not yet considered. In the years since, I have often found it useful when confronted with a perplexing problem to consider not only the evidence of what *is,* but also to look for what *is not.* Sometimes it is in the empty, blank places that we find truth staring back at us.

Amid all the preparations for the funeral, what was missing from the basilica?

"Innocent's body still lies in the chapel," I said slowly.

Cesare nodded. "It will be processed in after the mourners are assembled."

In that procession, the late Pope would be escorted by the highest prelates of the Church and the most honored lay attendants. All of whom would be assembling first in the Sistine Chapel.

"We may be looking in the wrong place," I said.

To reach the chapel, Cesare and I, along with several guards, had to leave the basilica and make our way through the Apostolic Palace. Our passage did not go unnoticed. Already word was spreading that Borgia's son was on the premises and that he had not come in peace. We were greeted with glares by priests and clerks alike, more than a few of whom made a show of pressing against the walls as we went by, as though to avoid being contaminated by contact with us.

Cesare did not so much ignore them as appear to be entirely oblivious to their existence. I envied that even as I struggled to keep up with him. Such was the forcefulness of his presence that when the captain of the guards in the chapel saw us coming and stepped forward to block our entry, a mere glance from Cesare froze him in place.

Looking back now, I think it is possible that Cesare had never been in the Sistine Chapel before. If that is true, it would be consistent with Borgia's policy of discretion regarding his children until he became pope, when all that changed so spectacularly. At any rate, Cesare paused before turning around slowly in a circle, staring at the magnificent frescoes decorating the walls.

In particular, the work depicting the Temptation of Christ seemed to attract him.

"Who painted that?" he asked.

"Sandro Botticelli," I replied.

What Cesare made of the Devil or the splendor of treasure the Fallen One offered to the Son of God escapes me. He seemed more curious about a small detail within the fresco, the appearance of a priest holding a bowl filled with blood.

"What's going on there?" he asked.

I had asked the same question of my father years before, and gave Cesare the answer he had given to me.

"See those people," I said, directing his attention to a small group of figures approaching the priest with animals. "They are Jews preparing to offer sacrifices. The scene reminds us that God allowed Abraham to spare his son, Isaac, by offering up a ram in his place.

But we are also to remember that God gave His own son to redeem us from sin."

What Cesare made of this matter of fathers and sons, and the sacrifices one did or did not make of the other remains a mystery to me. But I can say that he stared long and hard at the scene before returning his attention to the rest of the Chapel.

For my part, I seized hold of the thought that the scene might have some significance to Morozzi, that he might even have chosen it to frame his own sacrifice of a child. Admittedly, that was very slim, but it did give me enough hope to keep going.

The interior was empty except for Innocent's remains, the handful of guards keeping watch over them, and ourselves. Of Morozzi, there was no sign at all.

"There are wardrooms above us," I told Cesare. "We should look there." I had in my mind the memory of how Morozzi had appeared to Vittoro and myself on the walkway above the chapel.

"If you think it would be worthwhile," he replied but without enthusiasm. I could not blame him. Time was passing at a fearful clip and we were no closer to finding the mad monk than we had been hours before.

Even so, I was about to mount the staircase set into the wall at the north end of the chapel and leading upward to the wardroom when the sudden appearance of several men stopped me.

The guards Cesare had sent to the Dominican chapter house had returned. And they had brought Rocco with them.

35

I have walked with fear often enough to consider it an old companion, and I am no stranger to despair. But what I saw writ starkly on Rocco's face as he hurried across the width of the chapel made me feel as though I had been swept up by a gale that threatened to hurtle us all into the abyss.

"Is it true?" he demanded. "What the guards said? Is it true that Morozzi has taken a child?"

So agitated was he that Cesare moved to put himself between us. I gripped my unlikely protector's arm and dug in my heels to hold him in place.

"It may be true," I said cautiously. "What has happened?"

He tried to tell me but his breath caught and he was unable to speak. Finally, he gasped out a single word.

"Nando."

I will spare you the rest except to say that Rocco had received word from his mother the previous day that his son had gone off to fish in a nearby stream and had not returned. Fearing that Nando had come to harm—accidentally, as he thought then—Rocco hurried to La Giustiana, the village a few hours north of Rome where he was born and where his mother still lived. When the search for Nando proved fruitless, he returned to the city to seek help from me, only to be turned away at the palazzo. He then sought out Friar Guillaume. The two were trying to decide what to do when the men-at-arms sent by Cesare arrived.

"Nando is missing?" Poor stumbling thing that my brain had become, that was the best I could do.

"He is a good boy," Rocco said. His eyes glistened with tears only waiting to be shed upon confirmation of the tragedy that loomed before us all. "He would not go off without a word to anyone. Something has happened to him."

Too late, I recalled that the village was along the same road going north out of Rome as was the Orsinis' country estate. One as enterprising as Morozzi had shown himself to be could readily have intercepted the messenger carrying the latest missive to La Bella from her cuckolded husband and at the same time seized the child of the man he knew to be at the nexus of all those he despised and feared.

"I am so sorry."

The words were pitifully inadequate but the pain resonating within me was a far better measure of my guilt.

"I will do everything I can to see him returned safely to you."

Rather than being nailed to a cross, gasping out his life as he died in a horrible mockery of the death of our Lord.

God help me.

I mean that literally. I truly did beseech the Almighty's help, but, as usual, He seemed to be occupied elsewhere.

"Who is Nando?" Cesare asked.

"Rocco's son," I replied. "A child."

Make no mistake, Cesare was a selfish and ruthless man. The entire course of his life proves this. But for all that, he could on occasion actually be a man—and by that I do not mean that he possessed a scrotum and penis, as does the rudest hog rooting in a sty. He had an instinct to care for those weaker than himself, especially children, whom he liked and valued far more than he did most adults.

But just then he was very young and lacking the thin—in Cesare's case, extremely thin—veneer of civilization that most men manage to acquire as they pass through life.

That being the case, he gave voice to what was, in all honesty, my own instinctive response to Rocco's news.

"Merda."

I could not have put it better.

Very shortly thereafter, a frantic search of the wardrooms above the chapel produced no sign of Morozzi. We were back to where we had started, which is to say in the basilica.

"Why would he have taken Nando?" Rocco demanded as we stood before the main altar, near where the body of Innocent would be placed shortly at the start of the funeral rites. It was a reasonable question under the circumstances but not one I wanted to answer.

"He is mad," I said, and hoped that would suffice.

But he was also a man, not a magus. In order to carry out what I believed to be his plan, Morozzi would have to make a crucified child appear before a large crowd. How could he do that and escape without being detected?

A child, a cross. A single man needing to maneuver both within a vast space and before the eyes of hundreds.

I had ventured into the netherworld below Saint Peter's and discovered only that Morozzi had, in all likelihood, hidden Nando there briefly. I had found no sign of the child himself or of the cross upon which he would have to hang.

Where were they?

If not below then—

I looked up, into the deep shadows that hung beneath the roof of the basilica.

"What lies above?" I asked.

Cesare did not know, nor did any of us. But the same priest who had dared to challenge us in the sacristy was, when found at Cesare's order and hustled before him, willing enough to provide an answer.

"A garret," he gasped. "In poor repair. No one goes there."

"How do we reach it?" I asked. So anxious was I that I only just managed to stop myself from grabbing hold of the old man in an effort to shake the information out of him.

Though he might have been more tolerant than most of his brethren, being addressed without deference by a woman of no particular lineage was more than the priest could bear. A nervous tic sprang to life in his right eye. Glaring, he turned away from me and addressed himself pointedly to Cesare.

"Signore, we are about to perform the final sacraments for our late Holy Father! Surely you can understand that your presence here and that of your—" He paused, no doubt considering what he would like to call me. Some sense of self-preservation must have won out as he said only, "—companion is not appropriate?"

Cesare had many skills—I have alluded to several of them—but he was utterly lacking in even the rudiments of tact. Indeed, his notion of diplomacy revolved around the conviction that the best route to peace lies in grinding one's enemies into the ground so thoroughly that the very fact of their ever having existed will be forgotten on the wind.

But he was in Saint Peter's Basilica, next to Jerusalem the holiest place in all of Christendom. And if he caused any real problems, he would have no end of trouble from his father.

Accordingly, Cesare gritted his teeth and said, "Don't fuck with me, priest. Just show us how to get into the garret."

The old man turned white, then blazing red. Though he seemed to be having some difficulty breathing, he managed to point the way.

A short while later, I paused to reflect that the priest had told the truth about conditions in the upper reaches of Saint Peter's. Dark, damp, musty, filled with air so thick that I struggled to breathe, the garret seemed to contain the combined effluvia of a thousand years of human sweat, toil, prayers, and suffering. It was a veritable midden of dust so heavy that I sank in it up to my ankles, spiderwebs of a thickness to mimic walls, and trash—the castoffs of generations who, by the look of it, had mostly found the garret a convenient place to disport themselves in all manner of illicit ways. Heaven only knows how much worse it would have smelled if not for the gaping holes that let in the sky.

We had reached the garret up a narrow staircase concealed behind a pillar in the southeast corner of the basilica. The priest showed us the location of the entrance but did not accompany us. He did not wish us well, either, but I suppose he could be pardoned for the lapse. Cesare went first with Rocco right behind him. I followed along with several men-at-arms.

As we straightened and looked around, Rocco asked, "Why would Morozzi come up here? There must be far better places to hide."

I remained unwilling to tell him what we feared. Instead, I said only, "We have already looked below. Besides, Morozzi likes to do the unexpected."

Rocco nodded but he appeared unconvinced—and growing more desperate by the moment. His eyes were red-rimmed, he was unshaven, and his lips looked severely bitten, as though he had done so to keep from crying out.

As much to give him the relief of action as to hasten the search, I said, "We will make faster progress if we split up."

"Fine," Cesare said. "Glassmaker, two of my men will accompany you. Francesca, you come with me."

We went, picking our way down the long axis of the basilica. Perhaps inevitably in a building of such age, there was not a single open space but rather a vast maze of cubbyholes and cubicles alternating with long aisles. I suppose that at some time in the distant past, the garret had been used for storage. But as the building deteriorated and weather did its work, the floor became too weak and unstable to hold anything heavy.

Even, quite possibly, the weight of a single person.

"Careful," Cesare said, reaching out to steady me. The wood directly under my feet felt alarmingly soft.

"I had no idea it was this bad," I said.

While it was true that I had seen chunks of stone and brick fall from the basilica on occasion, and had heard even more stories about hapless visitors being struck by them, I hadn't really understood how dilapidated the immense building had become. For whatever reasons—repeated barbarian invasions, the shifting eastward of imperial authority into Byzantium, the abandonment of Rome during the Great Schism—the notion that a structure had to be maintained apparently had not occurred to the successors of Peter, who by all evidence had left it to rot. Rather than belabor the obvious metaphor for the condition of Holy Mother Church herself, I will say only that the place was a death trap.

Torches were out of the question in the garret, which, where it was not rotting, was tinder dry. We had to make our way as best we could by the shafts of sunlight penetrating through the holes in the roof. Some of these were little more than the size of pinpricks but others were as wide as a well-fed priest. Not unexpectedly, pigeons had taken up their roosts within the garret. It being daylight, most of the birds were below in the square or elsewhere looking for food, but the few that had remained took off in a great flutter of wings, leaving us to make our way through and around their copious droppings.

The basilica was more than three hundred and fifty feet in length—I knew this because my father had been interested enough in the ancient building to measure it with the help of a mathematician friend. The garret ran almost that entire distance. We had entered at the far side from the main altar. As we made our way slowly and laboriously, by necessity given the conditions we faced, I could hear the choir beginning to rehearse below.

"There can't be much time left," I said. My eyes smarted from the dust and grime. I blinked hard to clear them and saw, in the flicker of an instant, what I took to be movement about two-thirds of the way toward the far end of the garret. Either that or merely the fulfillment of my most fervent wish.

"What is that?" I asked.

Cesare looked in the same direction. The obscurity was very great. What I had seen might have been no more than the flutter of yet more pigeons or the stirring of dust.

"Shadows, nothing more?" he said.

In my desperation, I seized on his uncertainty as confirmation that whatever I had seen might be at least worth investigating. Tugging impatiently at the skirts that weighed me down, I pressed ahead.

And got no more than a half dozen yards or so before Cesare yanked me back. At the same time, he raised a hand, bringing his men to a halt.

Very softly, he said, "Don't make a sound. You're right, someone is there."

"Where?" I whispered, straining my eyes to see.

"Two hundred feet ahead of us, maybe less. If I'm right, that would put him directly above the main altar."

"It has to be Morozzi!"

Cesare nodded. He looked grimly satisfied. "Leave him to me."

I shook my head vehemently. "The moment he sees you, he will know himself to be in grave danger. There is no telling what he will do then. But he will not believe that he has anything to fear from a woman."

All that was true enough, but I will confess that I wanted to confront Morozzi myself. Call it hubris, vanity, or what you will, I could not be content to hide behind Cesare.

"Just give me a moment," I pleaded. "I can take him by surprise. Then you can overcome him."

"I can overcome him readily enough without you," Cesare protested.

"This isn't about your prowess! He has a child, for God's sake! We can't take the chance of Nando being hurt."

Assuming, of course, that he had not been already, but of that I could not think. Indeed, it was all I could do to wrench my arm free of Cesare's hold and plunge forward into the shadows.

My way was obstructed by a thick mass of webs that had blurred my vision of what lay beyond. To my horror, they clogged my nose and mouth, tangled in my hair, and seemed to grasp at every part of me like a thousand spectral fingers. So much for my overwrought imagination. A spider is only a spider, to be stepped on if dangerous and otherwise left alone. I struggled to remember that and kept going until finally, gasping and filthy, I was free.

Like so much in life, that was both good and bad. I could see into the distance much more clearly but at the same time, I could also be seen.

The figure still a hundred feet or so down the length of the basilica turned suddenly and looked toward me. He was hunched over something I could not make out, but as I watched, he straightened and let whatever he had held drop to the floor.

In the next instant, he started toward me.

I possess the normal instincts for self-preservation, at least I think I do, but there have been times when they are overridden by imperatives I cannot deny. This was one such.

Without thought or hesitation, heedless of Cesare's shout behind me, I raced forward. Twice, my feet broke through the floor and several times, I tripped badly enough to fear I was about to fall only to right myself at the last moment and keep going.

Quickly enough I saw, to my immense relief, that the figure I had seen was Morozzi. He was in his priestly garb, no doubt in order to pass without question in the basilica, but he was not alone. The small, huddled form of a child lay where he had dropped him.

"Bastard!" I screamed at the top of my lungs and—perhaps I truly am not entirely right in the head—launched myself into space and straight at him.

We collided with a heavy thud that sent both of us sprawling.

"Monster!" I grabbed hold of him by his golden hair, slamming his head against the floor. In all honesty, I could have done that over and over until his brains splattered over us both, but Morozzi had other ideas.

"Strega!" he howled and, having seized me by the shoulders, hurled me off him so hard that I landed a considerable distance away with such force as to rob me of breath.

As I struggled to straighten up and rejoin the fray, I was treated to the vision of Cesare, sword drawn, making straight for Morozzi. One horrified look at him was enough to send the mad priest fleeing, but not before he seized Nando.

The clamor had drawn Rocco's attention. Seeing what was happening, he joined Cesare in pursuit of Morozzi. I tried to do the same only to stumble and fall, sprawling facedown over something hard and oddly familiar. Raising myself enough to look at what was beneath me, I realized that I was stretched out on top of a wooden cross, of a size large enough to accommodate a child.

With a scream, I struggled to my feet and went after Morozzi. Caught as he was in the confines of the garret, surely we had him! He would have to be able to take flight like the archangel Saint Michael to escape us.

Or so I thought. One mad priest, one terrified little boy, one equally affrighted father, one warrior, half a dozen men-at-arms, and me . . . all in the maze that was the garret of Saint Peter's. All running—or in Nando's case being carried—over a dangerously weakened floor as below . . .

Who knows what was happening below? Did they look up and wonder at the strange sounds emanating from the starry heavens? Did they imagine devils had roosted there? I have no idea and I spared it no thought. All my attention was on rescuing Nando from Morozzi's grasp. Even capturing the mad priest came second to that.

As much as it pains me, I give Morozzi full credit. He thought not one or two steps but many steps ahead of me. Over time, I came to realize that he always had a multitude of plans layered one upon the other, to be executed as need arose. Had he turned his abilities in saner directions . . .

A pointless speculation. He was mad, and being mad, he thought only of his own survival. Confronted by both Cesare and Rocco, he turned like an animal at bay, his handsome face distorted in a hate-filled snarl.

"You will burn! The fires of damnation will consume you!"

Perhaps so, but before that happened, Morozzi had to face Cesare's sword. And Rocco's wrath.

Rocco almost reached him first. He was within an arm's length of Morozzi when the mad priest threw his burden at him and fled. I did not notice which direction he went, all my attention being focused on the boy. As Nando fell, the floor where he landed crumbled beneath him.

I saw it all as though time itself had slowed. The fraying of the wood, the way pieces of it rose at an angle to the floor, breaking off as they went, the collapse of what lay beneath and the sudden sight of space fading away an unknowable distance below.

Rocco turned from Morozzi and toward his son, but he was not close enough to stop Nando's fall. It was left to me to hurl myself across the floor, my arm thrusting through the opening to grasp the boy's shirt in the instant just before he would have passed beyond my reach.

Together, we slid toward the abyss.

"Francesca!" Rocco shouted my name, but I scarcely heard him. My breath and the frantic beating of my heart were all I knew, that and the fierce grip of my hand holding the child above the hundred-foot drop to the floor of the basilica.

I assume that we were seen for certain then. I assume eyes turned toward us. I assume there was a murmuring among those gathered below.

I assume because I do not know. No one has ever spoken of it. Perhaps we were not seen at all. Perhaps some fragment of plaster remained to conceal our presence. Perhaps there has been a conspiracy of silence drawn over that which no one wants to acknowledge almost happened that day in Saint Peter's.

Whatever the case, we slid, Nando and I, toward the hole that had opened up in the floor. I clung to him with one hand and tried to reach out desperately with my other to grasp hold of something, anything that would stop us.

And found Rocco's arm.

"Francesca," he said again as I grabbed him, "don't let go!"

I remember being startled and then, rather absurdly under the circumstances, offended at the notion that I could do any such thing. Did he have such scant confidence in me? The woman who had drawn him into the maze of deceit and treachery surrounding Innocent's death and in the process imperiled his son's life? How could he do other than expect the worst from me?

"Save him!" I screamed, and heard my voice as though from a great distance. "Don't let him fall!"

But in truth, we were both in danger of that fate. I could feel my fingers weakening—on Rocco and on Nando both—and knew it was only a matter of moments before all was lost.

"Save him!" I screamed again, and tried to twist around so that Nando was in easier reach of his father.

For just a moment, my gaze met Rocco's. I saw him hesitate, trying to measure how he might reach us both, but I was having none of that. With all my strength, what little remained, I pulled Nando up toward his father.

Rocco wrenched his eyes away and reached out, seizing his son in his strong and capable grasp. I heard the boy moan, heard his father breathe his name, heard, too, my own gasp as my hands gave way. All in an instant, I yielded the child to life and myself to whatever fate God chose to bestow upon me.

36

Cesare saved me.

At the last possible moment, he turned away from pursuing Morozzi and lunged toward the hole, grabbing hold of me just as I would have plummeted to certain death.

As he hauled me up, shaking and gasping, I glimpsed the back of the mad priest vanishing into the darkness. I tried to shout, to call attention to him, but my throat was clogged with dust and tight with terror. At any rate, it was too late. Although several of Cesare's men-at-arms went clattering after him, Morozzi was gone.

But Nando was alive and safe in his father's arms. The little boy appeared dazed but otherwise unharmed. Clutching his son, Rocco met my eyes over his tousled head. The joy of relief bubbling up within me vanished in the face of his dark stare. He looked at me with what I took to be well-deserved condemnation. Without a word, he turned his back and sped Nando away.

Vaguely I recall Cesare carrying me down the steps from the garret. He was muttering to himself as we went, something about the foolishness of women and of one woman in particular, but I scarcely heard him, so deep was I into the pain of losing Rocco as a friend and, forgive my foolish heart, perhaps more. So do the longings we shy from confiding even to ourselves vanish down dark tunnels into oblivion.

As for Cesare and I, we emerged into the basilica as it was filling with prelates and nobles arriving for the funeral. The sight of a glowering warrior carrying a dazed woman drew startled stares. He ignored them and pushed his way through the crowd until at last we reached blessedly fresh air.

Cesare set me down on the low wall surrounding a small fountain on the edge of the square. I huddled there, my arms wrapped around myself in a futile effort to stop the convulsive shaking that gripped me. He knelt, wet a cloth in the fountain, and slowly washed away the thick layer of grime covering my face. His touch was soothing and undemanding, very uncharacteristic of him.

"Are you hurt?" he asked when he had removed the worst of the dirt and filth, enough so that I could breathe more easily and open my eyes without wincing.

I shook my head. Rocco had broken my heart with a single glance, but aside from that, I was remarkably intact, as though Nature itself dismissed my suffering.

"You look hurt."

I said nothing, only shook my head again, but Cesare, who normally could be counted on to be oblivious to any concern not his own, chose that moment to become perceptive.

"It's that glassmaker, isn't it?"

Again, I tried to deny any such thing and might have succeeded had it not been for the trail of tears etching furrows down my still grimy cheeks.

"Ay, Francesca, *il mio dio*!"

"It doesn't matter," I said quickly, and balled my hands into fists, the better to scrub away my foolish tears. Somewhere in the days since I had first gone to Rocco for help, I had fallen into the trap of imagining that my life could be different from what it was. That the wall around me might crack open and that I might step out at last, not into the scene of my nightmare but into the light.

Instead, I had lured a good man into risking not only his own life but that of his son. I could not believe for a moment that Rocco would ever forgive me, nor did I imagine myself to be deserving of such forgiveness. Rather I had to confront the truth: Morozzi and I were alike at least in so far as we were both creatures of the dark, doomed to struggle within it until one of us, at least, was dead.

Cesare got to his feet and held out a hand. As I took it and rose, he asked reluctantly, "Will you be all right?"

If I had come to such a pass that Cesare Borgia was worried about my bruised heart, truly I was pitiable. My pride stung, a welcome pain in which I gladly took refuge.

"The less we are seen here," I said, "the better. We must return to the palazzo."

As I must return to who and what I truly was. Morozzi had been thwarted for the moment, but my father was far from avenged and, just as important, the great evil he had died trying to prevent would still be unleashed should Borgia lose the papacy.

Cesare's men-at-arms formed up around us, clearing our way through the crowd. Only a small fraction of the people gathered in the piazza in front of Saint Peter's would be admitted to the basilica for the funeral, but thousands more wanted to be close to the seat of power. Throngs were still arriving even as we attempted to leave, but it seemed that we were not alone in our eagerness to be gone from the area. A contingent of guards tromped past, escorting in their midst an elderly man in the black-and-white garb of a Dominican. Despite his age, he appeared to be departing in great haste.

Cesare stopped abruptly, his fixed stare drawing my attention to the man.

"Torquemada," he said under his breath.

I stared at the tall, pale friar passing directly in front of me. He had a thick boxer's nose and was bald save for a ring of hair above bushy eyebrows. So fierce was his expression that I suspect I would have noticed him under any circumstances.

"Are you sure?" I asked.

"I saw him once in Valencia when I was a child. My father pointed him out. He said then that no good would come of Ferdinand and Isabella's determination to blame the Jews for every ill, but I don't think even he imagined the depths to which they would sink."

Unable to help myself, I stared at the figure who haunted the nightmares of so many innocents.

He turned his head just then and for a moment, our eyes met. I would like to tell you that I saw the face of evil when I looked at the Grand Inquisitor, but in fact he seemed like so many men who serve Holy Mother Church: a bureaucrat for whom the suffering of humanity is of no account when compared to his own imagined vision of God's will. It is said that the Devil enters through back doors and in disguise but men such as Torquemada never seem to consider that. He is dead now, as I tell this tale. I wonder how warmly the One he served welcomed him into eternity.

Still in this world, he passed by in a rush, as though eager to absent himself now that what he had been led to expect was not occurring. Without a crucified child to proclaim as evidence of Jewish perfidy, he had nothing to look forward to from the citizens of Rome other than suspicion and humiliation. Morozzi had made an enemy of him, I judged. If Borgia survived to become pope, the mad priest would have to look elsewhere than to Spain for sanctuary. God willing, he would not find it.

As we left the environs of the Vatican, the bells of Saint Peter's began to toll, their dolorous cadence announcing that the funeral had begun. Great flocks of startled pigeons rose into the sky. For an instant, they seemed to obliterate the morning sun.

But no, that is not possible. Only poets claim that birds can do any such thing. It was the darkness within me that rose up and, for a time, blotted out all light and hope. If waves roil the river Styx, one such threatened to swamp me then.

How is that for poesy? The more mundane fact is that Cesare tossed me up into the saddle, swung up behind me, and, with the hard thrust of his spurs, took us back across the river to the palazzo at a trot.

Renaldo was waiting for us when we arrived.

"Where have you been?" the steward demanded with what seemed to me an excess of petulance. "His Eminence sent word that the patriarch of Venice has arrived. The conclave will begin day after tomorrow. There is much to be done and precious little time to do it in."

I did not have to approve of Renaldo's manner to know that he was right. Moreover, I knew that hard, relentless work offered me the only shelter from the grief tearing at me. Before Cesare could lower me from the saddle, I found my footing on the ground.

"I must see all, every bit of food, clothing, everything His Eminence intends to take with him."

"Half of it has already gone. You cannot expect His Eminence to wait on your pleasure and risk arriving like a ragtag gypsy, carrying bundles on his back."

"I can expect him to be sensible. He knows what is at stake. Morozzi—"

The priest had proven himself if not a master of the poisoner's art, no novice at it, either. With the tainted figs, he had killed Borgia's unborn child and come very close to killing La Bella herself. That he had used such a means rather than the lozenge in the locket he had taken from me told me that he was reserving it for a greater purpose.

I might be wrong, of course. Perhaps he intended to kill Borgia some other way and I was allowing myself to be misled. But everything I believed about the mad priest told me that he had not used the lozenge on La Bella because he intended it for Borgia.

The saving grace, so far as I could discern any, was that the combination of tartar emetic, dried paternoster pea, and star of Bethlehem that I had concocted was not a contact poison. It would be useless spread on fabric or any other surface Borgia would touch. That much might work in my favor. If I could be certain that the attack on Il Cardinale would come through his food or drink, at least I could concentrate my attentions where they would do the most good.

"What exactly has gone?" I demanded of Renaldo. "Any food, drink, anything of that kind must be recalled at once."

"Nothing like that," he assured me. "His bed, his clothes, certain items for his comfort and dignity, all from his own quarters here and therefore already inspected by you. Surely, that is acceptable?"

I did not know for certain if it was or not. I only knew that I had very little time and an immensely dangerous enemy who, in the face of his latest defeat, was likely to be more determined than ever to win at all costs.

"Come with me," I said and, without thinking to say a word to Cesare, I hurried off.

Sometime later, I was in the kitchens, inspecting the supplies being packed up to accompany Borgia into the conclave, when Vittoro appeared at my side.

"There you are," he said. "What's this I hear about Morozzi getting away again?"

Busy checking the seals on barrels of wine, I did not look up but said only, "At least his plan to incite Rome against the Jews was thwarted."

"So we have reached the endgame."

I did look up then, for I thought I caught a hint of relish in his words. He was a devoted chess player and as such, fully capable of appreciating the deep strategy Morozzi pursued, always looking many moves ahead.

But now, in less than two days—alarmingly less by the slanting of the sun—the princes of Holy Mother Church would be sealed away in conclave. Sometime after that—sooner rather than later if chaos was to be averted—a new pope would emerge to the acclaim of all Christendom.

"I've heard from your friend, David ben Eliezer," Vittoro said, once he was assured that he had my attention. "He says the word among the Jews is that della Rovere is prepared to do anything he must to assure that Borgia is defeated. He seeks that more even than his own election to the papacy."

"I do not doubt it." If it came to it, della Rovere was young enough that he could afford to wait. No doubt he hoped to elevate another caretaker pope in the mold of Innocent, someone he could control for his own benefit.

"Nor do I," Vittoro said, "but ben Eliezer is very specific. He says that della Rovere has gotten wind of Borgia's arrangement with the Jews. He is working frantically to assemble proof that will discredit Il Cardinale once and for all."

"Before he can be elected Pope."

"Exactly," Vittoro said. "According to ben Eliezer, della Rovere will stay his hand unless and until it appears that Borgia is about to be elected. Then he will strike without mercy. If he has the evidence, he will use that. Otherwise—"

"He could turn to Morozzi," I said, "but how? The cardinals will all be sealed in conclave—"

The sound of a throat being cleared drew us both up short. I had all but forgotten Renaldo. The steward looked anxious, as always, but also brimming with urgency he could scarcely contain.

"What do you know of this?" I asked.

"Why would I know anything?" he hedged.

"Because, dear Renaldo, we have established that very little escapes you. You are among friends. Tell us what you know."

The steward dabbed at the beads of sweat on his forehead, expanded his narrow chest, and said, "As it happens, I have heard one or two things."

"And that would be?"

"As you know, each prelate is to be accompanied by three attendants. Two of those serving della Rovere have been announced and are no surprise, they're both his secretaries. The name of the third has not been released but there are rumors. . . ."

"Morozzi," I said as did Vittoro in the same breath.

An instant later, Renaldo confirmed it.

It was the fulfillment of my worst fear. If Renaldo was right, Morozzi had contrived to place himself not only where he could do the most harm, but where I, as a woman, would not be able to reach him—inside the papal conclave itself.

"It is a risk for him," Vittoro observed, "should suspicions arise later surrounding the death of Il Cardinale."

"A risk he can afford to take," I said, "since Morozzi has the means to make it appear that I killed Borgia."

For once, I had managed to shock Vittoro. He stared at me. "What are you saying?"

Briefly, I confided my conviction that Morozzi intended to use both my locket and the lozenge he had taken from me to make it appear that I had struck down the very man I was charged to protect.

"Jesus weep," Vittoro said. He passed a hand over his face wearily.

There being nothing to add to that, I leaped ahead to what concerned me most. "Who will Borgia take into the conclave with him?"

"He has not said . . . exactly," Vittoro replied. The shifting of his gaze did not escape me.

"And that means . . . what?"

"It means that he is coming here, as soon as he can manage it, and he wants to be sure that you are on hand so that he can speak with you."

That suited me perfectly. I needed time alone with Borgia if I was to persuade him of the plan suddenly hatching in my mind.

"When you have finished with whatever it is you are doing," Vittoro said, "get some rest, have a bath, eat something but do not attempt to leave. I have enough to occupy me without chasing after you. Do we understand each other?"

I assured him that we did. When he was gone, I slumped against a vat of wine and looked at Renaldo.

"If we survive this, I will personally offer prayers of thanks to Saint Catherine of Siena and Saint Joan of Arc."

"Better you ask them now to help us and save the thanks for later," the ever practical steward pointed out.

If it is possible to pray while inspecting freshly butchered lamb, rounds of cheese, bushels of onions, and yet more wine, then I did so most fervently.

The day wore on. Borgia did not return to the palazzo. I supposed he was at the Curia, busy doing whatever he must to sway his fellow prelates to his cause. David sent a further message, carried by Benjamin, warning that della Rovere had dispatched several men to Siena. I had to hope that Cesare possessed the foresight to have left sufficient forces in that city to thwart any attempt to discover where the Jews' money had gone.

By early evening, exhaustion threatened to overwhelm me. I resolved to seek my bed for just a few hours. Renaldo sent me on my way, pointing out when I hesitated that I had checked the same bunch of basil four times. Not that basil is a particularly good hiding place for poison. Although strongly favored, its leaves, even when dried, tend to reveal the presence of any adulterant.

But I digress. Again, always, it is my curse. Suffice it to say that I went and—miracle of miracles—found that some kind soul had left a bath already prepared in my quarters. I soaked in it until the water was thoroughly cooled, then managed to dry myself, and tumbled into bed with no thought other than for blissful sleep.

Only to discover that I was not alone.

37

"You're incorrigible," I said, a statement of fact not to be mistaken for complaint. I was beyond even token protest, my body infused with that species of ease that comes in the aftermath of terror when fear, strength, will all drain away and leave only a strange, limp peace. Moreover, the truth is that I did not relish my own company just then, not awake or asleep.

Cesare lay with his arms folded behind his head, stretched out beneath a linen sheet that covered him no further than his hips. He must have bathed recently because his dark hair was still damp. His chest was bare except for the silver medallion of Saint Michael that he had taken to wearing of late, having declared his fealty to the warrior archangel.

In the shadows surrounding the bed, I could not make out his expression but I heard his smile. "Would you have me any other way?"

Wordlessly, I shook my head. The truth was that after my initial surprise, I felt only relief at his presence, that and the stirring of desire he inevitably provoked. I moved toward him or perhaps he reached out first, but in either case I was wrapped in his arms, held safe against his broad chest, his legs entwined with mine. How strange that I can still remember the heat of his skin, the smell of the sandalwood soap he used, the roughness under my questing fingers of the scar that ran along the right side of his rib cage, reminder of a sword fight when he was little more than a child that had almost killed him. All this I can recall precisely as though I had only to reach out my hand to be touching him again. Truly, memory is a cruel deceiver.

If his intent had been to remind me of how well suited we were to each other, he succeeded admirably. The burden on my heart from the loss of Rocco remained unchanged; I had no expectation that it would ever lessen. But the realization of that made it easier for me to accept the consolation of my dark lover.

Some while later—it must have been deep night by then—we lay sweat-slicked and sated yet both reluctant to sleep. Our hours together were too rare to yield any to Morpheus, that stealthy thief.

Cesare stirred beside me. "I should have gone after Morozzi. He is a threat to my father," he added as he stroked my breasts. "But the thought of you dying . . ."

I appreciated the sentiment, truly, but time was fleeting and did not wait upon small concerns, however much they mattered to me.

"The conclave—" I would have continued had Cesare not dropped his head and groaned. He was, I suspect, somewhat deflated by my lack of response to what was for him a veritable declaration of devotion.

"Oh, God, must we? Can we not, for just a little while, pretend none of that exists?"

There were times when I forgot that he was not yet seventeen. He was also unshaven and his beard scratched my skin. The weight of him, so pleasant in the throes of passion, left me feeling crushed. I gripped his hair in both hands and pulled him up so that he had to look at me.

"You can but I cannot. Your father is about to be sealed away with the most dangerous and conniving princes of Holy Mother Church. At least one of them is allied with a madman who has the means to kill Il Cardinale. It is my duty to prevent that. I would appreciate your advice."

"Kill della Rovere," he said without hesitation. Some have made the mistake of believing that Cesare was at heart a simple man, but I would say instead that he had a clarity of thought many of us would find enviable. Even so, there were times when he was wrong.

"I'm not sure that's the solution," I hedged.

He sighed. "You're a poisoner. Why are you so reluctant to kill people?"

"I am not—" Killing was, for me, not only a practical matter but, as I had discovered, a source of release and even pleasure. However much I wished myself not so afflicted, I cherished no hope that any amount of devotion, not to God or Borgia or anything else, could wash the darkness from my soul.

There being no reason to explain any of this to Cesare, I said only, "Killing isn't the best approach right now."

"Then how do you propose that we deal with this mess? Oh, I know, didn't Lucrezia tell me that you used to talk of running away to L'Angleterre and becoming a magus in the court of their king—what is his name, Henry something? Does that still appeal to you?"

"It might," I allowed, refusing to be embarrassed by my younger self. That is the problem with knowing people so long; they remember too much.

"Or better yet," I said, "we could make your father pope."

"You know he intends the same for me?"

I knew that Borgia intended his eldest son for the Church, but to hear Cesare speak so frankly of dynastic ambitions took me aback.

"Do you want to be pope someday?" I asked.

"God no!" There was no mistaking his fervency but lest I be left in any doubt, he added, "Give me a horse and a sword and I will remake the world, but for mercy's sake, leave God out of it."

"Yes, well, whatever your father plans, it will come to nothing if della Rovere manages to thwart him."

Cesare sighed and flopped over onto his back. I breathed in the sweat he had raised on me and asked, "Do you know what he intends?"

He turned, propping himself on his elbow, and met my gaze. "Who? My father or della Rovere?"

"Your father, of course. I care nothing for della Rovere. Il Cardinale knows the situation better than any of us. How does he plan to deal with it?"

"Hell if I know. I receive his orders, I carry them out, I hope he is pleased. Beyond that, he tells me nothing."

"You underestimate yourself. Did not your father send you to Siena? Obviously, he depends on you to handle delicate matters."

"He depends on me to frighten people so they don't get out of line. I'm very good at that. As to the rest"—he shrugged—"I suppose we will learn his plans in time. But for now . . ."

He moved against me and I welcomed him, for in the back of my mind was the thought that if Morozzi succeeded, I was unlikely ever to enjoy such pleasure again. Or anything else, for that matter.

When next I woke, sunlight was pouring through my windows and Cesare was gone. I had just enough time to wash and dress before Vittoro arrived to inform me that Il Cardinale required my presence.

In the final hours before the beginning of the conclave, the palazzo swarmed with activity. Men-at-arms were everywhere, servants hurried to and fro, and a veritable plague of clerks and secretaries seemed to have descended on us. All this was predictable enough but still startling. I was almost glad to reach the relative quiet of Borgia's offices.

He was busy when I arrived but I did not have long to wait before being ushered into his presence. Considering that he could not have had very much rest for days, he appeared remarkably robust. Crises always seemed to energize him, which was fortunate as there were so many throughout his life. When he saw me, he smiled and waved a hand, dismissing his secretaries, who went off with sullen glances in my direction.

"Francesca, you look very well. I must say that is a relief given what I had heard. You weren't injured then?"

It did not surprise me that he knew all that had happened in the basilica. Cesare would have reported to him directly while I was occupied with preparations for the conclave. I could only hope that Il Cardinale recognized the threat that Morozzi still presented.

I took the seat he indicated. "Not at all, Eminence, but thank you for your concern."

Borgia took his own chair and stared at me across the span of his desk. His scrutiny unnerved me but I hope I managed not to show it.

"Yes, well," he said. "Morozzi has certainly proven himself to be resourceful."

So did he acknowledge the plan to crucify a child and raise an enraged mob to destroy both Borgia and the Jews.

"And I fear he will continue to do so," I said. "You have heard the rumor that he will be in the conclave?"

I thought there little chance that I knew something Borgia did not and I was not disappointed. He nodded but appeared unperturbed.

"So I understand. He still has your locket and the lozenge, does he not?"

The reminder of my folly in allowing Morozzi to gain such an advantage still rankled. "We must assume that is the case."

"What then do you propose we do?"

"Everything that we possibly can to safeguard you, Eminence. But with Morozzi actually inside the conclave, I fear the precautions I have taken on your behalf will not be enough. He is, as you say, very resourceful. If he finds a way to substitute any item of food or drink intended for you—"

"Then we would have quite a problem, would we not?"

"Yes, Eminence," I said, and took a breath, ready to launch into the speech I had prepared to convince Il Cardinale to commit an act of such audacity that even he might balk.

"I see only one solution," Borgia declared.

I balked at cutting my hair. For all my relief that Borgia and I had turned out to be of the same mind on the matter of who should accompany him into the conclave, I drew the line there.

"I will braid it tightly and wind it around my head. So long as I keep a hat on, no one will be the wiser."

"Are you going to sleep in a hat?" Borgia inquired as I emerged from behind the screen where I had donned the mulberry red and gold livery worn by pages and other male servants in Il Cardinale's household. The sight of me seemed to amuse him.

"Why so uncomfortable, Francesca? This is hardly the first time you have worn boys' clothes."

That he knew about my sometime habit of wearing male garb did not surprise me. I had already suspected that the notion of smuggling me into the conclave had not sprung out of empty air, but I still felt compelled to warn him.

"You do realize that Morozzi intends to kill you in such a way that I will be blamed for your murder? My presence in the conclave will make it all the easier for him to convince people of that and in the process, shield della Rovere."

"All the more reason that he not succeed."

In the acknowledgment that our fates were well and truly intertwined, Borgia reached across his desk and poured wine for us both.

"Be of good cheer, Francesca," he said, handing me a goblet. "You are about to witness the awesome spectacle of God making his will known to the princes of his church. While it may appear less than edifying, I assure you that you will never forget it."

I muttered something to the effect that I would be pleasantly surprised if I lived to remember it at all before I threw back the wine and drank deeply. My stomach was empty; the wine hit it hard, but after a moment it surrendered.

As did I to whatever God intended for me.

Shortly after the sun rose on a new day, I—a mere woman, albeit in boys' garb—walked in the procession of prelates and attendants across the piazza in front of Saint Peter's into the Apostolic Palace and from there to the Sistine Chapel. The sweet, high voices of the *cantoretti* sang us on our way. The sun shone in brilliance as thousands gathered to applaud our passage amid prayers that the Almighty's will would be done.

Kneeling on the stone floor of the chapel, looked down upon by Moses, Jesus, the Apostles, and the Saints, I listened as the Mass of the Holy Spirit was celebrated. In his position as vice chancellor and dean of the College of Cardinals, Borgia should have led the Mass, but it was della Rovere who mounted the altar in red vestments. I was not alone in being taken aback. Several people near me exchanged startled glances and whispered comments. Did this disregard of protocol signal capitulation on Borgia's part? Was he acknowledging that his rival was preeminent among the cardinals? Or was it a clever step on his part, a show of diplomacy and willingness to compromise that demonstrated his fitness to be pope?

In the face of all that, very little attention was paid to the service itself until we all rose to receive communion. I took that opportunity to glance around quickly on the chance that I might see Morozzi, but there was no sign of him. The effort distracted me a little from the usual difficulties I have at such moments.

I managed the body of our Lord well enough and avoided all but a drop of the wine changed through the miracle of transubstantiation into our Savior's blood. Even so, my hands were clammy by the time I returned to my place and knelt once again. I was desperately worried that one of what I had come to think of as my "spells" might descend upon me but, mercy of God, none did.

The whispers were still going on when the Mass ended and the oration began. Tradition dictated that this be an address regarding the awesome responsibility entailed in the election of a new pope. Authority to select the speaker having rested with Borgia, necks craned to see whom he had chosen to honor. At the sight of Il Cardinale's fellow countryman, the Spanish ambassador, rising to mount the dais, a stir rippled through the crowd.

The ambassador did not disappoint. In the most forthright terms, he admonished the cardinals to put aside all personal considerations whether of ambition, personal rivalry, or ill will, and elect the man best suited by temperament and skill to lead Holy Mother Church. As it was well known that della Rovere's opposition to Borgia was entirely personal, there could be no doubt to whom the ambassador directed his exhortations.

At long last, it was over and we were allowed to rise for the singing of the Te Deum. As the prayer of thanksgiving ended, all those who would not be remaining within the conclave exited. The sound of the heavy wooden doors being slammed shut still reverberated around the chamber when we heard the clang of chains securing them.

We were sealed in—twenty-three cardinals, almost seventy attendants, one madman bent on murder, and myself.

So we would remain until God's will was done.

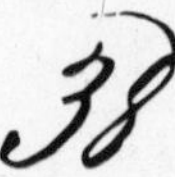

After the grandeur of the opening ceremony, the remainder of the first day of the conclave was devoted to the minutiae of an agreement limiting how many cardinals the new pope would be able to name over the course of his reign. This was exactly as tedious as it sounds. I paid very little attention to it.

Instead, I was occupied settling into our quarters. It has been given out that a dormitory of sorts was rigged up to accommodate the cardinals in Spartan circumstances during their deliberations. This is not strictly speaking true, at least not by my standards as to what constitutes Spartan.

As Vittoro and I had seen on our visit to the Sistine Chapel, a large adjacent hall had been converted into private apartments. Each comprised three rooms, the first providing the only access in or out of the apartment through a door that could be bolted. Here the attendants would sleep. Beyond was a larger and more gracious chamber in which the cardinal could eat, sleep, pray—should he be so inclined—and, most important, conduct private conversations. A third, much smaller chamber connected to the two principle rooms and was intended to aid the discreet flow of visitors. I claimed it for my own.

I was inclined to do so under any circumstances but my need was heightened by the fact that within hours of being sealed in the conclave, I discovered that my dalliances with Cesare had not borne fruit. Fortunately, I had had the foresight to plan for that contingency and was well provided with the necessary cloths, but as I have resolved to be entirely truthful here, I will say that the inevitable discomfort did nothing to improve my mood.

Despite my constant concern as to Morozzi's whereabouts and intentions, far more mundane matters could not be ignored. Borgia was expected to be in meetings for most of the day, but eventually he would retire and then he would have to eat. Simple food of the kind designed to make a display of humility was being provided to the conclave from the Vatican kitchens—bread, a bit of fish, a lentil potage, all passed through a slot in an otherwise secured door. The few cardinals known for their sanctity, and with no reason to fear poisoning, would make do with that. The rest had, like Borgia, provided for themselves.

While I have very few domestic skills I can, when pressed, put a meal on the table. Learning how to poison food may not be the most orthodox means of learning how to prepare it, but in my case it served well enough. Besides, it was suitable occupation for a page and would draw no scrutiny.

Facilities were limited—I had only a small brazier to cook over—but I contrived what I thought was a decent enough lamb stew. I was tasting it and adjusting the seasonings when Borgia arrived.

"What are you doing?" he asked. He looked tired but satisfied, from which I concluded things were going well. His secretaries hovered behind him. I was certain that they knew who I was but, sensibly, kept their knowledge to themselves.

"Making sure that I haven't poisoned you."

He raised a brow. "Are you inclined to do so?"

"Not at the moment." Hardly a politic answer, but my nerves were on edge. I was about to taste food that I was reasonably certain was safe in an effort to discover if I was wrong. Such circumstances do not make for good humor.

I will note in passing that while there may be poisoners who slough off the responsibility for tasting onto hapless servants, that is not the common practice. It is a matter of professional pride, and a show of professional confidence, to do one's own tasting. A wealthy patron, entrusting his and his family's life to the skills of a poisoner, will not long tolerate one who shows any hesitation in this matter.

I ladled a small amount of the stew into a bowl and began eating where I stood.

"How is it?" Borgia inquired after a few moments.

"Not bad. The meat is a little tough but it's edible."

More to the point, I felt fine. No burning of the mouth or throat, no sudden convulsion of the stomach, nothing to indicate there had been anything untoward in the ingredients I had used. I relaxed a little and even managed a slight smile.

Borgia said nothing about my willingness to die, if need be, to protect him, nor did I expect him to. He went on into his own quarters and, a short while later, called for his dinner. I brought it to him and, at his invitation, lingered as he ate.

"It's not bad," he said after he had taken several bites. "Clearly, we won't starve."

I inclined my head in thanks and refilled his goblet. "Just make sure that you don't eat or drink anything outside these rooms. If Morozzi really is here, he will contrive to poison you as far from della Rovere's quarters as possible. That being the case—"

"He is here," Borgia interjected. At my startled look, he added, "I caught a glimpse of him several hours ago and I don't think that was accidental. I believe he means for me to know that he is near."

"To distract you and perhaps even frighten you?"

Il Cardinale snorted and took another swallow of his wine. "If that is what he intends, he will be disappointed. It takes a great deal more to frighten me than a pretty priest mad with self-glory."

The description amused me enough that I almost smiled but, schooling myself to seriousness, said instead, "I pray you, Eminence, do not underestimate him. I have made that mistake and sorely regret it."

He looked at me shrewdly over the rim of his goblet. "You blame yourself for what happened at the basilica."

"How could I not?" I did not add that Rocco blamed me as well and that I deserved his condemnation.

"If you hadn't reasoned your way through to see Morozzi's plan, the boy would have died and we would all be dealing with chaos right now."

"If I had seen more reasonably in the beginning, the boy would never have been in danger to start with and Morozzi would have ceased to be a threat before now."

Borgia scraped up the last of his stew and leaned back in his chair. It was warm in the room despite the thick stone walls that kept much of the summer's heat at bay. The air scarcely moved. A drop of sweat crept down my back.

"So far as I can see," he said, "the only real mistake you made was in not telling me when Morozzi approached you, and for that you can be forgiven."

At my look of surprise, he added, "We have all made mistakes, each and every one of us. The trick is to not keep making them over and over."

"I don't," I said, not modestly but truthfully. "I keep finding new mistakes to make. I suspect that I have a genius for it."

Borgia chuckled. "You are young yet. Time will season you."

That he assumed I would have such time can be taken as a sign of confidence in his own ability to carry all before him. I could only hope that he was right. A short while later, he let me go, for which I was grateful. Anxiety as to what, if any, future lay ahead of me could not outweigh exhaustion. I had dragged a pallet from the attendants' room into the small chamber. Having left Borgia to his own rest, I fell onto it and was asleep almost instantly.

I knew nothing more until sometime in the depths of night when I awoke suddenly, uncertain of where I was. Several moments passed before I remembered and then a rush of fear went through me. I touched a hand to the broad felt hat that, awkward though it was to sleep in, concealed my hair. Reassured that it was in place, I drifted off again but slept lightly, mindful of the great struggle to come.

With the new day, the real work began. The merchants of this world will be cheered to know that God is, apparently, one of them. Everything I witnessed within the bazaar that was the papal conclave confirms this. If God truly moved through the princes of his Church, then God is a bargainer, a negotiator, a clever seller of goods, and an equally skilled purchaser of same. From all this, I have concluded that it is the merchants, rather than the meek, who will inherit the Earth. What they will do with it is anyone's guess.

It was a day of whispered conversations, of notes passed hand to hand, of surreptitious visits and huddles over goblets of wine. A day of smiles, cold and otherwise, of pressed handshakes and murmured confidences. A day in which immense amounts of money and vast properties were thrown down upon the table as so many chips and swept up as readily.

A day that seemed to leave Borgia well satisfied, for all that he ate only a little and retired to bed early.

On the next day, the first scrutiny, as it is called, was held.

Borgia lost.

He received seven votes but fourteen in all went to della Rovere and his surrogates. A two-thirds majority having been achieved by no man, the conclave continued.

What shall I tell you of the following day? Shall I speak of my mounting anxiety as the meetings, and the dealing, went on or of the many times I dared to peer outside Borgia's suite to try to assess what was happening elsewhere? Perhaps you would like to hear of who I saw coming and going between the various apartments—attendants, usually, carrying messages, but on occasion a cardinal himself, skittering quickly in the hope of not being seen or swaggering without shame. I had wondered at Borgia's determination to amass vast wealth on top of what he already possessed, but in those hours I came to understand why he had done it. I could inventory the exact payments made to so many princes of the Church, but as their venality is known to all, there seems no point.

Suffice it to say that very wealthy men became even wealthier over the course of a few crucial hours. But still it was not enough.

The second scrutiny was held in the evening of the third day. The tally was little changed from the first except that Borgia had gained a single vote. Negotiations continued through the night. There were rumors of a stalemate. I could only imagine the mood of the crowd gathered all this time in the piazza, waiting on the news that would tell them whether there would be order or chaos.

With all the coming and going within Il Cardinale's suite, I did not sleep. Early the next morning, I went to collect fresh bread provided by the Vatican kitchen, having confirmed the day before that the loaves were good enough not to offend Borgia's palate. By selecting several at random, I thought to minimize the chance that anyone could think of using them as a means of poisoning him—or me.

At the same time, I collected the letter slipped through the slot by an anonymous hand. Of course, Il Cardinale had established a means of communicating with the outside world even though sealed away in conclave. I would have expected nothing less.

I was about to go when I stopped short suddenly, my heart racing. A hint of camphor and citrus hung in the air. Turning, I only just managed to stifle a gasp. Morozzi stood directly behind me.

The golden angel looked entirely well and whole, untouched by his failure in the basilica. There was no doubt that he knew me for who I was. For a moment, I feared he was about to denounce me but he merely inclined his head and smiled pleasantly.

"Have you tried the bread?" he inquired. "It's surprisingly good."

Anyone listening to him would have mistaken his amicable manner toward a mere page as a sign of Christian kindness. I, however, understood him well enough.

"You can be assured that I will," I told him stiffly. "I taste everything meant for Il Cardinale."

"How very responsible of you. I hope he appreciates the risk you take." With a smile, he leaned forward and said close to my ear. "I hear his poisoner is a Jewess possessed by demons. If I were Borgia, I would fear her above all."

As he spoke, he drew my locket from beneath his cassock and held it so that I alone of those gathered nearby could see it.

An instant later, it had vanished back from whence it had come, close to what passed for his heart.

Bile rose in the back of my throat. I stumbled away, hoping against all hope that I had managed to conceal my fear from Morozzi but knowing too well that I had not.

My hands were still trembling a short time later when I brought Borgia his breakfast and the letter.

He glanced at me as he broke the seal and prepared to read. "Is something wrong?"

"I had an encounter with Morozzi."

He nodded but said nothing and gave his attention to the letter. After a moment, he remarked, "Cesare expresses his confidence that you are safeguarding me properly."

"Is he well?" I asked, as mildly as I could manage.

"Apparently so. Della Rovere's men are finding Siena an unfriendly place. No one wants to talk with them."

That was hardly surprising since, as Cesare himself had said, he was very good at frightening people. However, there was a darker side to the news.

"If della Rovere is unable to convince the cardinals not to elect you pope because of your dealings with the Jews, he will be left with only one other option."

Borgia finished reading and nodded. "He will have to let Morozzi kill me."

For a man standing on the brink of death, he seemed remarkably calm.

My own nerves were considerably more frayed. "The mad priest is here, he has my locket and its contents, and he has made it more than clear that he intends to act." Indeed, he had taunted me with his plan.

"I have no doubt that he does. The only question is how."

"Everything you eat, everything you drink, I test it all. But he knows that. Perhaps he intends to use a contact poison after all." The possibility haunted me.

"You did not think he had the skill for that. If he does use such a poison, there will be no direct link to you. Suspicion will fall on the man everyone knows has made himself my enemy, della Rovere."

"Except that I am here." I did not speak from concern for myself, at least not mainly, but rather to the point that my presence might embolden the mad priest to throw all caution to the wind and attack Borgia in any way he could, thinking to unmask me afterward and in the ensuing chaos, proclaim me a murderess.

"If the worst happens," Borgia said, "conceal yourself as best you can and wait for Vittoro. He will get you out."

I stared at him. "You have already thought of this."

"I may not be much of a priest but I am a very good administrator. I try to plan for all contingencies."

He got up to go without having breakfasted, from which I concluded he was not as impervious to the situation as he liked to appear.

"Wear the gloves," I called after him. I had insisted that he bring half a dozen pairs and keep one of them on at all times when he was outside the apartment. Further, I had instructed him—there is no other word for it—not to accept anything directly from the hand of another but to pass everything through his secretaries for my inspection. As a result, they, too, wore gloves.

Beyond that, he wore the formal vestments of his rank when outside his quarters, as did all the cardinals. The garments left no part of him uncovered save for his head.

Over his shoulder, he said, "Believe me, Francesca, I am in no rush to leave this world."

It was now the tenth of August, Anno Domini 1492. The cardinals had been in conclave four full days. All were growing restless, understanding as they did the need to protect the stability of the Church so lately healed from the Great Schism. Too long a delay in naming the new pope and far more than merely the populace of Rome would rise up in fear of a return to chaos. Frightened, angry people are unpredictable, and therefore all the more dangerous.

Accordingly, when the third scrutiny was held later that day, I was not especially surprised to learn that a clear favorite had emerged.

Borgia had fourteen votes, one short of the fifteen needed to become pope.

Morozzi had to strike soon.

"I am counting on you to keep him at bay long enough for me to win," Borgia said when he returned to his quarters briefly.

With that he was gone again, off to meet with one or another of the very few cardinals not yet pledged for or against him.

His secretaries went as well, leaving me alone in the silent apartment to ponder what I should do.

Or more particularly, what Morozzi would do.

How reluctant I was to put myself in the mad priest's mind yet how vital it was that I manage no less. I paced and fiddled, sighed and groaned, sat and stood, and at one point snatched off the hat I had come to loathe and yanked hard enough on my hair to bring tears to my eyes.

Finally, frustrated beyond bearing and deeply worried about Borgia, I left the apartment to see if I could learn anything about what was happening.

I was about halfway down the passage linking the cardinals'

quarters to the chapel itself when a party of several prelates and their attendants surged toward me from the opposite end. Quickly, I pressed back against the wall and averted my face as they passed, but not before I saw that della Rovere was in the lead. If you have seen the portrait Raphael did of him, you will think him a frail, white-bearded man of somber mien, and I suppose that he was by the time he sat for the painter. But that day he was not yet fifty years old and still endowed with vigor many a man of similar age would have envied. Without the concealment of a beard, his features could be seen to be somewhat soft, the eyes deep-set beneath jutting brows, and the mouth seemingly set in permanent disapproval.

He went by and the rest of his party with him, giving no sign of having noticed me. I breathed a sigh of relief and continued on, hoping to encounter one of Borgia's secretaries or, failing that, simply to loiter about and pick up what gossip I could. Much of the day had gone as I stewed over what to do. It was already past vespers. From what I could glean by listening here and there, no further vote was planned before the following morning.

That being the case, I assumed that Borgia would return soon to his apartment, expecting to find something to eat. I hurried back to be there when he arrived.

He looked tired but in no way downhearted as he pulled off his gloves, accepted the wine I poured for him, and took a seat.

Without preamble, he said, "I think Gherardo is senile."

It took me a moment to realize that he was referring to the aged patriarch of Venice for whose sake the conclave had been delayed.

"Half the time we're talking, he seems to think he's a boy back in Venice."

"Do you have his vote?" You would think that someone in my line of work would be a master—or mistress—of circumspection.

My father was such but it is a skill in which I remain lamentably lacking.

Fortunately, my directness did not faze Borgia. Indeed, he was to tell me later that he valued that quality in me almost more than any other.

"When he is in the here and now, I believe that I do."

I stepped back and stared at him. My heart was beating very fast. "Then it is done?"

He shrugged and accepted his wine. "If God wills it."

His manner did not fool me. I knew him too well not to realize that he was both deeply pleased and still apprehensive. How could he not be? He was so very close and yet—

"Della Rovere knows," I said, "or at least he suspects."

"What makes you say that?"

"I saw him in the passage a short time ago. He looked . . . upset."

"You know he is prone to constipation? Perhaps it was that."

I smiled despite myself. "No, I think it was of rather more import."

"We will vote again at break of day," Borgia said. "Shortly before then, I will go to see Gherardo again in hope of finding him still of the same mind, whatever that may be. In the meantime, I trust you, and the sturdy lock on the door, to keep me from harm."

I nodded and went about my tasks, seeing to his meal, but my thoughts were elsewhere. Whatever the state of his bowels, I was convinced that what I had seen on della Rovere's face meant that he knew the final blow was about to fall. Yet Morozzi seemed so supremely confident, mocking me with his assurance of success. As for the rest of us, we were all sealed away in a world where the only chance to commit murder and get away with it had to lie in making a stranger appear responsible.

"Della Rovere must know by now that his only way of stopping you from becoming pope is to let Morozzi kill you," I said.

"So it appears . . ." Borgia muttered. He seemed disinclined to go over yet again how close he was to the precipice.

"But," I went on, speaking as much to myself as to him, "for all that they have allied themselves, della Rovere and Morozzi don't really seek the same end."

This notion had been in my mind before, but I had given it no real attention. Now I forced myself to do so, turning it this way and that as the conviction grew in me that what separated the two men was at least as important as what united them.

The Cardinal peered at me. "What are you saying?"

I stared not at but through him and saw the dark and twisting labyrinth I had followed from the first day I met the mad priest and tried to divine his intentions. As though from a distance, I heard myself speak.

"Della Rovere wants to be pope, but he will settle for electing a surrogate who he can control. Morozzi, on the other hand, wants only to assure the election of a pope who can be convinced to sign the edict against the Jews. That could be anyone—not just della Rovere or his surrogate, anyone at all except you."

"I fail to see the difference. Both are determined to stop me from becoming pope."

"True, but you said yourself that Morozzi is not della Rovere's creature. Yet surely he has led the cardinal to believe otherwise or della Rovere would never have brought him into the conclave."

As I spoke those words, the final piece fell into place and the puzzle opened before me, revealing all it had concealed.

I turned, moving quickly, no longer thinking, knowing that every moment counted and dreading that I might already be too late.

39

Borgia followed me. He admitted afterward that he thought I had truly gone mad, all the more so when I burst into della Rovere's apartment, pushing past his attendants who had opened the door on my claim that I carried a message of vital importance. Once in, I lunged for the inner chamber, heedless as my hat flew off, and found his Eminence at his dinner.

"Don't," I screamed, but it was too late. He was already chewing.

"Spit it out," I ordered, and would have grabbed hold to force him to do so had not one of his secretaries tackled me from behind, thrown me to the floor, and sat on me.

With my chest all but crushed and the last of my breath almost gone, I cried out. "Morozzi doesn't need to kill Borgia! He only needs to make him unelectable!"

Della Rovere gaped at me. Around the morsel still in his mouth, he managed to say, "A woman? You are a woman!"

Sweet lord, you would have thought the gates of Hell had opened and a thousand demons had poured forth. In the uproar that followed the discovery of my sex, I managed to regain my feet despite the blows rained on me by the attendants and della Rovere himself, who rose expressly for that purpose and did not stint.

Only Borgia's bellow of outrage as he waded into the fray stopped the worst of it. He yanked me behind him and confronted his hated rival. Color flooded his face as he berated della Rovere.

"Did you not hear her, you fool? We know why you brought Morozzi here but he is not your creature, he never has been. He couldn't get to me but it serves him just as well to get to you!"

Della Rovere opened his mouth, no doubt to deliver a scathing reply, but no words came. His eyes widened hugely as he put a hand to his throat. A look of pure terror overcame him in the instant before he convulsed.

If there was chaos before, now there was pandemonium. Both of Borgia's secretaries had followed us. With della Rovere's two attendants, there were seven of us in the room. Only Borgia and I had kept our heads and of the pair of us, only I had any notion what to do.

"Get him onto the floor," I ordered and, after a moment's hesitation, I was obeyed. Terror over what was happening overcame all else, even the terror of women that seems to lurk in so many men. Della Rovere was breathing with great difficulty. His skin already felt chilled to my touch. Flecks of white shone at the corners of his mouth and his entire body was stiff, his back arching as another spasm went through him.

Yet he was still fully conscious, as the terror in his eyes made clear.

That reassured me that he could not possibly have ingested very much of the compound I had made.

"Loosen his clothes," I ordered one of his attendants. To one of Borgia's secretaries, I said, "Go back to the apartment. There is a brown leather bag in the small room. Bring it here *quickly.*"

The man sprinted off. When he was gone, Borgia leaned down close to me. With a slight nudge, he drew my attention to what he held nestled securely in the palm of his hand. My locket.

"How?" I mouthed the word.

He inclined his head in the direction of the table where della Rovere had been eating. Very quietly, he said, "Under there. Rather obvious but found beside a dead cardinal, it would have been effective."

"Morozzi—?"

"Gone, I'm sure."

And with him any immediate hope I had of avenging my father. For a moment, anguish filled me. Yet I am ever a patient woman. If I still managed to hoist Borgia onto Peter's Throne, at least I would thwart the mad priest's dream of death for the Jews and at the same time acquire a formidable weapon to assist me in hunting him. Justice may have been delayed but it would not be denied, not while I had breath.

With a glance at della Rovere, who I was certain could hear us both, Borgia said, "You realize that if you treat him and he dies, you can be blamed for his death?"

Whereas if I stopped right then, all anyone would know was that Il Cardinale and I had made a desperate but futile effort to prevent della Rovere from being poisoned. Borgia's enemy would be dead and he would be pope.

I will tell you honestly that I hesitated. For della Rovere to die by the very means he had intended to bring about Borgia's death and in all likelihood send me to the stake seemed just to me. It might even be called divine justice.

And yet—

I am certain that della Rovere knew exactly what was being decided, for he tried frantically to speak. Already he was in such extremis that no sound came from him other than strangled grunts.

Il Cardinale rose and stepped back. A moment longer, he looked at his great enemy, the man who had conspired to bring about his own death. And then he said, "Do what you can for him."

Do not ask me why he made the choice that he did. In all the years that followed, I never had the nerve to ask him. Suffice it to say that Borgia being Borgia, I trusted that he had his reasons.

I administered enough emetine to empty della Rovere's gut ten times over. The strain of that on top of what was already happening to him might prove too much for his heart to endure, but I felt that I had no choice. Every particle of the lozenge had to be expelled before it reached deeper into his body and wreaked havoc. Violent, repeated vomiting was the only means to save him.

The details being surpassingly unpleasant, I will say only that della Rovere bore it as well as any man might. The same cannot be said for the attendants who appeared so sickened by the spectacle that I feared they would begin vomiting in turn with no assistance from me.

As for Il Cardinale, when next I had a moment to look, he was gone.

In the early hours of the morning of the eleventh of August, Anno Domini 1492, the fourth and final vote took place. Fifteen votes went to Cardinal Rodrigo Borgia, the crucial margin of a single vote being provided by the aged patriarch of Venice who, it was said afterward, told several of his fellow cardinals what great friends he and Borgia had been when they were both boys all those years ago in Venice. To this day, it remains a mystery whom he actually thought he was voting for.

In a gesture of extraordinary magnanimity so uncharacteristic of him as to occasion great discussion, Cardinal Giuliano della Rovere, who it was remarked at the time did not look well, acceded to the motion to make the vote for Borgia unanimous.

At the throwing open of the windows facing the piazza and the shout: *"Habemus Papam!"* the crowd went wild. Rome—and all of Christendom—had been spared the chaos of a long, drawn-out contest for the papacy. The college of cardinals had chosen a man who, for all that he was a Spaniard, had at that time the love of the Roman people, who promptly fell to rejoicing with their customary enthusiasm.

As they did, Borgia was carried into Saint Peter's Basilica on the *sedia gestatoria,* the portable throne of the pope, and borne to the high altar where, in acclamation of his election, each of the cardinals offered his homage to him. How well della Rovere managed that I cannot tell you, the basilica being no place for a vomit-encrusted page who had forgotten to reclaim "his" hat.

I made my way back to the palazzo through streets filled with celebrants already falling upon the vast amounts of food and wine Borgia had arranged to have available in anticipation of his victory. Not far beyond the Pons Aelius, I happened upon Petrocchio, who was overseeing the event. The Maestro gave me a huge smile and despite my state, an equally enthusiastic embrace.

"He is Pope!" Petrocchio enthused. "Our very own Borgia is Pope!"

Pope he certainly was. As to whether he would ever be able to see beyond the interests of La Famiglia to be "our" Pope, that remained for us to discover.

I reached the palazzo to find the servants in a mad scramble to pack Borgia's belongings for transfer to his new home. Renaldo descended upon me, shocked by my appearance and wanting to know everything. I told him what I could but made short work of it and went as quickly as possible to my quarters. I had no idea where I would be going, but I trusted Borgia to contrive some convenient place to put me. Despite my fatigue, I did not delay securing my belongings, packing them away in my chest, and making sure that the puzzle lock was in place. Only then did I bathe and change into my own clothes.

I had barely finished when a maid knocked timidly at the door. Upon my opening it, she handed me two notes.

"These came for you, Madonna," she whispered without daring to look at me. Such was my reputation already, born in rumor but fed by truth. Very few people have looked me in the eye since then, at least not willingly. I live with that but I cannot be said to like it.

I opened the first of the notes after she had gone. Standing by the window, I scanned the single line neatly written:

M is making for Florence. I follow. You will hear when I know more. DbE

Florence, golden city of the Medici. What would the mad priest find there and what would it mean for all of us? At least I could count on David to leave no stone unturned in discovering what Morozzi planned next.

The second note was from Rocco. It said only that the apparatus I had ordered were ready and could be collected from his shop at my convenience.

I went there the next morning. I told myself that to fail to do so would be cowardice, but in truth I could not have stayed away.

Nando was playing out in front. He jumped up at the sight of me and ran into my arms. I knelt, clutching him tightly, and struggled not to weep at the sturdy feel of his small, blessedly alive self. My efforts were only partly successful. I was brushing the tears from my cheeks when Rocco emerged from the shop.

He stood for a moment in the sunlit street surrounded by the bustle of the city that was slowly returning to normal after the excesses of celebration. His face was solemn and his eyes watchful as he drew a coin from his pocket and sent it spinning through the air toward his son, who leaped to catch it.

"Tell Maria I want an especially good loaf," he instructed, "and get a biscotto for yourself while you're at it."

Nando ran off, leaving me staring dry-mouthed at his father. After a moment, Rocco stepped aside so that I could enter the shop. He followed, closing the door behind us.

Just over the threshold, I turned and blurted what was uppermost in my heart.

"I am so sorry."

He did not pretend to mistake my meaning but nodded. "When I thought of how close I came to losing him, I blamed you."

So I had seen on his face and so I had believed nothing could ever change. But hope can exist even in one such as myself, if only dimly. Gathering all my courage, I asked, "Do you still?"

He stared down at me and I had the sudden sense that he alone, of everyone I knew, saw me in a way that not even I could manage to do. Saw not the darkness within me that spawned fearsome nightmares and twisted visions I could not begin to grasp but rather the woman I longed to be. A woman of the light.

"You almost died saving him. Whatever else you did, I can never forget that."

"Morozzi got away. He is still out there—" I had saved the child and the Jews, but ultimately I had failed to avenge my father. The shadow over my life remained and with it the mystery of why I was as I was.

Rocco came toward me and took my hand. "We will deal with him, Francesca. He is not your enemy alone."

Not trusting myself to speak, I nodded and was glad when he drew me off to look at the apparatus he had made. I feigned interest in them until he said, "When you came to see me to order these, there was something you wanted to ask, wasn't there?"

I struggled to think, frankly not caring just then about anything other than what measure of his forgiveness I had achieved and what more might yet be attainable to me. But finally a memory surfaced. I started to dismiss it only to stop when I saw his seriousness.

"I wanted to ask if you knew whether it was true that my father belonged to a secret society of alchemists called Lux. I even wondered if you yourself might be a member."

"Are you busy tomorrow evening?"

The question caught me unawares. I was not clear how it followed from what I had just said. "I don't think so—"

"Then come here and you will find your answer."

Before I could begin to absorb his meaning, a child's footsteps sounded, running toward the shop. With a smile, Rocco said, "Just don't be surprised if some of those you meet are already known to you."

Nando burst in upon us then, bringing warm bread and eager chatter. Over his head, my gaze met Rocco's. In him I saw calm acceptance of the struggle that lay ahead but also the enduring hope that the future can be better, that light truly can triumph over dark.

Especially when a mistress of the dark wills it to be so.

AUTHOR'S NOTE

In the course of writing *Poison,* I relied mainly on the following works: Sarah Bradford's *Lucrezia Borgia: Life, Love, and Death in Renaissance Italy* and *Cesare Borgia: His Life and Times;* Ivan Cloulas's *The Borgias;* Marion Johnson's *The Borgias;* E. R. Chamberlin's *The Fall of the House of Borgia;* Clemente Fusero's *The Borgias;* Michael Edward Mallett's *The Borgias: The Rise and Fall of a Renaissance Dynasty;* and Christopher Hibbert's *The Borgias and Their Enemies.* As a primary source, Johann Burchard's *At the Court of the Borgia* was invaluable.

In addition, several people played key roles in bringing this book from the kernel of an idea to a completed work. I am especially grateful to my agent, Andrea Cirillo, for her constant patience and sound advice. Thanks also for the outstanding editorial support provided by Charles Spicer and Allison Caplin, and to marketing whiz Anne-Marie Tallberg, who so generously shared her expertise.

Author's Note

As always, my family coped wonderfully with a distracted writer muttering about poisons and other arcane means of inflicting death. Without their unfailing encouragement, this book and a great deal more would never have been accomplished.

The challenge in writing historical fiction is to weave together what is real and what can be imagined into a coherent and, one hopes, compelling story. Francesca herself is, of course, fictional, but much of *Poison* is based on real people and the events they took part in during the summer of 1492.

Pope Innocent VIII died on July 25 in that year after a long illness punctuated by an improvement in his health around the time that Francesca's father is depicted as having been murdered. In the final stage of his life, Innocent was rumored to take mothers' milk to stay alive. During his last days, he was also said to have ingested the blood of young boys in an effort to stave off death. As much as I would like to claim credit for coming up with such macabre devices, this is a case of history truly being stranger than fiction.

Poison was rumored to be the cause of the pope's demise, as it was widely believed to be the cause of many deaths in this period. While it is most likely that Innocent expired from natural causes, we can no more be certain of that than could Francesca.

Although there is no evidence that Innocent was considering a papal edict calling for expulsion of the Jews from all of Christendom, it is well known that he applauded the decision by Ferdinand and Isabella to force all the Jews of Spain to convert or leave their kingdom. The doctrine of anti-Semitism was ubiquitous throughout Europe at this time, but no institution supported it more vigorously or effectively than did the Catholic Church.

The events described as having occurred in La Guardia, Spain, and the story of the "Holy Child" are based on fact. Tomás Torquemada, the Grand Inquisitor of Spain, is a historical figure, but if he made a trip to Rome at the time of Innocent's death, no record remains of it.

The papal conclave that selected Innocent's successor is remembered as the most corrupt ever held. Rodrigo Borgia triumphed, becoming Pope Alexander VI not because he alone was willing to engage in bribery to attain votes but because he proved the most effective at understanding and exploiting the greed of his fellow princes of the Church. The vast wealth that Borgia used to secure his victory was rumored to have come in part from the Jews, in return for which he agreed to tolerate their presence in the Papal States and by extension in Christendom. If an attempt was made during the conclave to poison Borgia's great rival, Cardinal Giuliano della Rovere, that has escaped the notice of history.

Rodrigo Borgia and the most notorious of his children, Lucrezia and Cesare, have long been accused of using poison to advance their ambitions, in addition to a host of other crimes. It is my belief that Lucrezia was a victim of her father's unbridled lust for power and that she survived as long as she did despite, not because of, the corruption of her age. While Rodrigo and Cesare may have been amenable to using poison, they clearly preferred the more direct methods of bribery, intimidation, and, when necessary, open warfare.

Poison takes place near the beginning of the great struggle between the forces of the Renaissance and those of the Inquisition, a struggle that dominated Europe for centuries and played such a crucial role in shaping the world we know today. While an argument can be made that there were decent, well-intentioned people on both sides of this conflict, overwhelmingly the Inquisition represented an oppressive force willing to sacrifice even the hope of a better life for the many in order to maintain the power of the very few. The valiant men and women who stood against it, and who often paid for their courage with their lives, deserve to be remembered, but the victory they won must be earned again by every generation.

POISON

by Sara Poole

About the Author

- A Conversation with Sara Poole

Behind the Novel

- Historical Timeline
- "Pretty Poisons All in a Row"
  An Original Essay by the Author

Keep on Reading

- Recommended Reading
- Reading Group Questions

A Reading Group Gold Selection

For more reading group suggestions,
visit www.readinggroupgold.com.

ST. MARTIN'S GRIFFIN

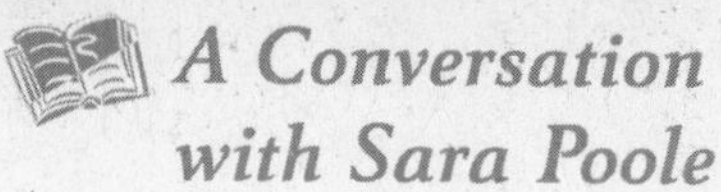

A Conversation with Sara Poole

Could you tell us a little bit about your background, and when you decided that you wanted to lead a literary life?

I grew up in a family of journalists who were taken aback when, at the tender age of twelve, I announced my intent to write fiction. I immediately set about doing so and have never stopped. Along the way, I've worked in advertising, public relations, and publishing, but fiction has always been my lodestone drawing me home. I can't imagine a life without it.

"Fiction has always been my lodestone drawing me home."

Is there a book that most influenced your life? Or inspired you to become a writer?

As a child, I read everything from Lewis Carroll to comic books (*Little Lulu* stands out in particular). I loved it all indiscriminately and gobbled up anything that fell into my hands. Somewhere along the way, I encountered Jean Plaidy in one or more of her various incarnations and became hooked on historical fiction.

Who are some of your favorite authors?

My favorite novel of all time is *Killer Angels* by Michael Shaara; in my opinion, it's the finest historical novel ever written. Apart from that, my favorite writers remain those I discovered early on—Jean Plaidy aka Victoria Holt and Philippa Carr, Daphne du Maurier, Anya Seton, and Mary Stewart, among others.

Who are some of your favorite historical figures?

Obviously, I have vast affection for the Borgias, although I can't say that I would have wanted to live under their rule. The combination of ruthless ambition, brilliant intellect, and unfettered sensuality that they embodied is enormously appealing from a writer's point of view. Apart from them, I love the Tudors, most particularly Elizabeth, who has to be regarded as a survivor of one of the most dysfunctional families ever.

What was the inspiration for *Poison* and its heroine, Francesca?

Several years ago, I became interested in the wild plants on my doorstep that in one form or another are poisonous. One evening, I mentioned this to my family at dinner, setting off a round of teasing about what I'd put in the food. Two words popped into my head: *woman poisoner.* In the strange way of such things, Francesca appeared shortly thereafter, virtually fully formed. I've had to run to keep up with her ever since.

Do you scrupulously adhere to historical fact in your novels, or do you take liberties if the story can benefit from the change? To what extent did you stick to the facts in writing *Poison*?

I try to stick very closely to the historical facts while weaving a thread of fiction through and around them. Nothing in *Poison* contradicts anything that happened in the summer of 1492. But as is always the case in such fraught times, much that did occur was hidden from public view and will never be known. It is in those secret, forgotten spaces that I found room to begin Francesca's story.

Much of the plot of *Poison* revolves around poison and its use by the leaders and politicians of Renaissance Italy. How much of this was historically accurate?

Because so many of the poisons available at the time produced symptoms similar to those caused by common diseases such as malaria and cholera, it is impossible to know how many deaths can be attributed to natural causes versus unnatural. What we do know is that people in all ranks of society believed that poison was in widespread use, and that many lived in terror of falling victim to it. In that climate of fear, families of means took steps to protect themselves, including employing experts

"It is impossible to know how many deaths can be attributed to natural causes versus unnatural."

capable of detecting the presence of poison in food, wine, fabric, etc. These men and women appear cloaked in household accounts as "perfumer," "herbalist," "apothecary," and so forth—occupations that concealed their true purpose. How many of them crossed the line between defending against poison and deploying it as a weapon remains a matter of speculation.

In your research of the poisons used in Renaissance Rome, what was the most interesting/surprising/shocking thing you learned?

For me, the role of poisons during the Renaissance turned out to be a window into the era as a whole through which I glimpsed the herculean struggle that went on between the forces of conservatism (i.e., much but by no means all of the Catholic Church) and the forces of modernization including the emerging merchant class. Previously, I'd had only a general sense of the competing visions that tugged at all corners of life and eventually ripped the fabric of the world. What struck me most were the eerie parallels to our own time when we seem to be experiencing equally profound and sweeping change with consequences we can speculate about but cannot yet really see.

There is a proverb attributed to the Chinese that is said to embody a curse: *May you live in interesting times.* The Borgias and their fellow travelers through the Renaissance certainly did, and so do we.

Why do you think readers are so drawn to historical fiction?

Historical fiction has been categorized as "infotainment" and there is something to that. In the vicarious experience of a far-flung time and place, we can find a better understanding not only of another age but of ourselves and our own world.

Are you currently working on another book? And if so, what—or who—is your subject?

Poison is the beginning of a series depicting the life of Francesca Giordano and her entanglements with the Borgias. The second book, *Serpent,* is completed. I am currently working on the third book in the series, *Malice.*

Historical Timeline

"[In] our own time . . . we seem to be experiencing . . . sweeping change with consequences we can speculate about but cannot yet really see."

March 31, 1492	Edict issued by Queen Isabella and King Ferdinand expelling all Jews from Spain
Spring, 1492	Pope Innocent VIII's health worsens; rumors spread that he is receiving mother's milk
	Jews fleeing Spain flood into Rome and elsewhere
Late Spring, 1492	Pope Innocent VIII's health improves
Early Summer, 1492	The Pope's health worsens once again; rumors spread that he is receiving the blood of young boys
July 25, 1492	Pope Innocent VIII dies, setting off the scramble to succeed him
July 31, 1492	Last day for Jews to leave Spain or face execution
August 3, 1492	Christopher Columbus sets sail from Spain but with attention focused on the death of the Pope, little notice is taken.

August 6, 1492	Papal conclave to elect the new Pope opens in Rome, for the first time in the Sistine Chapel
August 8, 1492	First "scrutiny" taken, no clear favorite for Pope; Borgia said to have placed third
August 9, 1492	Second "scrutiny" taken; Borgia gains slightly but clearly is not the favorite
August 10, 1492	Third "scrutiny" taken; Borgia gains significantly amid rumors of vote buying
August 11, 1492	Rodrigo Borgia is elected Pope, becoming Pope Alexander VI in what will become known as the most corrupt papal conclave in Church history

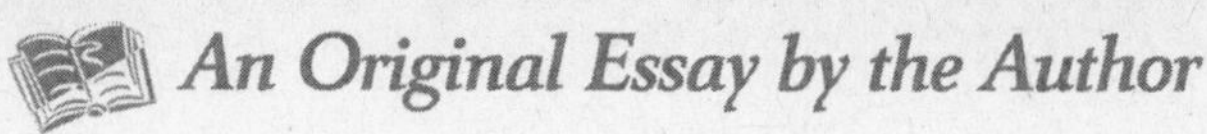

An Original Essay by the Author

Pretty Poisons All in a Row

Take a stroll through your local park, past an empty lot, or in your own backyard and you are likely to come across the deadly means of dispatching a fellow human being from this world. Poisons abound in nature, often coming in the form of lovely flowers, attractive berries, and seemingly harmless leaves and roots. The results vary from the relatively benign to the almost instantly fatal but the message from Mother Nature is the same: Beware!

"Our own backyards [are] a virtual pantry of poisons."

My own initiation into the ready availability of poisons all around us came a few years ago when I noticed a plant I hadn't seen before growing just a few feet from my doorstep. The plant with its distinctively curving leaves turned out to be jack-in-the-pulpit, as *Arisaema triphyllum* is commonly known. In identifying it, I learned that pretty jack contains calcium oxalate, which in small quantities will irritate the mouth, esophagus, and stomach while larger amounts cause swelling severe enough to cut off breathing.

That got me to wondering what else I might find amid the wild flowers and plants that I'd enjoyed in passing but rarely thought about. In short order, I discovered foxglove with its potentially deadly dose of digitalis; monkshood carrying lethal aconite; nightshade of the sweet but fatal berries; hallucinogenic and sometimes lethal jimsonweed; and much more. Many of these plants flourish because the omnipresent deer avoid them, thereby giving them an advantage over tastier edibles while making our own backyards and byways a virtual pantry of poisons.

In these days of modern forensics, toxicology analyses readily uncover the presence of deadly natural compounds, limiting the appeal for would-be murderers. But in the past, nature played a far more active role in homicides and executions. Hemlock, for example, killed Socrates. Arsenic was suspected in the death of Lorenzo de Medici (Lorenzo the Magnificent) and numerous other nobles of the time. Several popes were rumored to have been poisoned and far more feared that they would be. Much more recently, the deadly poison ricin, extracted from castor beans, has been used to kill at least one anti-Communist operative in Western Europe.

Even more than deliberate killings, accidental poisonings still occur with alarming regularity. Hikers and campers, swooning over the beauty of nature and unaware of the dangers, ingest substances that at best leave them mildly ill and at worst land them in the hospital. Children and pets are even more vulnerable, especially since deadly doses for them are much smaller. The lesson for all of us has to be that while we should enjoy nature by all means, we underestimate it at our own peril. Before you pluck that berry, sauté that mushroom, or toss what you think is an edible flower into your salad, stop and ask yourself: Is Mother Nature about to kill me?

Want to learn more? You'll find the author's "Poison of the Week" blog, a colorful pharmacopeia, and other poisonous delights at www.sarapoole.com.

Recommended Reading

Sarah Bradford
Lucrezia Borgia: Life, Love, and Death in Renaissance Italy
Cesare Borgia: His Life and Times

Johann Burchard
At the Court of the Borgia

E. R. Chamberlin
The Fall of the House of Borgia

Ivan Cloulas
The Borgias

Sarah Dunant
The Birth of Venus
Sacred Hearts
In the Company of the Courtesan

Clemente Fusero
The Borgias

C. W. Gortner
The Confessions of Catherine de Medici: A Novel

Christopher Hibbert
The Borgias and Their Enemies

Marion Johnson
The Borgias

Jeanne Kalogridis
The Borgia Bride: A Novel
The Devil's Queen: A Novel of Catherine de Medici

Michael Edward Mallett
The Borgias: The Rise and Fall of a Renaissance Dynasty

Reading Group Questions

1. Francesca Giordano lives at a time when civilization is being revitalized by new perceptions and ideas that threaten the existing power structure. How does the struggle between the two shape this story and the challenges that Francesca faces?

2. Over the course of this story, Francesca kills at least twice and possibly three times. Can her actions be justified morally?

3. While she yearns for the glassmaker, Rocco, and the life she could have had with him, Francesca does not hesitate to pursue a relationship with Cesare Borgia that is sexual and more. Is she hypocritical in having feelings for both men or is she drawn to each for different reasons?

4. Francesca has a complex relationship with her employer, Cardinal Rodrigo Borgia. How much do you think the Cardinal knows about Francesca's past? What role may he have played in the murder of her father?

5. In modern terms, Francesca suffers from post-traumatic shock related to an event early in her life. In a time before psychoanalysis, she can understand her condition only as the act of a supernatural agent, either God or the Devil. What factors in her life may prompt her to look elsewhere for the true cause of her distress as well as the path to resolving it?

6. The discovery that her late father was *converso,* a convert from Judaism to Christianity, shocks Francesca and makes her question what else he concealed from her. But it also opens her to new perspectives and relationships. Is the uncovering of hidden truths always beneficial or are there times when secrets should remain unspoken?

7. Francesca regards the priest Bernando Morozzi as the embodiment of evil, yet she also fears that they are alike in some ways. Is she right in either regard? In both?
8. Lucrezia Borgia is depicted very differently in this story from much of what has been written about her. Why do you think she has been portrayed in such dark terms historically? Did being a woman make her more vulnerable to exploitation by her family's enemies?
9. As Rodrigo's son, Cesare Borgia has access to great power, yet he cannot use it to claim the life he truly wants. What acts might his frustration give rise to?
10. Throughout this story, poison appears as a metaphor for the stain of corruption running through the highest levels of society. Is a similar metaphor appropriate in our own time and if so, where?
11. What role do you think the corruption of the popes and other high-ranking prelates of this time played in triggering the rebellion against Catholicism that we know as the Reformation? Were there internal reforms the Catholic leadership could have taken that might have prevented the Reformation from happening?
12. If Rodrigo Borgia's dream of a papal dynasty controlled by his family had succeeded, what would have been the implications for his time? For ours?